Dinah Lampitt was born in Essex but spent her childhood in a seventeenth-century cottage in Chiswick. She was educated at Putney High School and the Polytechnic and was fired with her love of history by an inspired teacher. She subsequently worked in Fleet Street for *Woman* magazine, *The Times* and the *Evening News*. She also undertook financial research for City Research while writing short stories for the *Evening News* and features for *She* and *Woman's World*. She has a daughter and a son and lives in Tunbridge Wells, Kent.

By the same author

Sutton Place
The Silver Swan

DINAH LAMPITT

Fortune's Soldier

GRAFTON BOOKS

A Division of the Collins Publishing Group

LONDON GLASGOW
TORONTO SYDNEY AUCKLAND

Grafton Books
A Division of the Collins Publishing Group
8 Grafton Street, London W1X 3LA

Published by Grafton Books 1987

First published in Great Britain by
Frederick Muller 1985

Copyright © Dinah Lampitt 1985

ISBN 0-586-07120-2

Printed and bound in Great Britain by
Cox & Wyman Ltd, Reading

Set in Times

To my Magic Three:

Bill Lampitt, the inspiration
Jacqueline Getty Phillips, the catalyst
Geoffrey Glassborow, the guru

and to

Heather Burbidge, Beryl Cross, Amanda Lampitt, Brett Lampitt, Erika Lock, Zak Packham, Deborah Richardson-Hill, Shirley Russell and the staff of Hastings Public Library for all their help and patience.

My thanks are also due to Maureen Bickford for access to the memorabilia of Lady Northcliffe; to Joan and Godfrey Shaw for the loan of Captain Francis Salvin's personal diaries; and to Colonel Maximilian Trofaier for his advice on the British soldiers of fortune in the Army of the Emperor of Austria.

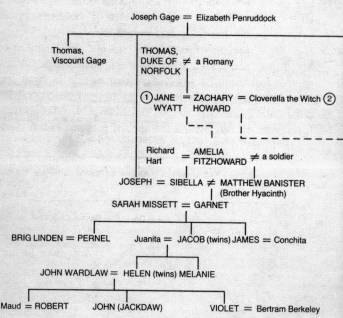

WALTER DENNYS = MARGARET

Grace Harper

son
(d.youn

Joseph Gage = Elizabeth Penruddock

Thomas,
Viscount Gage

THOMAS,
DUKE OF   ≠ a Romany
NORFOLK

① JANE   = ZACHARY = Cloverella the Witch ②
WYATT   HOWARD

Richard
Hart   = AMELIA
           FITZHOWARD   ≠ a soldier

JOSEPH = SIBELLA ≠ MATTHEW BANISTER
                   (Brother Hyacinth)

SARAH MISSETT = GARNET

BRIG LINDEN = PERNEL   Juanita = JACOB (twins) JAMES = Conchita

JOHN WARDLAW = HELEN (twins) MELANIE

Maud = ROBERT   JOHN (JACKDAW)   VIOLET = Bertram Berkeley

? ① ≠
JA

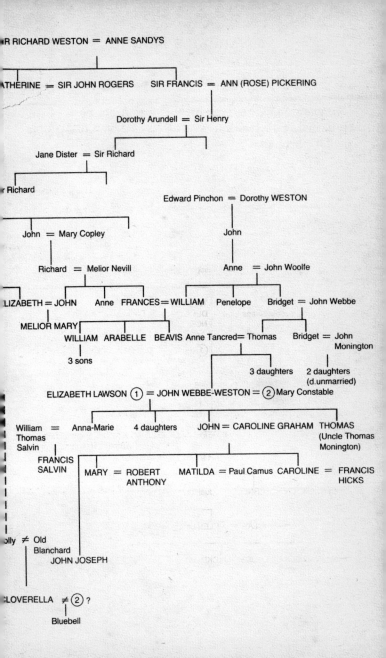

Author's Note

Fortune's Soldier is presented as fiction but most of the principal characters and events are based on actual people and happenings.

Prologue

The dream, in its way, was beautiful. He slid from his body as easily as a snake shedding a skin and looked about. Just beneath him a shell, once human, was lying upon a stark camp bed. But though he was aware that the poor corpse was himself, he cared not at all. He was free, ready to progress, to go adventuring.

Yet the pallor of the face – his own face – made him pause for a second. Once – could it really have been only two days ago? – it had been tanned and handsome; the eyes, closed firm in death, the clear dark blue of distant sea storms. But now he was cold and still and no one would call him fine any more.

And yet he knew that he had died at the thick of it – if that were meant to be a soldier's consolation. For through the flapping walls of the tent, the morning was made terrible with noise. Cannon shot and mortar pounded at the walls of a beleaguered fortress and bricks and stone cracked and splintered beneath their pitiless crunch.

But beneath that barrage of sound came a distant moan far more terrible. For cholera raged amongst the men of that encampment and the toughest and the strongest of a whole generation were calling out for help. What a terrible, wild and futile anthem it made – the guns and the screams and the sad harsh voices of the dying.

The dead soldier looked down upon his deathbed and knew why he must linger a moment more. He saw a woman, arms curled about her sleeping head, sitting in a chair by his side and leaning forward across his bed. Her hair glowed foxfire in the amber sun, her face was ivory streaked with dirt. She had nursed him as best she could and even now in her sleep held his chilling hand in her own. She was as warm of spirit as the sun-filled orchards of long ago, as loving as the splendid days of youth.

Without hesitation he forced his straying soul to enter once more the harness of his wasted body; would rather taste the bitter darkness than slip away without a word to her. The rasp was agony in his chest but he managed to speak.

'Horry!'

She opened her eyes. 'John Joseph.'

His eyes were searing with pain but he focused them upon her and she bent her head over him to hear the whistling voice.

'Leave Sutton Place, Horry. Leave that accursed house.'

As his fingers fell from hers he saw his wife clasp his lifeless form to her and weep aloud. And then, as if his sleeping mind could encompass no more, he woke up.

All about him the shapes of his nursery focused and took on meaning in the dim light of a lamp that his nanny kept burning at night. He made out his kite, his bowling hoop and his sister's dolls' house. And there too was her bed and in it the slumbering form of Mary herself.

They shared a room now that the two youngest – Matilda and Caroline – had come along. Not that there was really any need, for their new home – recently inherited by their father – was vast and dark and scaring. Rooms enough for each child to have its own bedroom – had they so wished. But who would want that in Sutton Place, that loomed so large over four small children?

John Joseph Webbe Weston sat up slightly and whispered to his sister.

'Mary!'

She sighed in her sleep and turned over.

'Mary!'

'What is it? You've woken me up. Is there a ghost?'

'No. But I've been dreaming again.'

She yawned. 'What?'

'I've been dreaming. That one where I die on the battlefield – though not of wounds – and my wife is there.'

'Oh, *that* one. I think it's silly. I don't like her.'

'My wife?'

'Yes.'

Despite her brother's solemn face Mary giggled. It was such silly talk coming from a boy of ten, especially as she was only eight herself.

'Is she fat?'

'No.' He looked cross. 'She's not. But, do you know, I've never seen her properly.'

'I thought you often dreamed of her.'

'Not of her in particular – but of dying. Mary, you're laughing.'

He leapt out of bed and hit her in the stomach with his pillow but she only giggled the more and pinched him through his nightshirt.

'Be quiet. You'll wake Nanny.'

'I hate her – she smells of ham. Why have you never seen your wife?'

'Her face is always turned away, somehow. But she's got red hair.'

'Ughh!'

'It's not ughh! It's beautiful.'

'Well I think it sounds horrible.' Her face grew still for a moment and she said, 'I believe it's this house that makes bad dreams. You didn't have them in London, did you?'

John Joseph was equally still as he answered, 'The

servants say this is an unlucky place. That the heir always dies.'

'But you're the heir now.'

'I know,' answered her brother – and without another word went back to his bed to stare into the darkness.

She was in a sea dream, a little trick of hers when she was in labour: in her body the waves of contraction rising and falling, and in her mind the playful billows of the sea and herself swimming boldly into them. Boldly, and without fear, because, belying her small stature and blonde ringleted hair, she had always taken life by the throat, determined to extract every ounce from her time on earth.

She smiled to herself, burying her face deeper into the pillow so that the midwife would not see. She knew that her silence worried the nurse – and she knew that this would be reported back to her husband and, in turn, make him rise moodily from his chair and pace the library of Strawberry Hill, lined with the books of his kinsman Horace Walpole.

She had taken him to the altar by storm. Insisted that he married her when she was pregnant with their second child, and thus forced her way into the aristocracy. And, though this had taken rather longer than she had hoped, it had all been part of her life's plan. For there was absolutely nothing that would have persuaded her to remain simple Miss Anne King, daughter of a nondescript army chaplain from Hastings. Ambition burned in her little body like a naughty furnace.

'My Lady, are you asleep?'

She opened her wide blue eyes and stared straight into those of the physician.

'No, Sir, I am not. I am contemplating getting shot of this child.'

He looked rather startled but took the rebuff in his stride. After all he had delivered her of three others – the two little boys already dead and in their graves – over the last six years.

'Yes, my Lady.'

'So return in an hour and then we'll make haste.'

'Yes, my Lady.'

'And, Dr Carteret, kindly see to it that the Earl does not consume too much brandy while he waits. But on the other hand do not let him go to sleep before the matter is resolved.'

The doctor smiled. The Countess Waldegrave's fragile appearance and china-blue eyes did not deceive him for a moment. He knew and appreciated a tough fighter when he saw one.

But when he was gone Anne sighed and turned her head into the pillow once more. The sea of birth was growing rough and she must swim into the great breakers before she could reach the shore. She bit her lip and heard the November wind whip up the Thames and roar at the casement of Horace Walpole's Gothic villa. A mighty pang caught her unawares and she fell beneath a foaming wave and cried out.

It seemed to her then that she had left her body for a moment and was standing in a nursery in a great gaunt house, looking at two sleeping children. The boy opened his eyes, said, 'Is that you, Mother? I have had such a bad dream,' and then went back to sleep. At that she started to weep but did not know why.

'There, there, Lady Waldegrave – don't take on. It will all be over in a moment. Just push a little more, my dear. Why, there's the head.'

Time had telescoped inwards; she had almost given birth to her sixth child. She strived obligingly and the midwife said, 'Why, it's a girl. A dear little soul. God bless her heart but she's got a mass of red hair.'

Anne was in full command of herself again as she said, 'Then that will be Horatia Elizabeth – a pretty name don't you think? Be so kind as to despatch a maid for the Earl and another to bring me some tea.'

The baby, wrapped in a white shawl, was passed to her and she looked at it appraisingly. A very fair-featured child with what would appear to be a determined mouth. It looked up at her with startled new-born eyes.

'Well, Miss,' said Anne, 'let us see what you make of the world.'

The Earl, looking owlish and smelling of the decanter, appeared in the doorway.

'James, my dear, come and meet your new daughter. She shall be known as Horatia.'

The Earl Waldegrave smiled and bowed. He had long since given up arguing with his wife about anything that he considered of no real importance to himself.

Jackdaw had never quite known what the blazing comets in his head signified. But since his third birthday – and that had been three years ago – he had felt the sensation of dancing stars four times. Immediately after they had faded, he had seen a picture reflected in a bright object which could not really have been there at all.

On the first occasion he had seen a vision of his cat going beneath the wheels of a carriage – four days later it had been dead; the second time a new-born girl had been lying in a white lace-trimmed cot, a mass of red hair fuzzing about the infant face. But the third image had frightened him, for his aunt – his mother's twin who had died when she was seventeen years old – had lingered in his doorway for a second before vanishing. She had smiled and stretched out her hand.

14

'Mother, why did she do that? I thought she was dead?'

'That only means on the other side of life, Jackdaw. You have a gift that allows you to see her.'

'What gift is that?'

'A family one, my dear – some of us have always had it, though I personally do not. We are descended from a Romany who lived over three hundred years ago. She had a child by the great Duke of Norfolk, who became an astrologer and mystic – Zachary was his name. That is what you have inherited.'

Jackdaw had nodded his head, glad that old wild blood ran on his mother's side. His father was remote – John Wardlaw, the army man – but Helen Gage, as she once had been, was warm and exciting, full of fire and dark as a raven, yet with bright light eyes.

Her father had been Jacob Gage – one of the three magic children of the house of FitzHoward. Her uncle had been his twin, James, and her aunt, Pernel – all of them fathered by Garnet Gage the Jacobite. Their grandfather – Helen's great-grandfather – had been the famous rake Joseph Gage, though Helen had once heard a horrible whisper, when she and her dead twin, Melanie, had been young girls, that he was not so in fact. There had been a terrible scandal in the family and somebody else – somebody altogether unknown – had been Garnet's true father. She had put this awful thought from her. She felt if she were not really descended from the legendary Joseph then she would rather not be alive.

But nobody had ever spoken of such a wicked thing in the confines of the family and she doubted that her grandfather, Garnet, had ever heard the evil rumour. She hoped not, for the idea would have destroyed him.

But whether her father, Jacob, had known the story was a different thing. If he had then he had said nothing and had gone on to have a brilliant career. First as a

Colonel in the Spanish Army, and then as a peer of the British realm, rewarded by George III – despite the known Jacobite leanings of the whole family – for a delicate mission which had brought about a trading treaty between Britain and Spain.

Jackdaw knew that all those old people were still alive. Not Joseph or Garnet, of course, but Great-Aunt Pernel and Great-Uncle James. And Grandfather Jacob, living in Dorset, and enjoying in his old age the life of an English aristocrat.

His wife, Lady Gage, was Castilian – the twin daughter of a Grandee – and it was from her that Helen, and Jackdaw too, had inherited their vivid dark looks. All together an attractive and brilliant family and small wonder that the Hon. Helen Gage and the Hon. Melanie Gage had been two of the most sought-after girls in English society.

And, indeed, even smaller wonder that John Wardlaw – brought up to be so prim and boring by his mean-hearted mother – had fallen madly in love with them. He would have married either gladly, been grateful if they had so much as given him a glance – which they never did – but after Melanie had died of high fever, Helen had, in fact, turned to the correct young soldier for her solace and he had gained his heart's dearest wish.

Jackdaw, the second-born of their children, always thought that he must have been a bitter blow to his father. Small and with one leg three inches shorter than the other, there was no possibility that he could follow the double family tradition and join the army. None the less, he had been christened John after his father. But his dark looks and quick eyes coupled with his name – John Wardlaw – soon earned him his nickname. He was the Jackdaw and it was left to his elder brother, Robert, to be big and amiable and just what their father wanted.

But Helen saw the potential in him. She had realized when he was a baby that he had not only taken after her side of the family in looks but also in the magic gift of second sight that had been theirs for centuries. So that he could walk properly she had had special shoes made for him, and very early on his brilliant brain had been obvious and she had taught him how to form characters, to read – and also to speak Spanish.

And now on this windy November night the comets were dancing in Jackdaw's head again. Round him he heard a roar like a dragon drawing breath and then, clearly visible in his sister's toy bell, he saw a reflection. First it was a baby, but this faded into a child with burnished hair, and blurred once more to become a grown woman whose wild tresses burst about her shoulders in a blaze of foxfire. He almost heard her name but the vision was beginning to fade from him.

He strained his nerves to stretching point.

'Who are you?' he said aloud.

A thousand million echoes were in the voice that answered, 'Horry.'

Part One

1

It was the most frightening thing Horry had ever seen. At one moment her brother had been laughing with her, picking her up in the air and throwing her above his head only to catch her again. At the next he had dropped her roughly and had fallen at her feet, frothing and foaming and choking upon his tongue, his body jerking as hard and as cruelly as a whiplash.

She had been too terrified to cry, simply staring at the unrecognizable creature threshing on the ground before her, and it had been her brother George who had saved the day. He had sprinted forward from where he was throwing a ball vigorously at their sister Annette Laura and jerked J.J.'s tongue from his mouth, pressing down hard upon it. With his other hand he rent J.J.'s collar like a rag as he pulled it away from his throat.

At the same time he called out to Annette, 'Take the children into the house. Quickly! And fetch Mother. J.J.'s having a fit.'

Horry had never heard the word before and that evening – long after J.J. had been carried into the house by a footman and the doctor had been sent for – she had asked the nursery maid what it meant.

'I can't tell you that, Lady Horatia. You must ask her Ladyship about it. Though little girls should be seen and not heard, you know.'

But as night fell and the Earl and Countess Waldegrave, on their way to dine with King George – the fourth to bear that title – made the formal round of the nurseries to bid sweet sleep to their five children, Horry spoke up.

21

'Mother, Father – what is a fit?'

The Earl, who was in Court dress – a white satin waistcoat embroidered with gold thread beneath a black and gold cut-away and an immense lace cravat – gave her a straight look. He had been the wildest youth in the world but had grown serious with the cares of family life. Yet Anne answered her at once.

'An illness, Horry. J.J. is attacked by it sometimes. It is called epilepsy.'

'She won't understand,' said the Earl.

'Don't be silly, James. I have never talked down to any of the children, as well you know. How else can they learn?'

They stood arguing quietly between themselves and Horatia thought that her mother must be the prettiest woman in the world. She had exchanged her blonde ringlets for the latest style of the Apollo knot, with artificial hair pinned on the back of her head to form a chignon, and curls over the forehead. This splendid creation was piled high with flowers and a tiara, and a goodly array of diamonds winked from her throat and ears. And to crown the effect of *beau monde* Anne wore the latest in skirt length so that her neat silk-clad ankles and minute black satin pumps were prettily displayed.

'I suppose you know best,' said the Earl eventually.

He was as handsome as their mother was beautiful. Thick black curling hair – now just starting to streak with grey – crowned his head and a pair of blazing blue eyes looked out from beneath curling jet lashes. J.J. and George had his looks exactly, though Annette Laura favoured her mother with golden hair and a deceptively mild moonstone gaze. Of the baby, Ida Anna, it was a little difficult to tell except that her eyes had a hazelish quality and she already had the habit of pouting her little rosebud mouth if refused what she wanted.

22

But Horatia, so everybody said, threw back to her grandmother – the celebrated and beautiful Lady Laura Waldegrave, great-niece of Horace Walpole. Painted by Joshua Reynolds and known as the exquisite of her day, she had brought up five young children on her own when her husband, the fourth Earl, had died after only seven years of marriage. Through her, Horry's father had inherited Strawberry Hill – Walpole's little Gothic castle on the Thames at Twickenham.

Blazing foxcub hair and mermaid eyes had been Horatia's inheritance from her grandmother, but her determined mouth came from Anne and her love of adventure from James, who had fought under the command of the Duke of Wellington and had taken wagers with his fellow officers as to how many girls he could impregnate in any one year. Unfortunately – or perhaps fortunately, as somebody had had to curb him – he had reckoned without the forcefulness of the diminutive Anne King.

His downfall had taken place in Paris where he had been stationed after Napoleon's ignominious defeat. The year had been 1812 and the entire city had been dancing in celebration, so when the chaplain's daughter with her childlike stature and downcast eyes had been allowed to attend a ball she had seemed easy meat for Lieutenant Colonel the Earl Waldegrave.

He often wondered how he could have made such an enormous error of judgement. No sooner had she laid hands on him in the dance than he was a puppet in the control of a master. Little Anne King was bored with her station in life and James was her salvation personified.

But the Earl had resisted. Lady Laura, his mother, would not approve of his marrying beneath his dignity, he had announced firmly when Anne had told him she was pregnant. So, to the shock of her father and the horror of the officers' wives, the chaplain's daughter had borne her first child – John James known as J.J. – out of wedlock.

'Will you marry her?' someone had asked.

'Of course not,' the Earl had answered loftily.

'Ah, there speaks one of the wild Waldegraves.'

He had not seemed quite so wild nor quite so rakish when Anne had stormed into the officers' mess and deposited a howling and definitely moist infant upon him while she went to visit the sick. Nor had he smiled so broadly when J.J.'s howls had woken the whole barracks in the small hours of a summer night. The Earl's son had been discovered in a basket with a note attached to his woollen jacket: 'Kindly feed your child at six. I cannot keep him indoors as my father is taken to his bed with a headache and must not be disturbed for the sake of his health.'

He should have ignored her, he told himself. Risen above it, pretended she did not exist. But it was not easy in the small army community, and anyway there was something fascinating about her now that she was no longer with child. And she had the prettiest thighs he had ever seen. Slim and brown and leading to the dearest little hips.

When she told him she was pregnant again he felt the perspiration of doom start out upon his upper lip.

'Well!' she had said, sitting in a chair as cool as you please and reminding him vividly of a child's porcelain doll.

'Well, what?'

'Is history to repeat itself or this time are you to father a child that can succeed you?'

She had made a telling point. J.J., by the very fact of his bastardy, was forever unable to inherit the earldom. Was the Earl to sire an entire litter of dependants or was he to put this one in line for the title?

'Well?'

Her exquisite little brows had risen virtually to her hair and her pale blonde ringlets had bobbed. The sixth Earl Waldegrave had swallowed miserably. He enjoyed his extravagant life and had no true wish to change. But she was very pretty and could arouse something in him that he had never experienced with other women.

'I don't know what my mother will say.'

'It is not your mother who is having the baby.'

They were married in Paris three weeks later and – as if Fate had intervened in some unnerving manner – four months afterwards, in January 1816, Lady Laura had died at Strawberry Hill. The way was clear for the Earl and the new Countess to return to England.

'But I can't marry you again the day after George is baptized,' James had protested vigorously to Anne's immediate suggestion upon arrival in her new home. 'What will society say?'

'It will say a great deal more if we are not seen to be married in the eyes of the polite world. Come, come, James. Such reticence is not like you.'

He was beaten again and so on June 11 the infant George, almost invisible in the massive Waldegrave christening robe, was baptized at Twickenham Church and on the following day John James, sixth Earl Waldegrave, married Anne, Countess Waldegrave. The bride wore cream lace caught tight and high beneath her bust, the skirt – with six ruffles at the end of it – falling to just above her dainty shoe. On her head she wore the tiara belonging to her late mother-in-law and from this a veil bunched out to her shoulders. She was the most beautiful bride Twickenham had seen in years and all the villagers cheered as the bells rang and the organ pealed and she stepped out into the sunlight. Nobody could quite understand why this second ceremony was really necessary, but then it was impossible anyway to follow the way in which the minds of the gentry worked.

And now the Earl and Countess stood, eleven years later, attired in Court dress, their orders on the blue ribands blazing upon their chests, and bade goodnight to the family that had followed. Of course, there were two that were not there. The Honourable William and the Honourable Frederick had both died in their first year, but Lady Annette Laura, Lady Horatia and the baby Lady Ida Anna had survived. The Earl often felt thankful that he had legitimized George in time, in view of what had followed.

'Will I catch fits?' said Horry.

'No, my dear,' answered Anne. 'You can't catch fits – they just happen.'

'Why do they happen to J.J.?'

'Enough,' said the Earl. 'There's been enough talk of this. Goodnight, Horatia.'

He could look handsome even when he frowned as he did now, deep blue eyes narrowed beneath the dark brows which pointed upward at the corners. His daughter looked up at him admiringly.

'Goodnight, Sir.'

He smiled as suddenly as he had looked angry.

'And be a good girl and quiet while I am out – or I shall tell the King.'

'Would he be cross?'

'Very.'

Down the slightly sloping floor of the dormitory, which glowed and smelled of a hundred years of beeswax, the marbles ran like a little avalanche. First the big blue one, then two little pearlies, then the red and the yellow, and finally the pride of the collection; the big green that

26

glowed like a panther's eye. Outside were the shouts of English boys as they charged about the playing fields of their long-founded school, but Jackdaw was unaware of them. In his mind he was hurtling down an emerald cascade and braving a jungle river, as he watched the spheres run the length of the sloping room and finally come to rest beneath a large and open casement.

He smiled to himself. He did not mind in the least that his slight disability – the limp that was unnoticeable when he wore his built-up shoe – did, in fact, preclude him from running about with his fellow scholars. Indeed he was rather glad. Let Rob, his amiable puppy of a brother, win the family sporting honours; he – Jackdaw – far preferred to walk and play alone.

The marbles chinked together with the angle of the floor and he dropped to his knees – a Chinese dragon spitting flame at its enemies – crawling to where they lay. Raising himself on to the window seat he lay stretched out in the autumn sunshine, the cushions comfortable beneath his back and head, his ankles crossed. Outside the shouts of the players drifted into the distance as the game concentrated itself round the farther goal.

Jackdaw raised the marble to his eye and peered into the world of green spirals and convolutes – some forgotten cavern, even perhaps the centre of the world itself. He was not altogether shocked to feel himself melting into the magic orb.

But to his amazement, when he passed through whatever barrier time and space and reality had set for him, it was not to find himself in – as he suspected – Merlin's most secret lair, but on the banks of a fast-flowing river where children swam naked. Brown bodies sent arcs of rainbow droplets high into the air as they dived into the water, and hairless little girls shrieked with fun as they splashed their elder brothers. Even the baby, sitting in her pretty laces, her boots neatly buttoned and pointing up to heaven, managed to get herself waterdewed and her nurse called out crossly, 'Lady Annette, you're making Lady Ida quite wet.'

The boys were well made, thought Jackdaw. The larger, whom the others called J.J., about sixteen with dark curling hair on his head and body; the other – George – so like J.J. that they were difficult to tell apart, except for a bluish streak in George's hair that ran from brow to nape. That they were high-spirited rogues, the pair of them, was obvious, and even as Jackdaw watched, J.J., hidden beneath the shelter of a willow branch, passed with satisfaction a cascading arc of water into the river below, while George fished into his trousers – lying roughly thrown upon the ground – for a bottle of spirits from which they both took a deep swig.

'In one end and out the other,' J.J. chuckled, squeezing out a few more drops.

'Lovely feeling,' answered his brother and joined him in the happy pastime.

Absolutely sure that they could not see him Jackdaw flicked their naked buttocks hard. Then, coming from behind the sheltering willow, he found himself face to face with *her*. The last time he had seen the child she had been reflected in a ball above Violet's cot and now she was before him – naked in the sunshine – her hair like mulled wine with the dampness that made it cling to curls around her shoulders, her eyes water jade reflecting the river light.

That she saw him for a moment he had no doubt, for she started and said, 'Who are you?'

Her elder sister, Annette Laura, about twelve, said, 'What is it, Horry?'

But the answer came, 'Nothing. I thought I saw a boy standing here. But it must have been a trick of my eye.'

'A ghost I expect.'

'A ghost?' said J.J., returning with George from behind the willow tree, looking well pleased with their schoolboy communings with nature.

'Nothing that *you'd* see.' Annette Laura was looking firmly at the bottle that George had thrust, once more, into his trouser pocket. 'You know that J.J. is not allowed to drink.'

'Be damned to that – it cures me. Now lower your voice or Parkins will be craking like a fishwife. Come on all of you, let's get back to Strawberry Hill. How about tea in my study, George, with a nice roaring fire?'

'And some hot toddy?'

'Just the thing. Annette Laura, don't make your mouth Miss Prim. When you've a husband to keep you in order you'll understand such things.'

They began to pack up their picnic, putting their clothes back on, but as Horatia went to go she turned back with a rather wistful glance.

'What is it?' said J.J., hoisting Ida Anna on to his broad shoulders. 'Seen your ghost again?'

He smiled as he said it, for J.J. believed in nothing but the total strength of one thing – himself, John James Waldegrave Esq. It amused him enormously – made the blazing blue eyes crease with hilarity – to think of his indolent father not stirring himself sufficiently to slip a marriage band on to Anne King's finger while *he* had been on the way, thus putting him in line for the Earldom and Strawberry Hill. Not that he cared a damn. All the privileges and none of the responsibilities as far as he could see. He chuckled aloud.

'Why are you laughing?' said Horry.

'Because I've decided against toddy. I'm going to crack a bottle of champagne when I get in.'

'Do you drink too much?'

'Far too much. Can you see your little ghost?'

Horatia stared hard. And Jackdaw in his strange time-less green marble world tried desperately to talk to her, make her look at him.

'No, he's gone – but not far away.'

J.J. patted his sister's gleaming head.

'Perhaps you'll meet him properly one day.'

'I hope so.'

'Well, I'm going for a walk even if you don't,' said Mary Webbe Weston.

John Joseph groaned aloud. For his fourteenth birth-day, two days before, his father had given him a great wooden box containing over a hundred tin soldiers garbed in bright red. A whole regiment was there – the Hussars – in force. And all he wanted to do now was set them up and let them fight a battle with Napoleon's rag tag and bobtail troops. As he moved them from place to place – complete with miniature horses and cannon – he would make the sound of mortar and grape-shot, booming away to himself until Mary would shout at him, Matilda would stamp her feet and Caroline would beg him to stop. Then his mother would intercede and the usual compromise would be reached. John Joseph must walk with the girls accompanied by the governess, and then he could play Beat Boney until bedtime.

'Always the same,' he would think. 'One day I'll join the proper army and get away from them all.'

And then he would remember his recurring dream – his fevered death, the woman with autumn hair – and shiver where he stood. And yet the idea of a military life attracted him; being a man amongst men, drinking till the cups were dry, eyeing the girls until they blushed.

'Are you coming or not?' said Mary.

'Not. Anyway it's raining.'

She looked out of the window crossly, saw that he was right and promptly came up with a counter-suggestion.

'Let's play hide-and-seek in the haunted Chapel – and frighten Caro until she screams.'

He shot her a contemptuous glance but none the less considered the idea silently. He knew he would get no peace from her until he agreed to one of her schemes – and playing in the ghastly rotting Chapel, which his father could not afford to restore, was as good a plan as any.

He paused, to keep her in suspense, and then said grandly, 'Very well,' adding, 'but then you must play soldiers with me after supper. And you shall take the part of Boney.'

'But I always do so! Could I not be Wellington for a change?'

'No,' he said.

'Please let me.' She was wheedling and grasping his jacket with her plump little hands. 'Let me, John Joseph.'

'Oh very well,' he said again. He was like that with women – as personified by his mother and sisters. Constantly agreeing to their pleas to gain a little peace.

Mary gave him a radiant smile, said, 'Come on, let's get the babies,' and began to hurry towards the nursery door.

They had always referred to their two younger sisters thus. Not that there was any vast gap in years between the four of them – John Joseph and Mary being four and two respectively when Matilda came along – but because the two younger sisters could not remember London. And London to John Joseph and Mary had been the height of sophisticated dwelling. They had both loathed Sutton Place on sight, and living there had proved to be even worse than either of them had imagined possible. Vast empty corridors, smoking chimneys, a Great Hall dim with antiquity and a Chapel that smelled of damp. That was their lot and they bitterly resented it.

'When it's mine,' John Joseph had been heard to mutter darkly, 'I shall burn it to the ground and clap my hands while it blazes.'

But now that he was fourteen he knew that he would not, that he would simply close it down and live elsewhere. He wondered if his yearning to join the Army was a symptom of his longing to get away from the sprawling mansion house that had been connected with his family for over three hundred years, or whether he was just born with a love of things military.

In either event he could not find it in him to like the house and as he and his sister walked down the corridor of the west wing, towards the room in which Matilda and Caroline could be found, he kicked the wall spitefully. As if it knew what he was thinking Sutton Place seemed to shudder and John Joseph felt suddenly guilty. After all, it was not the house's fault that it had been allowed to grow so miserable and dank. He supposed that when it had first been built and King Henry VIII and Anne Boleyn had come to visit – and that was what his father had told him so it must be true – the mansion would have been quite jolly and bright and full of bustling people. Hard to believe now but the fact remained.

'If you kick it like that,' Mary said maliciously, 'all the ghosts will come in the middle of the night and take you away. Even Sir Francis waving his head aloft.'

John Joseph gave her a black look.

'Ghosts are for girls,' he said.

They had reached the door of the smaller nursery and stared silently to where Matilda and Caroline sat at the table, pinafores covering their dresses, painting. They were as unalike as it was possible for sisters to be; Matilda round and brown – eyes, hair, skin – even her apron and

her little shoes. Caroline like cream – tresses of thick
wheat, light pupils, a complexion good enough to eat
with fruit salad. They seemed a pair of angels as they sat
there, totally unconscious of the presence of their brother
and sister – little pink tongues darting about in unison
with the effort of concentration.

Mary took a step into the room and said in her most
mealy-mouthed manner, 'May John Joseph and I take
the babies for a walk, if you please, Miss Huss?'

Their governess – poor long-suffering creature – only
twenty-five years old but already with the small desperate
manner of one who had never seen a gentleman's eye
bolden with interest, smiled nervously.

'But it is raining, Mary.'

John Joseph's sister bobbed a deprecating curtsey.

'We thought a stroll about the house, Ma'am.'

Miss Huss frowned in hesitation. She did not like Mary.
In fact she did not like children, detesting heartily the
fact that the Reverend Huss of Norfolk had secretly
drunk away her small miserable inheritance and left her –
his only daughter – in a position where she must teach
the monsters or be turned out upon the streets. She
sometimes dreamed that she *had* chosen the streets, saw
herself, in fevered fantasy, painted heavily and smelling
of musk, loitering in disused doorways and pulling up her
skirts for militia men.

'What?'

'Stroll in the Chapel, Ma'am. It was the Long Gallery
once, you know. In the days of yore.'

Forward brat, using that ridiculous language.

'You must speak properly, Mary. You are not expound-
ing from a history book.'

'But we are an historic family, Miss Huss.' The smug
little face was turned up to her. 'Are *you* of ancient
lineage, Ma'am?'

33

'No, Mary. No I am not. Just from a line of country parsons.' She stood up, brushing the folds of her skirt. 'Nothing as exciting as the great Westons of Sutton Place, I'm afraid.'

John Joseph's voice was quiet as he spoke.

'We are *not* part of the Weston family direct, Miss Huss. We inherited the house – and the name – by marriage only.'

She looked at him gratefully and saw a glint behind the deceptively mild eyes; eyes that were the blue of a seascape in winter. Enough would be enough with John Joseph, she thought. Women might chivvy him, push him, do what they liked with him, but there would come a moment when he would simply turn and say 'No'. A man to be reckoned with, would be John Joseph Webbe Weston. She smiled at him.

'Would *you* like to take the girls for a walk, John Joseph?'

'Not particularly, Ma'am. But I suppose the exercise might serve tolerably well on a rainy day. Besides which they could come to little harm and you could read for an hour.'

'I think you will be a diplomatist when you are grown.'

'Ma'am?'

'It is of no consequence. Matilda, Caroline – let me remove your pinafores. John Joseph is to take you for a turn about the house.'

'And I too,' said Mary.

Miss Huss determinedly ignored her.

2

The winter of 1829 was unusually warm, and snowdrops and crocuses had pushed their tentative heads through the rich garden soil of that monstrously delicious palace known as the Pavilion, the dearly beloved Brighton home of the poor dodderer who had been once the elegant and witty Prince Regent. Now, like slippered Pantaloon, George IV shuffled about the exquisitely kept paths, where every blade of grass faced in the same direction, sucking his gums and muttering to himself.

He had given England the unforgettable beauty of the Regency; his charm and culture had earned him the title 'First Gentleman of Europe'; without his patronage the world would have never seen the paintings of Lawrence nor the architecture of Nash. But now nobody cared for his life or for his death. His elegant clothes had given way to a food-stained dressing gown, his fashionable Romanesque hair-cut to a parody of sticky white spikes. He who had been England's darling Prince was stricken to the soul with the torment of the unloved.

'I think I'll spend Christmas here,' he said to himself. 'No, perhaps in London. Ah me – such decisions.'

But nobody heard or cared and he toddled off to pick himself a snowdrop to put in his nightcap.

A little further down the undulation of that most heavenly coastline, the sea was going out at Hastings. Nearest the shore the water lay like a merchant's bale of shimmering grey taffeta but further out small white breakers rolled in on the slant. Above them all the great White Rock dominated and the sun shining on it, in an oddly dappled way, gave the impression that a mergirl sat there, twining herself a seaweed coronet and glancing now and then towards the houses that were built in the shape of an inverted U on a small hill beneath the Castle.

Seated at breakfast in one of those houses, in a room with bow windows that swept from ceiling to floor that the sun and the view might be better enjoyed, was the Wardlaw family. Their oval mahogany table gleamed as if the wood still had life and white napery and silver dishes reflected every facet of the clear and delicate December morning.

It was a beautifully shaped room, its furnishings enhancing it like a stage setting. For that Helen, raising her elegant dark brows over a letter which had just been handed to her on a small bright tray, could be thanked. Crystal chandeliers played rainbow prisms and tinkled free as wind bells in the morning breeze, venetian teal draperies swayed against deep rose carpets, golden mirrors, holding candles in their carvings, twinkled a thousand reflections.

General Wardlaw was positioned at the head of the table, his back to the sea view, forgoing that ever-changing aspect in favour of sitting where the greatest light would be cast upon the face of his wife. The charming countenance, the sheen of swept-up hair, the slanting eyes, the merry mouth and seed-pearl teeth, set his blood racing even after all the years. He was not only happily married, he was physically in love. He would have sent the children and servants packing and kept her hungrily for himself if convention had not decreed otherwise.

The war between these rules and his passion for Helen was the most difficult thing with which John Wardlaw nowadays had to contend. Rigidly brought up by a mother whose religious mania pointed to the Will of the Lord in everything, he could either have gone under in a sea of drink and self-pity or become rigidly tough and wrest circumstance round his way, caring not a damn for anybody.

He had been saved from doing either by his meeting with the Gage twins and the subsequent death of one and his marriage to the other. From that time on he had been a different man. The pale, slightly truculent, blue eye; the heavy moustache and side-whiskers; the quick, determined walk, were all still there. But emotion had entered his soul and the man who stared down the table at his family, hearing the sea sounds blow in from the open window behind him, was that most contradictory of all things – a man of war in love.

'What is that letter you are reading with such interest, my dear?' he said.

Helen's answering smile made his heart thump and he had to cough into his napkin to hide the fact that he was reduced to the status of a moonstruck boy at even a glance from her.

'It is an invitation for Christmas.'

'From whom?'

'My kinsmen the Webbe Westons.'

'The ones who live in the great ruin near Guildford?'

'The very same. But despite the draughts – or perhaps because of them – ' only he caught her naughty innuendo and twitched his lips ' – they have children of comparable ages to ours and thought that it might be amusing for us all to be together. What do you think, my darling?'

'Umm . . .'

He hesitated, knowing full well as he did so that he would abide by Helen's wishes. If she had asked him to leap from Hastings' heights with her he would gladly have obliged.

'My love?'

He often wondered whether she was fully aware of the intensity of his feelings for her.

'Well, I imagine it would be somewhat cold. Did you not tell me the house was Elizabethan?'

'Even older. Built during the reign of Henry VIII. Of course if you would rather not . . .'

'I don't know. What do *you* wish, my dear?'

She turned to their three children. 'Rob, Violet, Jackdaw – let us hear from you?'

'Is the boy taller than I am?'

This from Robert – the eldest child – who, at nearly thirteen, was already a foot bigger than Jackdaw and broad in the shoulders. He had that slightly vacant air often possessed by those who concentrate enormously on games and running about, but for all that was very equable and good hearted.

'I should think probably so. He must be all of sixteen years. He has been away at school to escape from his horde of little sisters.'

Rob, imagining himself cutting a dash with the young ladies, said, 'I should like to go.' And Violet, thinking of taking her dolls on a journey and then letting them meet the dolls of her cousins, and all having jolly tea parties in the nursery, said, 'So should I.'

'And what of you, Jackdaw? You're very quiet.'

As always when she spoke to the younger of her two sons Helen's face softened slightly and John felt the usual tug of jealousy in his chest. How ridiculous to feel that about his own boy. His jewel-eyed, black-haired son who was so like his mother. And yet the truth was there. He could not bear her to look kindly on any other male, even the offspring of his wild and seething passion for her.

'Yes, come on. Speak up,' he said to cover his unforgivable feelings.

'What is the name of the house, Sir?'

'What a ridiculous question. I don't know. I've forgotten. Helen?'

'Sutton Place.'

'Then we *must* go.'

Helen merely smiled but the General decided to pursue the matter.

'Why do you say that? What is that supposed to mean? Where's the "must", John?'

He did not like calling him Jackdaw, thought it rather effeminate and girlish.

'I feel it would be a good thing to do.'

'Why?'

Jackdaw's gaze dropped to his plate and he swallowed uncomfortably. For all his clairvoyant gift, he was still only twelve years old. There was no explanation he could give to the bold military man who sat at the table's top. Yet he knew it was part of the vast play of events that he should go to Sutton Place and there meet someone with whom his life would be inextricably woven.

Jackdaw thought to himself that it must be she; of the fox's hair and seagreen eyes. That she must be one of the horde of sisters mentioned. That he would step through the doors of the ancient house and see her standing with all those others who had paraded before him through the mediumship of his funny schoolboy marble.

As usual when he thought about that extraordinary event his hand crept into the pocket of his jacket. He always kept it there – his primitive scrying glass – though he had seen nothing more in it from that day to this.

'Don't fiddle, boy, when I am speaking to you. I asked you a question. Why would it be a good thing to go to Sutton Place?'

The General became aware of Helen's dark stare

turning in his direction and his voice became fractionally more gentle. 'Come along, young man.'

He was perturbed by what he saw. Jackdaw's eyes flashed at him like two birds startled by a distant lightning fork.

'Because it would be! I am sorry, Father. That is all I have to say. I *would* like to go.'

The General opened his mouth to speak but Helen's light voice cut in.

'Then, my dear, if that is the consensus, I too would enjoy it. The matter rests with you.'

How she could twist and turn him! He nodded his head as if considering but his eyes were already blurring with the fierce feelings that her direct glance could arouse. He laughed shortly.

'Then go we shall.'

Jackdaw's bright and grateful smile was the reward that he did not even notice, so busy was he with gazing at Helen.

In the snow of the cold weather that had followed the unseasonably warm snap, the gates of Sutton Place looked, from the distant road, like black lace spread against the fragility of the whiteness beyond. But as the largest and most durable of General Wardlaw's coaches came trundling steadily upon its four solid wheels towards them, the gates took on another aspect. They soared high and black and forbidding, suggesting that beyond lay a building which was not to be entered lightly nor tampered with in any way.

'Good God,' said John Wardlaw, staring at the entrance – mouth very slightly a-gape. 'What sort of place is this, Helen? I thought the Webbe Westons were poor as mice.'

'They are, my dear, they are! I came here once when I was a girl – when the first John Webbe Weston was alive.

40

What a grand ruin! They have restored it as best they can but the house has simply burned their money up.'

'Oh dear! Will we get anything to eat?' said Violet.

The General laughed and scooped the little damsel, clad in lavender velvet and sporting a beribboned bonnet and black button boots, on to his knee.

'Of course we will, my bird. There, there. Do you hear her, sweetheart?'

Helen smiled and patted her daughter's plump little white-gloved hand.

'Don't be afraid, darling. There shall be plenty for us all. See, your brothers are jolly.'

And it was true, for Rob's big amiable face had taken on the sort of grin given to a marvellous toy as the gates swung open before them and the lodge keeper came to a ragged salute; and as for Jackdaw, he was alive with some inner thoughts, cheeks glowing at the strange cold prospect that lay before them.

As far as the eye could see the Home Park spread out hushed and still beneath the majesty of new-fallen snow. Colossal trees, beneath which Saxon Kings had slain the gasping wild boar, raised their stark fingers to capture the virgin flakes and, as the Wardlaw carriage clattered over a wooden bridge, they saw flowing ice-cold – embanked as it was by escarpments of frost – a fast-currented river. Of the house there was no sign as they twisted and turned about, but another wide bend revealed – towering up as grim and gaunt as any enchanted castle – the building in which they were to spend the next few days. Sutton Place, with all its great history, its panoply of Kings, its relentless heritage, lay before them.

It was obvious that it had at one time been four-sided, built round a quandrangle. But now only three wings remained. Where a mighty Gatehouse had once jutted aloft there was now emptiness. The wing from which so

41

many pairs of eyes had swept the landscape for the first glimpse of a rider bearing news had been finally razed. Sir Richard Weston's soaring gateway was no more.

Each one of the Wardlaws was utterly silent. Each, in his own way, dumbstruck at the magnitude of the building that met their separate gazes. Helen full of thoughts of the family Gage that had allied itself with the builders by the marriage of Elizabeth Gage to John Weston and who had, by this act, fallen beneath the spell of the house. They had broken away only through Joseph Gage's vow never to set foot within its walls again. He had gone for a soldier to the Queen of Spain and there raised Garnet, Helen's grandfather.

John Wardlaw brooded on the upkeep of such a heap. General of the British Army he might be, but his pay could never encompass a similar dwelling. Helen had told him once that old John Webbe Weston – father of the present incumbent – had wanted to pull the mansion house down and start afresh. He had inherited it, in the most ruinous condition, from his kinswoman Melior Mary who, so the General understood, had gone mad and lived as a recluse despite the fact that she had been the beauty of her day and pursued by many suitors.

'Strange affair,' he thought and shook his head slightly.

And the three children were pensive too. Rob thinking of all the good sport that could be had in this park; the running and leaping and the trees to climb.

And Violet prinking up the bonnet of her favourite doll and telling her she was better than any toy that could possibly be found in the enormous and forbidding house that was drawing so horribly near with each rattle of the wheels.

But Jackdaw dreamed of the autumn-haired girl. He knew that the chain of events which would lead him to her had been set in train, and that Sutton Place would reach out for him and, in some indefinable way, alter his life. But he was not aware, as yet, of how this would take place. Only the fact that a vital meeting awaited him had been revealed.

So it was with a sense of disappointment that he looked beyond the massive door which was swinging open – revealing a Great Hall vast as a cathedral – and saw a family of four children and two parents, none of whom resembled her at all. He felt cheated, misled, and it was only when a voice said, 'I'm John Joseph Webbe Weston. Are you the one they call Jackdaw?' that he knew that he was not.

This was why he had come. Here stood a boy who was to be more of a brother to him than poor dull Rob could ever hope to be. Here was his fraternal partner in the flesh.

'Yes, I'm Jackdaw,' he said.

'Good. Do you like playing army games?'

'With tin soldiers, do you mean?'

'Yes.'

'Rob might be better than I am. He's more of a sportsman.'

John Joseph grinned. 'One doesn't need sportsmanship for war manoeuvres. They come from thinking. I'll challenge you.'

'Very well.'

Jackdaw gave a funny jerky little bow. John Joseph's personality was tangible, full of life and sparkle. He was the sort of young man to whom people would listen with interest.

He stood quite tall for his age, already sporting the dashing good looks which all his life were to single him out from his fellows. His hair grew thickly and brown upon his head and his arresting eyes – the light blue of a winter sea, yet encircled by a rim of indigo – were set finely above a straight strong nose and a smiling, rather passionate, mouth. The heir to Sutton Place was almost as handsome as the first heir – Francis Weston, who had died beneath the axe blade.

But Jackdaw knew nothing, at this time, of the house's tragic history and he stood overawed by his kinsman. He would always be little Jackdaw, in his own eyes, and beside this lively, good-looking young man must cut a poor figure indeed.

'. . . you must be famished,' Mrs Webbe Weston was saying. 'As soon as you have seen your rooms we shall have tea. We live only in the West Wing now so you shouldn't get lost. It is such a pity that we can do little with the rest. But it isn't easy, it isn't easy.'

She shook her head apologetically. She was a fair, ineffectual woman with a weakly pretty face and a mouth that constantly moved either into a smile or a purse, dependent on her words.

'Yes, yes, yes,' said John Joseph's father – also called John Joseph. 'Distressing really. Beautiful once. But there you are. Can't be helped. Good after bad. Dear me.'

They all moved off to a staircase that lay on their right and began the ascent to the rooms above.

'Hope you'll enjoy yourselves,' said John Joseph the elder. 'Do our best. Good food, cold rooms. Nobody's fault.'

Mrs Webbe Weston gave a silly little laugh.

'And none of you children are to listen to ghost stories,' she said. 'Sutton Place is not that kind of house.'

'Pshaw, pshaw,' guffawed her husband, but Jackdaw shivered none the less as he looked back at the gloom of the shadowy Great Hall.

'Well, this is a nice turn of events to be sure,' said Anne, Countess Waldegrave.

'What?' said the Earl absently.

'There's a baby due to one of the maids at Christmas and she swears that it is J.J.'s.'

'He should deny it,' said the Earl without looking up.

'I beg your pardon?'

She had paused, her silver fork loaded with salmon soufflé half way to her mouth.

'Deny it. It's the only way.'

'How typical of you, John James.'

She always called him by his full name when she was angry, and the newspaper lowered a fraction to reveal his eyes – masked by half spectacles it was true but still an exciting shade of blue – peering at her over the top.

'The servants, my dear,' he said mildly and returned to his perusal of the news columns.

She glared at him furiously, for that was the way he had learned, over the years, to catch her out. For, for all his early wild behaviour – which his sons were fast learning to emulate – he had indisputably been born a member of the aristocracy and she had not. Miss Anne King of Hastings could – if the Earl so chose – be put in her place with a mere glance.

'James,' she said in a lowered voice, but still with urgency.

'Yes?' The newspaper did not shift.

'I really *must* speak to you.'

'Later, my dear. Later. Pray continue with your luncheon.'

'Oh, it really is too bad.'

The newspaper rustled slightly but did not otherwise respond.

'I am discussing our eldest son, Sir.'

'I see that the King is wintering at Brighton.'

'It is not the winter quarters of our Sovereign that concerns me, but the spring quarters of some little bastard not yet born.'

Just for a second the kingfisher eyes flashed from behind the printer's ink.

'Yes, my dear, that has been an occasional problem with you, as I remember it.'

The Countess jumped on to her satin-pumped feet, throwing her napkin down upon the table and steadfastly ignoring the principal footman who was holding his face aloft in studious contemplation of the ceiling.

'I have had enough, John James. Should you so wish you will find me in the withdrawing room. Good day to you.'

And she was gone in a furious flurry of skirts.

'Good day, my dear. Pour me some wine, Parkes, if you would be so kind. And see that it is properly chilled this time, the weather being so damned unseasonably warm. And send Jamieson to me if you please.'

And a few minutes later, when his personal valet hovered at his elbow, the Earl, still without looking up, said, 'Ask Master J.J. to join me in the library after luncheon and set two glasses with the brandy decanter, there's a good fellow.'

'Yes, my Lord.'

'And I shall require complete privacy, Jamieson.'

'Very good, my Lord.'

'That will be all at present.'

The servant bowed. 'I'll see to it directly, Sir.'

The Earl waved a thin white hand. 'And no word of warning to J.J. – simply find him and send him in. You understand.'

'Of course, my Lord.'

The Earl sighed slightly, raised his wine to his lips and then set about consuming his salmon soufflé with relish.

That Horace Walpole in the eighteenth century had thought Twickenham 'a seaport in miniature' was undoubted. And that the delightful village, with its breathtaking view across the river to the sweep of parklands beyond, was favoured by other elegants of his day was indisputable. Alexander Pope had established his famous villa there and Henrietta Howard – George II's amusing mistress – had lived nearby in Marble Hill.

But wittiest of them all had been Walpole himself, residing in his little Gothic castle known as Strawberry Hill, which lay amongst gardens of 'shady bowers, nodding groves and amaranthine shades'.

But as a family house it had its shortcomings. Living space was limited and the boisterous tribe Waldegrave sometimes found itself a little cramped when one disagreed with another – which was regularly; or Lady Ida Anna whined for attention – which was often; or the Countess was in a pet with her husband – which was every day.

But, just for the moment, there was tranquillity. It was Christmas Day and it was evening and they sat – all seven of them – in the famous Round Room, round a huge mahogany table groaning with crystal and silver, surrounded by a bevy of liveried servants and lit by candled chandeliers.

The Earl, making a vastly handsome figure in scarlet cutaway, stood for once with the polished carving knife and fork in his hands paring immensely thin slices from a dozen or so pheasants that lay nestling in a trencher before him. To his right was Annette, to his left Horatia with her Uncle William – the Earl's younger brother – beside her.

William and his wife were the only guests that night and the family sat packed close together in the intimacy of the turret, everything being jolly. Even J.J. had been forgiven his first serious transgression and the housemaid had been found lodgings in a cottage outside the village. And because she had been allowed to stay up late and sat perched next to her mother on an adult's chair piled with three silk cushions, four-year-old Ida Anna was holding forth.

'And I have been tho good,' she lisped, 'that I am the favouritetht baby in all the land.'

J.J. and George smiled indulgently with the elders but Annette's lips tightened while Horry pulled a face at her empty soup plate. Since Ida Anna had been born there had been no real peace for the two girls. The Countess, forever busy with the war of wits she and the Earl played out constantly and implacably, had virtually handed over her youngest child to the servants and her other daughters.

However, she beamed at the little wretch now and patted the silken head with a small beringed hand.

'And so you are, my precious,' she said.

Lady Ida Anna pulled her little rosebud lips into a simper and looked round, head on one side, to see the effect she was making. She was a tiny, pretty thing with her mother's fair hair and bright boot-button eyes. But she was already terribly spoiled and could get her own way with most merely by quivering her lips. Her habit when wheedling was to stand on one foot and curl the other round it, swaying slightly from side to side whilst staring at the floor. She was altogether an obnoxious child, though her parents would have been mortified by the very suggestion.

'I love Horry,' she went on. 'She ith my bethtitht thithter in all the world. I shall always play dolls with her, Mama.'

Horry stared uncomfortably into her lap while the elders cooed with delight.

'Oh, was ever a child so precious?' gushed William's wife. 'Why I could eat her up, I swear I could.'

'I wish she would,' mouthed Annette across the table, hoping that only Horry would see.

'What did you say, my dear?' asked the Earl.

Annette's moonstone eyes turned towards him innocently. 'I only said that Ida was so good, Papa.'

He was not at all convinced but was in no mood to make an issue of it and the meal continued without interruption. The pheasants – which had been preceded by lobster bisque, cod in oyster sauce, a saddle of mutton and sweetbreads larded in parsley – gave way to jelly of fruit, cheese-cake, meringue à la crème, ice pudding and beignet soufflé. A plum pudding was brought in on fire with brandy and finally, when all were truly replete, the Countess rose and led her sister-in-law and her three daughters to the Holbein Room where they might talk freely while the Earl and his brother, with J.J. and George, lingered over fine port.

'The King's in poor health, William,' said the Earl. 'I fear that this could be his last Christmas.'

'And they say at Eton,' said J.J., 'that there'll be a woman on the throne of England before a dozen years are out. And how will we all like that?'

'Tolerably well, I dare say.' The Earl leant back in his chair and crossed one elegantly clad leg over the other. 'In fact England does very well under a Queen. Think of Elizabeth.'

'But Father – ' J.J.'s cheeks were bright with wine and he was speaking rather more loudly than usual ' – what do we know of the Princess? Have you ever seen her?'

'I admit her mother keeps her secluded in Kensington Palace. No, I've never laid eyes on her. William?'

'No, nor I. How old is she? Eight, nine?'

'She's a year younger than Annette – ten.'

'I hope the poor child reaches a decent age before responsibilities are thrust upon her.'

'We can hope,' said the Earl.

In many houses throughout the land, including Sutton Place, exactly the same conversation was taking place.

'Good thing,' said Mr Webbe Weston. 'Make a change. Good Queen Bess. Fine Queen Anne. All that.'

'It will seem strange to have a Queen though, John. I mean we are no longer used to it.'

Mrs Webbe Weston looked round her Boxing Day tea table with a deprecating smile. She had the knack of making even a fairly intelligent remark sound boring and all her family and guests now stared back at her owlishly.

'Well,' said General Wardlaw eventually, 'the King is not dead yet and Prince William, his brother, is only sixty-four. They could go on for years.'

'But obviously won't,' said Helen. 'Victoria will come to the throne whilst still a girl, you mark my words.'

As always when she spoke the General feasted his eyes on her in a way that Mrs Webbe Weston thought 'unhealthy'. This train of ideas was only interrupted by her husband's rumbling into a laugh and saying, 'Funny situation. Prince William's little bastards. Not an heir among 'em! Ha, ha! Dashed odd.'

His wife rounded on him, her silly mouth pulled down crossly.

'John! Really! Such a display! Little pitchers have big ears, you know.'

'What does that mean, Mama?' said Violet.

'It means that you talk too much,' Helen answered.

'It means that Prince William has children but they can't succeed to the throne,' said John Joseph.

'Oh dear,' thought Jackdaw. 'She's going to ask why.

50

You can see John Joseph has been away at school. He doesn't know much about girls.'

Violet hesitated and in his anxiety Jackdaw thrust a piece of mince pie from his own plate into her mouth. Her eyes rolled protestingly and the General said, 'What's the matter with you, boy? Have you taken leave of your senses as well as your manners?'

Jackdaw went scarlet – all too conscious of the gaze of his idol John Joseph upon him – and said, 'No, Sir.'

'Then what are you doing to your sister?'

'He was feeding her with his own food,' said Helen very rapidly. 'I think it considerate of him. Thank you, Jackdaw.'

He looked at her gratefuly, gulping his cup of tea noisily in embarrassment.

'Oh,' said Mrs Webbe Weston uncertainly. 'Yes. To be sure. Well, you must all hurry and finish your repast because the estate workers will be up soon.' She turned to Helen. 'Such a nuisance really, but then it's been a custom here since ancient times. Long ago they used to dance in the old barn, but that tradition ended when poor Miss Melior Mary grew old. Such a shame. Anyway, nowadays they come up for a kitchen supper and then the children are allowed to play for a while. Not that there are many of them left with everything dwindling so.' She gave an apologetic laugh.

'Quite true,' said her husband. 'Money draining. Hard times. Can't go on for ever.'

It was not clear whether he meant that the end of his resources was in sight or that his luck was about to turn, and nobody thought it delicate to enquire. In the slight silence that followed Violet gave a convulsive gulp and said, 'Can we play in all the house, please Ma'am?'

Mrs Webbe Weston hesitated. 'Well, the East Wing is in a poor state . . .'

'Oh, let them see it, Mama,' put in John Joseph. 'They can't come to much harm. After all, Miss Huss is here.'

The wretched governess, who had been sitting at the table without uttering, now raised her head and gave an unenthusiastic nod.

'Very well,' said his mother. 'But nobody is to go into the Chapel. It is far too damp. Besides – ' she added piously, 'it is not right that children should play in a place of worship.'

'Used it not to be a Long Gallery?' This from Helen.

'Originally, yes. It was Cousin Melior Mary who had it changed. She grew very odd in her declining years, you know.'

'Somebody once told me it was haunted.'

Mrs Webbe Weston looked uncomfortable and said, '*Les enfants*, Helen!'

John Joseph, who seemed intent on mischief, said, 'It is. By a jester. May I take the boys on a ghost hunt, Mother?'

'No you may not. Such talk! Come Helen, children. Let us see what has been prepared below. I ordered some hams and beef sides. I do hope there will be enough.'

She looked suddenly distraught and Jackdaw had a fleeting moment of pity for her. It was obvious that the Webbe Westons had fallen into dire straits, that Sutton Place was bleeding them white. He wondered if they would be able to continue to live there in such awful and harrowing penury.

But below stairs a considerable effort had been made. A large table, spread with a darned but none the less crisp cloth, had been laid with a plain yet plentiful feast. A haunch of mutton added to the choice of meats, and leveret and chicken pies were packed closely by cheeses, puddings and tarts. Jugs of ale stood at the ready and there were cordials and sweets for the children. Above all loomed a large Christmas cake iced and decorated with the words Yuletide Greetings.

Standing and staring at the collation, caps in hands and shuffling a little, were two dozen or so assorted men, women and children. These were the servants, gardeners and farm labourers who nowadays comprised the staff of Sutton Place. Three hundred years before Sir Richard Weston's lads had swarmed the house in their dozens, and even when the last of the male line – John Weston – had taken his adopted daughter Sibella to her wedding at Holy Trinity, she had been preceded by eighty marching people from the estate. But now only this diminished collection was left. None the less they shouted a brave Huzzah for the Master and Mistress, and as Mr Webbe Weston cried jovially, 'Merry Christmas. Be seated all. Hot punch. Ha ha!' a fiddle struck up.

Jackdaw had never seen anything quite like it; the rosy-cheeked children scrambling for places nearest the cake and the adults jostling one another at the punch bowl. And they certainly made up in noise for what they lacked in numbers; giggles and shouts, laughs and the odd muffled curse filled the huge kitchen. Sutton Place might have fallen on hard times but these people were determined to enjoy themselves.

John Joseph stood amongst them in the most carefree manner, lifting the smaller children into their chairs and even going so far as to push one fat boy out of his seat that a tiny and pale lame child might have a place.

'Why is he like that?' Jackdaw whispered. 'What caused such a thing?'

He stared at the crushed and broken leg which hung, smaller than the other, above the ground, and was painfully reminded of his own deformity. Surreptitiously he hid his built-up shoe beneath the flowing tablecloth.

'He was caught in a man trap.'

'A what?'

'A trap for men. It is set to catch poachers. It has iron teeth which sink into the flesh and break the leg.'

'Ugh!'

'The last poacher caught on the estate was transported for ten years.'

'It seems very cruel – all of it.'

John Joseph's eyes were suddenly bleak. This is a cruel house, Jackdaw.'

'What do you mean?'

'Nothing goes right here. There's supposedly a curse on the Lord of the Manor.'

Behind John Joseph's head a copper pitcher blurred as a picture began to form in it. The stars danced in Jackdaw's head.

'A curse of ancient times,' John Joseph went on, unaware of Jackdaw's fixed and unblinking gaze. 'They say it strikes the lord and heir – that the heir dies young in many cases; that the lord has no good fortune. Look at my father. He had never a debt till he inherited this place. Now he is practically ruined. What are you staring at?'

Jackdaw did not answer and John Joseph followed the direction of his eyes – nothing except for the copper pans that hung upon the wooden beams. He looked at the boy rather sharply. He thought him a funny little creature, well suited to his name with those bright eyes and dark clever appearance.

'Hey, wake up,' he said.

Jackdaw gazed at him dreamily and a shiver went through the elder boy's frame. Just for a minute he sensed something of the ancient power that was crackling in the atmosphere and then, just as swiftly, it was over. Jackdaw shook his head, went bright red before the gaze of him whom he – Jackdaw – considered quite the best-looking, most intelligent youth in the world and said, 'I'm sorry.'

'What were you staring at?'

Jackdaw mumbled confusedly, 'Sometimes I see things. Reflections. I can't explain.'

John Joseph hesitated, his eyes wave-blue in the smoky light. It was his instinct to find out more, to get things sorted out, but he could see that his kinsman was uncomfortable, shifting from foot to foot.

'Will you tell me of it one day?'

'I'll try to.'

In a rustle of hyacinth-scented clothes Helen was suddenly at their side.

'Is everything all right?' she said.

Her smile was for them both but John Joseph knew that really her question was for her son – that she cared deeply for her strange brilliant boy. He thought briefly about his own mother with her silly mouth and affected laugh and he envied Jackdaw the raven-haired half Spaniard who was Helen. He felt terribly flustered suddenly as she leant forward and touched his arm.

'John Joseph, Jackdaw is not being a nuisance, is he?'

'Oh no, not at all, Ma'am.'

He knew that he was being over-formal as he drew himself up and gave a slight bow, hoping desperately that she was not laughing at him. But if she was she did not show it, for she touched him lightly under the chin with her fingers and said, 'You will be a good friend to him, I feel sure. Though four years separate you I think he is probably quite wise for his age.'

'Yes, Ma'am.'

He felt an idiot. The wretched false politeness was choking him. Helen slanted her eyes at him and John Joseph felt himself grow pink.

'I feel glad that he has you to talk to. He and Rob are so different that one would hardly take them for brothers.'

'No, Ma'am.'

John Joseph's heart had begun to thump in the most unnerving manner and he found himself unable to look at his pretty kinswoman.

'So, it is settled. You and Jackdaw will always be good friends?'

If her son had been hideous and stupid John Joseph would have said 'Yes' just to please her. But his blushing agreement was interrupted by the arrival of Jackdaw's father who – in John Joseph's view – was boring and opinionated and not fit to carry her gloves.

'All enjoying yourselves?' said the General jovially, meanwhile shooting John Joseph a most poisonous glance which set the poor young man reeling with shock.

'Yes, my dear, we are. And what of you?'

'Tolerably well, tolerably well.'

The General's eye ran over the feasting labourers with distaste. He hated rabble and disorder and felt that there was no man alive who would not benefit from being in the Army. He fixed John Joseph with a piercing look and said, 'Do you intend to serve your country, young man?'

'If I did, Sir, I would like to rise high and I do not think that would be possible for a Catholic.'

John Joseph had recovered his composure and his answer was barbed. The General had forgotten that the Webbe Westons of Sutton Place were still staunchly allied to the Church of Rome.

'Er . . . yes . . . of course Catholics are not *precluded* from becoming officers – '

'But would not be encouraged, Sir?'

'Well – '

The General was more than relieved to hear at that moment Mrs Webbe Weston's silly voice calling out shrilly for games for the children and dancing for the grown-ups.

'Perhaps not,' he muttered into his hand, and was just about to bow to his wife and carry her off to the jig when John Joseph did so in his place. To the older man's fury and dismay, Helen was whisked from under his very nose.

'You had better go and play with the young ones,' he said to Jackdaw to cover his annoyance. 'Look, there they go without you. Hurry up, Miss Huss is beckoning.'

And sure enough the governess, looking as desperate and long-faced as a herded sheep, was leading the way out of the kitchens surrounded by a bevy of eager youngsters.

'*Must* I go, Father?'

'Yes, of course you must. Just because your cousin – or whatever he is – ' the General gave a glare in the direction of the dancing figures of John Joseph and Helen ' – considers himself old enough to stay here, don't let that give you ideas. Off you go like your brother and sister.'

'But it's *dangerous*, Sir.'

'What do you mean, dangerous?' General Wardlaw looked at the end of his patience. 'What is dangerous about playing with your contemporaries, pray? Sometimes I despair of you, John. Have I sired a nincompoop?'

'No, Sir. But just now I had this mental picture of a coffin lid closing.'

The General lost his temper.

'Jackdaw, be off! I am tired of you and your fancies. It is quite wrong of your mother to encourage you in them. I shall speak to her most severely about it. I shall also seriously consider sending you to a harder school altogether. Why if it weren't for your damned short leg I'd have you down for the Army.'

For all his bluster the General was very far from

insensitive and to see his younger son lose colour to the lips was unbearable.

'Jackdaw!' he called.

But too late. His boy had hurried from the room holding back the hot tears that threatened to disgrace him in public.

The Boxing Day party was over and Mr and Mrs Webbe Weston stood at the kitchen door with their four children bidding goodbye to their cheerfully departing guests. The hot punch and ale had had a predictably festive effect, and there was a good deal of laughter and one or two voices raised in song as the workers filed out into a night sharp with stars and loud with the song of an old blind fox.

In groups of family or friends the estate labourers went off into the darkness to farms and dwellings that had been built in Sir Richard Weston's day and bore names like Bull Lane Cottage, Ladygrove Farm and Oak House. It was not till they had all gone that John Joseph said, 'Where is Sam Clopper? I didn't see him leave.'

'Sam?' repeated his mother.

She hadn't really been looking for the small lame figure that so easily could have been missed amongst the jostling adults. He really was of little concern to her – in fact she secretly found the sad-faced cripple rather revolting – and as long as he was kept clothed and fed, which it was her duty to oversee as he was orphaned and she the Lady of the Manor, she never thought about him.

'Who?' said Mr Webbe Weston.

'Clopper, Father. The boy who was crippled in the man trap. His great-grandmother once served Cousin Melior Mary's mother. He said there had been a Clopper at Sutton Place since the old Jacobite days, if you remember.'

'Oh, him.'

'Yes him. Did you see him go?'

'No. Fallen asleep I expect. Weak as a cat. Poor thing.'

'Ought we to look for him?'

'Not now, John Joseph. I really am too tired. Anyway I do believe I saw him leaving with the Blanchards. Now come into the house, do.'

The quick heavy scent of hyacinths told John Joseph that Helen had come to stand behind the family group and he turned his head to look at her. The dark eyes were brimming with some secret emotion as she said, 'Jackdaw sends his apologies to you all. He was seized with a headache whilst playing hide-and-seek and has taken to his bed.'

'Is he ill?'

'No. Just tired.'

'He does this sometimes,' said General Wardlaw's voice out of the darkness. 'He is too sensitive by half.'

'He has the old Romany gift,' said Helen dreamily. 'You know of the Gage connection with the FitzHowards, Caroline?'

'I've heard something of it,' answered Mrs Webbe Weston. She sounded rather petulant. 'Shall we go in?'

They all turned away into the pan-bright kitchen not thinking any more of Sam Clopper or his whereabouts. But in the gloom of Sutton Park the blind fox gave a sharp sad cry as he headed, sightlessly, for his lonely lair.

3

The sounds of the summer river drifted through the open
nursery window – the plop of oars, the muted distant
laughter, a pleasing baritone voice raised in song. And
beneath these – in steady rhythmic chorus – the carolling
of sun-warmed birds, the distant low of cattle from the
pastures of Marble Hill, the bubble and flow of the lovely
Thames itself.

Horatia sighed and wrote in her exercise book, 'James
Waldegrave, second Earl Waldegrave, was born on March
14, 1715, and was George II's most intimate friend and
adviser. He died of smallpox on April 28, 1763. Had he
lived longer Walpole thinks he must have become the
head of the Whigs. Walpole had brought about the
marriage of the Earl to his natural niece Maria in 1759.'

Horry put down her scriver and crossed to the window.
It was through that marriage – the bastard daughter of
Horace Walpole's brother to the second Earl Waldegrave
– that they had inherited dear little Strawberry Hill. The
house from whose grounds her brothers and sisters were,
presently, playing on the river and in which she, through
no fault of her own, had been kept indoors on such a
lovely day to write a brief family history.

It had been Annette who had rigged the bucket of
water on the nursery door to soak Ida Anna as she came
through it; and it had been Annette who had cast her
moonstone eyes to the floor and meekly curtsied when
the Earl had unexpectedly walked in and been drenched
to the skin. And it had been Horry who had giggled as he

had said, 'God damn and blast! Who is responsible for this?'

It was the contrast of his customary elegance with his flattened hair and dripping clothes that had seemed so ludicrous to her. Instead of apologizing and saving the day, she had laughed all the more, clutching her sides in a terrible combination of pain and fun.

'Oh, you do look a-wry, Father,' she had chortled.

'We'll see who shall be a-wry, Miss,' he had snarled; very, very cross.

And now here she was. A prisoner on the hottest day of the year while Annette sported on the water dressed in cool muslin. Horatia sighed again and returned to her table.

She wrote with a flourish, 'At the time of the second Earl's marriage to Maria Walpole he was as old again as she and of no agreeable figure. Yet for character he was the first match in England.' Her tongue poked out of her mouth in concentration. 'But Lady Waldegrave, since the death of Lady Coventry, was allowed the handsomest woman in England and her only fault was her extravagance. Sir Joshua Reynolds painted her portrait seven times and after her husband's death she was courted by the Duke of Portland but secretly married Prince William Henry, Duke of Gloucester. The marriage was for a long time unrecognized by the royal family.'

Horatia paused. She had a fondness for her notorious great-great-aunt, a wish that she – Horry – might do something to emulate her; lead a wild, adventurous life. But small hope of that as the youngest but one daughter of an impecunious Earl. Finding good matches for girls without fortunes was no easy task – even if they did bear the proud and ancient name of Waldegrave.

Suddenly deflated, she bent once more over her exercise book and wrote, 'The second Earl having no male issue, the Earldom passed to his brother James who was master of the horse to Queen Charlotte. He died of apoplexy in his carriage near Reading, and was succeeded by his son George who had married his beautiful cousin Lady Laura Waldegrave.'

Horatia smiled. This was the grandmother she so closely resembled; the grandmother who had come to Strawberry Hill as a widow with her two surviving children, one of whom – Horatia's uncle and the fifth Earl – drowned in the river while still at school at Eton, aged only ten.

It had been this ghastly accident which had put her own father in line for the title, and because of it the Earl, whom she could glimpse now if she stared sideways out of the window, would never go near the water. While the others took the boat out he preferred to sit in the sun with his shirt open and his coat removed. And because of it he had let them all learn to swim – naked and uninhibited – from the earliest age possible.

Horatia picked up her pen once more. 'The legendary – ' she liked that word ' – Lady Laura was the mother of John James, the sixth and present Earl, who is the father (naturally) of John James Waldegrave Esq, George, Viscount Chewton, Lady Annette, Hon. William (deceased), Hon. Frederick (deceased), Lady Horatia (myself) and Lady Ida.

'Signed, Horatia Elizabeth Waldegrave, in the year of our Lord 1831 and the reign of His Most Gracious Majesty William IV.'

She had finished and now was obliged to stay in her room until summoned. But her next sortie to the window caught the Earl's eye, for she saw him look up at her. She dodged out of sight but heard him call, 'Horry! Horry! What are you doing?'

She went slowly and deliberately down the stairs,

through the Little Parlour and out into the sunshine, blinking a little at the brightness.

'Well?'

'I've finished, Sir.'

'Have you now? What did you write?'

'All about Great-Great-Aunt Maria and the Earl who died of apoplexy in his carriage and my beautiful grandmother. All those things. Shall I fetch my copy book for you?'

The Earl ran the back of his hand across his brow.

'No, not now. I'll look at it tonight.'

'Can I go to the river?'

'In a minute. But first you can talk to me.' He patted the lawn next to him. 'You may sit here. Your mother is resting in the shade and will not see you spoil your frock.'

She settled at his feet and he stroked her hair as if she were a kitten.

'Your head is on fire.'

'Really?'

He laughed. 'No, not really. It is just the colour in the sunshine.' The Earl closed his eyes.

'Am I like the beautiful Lady Laura?'

He nodded smiling. 'Yes, you are the image of the beautiful Lady Laura.'

'Why didn't you come back to see her after you were stationed in Paris?'

'She didn't approve of your mother. I was torn.'

Horatia looked at him closely. He was very handsome, his face already going brown in the sun. Yet somehow she didn't quite believe what he had just said. She felt his looks belied him. There was still that air of recklessness about him which positively vibrated from his sons J.J. and George.

'Did you love Mama very much?'

He opened his eyes and – as always – she was startled by the vividness of the blue.

'Yes.'

But there was a grin somewhere that he wouldn't allow out. Horatia knew full well that he had been captured into marriage by the determined hot head her mother had once been and it gave her a moment's alarm.

'Do you love *me*?'

The Earl's face grew completely serious.

'I love all my children, Horatia. Even that little pest Ida Anna. Oh, I know that pail of water was meant for her. I may be getting old but I am far from stupid. Yes, I care deeply for you all. I was not cut out for fatherhood but as it has been wished upon me so many, *many* times I have taken to it like a duck to water.'

He swung her up on to his knee and kissed her smackingly on the cheek.

'You are a good girl, Horry. And very pretty. How old are you now – I lose count amongst you all?'

'Eight, Sir.'

'Eight, eh? Well, ten years will see you into a great match I dare say.'

'I should like that. I should like to marry an adventurous man. An admiral or a cavalry officer or something of that kind.'

'Then do so, Horatia. Remember that you can do anything you set your mind to if you really want it enough.'

'Did *you*?'

The grin burst forth like a sun and the Earl slapped his thigh.

'No, of course I didn't, you little minx. The last person you want to emulate in this wicked world is your poor old father.' He roared with laughter. 'But no fear of that. If you are anything like your mother you'll end up with the First Lord or a Field Marshal.'

Horatia put her arms round his neck.

'I don't think I'll go to the river after all. It is so rarely that I get the chance to talk privately with you.'

The sixth Earl Waldegrave winked at her.

'People have been saying that to me for years,' he said.

'Going home. Tired out. Rum do. There 'tis! Ride on, boy. Ride on.'

And with those words Mr Webbe Weston turned his chestnut hunter and trotted off through the parkland.

Summer had come in glory to Sutton Place and as the sweltering heat of the day blazed forth John Joseph, thinking he might enjoy a swim, headed for the River Wey, canalized to run through the meadows of the Home Park by Sir Richard Weston the agriculturalist, before the Civil War. It trickled and flowed through green grass banks and beneath a little wooden bridge which the heir to the manor house now crossed, his horse's hooves clattering into an echo beneath its ancient and moss-covered planks.

Everywhere was the hum and buzz of high season. Two brown butterflies circled above the horse's mane; swallows curved and caressed an arc in the blue above; the swans upon the river curled back their sinuous necks that their beaks might grow warm before they dipped them in the cool clear waters beneath. And from some-where distant drifted the notes of an unearthly flute – all part of the illusion of that lazy heat-filled afternoon.

Yet when John Joseph dismounted and sat down to soak in the sun's life-giving rays the sound persisted. None the less he rolled his coat into a pillow and, placing it beneath his head, closed his eyes. Whether the music was real or imaginary was of little importance to him in that wonderful and languorous heat haze.

But despite the outward calm his thoughts raced. Last night he had had the dream again; the first time since Sam Clopper's disappearance two years before. He had been once more on that fever-laden battlefield; had heard the dying soldier – himself – whistle and croak his last words to the exhausted girl who sat beside him; had heard Sutton Place called accursed. But was it?

John Joseph moved uncomfortably where he lay. There had been so much tragedy over the centuries – deaths, madness, even incarceration in the case of poor sad Melior Mary – that the legend of the curse of Queen Edith upon the Lord of the Manor seemed real enough. And now he was eighteen and had left school and was himself at the immediate mercy of the house.

'Do you believe Sutton Place to be bewitched, Father?' he had said the night before, when they were alone after dining.

'Don't know. Funny place. Started life. No debts. Ruined now. Must let it. Take tenants. Only hope.'

'But what of me, Sir? Where's my future to be? Am I just to be a glorified estate manager?'

Mr Webbe Weston had looked glum.

'Suppose so. Terrible prospect. Poor boy.'

John Joseph had tossed down a glass of port in one.

'The British Army is hopeless. They'll never let a Catholic rise through the ranks. Perhaps I should go abroad.'

Mr Webbe Weston had made a clucking sound, shaking his head from side to side.

'Professions no good?'

'No, Sir. I've always wanted a military life – though I believe it might kill me in the end,' he had added in a softer voice.

Mr Webbe Weston had not heard him.

'Fine life. Yes. Man. Fresh air. Earning respect. Well done.'

John Joseph had poured himself another glass from the ruby decanter.

'So the house has found another way to topple the Lord of the Manor,' he had said reflectively.

'Eh?'

'*You*, Father. It has ruined you, taken all your money, driven you out.'

'Yes.'

'But I am still the heir to the wretched place, damn it.'

'Of course. Always have been.'

John Joseph had given up. 'Perhaps I am being foolish.'

But he had thought that his cousins Helen and Jackdaw would have understood. Not that he had seen anything of them since that fateful Christmas long ago.

The flute playing seemed to be growing louder and John Joseph's eyes flicked open, his pupils turning to black pinpoints in the heart of his arctic and indigo irises. Coming towards him was a motley figure, which in the distance was difficult to assess as regarded age or sex. It wore a big red hat pulled well down over its face and had a cloak that swept to the ground as it moved. The flute was at its lips and it seemed the very personification of a pied piper.

John Joseph stared in astonishment but the figure remained apparently unaware of his gaping and approached so near that he was able to see that it was not, after all, a patchwork player but a nut-brown maid who strolled along so rakishly. Her merry eyes, bright as two hazelnuts, shone in a tanned little face that was as streaked with dirt as John Joseph's was clean, and her small brown hands worked over the flute as fast as two scampering mice.

'Hello,' she said, catching his eye. 'I am Cloverella. And you must be Master John Joseph.'

He couldn't believe that she was real and sat where he was, dumbfounded – all thoughts of manners and leaping to his feet totally vanished from his head.

'Did I startle you? I'm sorry for that. The fact is you won't have seen me around here before because I'm new.'

'Oh yes?' was all he could manage, in a voice which sounded to him like that of a piping boy soprano.

She sat down beside him and he glimpsed two dirty feet and a pair of sunbrowned legs.

'Yes. I'm old man Blanchard's bastard girl. I walked all the way from Wiltshire to find him when my mother died. I wouldn't let the mean old bugger see me starve. Would you have done?'

'Er, no.'

'That's what I thought. But when I got here he told me that the big house was in rack and ruin and there'd be no work for the likes of me. But I told him I'm no gill-flirt. I don't need wages, just a place to put my bones at night. Want a puff?'

She produced a clay pipe from the depths of her garments and fell to smoking it at great speed.

'No thank you.'

'Don't say much, do you!'

John Joseph sat up straight, putting on his riding jacket.

'I would like to remind you, Miss Blanchard, that you are speaking to your employer's son.'

She roared with laughter and he saw the flash of goodly shaped white teeth in the midst of all the dirt.

'Bugger me! You're all puffed up with fury. I'll be on my way then.' She stood up and gave a quick burst at the flute. 'Good day to you, Sir. No offence.'

And she was off, walking briskly along the river bank

and playing away to her heart's content. John Joseph stared for a moment at her departing back before jumping to his feet and pursuing her.

'Miss Blanchard! Miss Blanchard!'

'Cloverella to you.'

'Cloverella – '

'Yes?'

'Stay and talk to me. You're the liveliest company I've had in an age.'

'That I'll reckon to be true. All right, I will. Want a swim? I haven't washed in a week and I feel a bit mucky. Do I look it?'

'Yes, you do.'

'Then here goes.'

She threw her hat into a hawthorn bush and John Joseph was surprised to see a tumble of wild black curls fall about her shoulders.

'You've got beautiful hair,' he said.

'So I've been told. Do you swim naked?'

'Good Lord, no.'

'Well I do. It's the only way I know of washing. Begging your pardon but there it is.'

The cloak went flying, followed by a tattered skirt and blouse. As he might have suspected she had no concern with underwear and stood before him small, brown and nude.

'I've never seen a woman with nothing on.'

'Well you have now. Don't stare. Didn't your teachers tell you it was rude?'

And with that she jumped into the river feet first.

John Joseph stood gawping on the bank as she surfaced and stood up.

'It's shallow here. Come on. I won't harm you.'

Rather reluctantly he removed his jacket, shirt and

trousers till he stood in his hose and undergarments, then he dived in. Cloverella's peals of laughter filled the day.

'Oh, Mr John Joseph,' she said. 'You do look funny.'

They swam for ten minutes in silence. But, finally, even those hot summer waters grew chill and Cloverella stepped out on to the bank, drying herself with her skirt. 'I reckon that was a good swim,' she said. 'Do I look a bit cleaner?'

She stood with her back to John Joseph, laughing to herself in the sunshine, knowing that he could not take his eyes from the novelty of female nakedness so casually displayed before him.

'Yes, I think so.'

'Not sure? Do you want me to turn around?'

'If you do by God I'll tumble you to the ground, you wanton.'

'Oh ho ho! There's fiery talk from the Master's virgin son.'

She spun on her heel and grinned up at him saucily. She must have known that she was utterly desirable to stand like that, her hands behind her back, her face raised to his, her eyes twinkling all the naughtiness in the world.

'Virgin I might be but I can do my best, Miss Blanchard.'

'I'm sure you could, Mr Webbe Weston.'

'Do you want me to prove it?'

'Why not? A fine young man like you could do a lot worse than learn the ways of the world from a girl like me.'

'Then show me what to do.'

'Well, first you kiss me – ' her lips were like her name, warm and sweet-tasting ' – and then you put your arms round me like this.' Her skin was glowing and soft as honey against his fingers.

'Oh Cloverella. I'm as hard as you are smooth. There – feel for yourself.'

'Oh, John Joseph – what a lovely man you are!'

He laughed delightedly – and it was incredible to feel her slipping and sliding down beneath him so that she was lying in the grass of the river bank. He had never known anything quite so joyful, then, as the stripping off of his few remaining clothes and her cries of delight as she saw him for the first time.

He knelt down beside her. 'I hope I won't disappoint you.'

'If you do this time there will be other occasions when you do not.'

'*Many* other occasions?'

'That's for you to say – you're the Master's son, after all.'

He could speak no further. All he wanted was to sink his shaft within her and forget everything – Sutton Place, his father's debts, all – in the completely carnal pleasure of her unrestrained lovemaking. He had never known such delight as the first springing of his seed within a woman's body. And yet, even then, even in that moment when the unrelenting ache in his groin was transformed into a hot fountain of delight, purity and wickedness, he thought of the girl of whom he dreamed – and of the times of rapture that they would one day share together.

'Quite remarkable, General Wardlaw. It really is quite remarkable.'

'Oh really? Well I can only say I am gratified. Extremely so. Well done, John. Well done.'

The General stood with his back to the light thrown from the senior tutor's study window staring, rather nonplussed, into the face of Jackdaw's principal teacher.

'Yes, Sir, you should be proud of him. I can honestly

71

say that I have never had a pupil of fourteen as advanced as he. Of course he already had a fluent command of Spanish when he came to Winchester, but now he has added French, German and Italian to that. He is also starting the study of Russian next term. He is a credit to the school.'

'I never realized this about him.'

'It is a natural gift, General. A natural gift.'

They spoke about Jackdaw as if he were not present and he eventually felt obliged to say, 'Thank you, Sirs', to attract the attention of at least one of them. They turned together and chorused, 'Proud of you, lad,' for all the world as if they had practised speaking in unison.

Jackdaw bowed gravely and for the first time in his life the General felt a stirring of a different emotion when he looked at the son whom he had secretly always labelled as 'lame'.

'Well, John, I must say it was a good decision of mine to send you to Winchester. I thought the school would bring out the best in you.'

'The gift of languages has always been there, General,' said the tutor smoothly. 'It would have come out whichever school the boy attended.'

'None the less, Winchester has changed him. He used to be full of nonsense, Dr Fiske. Daydreaming, that sort of thing. I'll be honest with you. Two years ago I was very worried about him.'

'In what way pray?'

'He had stuffed his head full of – mysteries, as he called them.'

Dr Fiske looked blank and it was Jackdaw who put in, 'I had premonitions, Sir. My father considered it unhealthy.'

The tutor nodded and put his fingertips together without passing comment.

'Anyway, I trust that is all over now,' said the General briskly. 'Too many other things to think about now, eh John? French, German, and Italian – and all in this short time.'

He looked at Jackdaw narrowly; noticing again the sheen of black hair, the jewel-bright eyes.

'You grow more and more like your mother,' he said.

'She was unable to come today.' It was half a question, half a statement from the tutor.

'She is slightly indisposed, that is all.' He saw Jackdaw frown and added, 'A slight chill. Nothing to concern yourself with. Well, I must take my leave of you. Keep up the good work, my boy.'

After he had gone Jackdaw remained in silence, looking at his teacher.

'Tell me of your premonitions,' said the older man eventually.

'I'd rather not, Sir.'

'Are they very personal to you?'

'Yes, Sir.'

How could he even speak of something he did not understand himself, even to this man of whom he was fond; the man who had moulded him into an astounding student of languages.

'May I go now, Sir?'

'Yes, Wardlaw. You are dismissed.'

He bowed again, that odd solemn bow of his, and went to his dormitory. For once it was empty – every boy in the school engaged with parents and teachers.

Jackdaw sat down on his bed and took from the depths of his jacket's most cavernous pocket the old green marble which had, just once, transported him into a world in which a laughing family of children had played naked in the river. He had never seen her – the foxfire girl – since. Nor had he even dreamed of her. It was as if she had, after that incredible happening, gone from him for good.

He wondered if he had stopped himself from being clear sighted. If that last frightening vision of a coffin lid closing had been too much to stand and his mind had rebelled. He had seen it in the shine of a copper pan hanging in Sutton Place's kitchen on the night of Sam Clopper's disappearance, and had known then that Sam was dead. But when the people from the estate had dragged the river and beaten the forest Jackdaw had been unable to help them; his ancient power gone away, apparently by his own command.

Now, almost out of habit, he raised the glass sphere to his eye. Immediately, as if to answer all the questions he had just been asking himself, Helen was there – and he could see in a single glance that she was battling for her life. Her white face lay on its lace pillow, cold and clammy with an evil sweat, her breathing shallow and laboured. A doctor hung over her anxiously – his ear to her heart – holding her thin and childlike wrist in his fingers and then shaking his head.

Jackdaw sprang to his feet, knowing at once what he must do.

'Stop General Wardlaw's carriage,' he shouted to a startled fellow pupil coming through the door. 'Go on man, run. Can't you see I'm bloody lame?'

But for all that he was not far behind the boy as the General's horses reared in the traces and pulled to a halt.

'What the devil's going on?' Wardlaw seemed to have retreated behind his whiskers in his annoyance.

'It's Mother, Sir – she's dying.'

'What?'

'She's dying.'

Without further explanation his son put his good foot on to the wheel and heaved himself within.

'Has there been a message to the school?'

'Yes,' answered Jackdaw tersely. 'Yes, there has.' He turned on his father a glaring fierce look that had a hint of danger at its heart. 'Now drive on, Sir. At once, Sir.'

'But . . .'

'Say nothing. We are leaving for Hastings.'

And with that Jackdaw leant abruptly across his father – as if he cared not a damn for him nor the protesting sounds that were coming from his lips – and shouted in the coachman's ear, 'Make haste. Mrs Wardlaw is within hours of her death.'

In the face of such remorseless determination his father could do nothing but sit in impotent silence as they sped off into the summer evening.

4

That night the sea and the sky were all one, merged into a bowl of sapphire with nothing to light them but the star of Venus arm in arm with a crescent moon. Beneath, the waves did not stir, warmed into a summer daze by the heat of the newly dead day. There was nothing to awaken them, nothing to disturb their eternal tranquillity but man, the great despoiler, himself.

And as Jackdaw's carriage rounded the bend of the lantern-lit sweep that led to his house beneath the cliffs, his head turned for a moment to God's eternal message, spelled out so simply by the chant of the sea, the chorus of the universe.

But this night he could not be part of it, did not care for the huge incomprehensible signal that was being so relentlessly voiced by the whole vast concept. For he was as sure as he had breath that Helen's identical twin had come for her; that Melanie had tired of being alone in the shadows and had come forth, laughing and teasing, to take her other self with her. In fact he almost saw her as he stepped through the front door, a swish of argent taffeta upon the top stair before he looked again and saw it was not there.

As Jackdaw went in, Helen's room was full of the scent of hyacinths and everywhere was a rushing and rustling of darting cold currents.

'Melanie?' said Jackdaw.

She did not answer him but the pendants of the glass chandeliers tinkled together like laughter.

'Melanie, you can't have her. This is a wicked trick you're playing.'

There was no response save for the guttering of the candle that stood by Helen's bed and a shifting of the bed cover. A cold invisible hand was laid upon his arm and a voice as light as a leaf seemed to say, 'But she and I are one.'

'You do not share the same soul, Melanie,' he answered softly.

The curtains swished and blew outwards and Jackdaw felt a touch of panic. The spirit of his aunt was determined to have that of his mother for its companion. As if she had heard something Helen gave a tiny sigh and her eyelids slowly flicked open. Jackdaw caught her up into his arms and said in an urgent tone, 'Mother, please. If you can hear me at all just say these two words – "Melanie, begone." Say them, I implore you.'

She stared at him lifelessly.

'Just say them if you want to live. Here, I'll help you sit up. Just whisper them, mouth them, anything.'

Helen leant against him. 'Melanie . . . be . . . gone.'

The sound was an agonized, barely audible rasp and after she had finished speaking she collapsed unconscious once more.

But the room had gone cold as midnight. There was no sound except that of rustling taffeta and just for a second Jackdaw caught a glimpse of swirling silver. Then the bedroom door flung open of its own volition and a second or two later he heard the front door hurl open – and then close. Melanie had left the house for ever.

'I really do declare,' said Mrs Webbe Weston in a high voice, 'that I shall faint with the sheer strain of it all. I have never been strong, you know. Never. And now I have to cope with giving up my home – at my age. What

77

will become of us in Pomona House? The place is a mere box compared with this.'

She sat hard upon a tea chest, pulling her silly mouth down at the corners and dashing at her cheeks with reddened knuckles.

'Terribly grim,' said her husband, shifting from one gaitered leg to the other. 'Awfully sorry. So sorry. Oh dear!'

He strode away, his sensible legs squeaking in his boots as he walked.

'I don't know what to do,' Mrs Webbe Weston moaned.

Her three daughters – Mary, Matilda and Caroline – stood staring at her blankly while Miss Huss, the governess, glared in mute but militant disapproval. She had been given notice; told she must leave because they could no longer afford· her miserable wage and she – idiot though she had berated herself – had taken a cut in her pittance rather than lose her place. She despised her soul for it; thought herself a cringer, a weakling. But what to do? Wasn't she a bit old now, a bit past going on to the streets with painted face and gartered stockings, calling out to military men? Yet how she longed for it. The awful exciting smell of cheap scents, unwashed bodies and lust.

'Miss Huss!'

She jerked herself into awareness. It was John Joseph calling out – and a fine young man he had become these days, with some new indefinable self-confidence. She smiled at him nervously, wondering, just for a brief exhilarating second, what he would do if she invited him to take tea with her and then threw her skirts above her head.

'Miss Huss?'

Was he looking at her oddly?

'Yes, John Joseph?'

'Could you get some smelling salts for my mother? I believe she is greatly distressed by this move. More than she will admit.'

As Mrs Webbe Weston was already weeping as copiously as a fountain Miss Huss wondered how much further emotion could possibly be displayed by her employer. However she said nothing and was creeping, mouse-like, to her bedroom when she saw Cloverella Blanchard – clad from head to foot in flowing scarves of apple green tawny – struggle through the Middle Enter carrying a vast tray of cakes.

'Oh, Cloverella,' she said, 'I do not think this is quite the right time to call.'

It was sweet meat indeed to wield some pathetic authority but Cloverella appeared undaunted, said, 'Very good, Miss,' and turned to go. However, behind her Miss Huss heard John Joseph say, 'It's all right, Miss Blanchard. You may leave them over there.' And the governess, wheeling sharply, was left in no doubt at all that the son of the house had bestowed on the ragamuffin girl a naughty wink.

She stared in horror as Cloverella reciprocated and then – had there ever been such a flagrant display? – heard her whisper, 'Later.'

It was too bad. Before she had time to think the word 'Really!' had risen, unbidden, to Miss Huss's lips.

'Is anything wrong?' said John Joseph politely.

'Er – no. That is – yes. John Joseph, I feel I must speak. Your mother would be so distressed and it is my duty . . . The fact is that you are delicately reared and that wicked girl . . . Why, she is nothing more or less than a gypsy slut.' She blushed scarlet with her fevered thoughts. 'I do hope . . . John Joseph, nothing has *taken place*?'

The seascape eyes looked at her enigmatically.

79

'What sort of thing?'

The governess shifted miserably where she stood, well aware that Mary – horrid little pig – had sensed a serious note in their conversation, though unable to hear a word, and was staring beadily in their direction.

'You know very well what I mean. I should not have to speak to you like this. It is the duty of your father.'

John Joseph took her hand in his and said with apparent sincerity, 'So it is, Miss Huss. I shall go and talk to him immediately. Thank you for your concern.'

It was not the response she had expected and she felt herself growing more and more flustered and starting to dither. Meanwhile John Joseph stayed holding her hand and looking at her sympathetically, shaking his head.

She snatched her fingers away.

'Well, go then. I've a great deal to do, John Joseph. Everything must be crated and carted by nightfall and as for you . . .'

'Yes, Miss Huss?'

'Oh, don't stare at me so.'

She turned in a whirl and hurried through the Middle Enter, her lips compressed tightly together.

Outside she shivered with the first hint of autumn in the September shadow of the courtyard. Once it had been a quadrangle; a quadrangle through which had ridden many leading players in the pageant of English history – Kings, Queens, statesmen and soldiers.

And not only they but also the common people had stood there. Armies of servants had bustled and swept and held the horses' heads while great men and women had descended and walked through that mighty door, out of which the insignificant figure of the governess now hurried.

Artisans had built the walls, masons had carved the stone. The ordinary folk of England – the laughing, sweating, suffering, flea-bitten population – had come to Sutton Place to work or watch men of rank at play. Plagues had killed them, wars had decimated them, yet Sutton Place still stood, posing a question by its very invulnerability: was it, in truth, the master of those who had dwelled within?

Something of this occurred to poor Miss Huss as she twittered and fluttered round the courtyard like an anxious bird, looking fearfully up at the soaring walls as if they would close around her at any moment; the windows staring back at her as blankly as unfriendly eyes.

'I'm glad we're going,' she exclaimed aloud. 'Anything will be better than this grim place.'

And then she jumped violently as someone said, right behind her, 'Miss Huss.'

Just for a fleeting second she had the notion that the house had a voice and was about to take her to task, but when she wheeled round she saw that it was only Cloverella Blanchard standing in the shade of the West Wing.

'Oh, you made me jump,' the governess said. 'What do you want, Cloverella? You shouldn't lurk about like that, frightening people.'

'Sorry, Miss,' answered the ragamuffin, dropping a small curtsey. 'It's just that I wondered if we might speak together for a moment.

'Yes, I suppose so. But I am very busy, you know. Mrs Webbe Weston is extremely upset and the whole responsibility of the move has fallen on my shoulders.'

'I dare say the Mistress will be able to spare you for a few minutes. Shall we step into the garden? It's more peaceful there.'

'Well, I . . .'

She wanted to say no, but Cloverella's merry hazelnut eyes were twinkling like a squirrel's and it was hard to refuse. Miss Huss reluctantly fell into step, feeling a fool when the wretched girl produced her battered flute and began to jig along in time to the music.

'Cloverella, really! We can be seen from the house.'

'That doesn't matter, Miss. Anyway, they're busy with the move, as you said yourself, and won't have time to be staring at us. Come on, Miss, dance a step or two.'

'No I won't. How can you be so silly? I must remind you that I am the governess and here to set an example.'

Cloverella turned to look at her, her black curls bouncing about her shoulders as she did so.

'Well then you should be more cheerful. You don't want them all growing up miserable, do you?'

'How dare you!'

'It's true, Miss. But I suppose you haven't a great deal to be cheerful about. Life didn't deal you out very good playing cards, did it?'

Miss Huss stopped in her tracks, her one desire to hit the dark little face that stared up at her so knowingly.

'What do you understand of it? How *can* you speak to me like this?'

'Because I want to help you. You weren't cut out for this life, Miss Huss. You should have married a curate and raised boys. Now then . . .' Cloverella's grubby hand fished into the depths of a vast pocket '. . . take this.'

She handed Miss Huss a particularly revolting toffee wrapped in a tattered piece of handkerchief.

'What is it?'

'You give that to the man of your choice and he won't be able to resist you.'

The governess threw it from her as if it were a snake.

'Cloverella, I'm shocked. You are speaking of spells and magic and things un-Christian.'

A very odd expression crossed Cloverella's face.

'Oh, so it's un-Christian, is it? It is wrong to help people, I suppose? Miss Huss, you know very little.'

'I know that to worship Satan is wrong.'

Just for a moment Cloverella looked very angry.

'I *don't* worship Satan, Miss. I worship God because He gave me life and wit; He gave me the chance to be outside in the sunshine and dance to my flute; He gave me breath, Miss, and He gave me the chance to take hold of Fate and do my best with it. I don't pity you, Miss. We all have opportunities and you – you are so busy bemoaning your lot that you don't give a bugger about taking them. Well then I'll have back my magic sweet and wish you the time of day.'

'Cloverella . . .'

'Yes?'

'May I keep it?'

'But you think it's ungodly.'

'Yes . . . No . . . I'm not sure.'

Cloverella pressed the toffee back into Miss Huss's palm.

'Listen, you foolish creature. It has been blessed with laughter and merriment – sounds the Devil doesn't like to hear. But I tell you this. It won't work unless you play your part.'

'What do you mean?'

'Learn to give out jollity; you'll get it back, I promise you. Now I'm going. I've spoken enough for one day. Keep the sweet and when you meet him, think of me.'

And Cloverella was off, her flute at her lips with a bravura trill, skipping into the forest with only the cry of 'Farewell, Miss Huss' to ring in the ears of the startled governess.

'No,' said the Earl.

'But James . . .'

'Anne, I said no. I don't want J.J. here any longer. It

is high time that he set up on his own. Anyway he makes too much noise.'

'But his health . . .'

The Earl looked up over his half spectacles and frowned. 'When he stops drinking so much it will improve.'

The Earl and Countess Waldegrave were in their bedroom at Strawberry Hill. In fact the Earl was in bed, propped comfortably against a cluster of lace-trimmed pillows and reading his customary newspaper, whilst the Countess sat at her dressing table brushing her light hair and peering at herself in the mirror for any sign of advancing years.

The bedroom was octagonal and was known as the Tribune – a name given to it by Walpole himself. It was set in one of the little castle's Gothic turrets and Anne – in a fit of enthusiasm upon her first arriving as mistress of the house – had clad the walls in blue and watered silk. The result was voluptuous, a veritable love nest, particularly when the merry log fire crackled in the grate like dragon's breath. She often blamed the five children that had been born after taking up residence on the watered silk, but at the moment nothing would have induced her to let the Earl so much as wink in her direction.

'Do you know, James,' she said now, looking at his reflection in the glass, 'you seem quite old when you glower. I personally try to keep my features composed. It is so much more attractive.'

'Really?' said the Earl without glancing.

'Yes. Also there is the fact that the eyes mirror the soul and if one is constantly glaring and squinting, people could not be blamed for thinking that one harboured something dark and demonic in one's depths.'

'Quite.'

'I do hope that none of the children will inherit this habit of yours. Of course poor J.J. cannot help contorting when he has a fit – oh, to think of his being alone when that should happen! – but if one of the girls should begin to resemble you! I dread to think about it.'

'Indeed.'

'I do believe that you are not listening.'

'I am. You have said that J.J. might be alone when he has a fit and my answer to that is the young rake is surrounded by doxies and drunks half the day and all the night. He'll fare very well at Navestock.'

'But Essex is so far away.'

'Rubbish.'

'Why is it,' said Anne with a sigh and more than a grain of truth, 'that parents who were the biggest libertines of their day are always the hardest task masters with their children?'

'Because,' answered the Earl, laying down his paper at last, 'they are only too aware that their children might take after them.' He eyed her up and down. 'You still turn a trim figure, my dear. Come and kiss me.'

'No, I won't. You are a wretched grump and a cruel father.'

'I see.'

'And beside you have grown so uncommonly ugly with all this frowning that I would as soon kiss a toad.'

The Earl took off his spectacles. He had no more grown ugly than Anne and as his piercing blue gaze fixed itself upon her, she blushed in discomfort.

'So you find me repellent?'

'Yes, horrible.'

She turned back to the mirror but was beginning to burn with the exultant excitement he could always arouse in her. In the glass she saw him get out of bed, his purple dressing gown brushing against the floor as he stood upright.

'Truly, truly hideous?'

'Yes.'

'Then I must use either force or persuasion to induce you to make love to me?'

The elation between them was crackling in the atmosphere.

'Yes.'

'Very well.'

He came up so close to her that a ribbon could not have gone between them.

'Shall I rape you, Countess – briskly, maritally, and without mercy?'

'No,' she breathed against the dark hair on his chest. 'Rape me with love.'

'Very well.'

She was off her feet and in the middle of their great bed before she could draw another breath. The Earl threw his gown to the floor and stood naked before her, smiling as insolently as he had on the day they first met. She flew at him but he caught both her hands in one of his and with the other lifted her on to his shaft. She was powerless as he moved inside her, first lazily as if he did not care – and then harder and harder and harder.

'Am I ugly, you little vixen?' he said in her ear.

'Yes.'

'Every bit of me?'

She could not answer.

'Even this bit?' He thrust so deep that she felt passion's culmination start inside her. 'Well?'

'I love you,' was all she could gasp.

'And I love you – damn you, blast you, pretty Anne King.'

They both cried out together as what was left of his

control deserted him and he pushed both of them ruthlessly over the cliffs of passion and into the tumultuous seas of rapture that roared beneath.

In the large bedroom to the front of Strawberry Hill, which Horatia shared with Annette and Ida Anna, she heard her parents shout out. Staring at the moon-silver ceiling, wide-eyed and sleepless, she wondered why they were arguing at this hour of the night. She also wondered why the house seemed pulsating with life when it should have been quiet and sleeping.

In the moonlight she called softly, 'Annette, are you awake?'

But there was no answer, only Ida Anna sighing and turning over in her bed. Putting her head cautiously over the counterpane, Horry stared about her. The room was as brightly lit, in a sharp platinum way, as ever it was in the daylight. Picked out by the moon's rays Horry could see the beds of her sisters and the fine lines of the Chippendale bedroom furniture which her family had collected over the years. Nothing moved anywhere and yet there was still that unearthly, almost tangible, feeling of stirring.

Without making a sound Horatia swung her legs over the side of the bed until her feet touched the Turkey carpet. Nothing seemed to breathe – including herself – as she slipped her woollen dressing gown about her shoulders and made for the door.

But once there she lost heart. For all its brilliance the September evening was chilly and she shivered as she stood at the top of the stairs. Beneath her she could see what Walpole had described as 'lean windows fattened with rich saints in painted glass' and – beyond three open archways – her kinsman's collection of relics of the Holy Wars. In the odd light the old coats of mail – mounted on dummy figures – took on a sinister life of their own and

Horry quivered at the very thought of walking past them. Instead she turned right and peeped for a moment into the famous Breakfast Room, Horace Walpole's favourite place in the entire building.

The thick velvet curtains had been drawn against the night and she imagined that her parents must have retired there after dining. Feeling her way with the familiarity of one who has known every inch from babyhood, Horatia crossed to the windows and drew back the drapery. Instantly everything was flooded with silver and even Walpole's sofa and the ancient marble urn in which he had kept his canister of Fribourg's *tabac d'étrennes* snuff, were transformed. For a minute Horatia wondered if he was in there with her, watching and smiling in the moonlight. In fact she wheeled sharply and drew a breath that was razor sharp, as a black shadow stirred itself and seemed to take shape on one of the sofas. But the arch of its back and the blink of an emerald eye told her that it was only her mother's cat spending a forbidden night within the confines of the house.

Suddenly nervous, she left the room intending to return to her bed, but as she regained the top of the stairs she heard a sound that made her freeze from head to foot – somebody was laughing, very quietly but very definitely, in the Gallery. She longed to move, but fear or curiosity – or both – kept her where she was.

She wondered if her mother and the Earl were perhaps up and kissing – a risky business, for Annette had told her that if a man kissed a woman she had a baby. Or was it a thief come to steal Horace Walpole's famous collection? Or was the shade of her ancestor walking in the Gallery and not the Breakfast Room at all?

A sudden burst of courage jettisoned her forward and down the passage, passing the Holbein Room – no longer a sitting room but now the place where George and J.J.

slept – on her right. To the left the door of the Gallery loomed large and, grasping the knob in brave fingers, she turned it silently.

The outlines of the extraordinary salon with its ornately moulded ceiling, carved woodwork, great carpet and mass of paintings, became clear to her at once in the argent light. She saw also that a high-backed sofa had been pulled before the fire and that on the floor, to the right of it, was a silver tray bearing several decanters and a selection of glasses. And as to who was drinking there was little doubt, for J.J.'s bare forearm – his shirt sleeve rolled up to his elbow – suddenly appeared in view, tipping out three glasses of port.

The soft laughter re-echoed and it became apparent to Horatia's horrified ears that J.J. was lying on the sofa with two females at the same time. Then – oh extraordinary and inexplicable happening! – a white petticoat, of the type worn by the maidservants, was thrown over the sofa back and a voice said, 'Come on, Master J.J. It's my turn now.'

Horry could listen to no more. She understood nothing except that J.J. was behaving 'badly', as her parents called it. She sped from the Gallery on bare silent feet. But something must have sounded for she heard J.J. call out, 'Who's there? God damn it, what's going on?'

She made no reply but scuttled into bed like a mouse, pulling the coverlet over her head and thinking of her parents' shout, J.J.'s soft laughter, the giggling of the maids. Things she did not comprehend were at work in Strawberry Hill that autumn night; things that made her fearful but curious, disturbed yet frighteningly excited.

Up in the mighty elm tree, whose boughs swept so near the drive of Sutton Place that anyone who bothered to climb would have a clear view of what was going on in the great house, sat Cloverella Blanchard; her bare legs dangling over the branch, her fingers working merrily on her ancient flute and her observant eyes fixing in a long appraising stare.

She saw the comings and goings, heard the shrieks and sighs, the weepings and the chucklings, that are an inherent part of the ritual of moving home. And she watched, without apparent emotion, the last personal possessions being stowed upon the hand cart. Then her flute was silent as first Mary, then Caroline, then Matilda, followed by a weeping Mrs Webbe Weston and finally a fluttering Miss Huss, piled into the carriage. She smiled as Mr Webbe Weston, gaitered leg swung well into the air, mounted his horse for fear of the crush.

She saw, her reed still quiet in her lap, John Joseph stand in the Middle Enter and wave his hand until the pathetic procession had plodded out of sight. Then she watched him turn back and enter the house for one last long look. The Westons had built Sutton Place in 1523; now – three hundred and eight years later – the last of their lineage, their kinsmen by marriage and distant cousinship, were leaving. The cycle was over – the age of tenants and strangers was about to begin.

5

'Jackdaw? What the deuce, it can't be! But it *is* you!'

The small elegant figure walking before John Joseph down Drury Lane, swinging its cane and occasionally throwing its wide-crowned top hat in the air, turned in its tracks. There was a moment's pause before it let out a loud shout of, 'John Joseph, by God! I thought I'd never see you again. How are you?' and they fell upon each other, slapping backs and shaking hands like long-lost brothers. Then, after a while, they stood at arm's length to appraise the difference that four years had brought about.

They were both young men now, handsome in their different ways. John Joseph dashing and fine with beautiful eyes and a sensual mouth; Jackdaw small and dark as his namesake, and dressed like a dandy in trousers and half-boots and a nipped-waist coat with padded shoulders.

'You've changed,' said John Joseph. 'What have you been up to?'

'I left school at the end of last year. I've been in Russia.'

'What for? No, don't tell me now. I'm off to my club. Come with me – or do you have an appointment?'

Jackdaw shook his head. 'I've already kept one. John Joseph, I was seen this morning by the General Command. I'm to join the Army!'

John Joseph gaped and Jackdaw added hurriedly, 'No, I still limp. But it is for something special. I'll tell you in a minute. How far is your place?'

'Just round the corner. It is nothing very grand, I'm afraid. We are not quite up to the scratch of White's.'

'Who cares? A drink is a drink – and I've the rest of the day free to celebrate.'

'Then what better! Come on, you wretch – I'm riddled with envy.'

Arms round each other's shoulders and laughing as if it were still that far-away Christmas when they had first met, the pair stepped briskly down Maiden Lane and into a small but prettily pillared room. The discreet pink shades over the candelabra and the presence of two ladies with high-built and feathered hairstyles caused Jackdaw's eyebrows to rise but John Joseph whispered to him with a grin, 'No, it is not what you think – though I believe that would be available if you desired it. The place is owned by a Mrs Fitz and those are her two daughters, so take that lecherous look off your face.'

Jackdaw shook his head, his eyes slightly rueful.

'Alas, I still lead a sheltered life, John Joseph. Russia was dark with mystery – and its women remained so as well. Perhaps the Army will broaden my education.'

'You can wager on it. Now tell me how you managed to pull your posting off, you lucky fox.'

'Well, they don't want me for my physical prowess. No, it is just that I speak ten languages.'

'Good God – I didn't know. What are they?'

'The usual European plus Russian – that's why I was there, to become fluent – Hungarian, Polish, Portuguese, Rumanian. I am starting on the Easterns next year.'

John Joseph sat back in his chair and drained his glass of wine.

'I had no idea you were that clever. So why do the Army require your services – to be a spy?'

'Yes, actually. In the event of hostilities I am to go

behind the lines. I am also to assist with translations and the questioning of prisoners-of-war.'

John Joseph looked suddenly sad. 'I wish to God it was me. I would change places with you any day. Damn it, Jackdaw, I don't see where my future lies. Being a Catholic precludes me from so much – yet I can't go on like this. Quite honestly I am nothing but a land bailiff. I see the tenants into Sutton Place and see them out again. I check inventories and ride about collecting rents. It's a hideous existence. I would do anything to be an Army man but what hope have I as a British officer?'

Jackdaw finished his glass and poured another.

'Have you thought of foreign service?' he said. 'How old are you now?'

'Twenty.'

'Then apply to a Catholic country. Spain – or perhaps Austria.'

'Do you think there's a chance?'

'Of course. You know how many mercenaries there are in both those armies. My great-great-grandfather fought for the Spanish Queen when he lost his fortune.'

'Then perhaps I should emulate him, for we most certainly have lost ours. Jackdaw, we live in Pomona House in the Home Park these days. We have had to let Sutton Place.'

'I know. My father wrote to yours two years ago when you were on the point of moving . . .'

'And my mother threw an hysteric that lasted all summer long. Yes, I remember vividly. But you must come and stay next week. Are you able to?'

'Yes. My enrolment is not for another twenty-one days. I have that time to say goodbye to my wives and sweethearts – if only there were any.'

'I think,' said John Joseph, peering up over imaginary spectacles and giving a wink, 'that I must introduce you to Cloverella Blanchard. I think you two might get on very well together. After all she is descended from magic stock too.'

'Cloverella,' answered Jackdaw slowly. 'I seem somehow to know that name.'

Beneath a tree in a shady bower at Strawberry Hill, Lady Horatia Waldegrave lay sleeping. At some distance away her sister Annette – now fifteen and considered fair of feature – sat busy at her embroidery, and even further off, Lady Ida Anna dug in the ground and made sandshapes with an old cake tin. They were all that was left of the family at home, for J.J. now had his own household on the Earl's estates at Navestock in Essex and George, who had left Eton, was on the Continent doing the Grand Tour.

Things had grown quiet – and definitely boring – since the departure of the two boys and Annette, her light blue eyes apparently fixed on the delicate stitching of a golden humming bird, was in fact busy watching the gardener's boy. She wondered what it would be like to kiss him – for though he was a labourer and really rather stupid looking he was big and strong and broad, and would make a pleasant diversion in the monotony of her everyday life.

She had, at one time, been close to Horatia but now the change in Annette's body, and the commencement of the moon's cycle within, had put her on a different plane. Instead of one of the little girls of the household she had become the eldest unmarried daughter at home. Within the next two years the governess would have done with her and then she could be introduced by her parents to polite society and the marriage market. She felt she could hardly wait.

But Horatia – fast asleep and dreaming peacelessly – sensed none of those things. She wandered, at first, on the banks of a great and fast-flowing river. Not her own dearly loved Thames, nor even a river she had ever seen before – but somewhere alien and foreign to her. And though it flowed through green and flower-strewn pastures where cattle bent their heads in idyllic grazing, somewhere – not too far distant – roared the sound of battle. She heard the whine of shot, the boom of cannon, the constant shouts and screams of men.

And – most frighteningly – she suffered in the midst of that tumult a terrible sense of loneliness. No – worse than that – of separation, of bereavement. She knew what it was like, as she walked along the banks of that strange river, to be completely solitary. She felt that she would be alone for the rest of her life.

The dream changed and melted. She stood now before an altar in a chapel that lay above the sea's sweep, at her side a man whose face was turned away.

'Oh, my love,' she said, 'who are you, what is happening to me?'

'Don't be afraid, Horry,' he answered. 'Give me your hand and let me break the spell.'

'But I am frightened.'

'Trust me,' he said.

And with that he led her out and she stood in a welter of bell sound, watching the gulls wheel beneath a cloudless sky and the sea pound against a great white rock. Far in the distance a solitary figure walked down the sand and out of her line of vision.

'Who was that?' she said to the bridegroom.

'He who has stepped out,' he answered. And with that he began to weep silently.

The dream changed once more and she found herself standing before a forbidding house that loomed against the sky like a tower. She was alone again, only she and the mansion in all the empty world. She knew somehow that she must not go in – for if she did she would never come out again. But a yawning door situated quite centrally in the building swung open before her as she watched it.

'Who's there?' she called out.

But there was no answer. Then she saw in horror that a figure was forming and had come to stand upon the step, grinning at her. She could not look at it. It was cruelty in the flesh. It reeked of death and despair – and yet it smiled and beckoned.

'I will not enter,' she shouted out.

But it stood there, immutable, grimacing at her futility.

'Who will help me?' she called in desperation. But only her own voice echoed back off the heartless stonework.

She turned to run but her way was barred by a thick forest that had suddenly grown up round the house and almost hidden it from sight. And that was how she woke, struggling with a branch of a shadowy tree that had bent in the wind and brushed against her face.

'What is it, Horry?' said Annette. 'You're making the most dreadful noise.'

'I've been dreaming. Frightening things. I dreamt of getting married too. That wasn't frightening – just strange.'

'Well, you can't dream of it yet,' answered Annette. 'Remember the rule. The eldest must wed before the others. Did you dream of my wedding as well?'

'No – just mine and the bridegroom's.'

'Who was he?'

'Only a dream person,' answered Horatia.

Dawn over Drury Lane was enlivened that next summer morning by an extraordinary sight. Staggering forth, arms supporting one another, and mixing none too readily with the crowd of hawkers, milkmaids, beggars and starved humanity which was already thronging the streets of London, were two young gentlemen obviously the worse for a night of debauchery. One – John Joseph – was minus his cravat whilst the other's – Jackdaw's – hat was rammed down over his eyes in an inelegant manner. Furthermore the younger man was only wearing one boot, his right foot being clad simply in a silk sock.

'Well?' said John Joseph.

'Well what?'

'Do you feel a man at last? By the way the two Misses Fitz dived upon you I thought never to see you alive again.'

Jackdaw winced. 'My head is throbbing fit to burst.'

'Not only your head I should imagine!' John Joseph retorted rudely.

Jackdaw laughed.

'Now, how are you travelling to Hastings?'

'By chaise. I don't think my head and I would stay together if I attempted the railway.'

'Never mind. They'll have it right one of these days. So, I shall see you at Pomona House next week?'

'Indeed you shall. Will we be able to go inside Sutton Place?'

'There's a new tenant arriving within the next two or three days. But we can present our compliments no doubt.'

'Good. Despite its discomforts I have some fond memories of it.'

'Very well. My kindest regards to your mother – and to the General of course.'

'Of course.'

Jackdaw gave one of his odd little bows and groaned as his head hammered in response. Then he disappeared into the crowd, his limp pronounced by the fact that his built-up boot had gone astray and was – at that very moment – adorning the bedroom of the elder Miss Fitz, filled with flowers and tied about with John Joseph's cravat.

Five hours later he arrived at Hastings wishing that he had taken the railroad after all. Since George Stephenson had won the Rainhill Trials four years earlier – in 1829 – with the fabulous Rocket, railways were springing up all over the country, starting with the line from Liverpool to Manchester which had been opened to the public on September 15, 1830. And though he could not have completed his journey Jackdaw would have saved himself a tedious hour or so.

Therefore, as he disembarked outside his house in the hill-hung crescent, he glanced at his watch and – realizing that he had been away for nearly forty-eight hours – crept surreptitiously down the area steps to the servants' entrance. Admonishing all who met him to silence, he was on his way to his bedroom to restore his battered appearance when he heard Helen call out from her sitting room, 'Violet, is that you?'

'No Mother,' shouted the pretty creature from behind her brother. 'It is Jackdaw creeping up the stairs like a scallowag. He is all in disarray and has a lady's stocking peeping out from his top pocket.'

Helen's light laugh rang out. 'Has he now! Come here, both of you.'

She was sitting in her favourite window seat where she had been engaged on gazing out into the sea-bright distance, a small telescope lying in her hand to aid her. But now she turned to look at her children with eyes bright as a bird's.

Since her illness two years ago she had grown a little thinner, a little more fragile. Yet she had lost none of her old attractiveness, nor still – or so Jackdaw thought – did she look very much over twenty-five. No wonder his father gazed upon her to this day with unconcealed infatuation. But the General was away in barracks and at the present moment Jackdaw was the acting head of the household.

So it was a little guiltily that he said, 'I am so sorry to have been out last night. Forgive me.'

But Helen merely smiled and answered, 'I gather from your appearance that you have been celebrating. Jackdaw, have they taken you in the Army? Was the interview successful?'

'Yes.' He picked her up in his arms, swinging her out of her chair. 'Yes, yes, yes, my darling Mama. I am John Wardlaw – soldier.'

Violet let out a squeal and jumped where she stood, her tight black curls bouncing about her little face.

'What wonderful news! Your father will be so proud of you. I shall write to him immediately.'

Jackdaw stood his mother gently upon her feet.

'Yes,' he said slowly, 'I will too. As soon as I have changed.'

He was aware, even as he said it, that the General would receive the letters with mixed feelings: could imagine the bewhiskered face drawing set, the truculent eye changing expression as he read that all his predictions had been wrong; that his lame son had followed him in the great family tradition and gone to be a soldier for King William IV. Jackdaw knew as well as if he had been present that General Wardlaw would once more feel the terrible tug of jealousy at his heart – and then curse himself for it. Poor wretched man!

Helen said with a straight face, 'So a new era has begun for you, my son.'

He looked at her quizzically, but there was only the merest hint of a twinkle as she went on, 'We will all have to regard you as an officer and a man of the world from now on, I see.'

The Chapel had – if anything – grown slightly worse since Melior Mary, in a fit of ungovernable religious mania, had desecrated the Long Gallery and turned it into a house of prayer. Down the whole of one wall ugly patches of mould, with their accompanying damp smell, were visible and flecks of fungus were eating into the canvases of the many and ghastly pictures of martyred saints and suffering Christs hung about the place.

The lofty windows with their finely moulded sills – once the pride of the English craftsmen who had made them to the architect da Trevizi's design – were now virtually blocked up by interweaving tendrils and foliage of ivy, and the light that they threw was dim and full of shadows.

And it was at one of these shadows that Cloverella – who had been given the unenviable job of cleaning up the mansion house for the new tenant – now stared in horror. It seemed to her that a small pale boy stood there. A boy whose mutilated leg hung above the ground like a crushed matchstick and whose pitiful eyes gazed at her beseechingly, while his features were contorted into such a grimace of fear and agony that she thought she would faint just looking at it.

Wheeling, a frantic scream upon her lips, the servant practically jumped the length of the Great Staircase to arrive panting and trembling in the Hall beneath.

'Good gracious!' said a modulated voice, with the merest hint of an Irish accent in its tones. 'Really!'

Pushing her escaping hair off her face and back into her mob cap, Cloverella peered towards the Middle Enter. A woman stood there, her back to the light.

'This *is* Sutton Place, isn't it?' the stranger went on as

if she could not believe that such an exhibition of careless behaviour or such a scruffy urchin could possibly be associated with so grand a house.

'Yes, Miss,' said Cloverella.

'Mrs! Mrs Augustus Trevelyan.'

The woman stepped forward and the light from the stained glass fell on her, showing her clearly to Cloverella's unblinking gaze. She stood quite tall – possibly as much as five feet seven – and was as slim and willowy as a nymph, even her hands being long and thin and her feet, in their neat boots, narrow and pointed. Her many-caped pelisse of purple silk did nothing to detract from her slenderness, nor did the leg-of-mutton sleeves hide her shapely arms. As she moved forward – which she did now – she swayed slightly and a distinctive scent of gardenias wafted from her heavy skirts.

'And you must be the serving girl,' she said.

Her speech was extremely cultured; careful almost, as if she took pride in her beautifully modulated tones.

Cloverella rubbed the back of her hand over her cheek, making a smudge of dirt streak right across her face.

'Yes, Miss – er, Mrs.'

'Well, we shall have to improve your appearance, won't we? I dare say with a good scrub and a neat uniform you might look quite presentable. Of course, I shall be bringing my personal staff with me, but Mr Webbe Weston did say that the domestics and labourers would be provided by the estate.'

Cloverella's face cleared. 'Oh, you must be the new tenant. I'd expected someone older. Old Blanchard said it was a widow woman who was renting the house.'

Mrs Trevelyan smiled sweetly, the sort of smile given to a child or simpleton.

'I am afraid, my dear, that one can be a widow even when one is as young as I.'

'Oh – you don't look *that* young. Just not old, that's all.'

Mrs Trevelyan gave a tinkling little laugh.

'This really isn't the sort of conversation for mistress and servant, my dear. Or perhaps you didn't know that. Never mind, with my guidance you will be fit to go into service one day, I promise you. Now what is your name?'

'Cloverella. Cloverella Blanchard. I'm the old man's bastard.'

Mrs Trevelyan winced, her soft blue eyes rolling upward slightly.

'We don't use that kind of word in polite conversation, Cloverella. I can see that we shall have to keep you firmly below stairs for the time being. Now, how much more work do you have to do? I must say that the place looks none too clean.'

She ran a gloved finger along the window sill, leaving a trail in the dust.

'Several hours more, Mam. But then we weren't expecting you until tomorrow.'

'I am staying at the Angel in Guildford for a few days while my things are sent on from Manchester. The first of them will come up in the morning and I shall spend tomorrow night here. I shall move in properly over the following two days.'

She smiled a sugar smile.

'I shall be off now; I've a deal of organizing to do. When you have finished cleaning be sure to lock up – and if you see Mr Webbe Weston would you ask him to call on me that we may discuss the fine details?'

'It will be Mr Webbe Weston Junior who'll come. He is the estate agent now.'

Mrs Trevelyan waved a gloved hand.

'Whoever! Now, Cloverella, I would like fresh flowers in every room – gardenias in the room in which I shall

102

sleep, which is the largest in the West Wing. And get the gardener to cut back the ivy from that wretched Chapel. I know it is open to the public but that does not alter the fact that it is still in my house.'

'The house you are renting,' said Cloverella.

Mrs Trevelyan arched her cheek bones. 'Quite. Now before you report tomorrow morning to help with the hand carts I would like you to have a bath.'

'I don't have those, Mam. I swim in the river with no clothes on. Won't that do?'

'No. I mean the tin bath with hot water. Otherwise, Cloverella, I shall have to speak of it to Mr Webbe Weston.'

Cloverella giggled. 'He swims too, Mam.'

Mrs Trevelyan chose to ignore that, merely patting her honey-coloured hair to ensure its swept-up smoothness beneath her purple flowered hat.

'I must say adieu. Don't frown, Cloverella. I am sure that a fine strong girl like you will suit very nicely. Good day to you.'

Leaning on her parasol she turned and walked sway-ingly out of the Middle Enter. The scent of gardenias was everywhere.

'Well!' said Cloverella. 'I wonder what her husband died of. Choked on honey, most like.'

And picking up her pail and mop she made her way crossly to the West Wing, putting as much distance as possible between herself and the Chapel – and the retreat-ing form of Mrs Trevelyan which was by now bowling down the drive in a trim trap, her slender back and neck held in perfect and lady-like straightness.

With his slightly old-fashioned mistrust of the railway system, Jackdaw chose to make the journey from Hastings to Guildford in a light one-horse travelling coach from

103

his father's stable. And consequently, having rested overnight, it was mid-morning when he finally turned through
the wrought-iron gates and clipped down the drive.

In his memory he was back four years, thinking of the
grandeur of the Home Park under snow and the gaunt
castle that was Sutton Place in winter. But now everything
was bright with sunshine, except where the fully leafed
trees formed a tunnel of green as he drove beneath.

He found his thoughts wandering frighteningly. He
remembered that game of hide-and-seek during which
Sam Clopper had disappeared and which he had only
managed to avoid by pleading a headache. He remembered, too, the flash of clairvoyance that had shown him
a coffin lid closing just before the game had begun. And
how they had never found Sam Clopper and, as far as he
knew, had not done so to this day.

And then he thought of his own mysterious gift and
wondered why it had gone away again since that one
brief vision of Helen on her deathbed. He had not seen
the red-headed girl for years and nowadays he doubted
her existence. She was a dream of childhood, a vision
come to taunt a little boy with too much imagination.

And yet that time when – through the mediumship of
his marble – he had stood on the riverbank and watched
her and her naughty brothers. It had seemed so real and
she, in turn, had seemed so aware of his presence.

'Hell!' said Jackdaw out loud.

Sutton Place was just coming into view round the bend
of the drive and he slowed the carriage to walking pace.
He had never seen it in summer before and the glow of
the brickwork was russet in the brightness. Like the girl's
hair. He suddenly had the overwhelming feeling that she
was real, a creature of flesh and blood like himself, and
that Sutton Place was the link between them.

'I'll meet you one day,' he said, and was rather startled

to see a gardener's boy – of particularly stupid mien – gazing at him in astonishment.

'Oh yes,' Jackdaw went on, unreasonably annoyed by the cod-like stare, 'I'll meet you. But who are you? Is it *you*, Sir? Are ye he whom I seek? Come here, my boy.'

He grinned and beckoned evilly and the lad lurched off into the Forest, shouting, 'Go away! I've heard about men like you. My Da will come and hit you.'

'And I,' shouted Jackdaw, bursting into song, 'will thicken his ear-o! Yes, yes, his ear; tra la la, la la, la!'

'For God's sake,' said John Joseph's voice behind him, 'stop frightening the servants. We have few enough left as it is.'

For no reason immensely jolly all of a sudden, Jackdaw gave a hoot of laughter and turned to see his friend trotting up on a great bay hunter and looking very fine in a periwinkle blue cutaway and black top hat.

'Well, there's one I would prefer not to drive off,' he answered with a wink. 'And that's Cloverella Blanchard. Where is she?'

John Joseph laughed. 'Grumbling fit to burst at present. The new tenant has got her running like a hare. She's never worked so hard in her life. Jackdaw, how are you?'

'Excessively well. Who *is* the new tenant?'

'Didn't I say? A Mrs Marguerite Trevelyan – widow of the late Augustus Trevelyan, merchant of Liverpool and a stockholder of the Liverpool and Manchester railway.'

Jackdaw whistled softly. 'Worth a guinea or two, then?'

'So it is said. She has rented Sutton Place in order to entertain her friends quietly – as befits her widowed status.'

'What is she like?'

'I don't know. I haven't met her yet – but reports vary. My father said, "Dashed handsome," my mother said,

"Expensive clothes." But Cloverella said, "Not what she seems," so . . .'

'So, worth a visit.'

'I am to call tonight to discuss the rental agreement. I might well ask you to accompany me.'

'I should be delighted.' Just as Jackdaw said this the most vivid feeling of ill-ease overtook him. Something, somewhere, had taken the wrong turn. One of fortune's wheels had started off on the wrong tangent. He stared at John Joseph not quite sure what to add.

'You don't seem very delighted.'

'I'm sorry. Something walked over my grave.'

John Joseph turned away abruptly, heading his bay for the Home Park and Pomona House.

'You haven't changed, have you?' he said. 'Always one to add a strange note. You depress me sometimes, Jackdaw.'

'I don't mean to. But occasionally I get these feelings.'

'I know only too well.'

'Do you remember the night Sam Clopper vanished? That was the very last time I had a vision, except when my mother was ill.'

John Joseph's face took on a strained expression.

'Cloverella told me she saw a ghost in the Chapel a few days ago.'

'Would that have been the legendary Giles?'

'No, strangely enough it wasn't. She said it was a crippled boy with a sad white face. She said he limped towards her with his arms outstretched and a look of such anguish upon his face. Jackdaw, it made me feel sick to hear it. Somewhere, somehow, Sam must have died in misery in Sutton Place.'

'He still hasn't been found?'

'No.'

Pomona House – its elegant Georgian façade looking

effete in comparison with that of the manor house – was visible in the distance.

'God, I hate this place,' said John Joseph.

'The smaller house, you mean?'

'No, just *here*; Sutton; Guildford. I wish I was a thousand miles away. I wish I was anybody else.' One of the violent swings of mood that occasionally threw John Joseph off course had beset him.

'Why?'

'You know why. Jackdaw, I want to get on in life. I want to be an Army man and make my mark – not be stuck here as some futureless and snivelling little estate agent, whimpering round tenants and running to the bottle every five minutes for consolation. Yet however hard I try I feel I am a marked man. I am heir to a curse. How can I succeed at anything?'

Jackdaw gave him a piercing look. 'I've told you before – get away. Go abroad and make your life far from Sutton Place. And if you feel it such a bird of ill omen, sell the house when it becomes yours. We are all masters of our fate to some extent.'

'That's what Cloverella says.'

'Then she speaks good sense.'

The seascape eyes regarded Jackdaw with no warmth. 'It is not easy in this situation, believe me.'

Jackdaw would have liked to tell his friend that his fears were groundless; that the curse of Sutton Place was nothing but a set of coincidences strung together over the centuries and dwelled on by those with nothing better to do with their time. But he could not do so. He knew perfectly well that the house was brimming with force; defying anyone who owned it to deny its omnipotence. He was glad that the front door of Pomona House was opening, stopping any further attempt at conversation.

Mrs Webbe Weston waved a feeble hand.

'Oh, Jackdaw. How nice. My goodness me but you have grown up. It makes one feel old to see it. I do hope we won't be too dull here for you. Of course this house is terribly cramped in comparison to what we have lost.' She rolled her eyes piteously and laid her hand upon her breast. 'But you know how things are – needs must when the Devil drives. I do hope there will be enough for luncheon.'

She hadn't changed a bit, still as silly-mouthed and ineffectual as ever.

'The girls are at home, of course,' she went on. 'But you'll see some changes there. Mary is eighteen now – and quite the beauty.' A calculating look appeared behind her vacuous eye and Jackdaw realized with a shock that he was being assessed as possible husband material. 'Oh yes, she's lovely, isn't she my dear?'

This question was addressed to Mr Webbe Weston who had appeared, red-faced and trudging, round the side of the house.

'Oh yes, capital. Nest of charmers. Ha Ha, Jackdaw!'

Jackdaw fingered his cravat and John Joseph stared at the ground.

'Come in, come in.' Mrs Webbe Weston was gushing now as her new train of thoughts took a grip. 'This really *is* a special occasion. Fancy, four years since we all met. What a happy chance that you ran into John Joseph in London. And what wonderful news that you will be entering the Army. Your family must be delighted. How is dear Helen?'

All the while she had been ushering her guest into a drawing room where a half-filled decanter of sherry and four glasses stood on a sideboard in preparation.

'John Joseph,' Mrs Webbe Weston's laugh trilled archly, 'ask Mary to step in here to greet her old friend. And tell Amy to bring more glasses. Sit down, Jackdaw, so. What a pleasure. Do you think, dear . . .' this last remark addressed to her husband '. . . that we might bring another bottle up from the cellar as it is so long since we have seen dear Jackdaw?'

'Splendid, yes. Nest of *charmers*! Eh, Jackdaw?'

He slapped his thigh and disappeared, rumbling with laughter. And it was while he was gone that poor Mary flew into the room and stopped short, her face going pink, on seeing Jackdaw sitting there.

She thought he had grown terribly handsome and loved the way his eyes seemed full of sparkling lights when he smiled. She also liked the curl of his dark hair about his ears and his small, elegant figure. Impressionable and cut off from more eligible young men by the fact that her parents could barely afford to entertain, Mary fell a little in love.

Jackdaw sprang to his feet and gave one of his formal bows and then kissed Mary's hand, at which she went pinker and pinker. She had not turned into a beauty at all but was a pleasant looking girl with a plump pretty figure. But she had very full and exciting breasts, Jackdaw could not help but notice.

'How do you do, Jackdaw?' she said.

'Very well, Mary. How wonderful to see you after so many years.'

She blushed again. 'I'm afraid we're not very good hosts these days. We don't have a great deal of company.'

'Nonsense.' Mr Webbe Weston had come back into the room bearing a dusty bottle of indifferent sherry. 'Enjoy friends. Especially kin. Distant cousins. Eh?' He gave a terribly knowing wink in the direction of his wife and rumbled into another laugh. 'Shot pheasants. Eat 'em tonight. Gala occasion.'

'Don't forget that I have to call on Mrs Trevelyan at

six,' John Joseph put in. 'And I thought I'd take Jackdaw with me. He wants to get a look at Sutton Place.'

'It's clean. New broom.' Mr Webbe Weston laughed uproariously at his own joke. 'Fine woman. Dashed fine.'

The door opened again and Matilda and Caroline rushed in shouting, 'Is Jackdaw here? You've grown up!'

The passing of time had made them even more unalike than they had been as children. Matilda had grown rounder and browner, for she had taken to wearing earth-coloured clothes which did nothing at all to make her more comely. Caroline, on the other hand, had traded on her wheaten looks and had a mass of fair curls tumbling from an Apollo knot whilst darkening her eyebrows above her light pupils. There could be no argument that, of the three girls, it was she who had emerged as the Beauty.

They all sat smiling at one another, sipping the over-sweet liquid, until Jackdaw said, 'Where is Miss Huss?'

There was a pause followed by a gale of laughter.

'You mean Lady Gunn,' said John Joseph.

'Lady Gunn?'

'She has married Sir Roly Gunn – a bachelor of strange reputation – whose horse threw him outside our very front door.'

Jackdaw stared astounded and John Joseph took up the story.

'It was quite the most incredible thing. This beastly old man – all of fifty and with a fierce reputation for seductions . . . begging your pardon, Mother. I do realize the girls are present . . . limped in here all battered and bruised. And within twenty-four hours he had proposed to Huss. It was just as if he were bewitched. The old lecher . . . sorry, Mother . . . was positively seething with passion. I've never seen anything like it.'

'Spellbound. Quite,' said Mr Webbe Weston. 'Extra-ordinary. Rum really.'

110

'Good Heavens. I can't imagine Miss Huss as Lady Gunn.'

'From fish to armament in one magic stride,' said John Joseph – and they all laughed.

But later as they trotted towards Sutton Place to call on Mrs Trevelyan, John Joseph said, 'Do you know it really was a strange affair – the governess and Roly Gunn. If she hadn't been who she was I would swear that she'd used a love potion on him. He was such a stinking old ram. The last person to fall for a bag of bones like Huss. Mind you, she had a funny look in her eye, didn't you think so?'

'No,' said Jackdaw. 'I didn't. But then I was very young at the time and not nearly as worldly as you.'

'It was a feverish expression. Ah well, perhaps she and Roly are having a fine time between the sheets.'

They rode on pleasantly together in the dapple of early evening, watching a heron swoop down over the River Wey to seize a lively fish and a lark ascending to the limits of the sky.

As always when he glimpsed Sutton Place Jackdaw found himself breathing a little faster. John Joseph, seeing this, said, 'It moves you, doesn't it, that great heap?'

'I find the house very profound, yes.'

'Will you buy it off me when you've amassed a fortune as a spy and risen to the rank of Field Marshal?'

The 'no' was out of Jackdaw's mouth a little too fast.

'I thought not – for all your admiration of it you wouldn't want to own the wretched place.'

It was undeniably true so Jackdaw said nothing. Once again a feeling was nagging at his spine, a feeling that trouble lurked somewhere – and not too far away at that. He wondered if perhaps the arrival of Mrs Trevelyan into the dull lives of the Webbe Westons was potentially dangerous and hoped that perhaps his sixth sense would

111

give him the answer. But as he followed John Joseph and a pompous butler into a small salon that – so he believed – had once belonged to Elizabeth Weston, the mother of Melior Mary, his old clairvoyance still eluded him.

'If you would take a seat, gentlemen. Mrs Trevelyan will join you in a moment.'

John Joseph stared round in amazement. Something of the old style had returned to the mansion house – or to this room at least. At the mullioned windows, which looked out over both the courtyard and the Park – exactly the same view as that from the Long Gallery but in the other wing – the new tenant had hung powder-blue velvet curtains. For light fittings she had chosen shell pink and a white jardiniere, beside a cherry-wood desk, was tightly packed with ferns and indoor flowers. What had been rotting but a short month before was now revived. Mrs Trevelyan had transformed her sitting room into a deliciously feminine retreat.

The heir was just about to remark on the change in the manor house when a rustle in the doorway told him that they were no longer alone. He stood up and bowed his head slightly and then, on looking up, found himself gazing into the eyes of the new tenant of Sutton Place. She smiled briefly and then decorously cast her glance to the floor. Beneath the harsh material of his riding jacket John Joseph felt his heart-beat getting faster.

Marguerite Trevelyan, as befitted her widowed status, was wearing purple – only this or black being considered good taste. But what a colour it was! She stood, the evening light falling softly upon her, as beautiful as a Parma violet, her thick honeyed hair decorated with flowers of the same name. In her long tapering fingers she carried a tiny fan of lace, and satin shoes of a matching shade encased her narrow feet.

112

'Gentlemen, do sit down,' she said with a little laugh. 'I am Marguerite Trevelyan. Mr Weston?'

She advanced towards Jackdaw with her hand outstretched. They were the same height to the last fraction of an inch and their eyes met fully. Instantly he did not trust her. There was something in that pale blue look that gave him a lurch of unease.

He made, for him, a very formal bow.

'No, Ma'am. John Wardlaw, at your service. I took the liberty of calling with Mr Webbe Weston. I stayed at Sutton Place during my boyhood and have fond memories of the place.'

Out of the corner of his eye he saw John Joseph look slightly startled at the stiffness of Jackdaw's speech. But, more tellingly, for a split second he saw relief pass over Mrs Trevelyan's face that he was not her landlord. She had taken as instantaneous a dislike to him as he had to her.

She turned round then and laid her hand – very, very briefly – in that of John Joseph. Jackdaw noticed that, quite involuntarily, his friend's fingers fractionally tightened before Mrs Trevelyan withdrew hers, fluttering as delicately as any bird.

'Please,' she said again, 'do sit down. I am so delighted to make your acquaintance, Mr Webbe Weston. I was going to make a point of calling upon your Mama in the morning and inviting you all to dine with me.'

He recaptured her hand and brushed his lips against it.

He was trembling very slightly as he said, 'It will be our pleasure to do so, Mrs Trevelyan. Please be assured that we will be your servants in all things.'

6

'Well, I've never seen such a to-do,' said Caroline Webbe Weston, pushing a straying curl from her eyes as she wrestled with Mary's gown. 'From the way you're all going on anyone would think you were to dine with the King. I only thank Heaven that Mama turned the invitation down. We would never have got her dressed, never!'

She was kneeling on the floor, struggling to make her sister look presentable in an evening frock that had once belonged to their aunt, and which had been renovated in a panic during the twelve hours since Mrs Trevelyan had called with her invitation to dinner.

'Thank goodness Matilda and I were considered too young to be included. God alone knows what *we* would have worn – old curtains I should think.'

'It *is* awful,' Mary agreed, swaying round to see her reflection in a long mirror. 'Aunt Bridget is practically flat-chested and here am I squeezed in like a sausage. Oh Caroline, I know I look a sight and Mrs Trevelyan is so terribly beautiful.'

'I think she is insipid.' Caroline's voice was muffled as she now had her head beneath Mary's hem, doing some last-minute stitching. 'Not all men like thin women. Jackdaw, for example, admires your breasts.'

Mary went the colour of a poppy. 'Caroline, what an awful thing to say. How could you!' There was a slight pause and then she added, 'What ever makes you think that?'

'I've noticed him looking.'

'Really?'

'Yes, really. Mary, you're quite red. I believe you're in love with him. I wondered why you were making such a fuss at not being able to have a new dress.'

'Only because I didn't want to look shabby in comparison with Mrs Trevelyan.'

'Hum. Well, whatever the reason, you needn't worry about her. She's in mourning.'

'Yes,' said Mary – unconvinced.

But mourning or no mourning, as the three guests – John Joseph, Jackdaw and Mary – sat expectantly in Mrs Trevelyan's saloon, there was not one of them who did not stare in amazement at the vision that rustled in a minute or two late, a favourite trick of hers.

She had, for this night, pushed purple – a widow's only second choice of colour – to the very limit of its shading. Her taffeta gown, scooped so low at the front that her shoulders were bare, was a delicate shade of lilac, and strewn all over the skirt, as if she had been standing in a shower of petals, were a hundred little violets. The same flowers bedecked an ivory comb that secured her Grecian hairstyle and her honey-coloured curls were tied with satin ribbons the colour of lupins. She was entrancing, reducing Mary, in her aunt's cast-off salmon pink, to the status of a frump.

'My dears,' she said, 'how wonderful that you could come. But I am so sorry that your Mama and Papa were unable to be with you.'

John Joseph, who had risen politely, said, 'They go out very rarely. Mother has suffered with her nerves somewhat of late. They send their deepest apologies.'

Mrs Trevelyan gave a brilliant smile and addressed herself to poor Mary who sat, her hands in her lap, staring at her hostess.

'Then we shall just have to entertain these two handsome gentlemen on our own, won't we my dear? Come, let us have some refreshment before we dine.'

The pompous butler was through the door as if he had been waiting for the summons and they all found themselves with an excellent sherry in a crystal glass, served somewhat colder than any of them were used.

'My late husband always liked his sherry chilled,' Mrs Trevelyan said by way of explanation. 'I believe he got the idea whilst living abroad. I miss him sorely, of course. But then he was very much older than I.'

She gave a courageous smile and John Joseph longed for nothing more, at that moment, than to take her hand and comfort her. Yet, at the same time, he was glad to hear that the late Augustus Trevelyan had been of declining years. The thought of all that fragile loveliness subjected to the rough ardour of a young man made him hot with emotion. Yet, contradictorily, neither could he bear the thought of old decaying hands fondling Mrs Trevelyan.

Staring at her, at the tiny waist enclosed in its sheathlike bodice, seeing the top of the little pear-shaped breasts peeping over a froth of violet embroidered lace, he felt his heart quicken again. He had never been so aroused. The totally outrageous thought of sinking his shaft within her came to him unbidden, disturbing him so much that he blushed red as his sister.

He realized that his hostess had been saying something to him and, gulping like an idiot, answered, 'I'm terribly sorry. I didn't quite catch that.'

'My goodness.' Her silvery little laugh tinkled. 'What a brown study! I was just saying to Mary that I thought gentlemen might find this room too feminine in its decoration.'

'It is charming in my opinion.'

116

He knew he was being flattering, trying to earn himself good points, and he felt Jackdaw's eyes fix on him. He caught the look and was angry to see that it was one of amusement. He felt highly irritated with his kinsman and half turned his back on him.

Mary cleared her throat. 'I do hope my mother will feel well enough to visit you soon, Mrs Trevelyan. You really have improved poor Sutton Place enormously.'

'She shall come to tea as soon as she is up to it. And later on I will show you round – if I may – so that you may see one or two small alterations that I have made.'

In the doorway the butler announced, 'Dinner is served,' and John Joseph was bowing before Marguerite and offering her his arm.

'I do want you to still consider Sutton Place your home,' she said as they descended the West Staircase, Jackdaw and Mary just behind them. 'You may call whenever you wish.'

She smiled up into John Joseph's eyes and all he could think was that emotion had gone mad; for he wanted to cherish her, ravish her, enslave her and put her on a pedestal, all in one.

The wood-carved dining room in the West Wing to which they now proceeded had, in the days of Sir Richard Weston, been nothing but a buttery. But over a hundred years before – in 1724 – John Weston, the last male of the direct line and father of Melior Mary, had had it restored and panelled in oak.

Tonight it lay – candlelit and beautiful – beneath the auspices of Mrs Marguerite Trevelyan: the massively long wood table polished by a hardworking pair of hands – John Joseph suspected Cloverella's – until it shone like iced mahogany. And this theme of things wintry and glistening was continued all around the room. The candles gleamed in fluted glass holders; the napery shone like newly-fallen snow; the cutlery sparkled clear as a winter moon.

And, like springtime in frost, there were flowers. Crowding the dinner table, jostling in shallow jardinieres, transforming John Weston's eating place into a veritable hot-house, was a profusion of all the blooms the garden could provide. And some brought from outside Sutton Place, Mary thought; for Mrs Trevelyan's favourite gardenias – one of which was pinned above the delicacy of her bosom – pervaded the atmosphere with their insistent and sensuous aroma.

'Oh Mrs Trevelyan – it looks lovely! The house is much nicer than when we lived here.'

'Thank you, Mary. I do hope you will come often with John Joseph – and your dear parents of course – to visit me.'

'I should love to.'

'Splendid, my dear. I am rather solitary these days. I pray you won't find me and my humble board dull.'

As the 'humble board' consisted of consommé, filets de sole en coupe à la Venitienne, a dozen partridges à la Roi Soleil, a carved ice swan bearing a fruit salad on its back, cheeses, cakes of every imaginable shape and delicacy and little sweets shaped like flowers, it was difficult to make any sensible reply. Mary contented herself with lowering her eyes to her plate and eating everything put before her, only stopping to steal a glance at Jackdaw from time to time, as if for reassurance.

He, however, remained unusually quiet, contenting himself with listening to John Joseph and Mrs Trevelyan discussing the rival delights of various plays and operas they had visited in London.

At one point Mary sighed and said, 'I do wish that I had seen those things. It is so difficult to keep up with the events when one lives in the country.'

And it was then that Jackdaw said, 'I would be honoured if I might escort you to the theatre. I have another week before I have to report to barracks.'

As Mary blushed and muttered that she would have to consult her mother, Mrs Trevelyan said, 'Barracks? Are you going for a soldier, Mr Wardlaw?'

There was a curious expression on her face; if John Joseph had not known that she was the sweetest woman alive he might have thought her faintly mocking.

But when Jackdaw answered her it was with a laugh.

'Yes, can you imagine! Even mice have their place in military life, it would appear.'

John Joseph cut in with, 'Jackdaw can speak ten languages, Mrs Trevelyan. He is needed for his special ability.'

And Mary added rapidly, 'He is a very clever man.'

Mrs Trevelyan replied coolly, 'I did not doubt it for a second. Shall we retire, Mary, and leave the gentlemen to their port?' She paused in the doorway, the smell of gardenias all about her. 'We shall be in my sitting room when you have finished, John Joseph.'

The very way she spoke his name had almost a conspiratorial manner about it; as if he were playing the role of host not guest. But once seated in her room she patted the place beside her on the sofa and said, 'Come, sit here Mary, and tell me all about yourselves.'

'There is little to tell. We are a very boring family who have fallen on hard times and have been forced to let our only asset – Sutton Place – to tenants in order to make ends meet.'

'Yes, that is most sad for your parents. But what of you children? There are four of you, are there not?'

'Yes. We have two younger sisters – Matilda and Caroline.'

'And John Joseph is the eldest?'

'Yes, he is twenty and I eighteen.'

Mrs Trevelyan smiled. 'Ah youth, youth! A bird that can never be recaptured once it has flown.'

It was half in Mary's mind to say that her hostess did not look old and, in fact, was probably little over thirty, but the guest felt that this would be going beyond the limits of good manners. Instead she said, 'You are very beautiful, Ma'am, if it is not impolite of me to say so.'

Mrs Trevelyan laughed and pinched Mary lightly under the chin.

'Sweet child. And has Sutton Place been long in your family?'

'Yes and no. We are not directly descended from the line of Sir Richard Weston the builder. We have two links with him – one through marriage and the other through distant cousinship. My grandfather – John Webbe – took the name of Weston in order to inherit from his kinswoman Melior Mary Weston.'

'I see. Had she no children of her own?'

'She never married.' Mary shifted position very slightly, the pink dress falling in more attractive folds as she leant forward. 'There is supposed to be a curse on Sutton Place, you know.'

The room went very quiet, the only sound Marguerite Trevelyan's intake of breath.

'Really? Tell me of it.'

'The Lord of the Manor of Sutton has no good luck – or so they say. Right from before the Norman Conquest it has been a doomed place. It is the legend that the Queen of England herself put on the malediction.'

Mrs Trevelyan opened her little reticule and dabbed her lip with a lace handkerchief.

'How interesting. Which Queen would that have been?'

'Queen Edith – the wife of Edward the Confessor. It's an old story. I don't know if there is any truth in it.'

'Has the house proved unlucky?'

'Yes,' said Mary slowly. 'I think it has. The first heir died on the block accused of adultery with Anne Boleyn. I do hope it does not offend you to speak of it?'

Mrs Trevelyan shook her head.

'And since then nothing has really gone right here. Of course we haven't died or anything like that but my father has lost his fortune and come right down in the world.'

'And could the curse affect me?'

Mary gazed at her with serious eyes. 'I don't know. You would have to ask Jackdaw.'

'Jackdaw?' Mrs Trevelyan looked incredulous. 'You mean John Wardlaw, your friend?'

'Yes.'

'But what has he to do with it?'

'He has second sight,' said Mary simply. 'You know, the old Romany gift. He sees lots of things. He could tell you whether the house is out to catch you.'

Mrs Trevelyan laughed and shivered simultaneously.

'What an interesting young man. I shall ask him to read my palm when he rejoins us. Does he practise that kind of thing?'

'I have never seen him do so. But then we have been out of touch for four years. And now he is – grown-up. Who knows?'

Mary blushed and looked at her lap and Mrs Trevelyan laughed again.

'I think you have a soft spot in your heart for him.'

Mary, shooting her a glance of consternation was about to reply when the door was tapped lightly and John Joseph and Jackdaw came into the room.

'So you did not linger long,' said Mrs Trevelyan. She turned to Jackdaw with a smile. 'Mr Wardlaw, I believe I have underestimated you.'

He gave her a quizzical look. 'Really, Mrs Trevelyan? How is that?'

'Mary has been telling me that you are not only a linguist. She says you have the gift of clairvoyance.'

'I did long ago. It seems to have departed in recent years. But why does that interest you?'

'I don't know really. Perhaps because I would like to have prior knowledge of the direction in which Fate will take me. Will you read my future? Am I to be affected by the curse of Sutton Place?'

John Joseph leant forward in his chair, his hands suddenly clenching.

'How did you know about that? Marguerite, who has been talking to you?'

Realizing with a lurching heart that he had said her name out loud the wretched young man looked at the floor in misery, not daring to catch anyone's eye. Mrs Trevelyan passed over the gaffe as if it had not taken place.

'Nobody has been talking to me, as you say, John Joseph. The subject came up quite naturally in conversation between Mary and myself. And you are not to look at her crossly. Somebody would have told me of it sooner or later.'

Jackdaw, seeing his friend's wretched face, spoke up rather rapidly.

'I have never told fortunes – as it is called.'

'Could you not try?'

'If I do we must be alone.'

Mrs Trevelyan's fine eyebrows rose and Jackdaw added, 'If I see certain events, you might not wish them discussed before your guests.'

The widow nodded her head slowly. 'Mary, John Joseph – would you humour me in this? I have always found such things so fascinating. You may have noticed that I have had a pianoforte placed in the Great Hall – a Broadwood, you know – and I wonder if you would mind amusing yourselves for ten minutes.'

John Joseph stood up at once and, after a second or two, Mary – rather reluctantly – did so as well.

'I promise I shall not keep him longer than necessary,' said Mrs Trevelyan, giving them a smile that made John Joseph's heart race again.

'Oh, don't worry,' answered Mary – and went so red that she had to fly out of the room to hide her burning cheeks.

'A charming young couple,' said Mrs Trevelyan, staring after their departing backs. 'I am so fortunate to have them as landlords.'

She and Jackdaw eyed each other closely behind their smiles.

'Well,' she said, 'do you wish to see my palms? Or I have some playing cards if that would be better.'

'Mrs Trevelyan,' answered Jackdaw. 'I have never done this before in my life – but I will try. Let me look into that silver dish.'

She laughed a little mockingly. 'A surrogate crystal ball?'

'Something of that nature. Here, put your hand on it first. Try to be quiet.'

She gave him a sharp glance at the abrupt way he spoke, but saw that he was serious. From downstairs the sound of the piano – rather laboriously played – drifted up to where they sat. There was no other noise except the differing rhythms of their breathing.

'Does the name Fish Street mean anything to you?' said Jackdaw softly.

Mrs Trevelyan drew in a sharp breath and looked at him with a narrow eye; other than that she made no reply.

'I see six poor children,' he went on. 'I see a mother dead before the youngest was two. I see a pretty young girl, Mrs Trevelyan. I see the Alhambra Theatre, Manchester.'

'I don't know what you mean.'

'No? Ah well. I see lights and music and ballet girls . . .'

'Enough!' She withdrew her hand abruptly from the salver. 'Is that all you can talk about, the past? Do you see nothing of what lies ahead?'

'I see great riches, Mrs Trevelyan – and a broken heart.'

'Whose? Mine?'

'No, not yours.' Jackdaw shook his head. 'You will always triumph. Yours is a soul of steel – you are a dangerous woman for men to know.'

She leaned forward so that her eyes were an inch from his.

'Yes,' she said, 'I am. You just try, Mister, clawing your way up from a slum's gutter. You just bloody try.'

'Don't destroy John Joseph.'

'Destroy? A man? They're all tarred with the same brush! Even you, with your pretty looks and your sad little limp.'

'How poetically put.'

'I am bored with this conversation,' said Marguerite Trevelyan, suddenly standing up. 'And with you. After you leave my house this evening you will not be welcome to call again.'

'Sutton Place is *not* your house,' Jackdaw answered, also rising. 'Nor will it ever be so. Be careful what you say and do here, Mrs Trevelyan. Sometimes I think it watches.'

She turned away in a flurry of petticoats, then stoped, her hand on the door knob.

'You breathe a word of this at your peril,' she said.

Jackdaw gave a jerky bow. 'What I learn through clairvoyance must be kept a secret. But even if I were to blurt everything it would make no difference. You must know as well as I do that John Joseph is already enchanted with you.'

She made no answer, simply flinging the door open and running down the corridor towards the stairs. The piano music finished abruptly as she called out gaily, 'Hello there, my dears. No don't stop playing. I love the sound. Let us all sing together.'

Jackdaw walked slowly along behind her, reluctantly meaning to join them but instead – not knowing quite why he did so – stepping into the West Musicians' Gallery which let him look down on the scene below without being observed. Not altogether to his surprise he saw that somebody was already sitting there, black curls just hidden by the shadows.

'Cloverella?' he said.

'Jackdaw?'

They had never set eyes on each other before but she rose and took his hand like a long-lost friend.

'I have heard so much of you from the Webbe Westons.'

'And I you.'

'Is it possible that we know each other?'

Much to his astonishment Cloverella answered, 'Yes. It is certain that I am familiar to you because we are kinfolk.'

'Related?'

'Aye. You are a descendant of Dr Zachary through Sibella Gage and her mother Amelia FitzHoward, are you not?'

'Yes.'

'Then we are twenty-second cousins – or something as remote.'

Jackdaw gaped at her. 'Why? Who are *you*?'

'I am also one of his tribe. By his second wife Cloverella the Witch.'

'He married twice?'

'Yes, but surely you knew that? His first wife Jane died of the Sweat.'

Jackdaw sat down rather fast on an old gilt chair that had stood in the Gallery since the days of Melior Mary.

'I am amazed,' he said. 'Yet I feel that I have perhaps heard something of the story in the old family tales. Was Cloverella the Witch not astrologer to the great Seymour family?'

'That she was,' answered Miss Blanchard with a chuckle. 'Mortal enemies of the Howard clan, they were. There were some fine goings-on – and yet was there ever such an alliance?'

'I can well imagine. So – greetings, my little hazelnut cousin! Am I allowed a fraternal kiss?'

She put her rosy mouth to his and held it there for one second longer than was decent between relatives.

'You're wicked,' said Jackdaw.

She laughed. 'I know. But not like her down there.'

She motioned to the Great Hall that lay below. Jackdaw followed the movement, keeping his dark head low, and peeped over the balustrade.

Directly beneath him was the Broadwood pianoforte, seated at it Mary. John Joseph and Marguerite Trevelyan stood just behind her, not touching and yet touching tremendously with the feeling that was passing from one to the other. The young man leant forward slightly, turning the music for his sister, while Marguerite had her sweet voice raised in song.

'Dear, dear!' said Jackdaw.

'Yes, indeed! Have you inherited the sight from your old blood?'

'I have – but not consistently. It has been gone for four years – except for a brief time when my mother was ill – but tonight it came back when Mrs Trevelyan wanted her future read. Why is that?'

'You have not fully developed. You are afraid of the power perhaps.'

'Yes,' said Jackdaw slowly, 'I think so. It frightened me witless on the night Sam Clopper disappeared.'

'He's in the Chapel somewhere,' Cloverella answered surprisingly. 'I saw him up there. I was waiting for you to come, Jackdaw, that we might find his poor bones and lay them to rest with Christian rite.'

'When do you want to search?'

'I would go now but they might see us.'

The distant cousins looked down with one thought at the little musical gathering below them. John Joseph was singing a solo in a light baritone and Mrs Trevelyan had taken a seat nearby, gazing steadfastly into her lap.

'What is going to happen there?' said Jackdaw. '*Will* she break his heart?'

Cloverella blushed a little. 'W-e-ll, I am not as gifted as my ancestress, but I do believe she will.' She sighed. 'Poor John Joseph.'

Beneath them the soirée was breaking up as Marguerite led the way, her full skirt sweeping behind her, in the direction of the West Staircase and out of the line of vision of the Musicians' Gallery. Somewhere they heard Mary's voice call out, 'Jackdaw!'

'Now's our chance,' said Cloverella. 'Are you game to go searching? I've a good idea where Sam is.'

'All right. But I daren't be too long. It would be rude.'

'Move fast then. They are in her sitting room. We can creep down the stairs without them knowing.'

127

The two descendants of Dr Zachary joined hands in the shadows and went across the Great Hall, peeping into John Weston's library on their left, up the Great Staircase and beyond into what had once been the Long Gallery.

The smell of rot was so pungent that Jackdaw had the grim thought poor Sam could have mouldered away anywhere within without causing undue attention.

'Is there any light up here?' he whispered, to hide his feelings from Cloverella.

'Only the Chapel candles. Wait, I'll light some.'

In the darkness he heard her strike a tinder and saw, as the pools of flame lengthened, just how terrible the great Gallery had become.

'It's a sin,' he said. 'This place was made for joy and laughter.'

Behind him a stick rattled along the Chapel wall. He started violently, turning ready to defend himself. There was nothing.

'What was that?'

'Only Giles. Take no notice of him, he's harmless. He's not been here much since this became a place of worship.'

'Worship!' Jackdaw answered with bitterness. 'How one could praise God in such a dwelling defeats me.'

Cloverella turned to face him and suddenly, there in the dim candlelight, they were very alike; dark as rooks – and magical.

'We know about worshipping God, don't we? The God of ancient lore and light.'

'Was Cloverella a white witch?'

'Very much so. Like Dr Zachary's mother she had the power without becoming a Mistress of Satan.'

'Will you do your best to protect John Joseph?'

'Yes. But Jackdaw, I believe the die is cast. It is his fate to love Marguerite and to know bitterness.'

'Probably. Cloverella, where did you see . . .'

'The ghost? Over there. Follow me.'

She led him to a spot beyond the altar where the shadows lay like ink pools. Snatching up one of the candles, Jackdaw peered within.

'There's nothing there – only an old oak chest.'

'We must open it.'

'You don't think . . .? Oh my God!' He heaved at the lid but it was shut solid, jammed in some way. 'Help me push.'

Her fingers were like little claws as she grabbed the top and Jackdaw was violently reminded of his vision in the kitchens of Sutton Place – the coffin lid closing irrevocably. There was a creak and a whirl of dust and the hinges finally moved.

'Don't look', said Jackdaw.

'I'm not afraid. He can't hurt me.'

But none the less she shuddered and turned into Jackdaw's shoulder at the sight of the little deformed skeleton that lay within.

They had found Sam Clopper.

7

Four months after they buried the lost boy the first snow of winter came. Caroline Webbe Weston stood before the little mouldering grave and threw winter roses on to the white earth. They lay there like drops of blood, seeming to tincture the ground. And as she watched they formed into shapes, dazzling her and making her eyes full of tears.

'Oh Sam, Sam,' she said with a sigh, but nothing answered her except a churchyard rook.

She drove back to Sutton Park in the pony and trap – blinded by the dancing flakes and frozen by the cold – and thought not only of her future and that of her family but that of England as well. The Great Reform Bill passed the year before – in 1832 – had heralded a revolution in society. The middle classes had been enfranchized; ordinary people like the curate could now go and vote.

Not only that. The railways had come to break up the countryside; the population was increasing; James Nasmyth was perfecting a steam hammer that could forge a mighty casting or crack an egg. Nothing would ever be the same again.

Caroline's thoughts turned to the monarchy; to the lonely girl who lived with her German mother in Kensington Palace and would, one day soon now, rule them all. Some people said that the new age had begun with locomotion, that the old days of wicked George IV and his brother William – the Sailor King – were over. They already thought of themselves as the early Victorians.

With a burst of confidence Caroline pictured the country beneath a young and attractive Queen. Surely, she thought, one of the most fascinating epochs in British history was about to begin.

'Gee up, Jessie,' she said to the pony and turned into the Home Park – and crumpets for tea.

Standing at her bedroom window, watching the countryside turning white for miles around, Marguerite Trevelyan saw the trap go by and knocked and waved her hand. But, of course, Caroline did not hear her and went bowling on past Sutton Place without even looking up from the depths of her sober black hood.

Bored, Marguerite sighed and consulted the gold watch pinned on to her bodice. Another hour until she could decently ring for tea. She felt she could weep with the sheer quiet and stillness of the house. In fact it often unnerved her, spending so much time alone in such a vast and echoing mansion.

'Thank God it's Christmas next week,' she said aloud. 'At least I can invite the County without appearing unseemly.'

She stared at her reflection in the glass, garbed in black from head to toe.

'Well, widow woman,' she said to it. 'You've another five years left till you see forty – another five years to make yourself a good match. For, as God is my judge, I've no intention of wearing drab colours and living nun-like the rest of my days. I would as soon flout convention and appear in this . . .'

She turned to her wardrobe and from its depths dragged out a box with a French label upon it. Laying it on her bed, she reached within the mounds of tissue paper and drew out an evening gown which she held against her: yards of voluptuous crimson floated like a wisp while – so stark that it was shocking – white bands of dove's feathers formed thin straps to cover the shoulders.

'. . . and be ousted by polite society.'

She whirled about as if she were dancing, and then, on a sudden impulse, drew out a midnight blue riding habit.

'I've had enough of black for one day,' she said, still speaking aloud. 'Anyway, who's to see me when I ride alone?'

As quickly as she thought of it she rang her bell and when her maid appeared said, 'Help me change. I've decided to go riding.'

'But Ma'am, it's snowing heavily.'

'I don't care. Lace me in tightly. I've still a smaller waist than most.'

She stood before the maid naked except for her stockings and garters.

'But Ma'am, are you to wear nothing underneath on this cold day?'

'No, nothing. It fits better like this. Go on, don't stare.'

'Yes, Mrs Trevelyan.'

Twenty minutes later she was in the side saddle, her habit like a second skin as she had hoped, her veiled hat with its plume of little feathers perched jauntily on her head, her honeyed hair snatched into a blue snood.

'You can't ride alone, Ma'am,' said the groom, staring at her in covert admiration. 'It's far too treacherous underfoot.'

'Nonsense,' she answered. 'I rode in worse weather than this when I lived in the North. I shall be back within an hour.'

'Mind you do, Ma'am. It'll be dark early today.'

She smiled and nodded and trotted off across the cobbles in the direction of the River Wey. But once there she changed course swiftly. It was her foremost intention to go to Pomona House, pleading sudden fatigue caused by the weather, and there to beg a cup of tea. And to see John Joseph, naturally, and tease him lightly for not calling upon her.

She must skirt Sutton Place through the trees, if she were not to be observed doubling back on her tracks, so she bent low in the saddle and let her mare pick its way beneath the snow-heavy branches. Everything was still and silent – as white and quiet as the beginning of time. So much so that the hare, starting and startled beneath the horse's hooves, was a horrid shock.

Her mare reared in fright so that Marguerite fell forward across its neck and was in danger of being thrown as it bolted. But she was an excellent horsewoman, strong and courageous, and one gloved hand shot out to grasp the neck-rein with which she always had her mounts harnessed. The other took the reins tight and firmly and she crouched low so that her head was beneath the lethal knock of the flying branches.

She shot through the forest like a jockey at Ascot Races, her heart pounding, her breath coming in gasps, her one thought to save herself till the animal ran itself out. Behind her there was a thudding sound which she thought at first was blood in her ears but which she realized, after her mount began to run even faster, was the sound of other hooves. There was another rider out that bleak day.

She could not glance over her shoulder, all her attention being needed to save herself from decapitation, and it wasn't until the horseman drew alongside that she glimpsed the black steed of John Joseph. He raced along beside her, shouting something which she could not catch. But, whatever he said, there was nothing he could do to help her until they had escaped the forest – and she was glad to see the parkland thinning out as they left the hunting land of the old Kings behind them.

They were in the Home Park proper now and the outbuildings of one of the farms were visible in the distance. John Joseph's left hand shot out and he grabbed the mare's bridle, circling his own horse so that the runaway was led out to the right.

'Hang on, Mrs Trevelyan,' he shouted.

She nodded her head, not having enough breath left in her body to speak.

'She'll slow soon.'

Once again she nodded and, sure enough, felt the pace of her mount begin to decrease and, a minute or so later, stop altogether. The marc stood, frothing and foam flecked and gasping for breath, rolling its eyes wildly.

'Here, get off. She looks fit to drop.'

He held his arms up and Marguerite Trevelyan kicked loose her stirrup and slid into his grasp. Beneath the velvet habit her nakedness must have been tangible as his fingers gripped her waist to lift her down. He was too embarrassed to know what to do and a fierce colour blazed in his cheeks. He would have let her go abruptly but she laid both her elegant hands on his.

'Thank you for saving me.'

'It was nothing.'

'Why don't you look at me?'

He did, falteringly; his eyes as clouded as a winter sea. She saw at once that he was wretched.

'What is the matter, John Joseph?'

His hands stirred to drop by his sides but she imprisoned them, tightening her hold.

'Answer me.'

'Mrs Trevelyan, I . . .'

She laughed under her breath. He was like an open book, torn in two with desire and the simultaneous insecurity of youth.

134

'Come, come – don't be shy with me. I always wear few clothes when riding. It makes for freedom of movement.'

It was a provocative remark from a widow to a man fifteen years her junior and she saw a certain look come into his eye. She wondered, briefly, how many times she had seen that expression before – and from how many different men.

'I see.'

He did not really, and was beginning to wonder if she was giving him a hidden message. And yet he idolized her so, would never dare lay so much as a finger upon her. Beneath hers, his hands began to shake.

Once again Marguerite Trevelyan smiled to herself. It was so obvious – the way this catch must be reeled in. He must take her by storm, apologize, be forgiven – and then go on ravishing and relenting until she tired of the game. With a little sigh she pretended to lose consciousness in his arms.

He was consternation personified.

'Marguerite, my darling. Oh my God!'

He began to pat at her hands and then her cheeks. Giving a little moan, but not opening her eyes, she started to tear at her collar as if struggling for air. Immediately his trembling fingers were at the buttons, wrenching at them awkwardly. One, two undone – and the plunge between her breasts was exposed. As if he could not help himself John Joseph lowered his head and ran his tongue down the delicious valley, tasting her sweat and all the lovely essence of her.

Gasping as if she were about to choke, Marguerite undid the third button herself. Her naked breasts came into full view, the nipples hard and tight in the icy air. With a groan John Joseph stood stock still, holding her firmly against him. Then he fell to caressing her, kissing and taking her nipples gently into his mouth.

'Oh, I must have swooned,' said Marguerite faintly.

John Joseph jerked away from her, guiltily trying to close up her bodice.

'Yes, yes – you did.'

'How foolish. But I feel so weak. I think I must lie down before I can proceed any further.'

'Should we not go to Pomona House? It is no distance and Caroline can look after you. I believe she is at home, though Mother and the others are out on a visit.'

'No, no,' said Marguerite quickly. 'I must rest *now*. Isn't that Blanchard's barn over there? Just help me that far and leave me to lie down. You can go home then, poor dear boy. I apologize for being such a nuisance.'

'You could never be that, Mrs Trevelyan.'

'I think after this adventure you might call me Marguerite.'

'Thank you.' He was going red with guilt. 'Are you able to walk?'

Marguerite cautiously put one foot before the other but her knees buckled beneath her and John Joseph found her in his arms once more.

'Do you think you might carry me? I believe that I am no great weight. If you tether the mare near the barn I shall try to ride back when my strength is returned.'

All the time she had been having this conversation Marguerite had been leaning against John Joseph's shoulder, one arm about his neck. Now he picked her up and carried her towards the long low building – put up at the same time as Sutton Place – where Blanchard kept his hay and animal feeds. The lovely golden smell of straw greeted them as John Joseph stooped his way through the low door and put his father's tenant down to sit upon a bale.

He was in torment. If she had been Cloverella – or any other of the farm girls – he would have asked for her

136

favour, and put an end to his barely controllable lust. But she was not. She was a lady, high born and delicate into the bargain. How he could have taken such advantage when she fainted, he would never know. But her buttons were still undone and now, as she lay back, he had another tantalizing glimpse of those beautiful breasts.

'Mrs Trevelyan . . . Marguerite . . .' he said, turning to stare out of the barn door through which could be glimpsed the dying winter sun, 'I think I will have to go now. I will fetch help, of course.'

She struggled to sit up slightly.

'Oh must you? I see that the night is drawing in. I think I might be the smallest bit afraid – alone here and in the dark.'

He turned back to look at her, then dropped on to one knee so that his eyes were level with hers.

'I can't bear the thought of that – and yet *I* am afraid to stay.'

She pretended to misunderstand and gave a little laugh. '*You* are afraid of the dark, John Joseph?'

'No . . . oh, damn it . . . I am afraid of *you*.'

'Of *me*?'

Her eyes widened like two blue circles. He swallowed miserably.

'Mrs Trevelyan, I can't help myself. I have fallen in love with you.'

Her tinkling laugh rang out and she gave a gentle smile. 'What nonsense is this? Here, foolish boy, come sit beside me.'

She patted the bale of straw and John Joseph obeyed. Then she leant back very slightly, supporting herself on straight arms. Once again her breasts were visible through her open neckline. She shook her head at him in mock reproof.

'You naughty boy . . .'

137

But she never finished. She had teased long enough and John Joseph's mouth – hard as a rock in his anxiety – sought hers in a frenzied kiss. He was astonished to feel her lips part to return him the most sensual embrace he had ever received.

His hands, clumsy as a schoolboy's, felt for her nipples and he heard the fabric of her riding habit tear beneath his touch. She lay naked to the waist before him; to contain himself now was an impossibility. He took her body to his and pushed his shaft into her remorselessly, not caring a damn for her feeble cries of protest.

But afterwards, in the dark shadows of Blanchard's frost-lit barn, he wept that he could have handled her so roughly, begged her pardon for what he considered was tantamount to rape. And her sweet smile of understanding moved him beyond words. He knew that he could never, ever, again love anyone with the blatant adoration that he felt for the entrancing Marguerite Trevelyan.

Three other people, in whose lives Sutton Place was destined to play a great part, lay sleeping as the stars came up over Blanchard's barn that night. And all three of them – though far removed from one another geographically – were dreaming.

Jackdaw, sent to Spain to translate from her native tongue the words of Queen Regent Christina, slept in his dress uniform of the 9th Lancers. He had sat next to Lord Palmerston's envoy at the formal state banquet and repeated the Queen's conversation word for word in English. And afterwards he had fallen asleep, his mind buzzing with the proposed alliance between Britain, France, Spain and Portugal against the Pretenders Don Carlos and Don Miguel, and wondering why a diplomatic translator would not have sufficed in his stead.

'Because you look so charming in your uniform,' Helen

had told him before he had sailed – and even the General had muttered agreement into his whiskers.

And Jackdaw thought they were probably right. Mature the Queen Regent might be, heavily involved with state affairs she was, but still she had a crinkle in the corner of her eye for him. And he had remembered then the favour his great-great-grandfather Joseph Gage had found at the hands of an earlier Spanish Queen – Elizabeth Farnese – and had allowed himself the liberty of executing one of his jerky bows. He had been rewarded with a rare but flashing smile from Queen Mother Christina.

And now he slept in a chair, still clutching a brandy bottle. He dreamt that he stood on the beach at Hastings looking out towards the White Rock. Two people had climbed to the top of it and they beckoned him to come and join them. But the ascent looked terrible to him and as he waded out to get there, for the tide was running at full swell, he felt that he would never achieve the summit.

One of the people leaned over the edge – high, high above him – and said, 'Come on Jackdaw – you're late,' and he realized it was *she*. Even though he was dreaming he felt his heart lurch. It had been years since he had first seen her vision as a new-born baby – and now here she was, grown-up. She stood up to speak to him, balancing on the rock's very cliff, and he noticed that her hair had grown even more abundant, falling round her shoulders in unbounded tresses. She wore a light green shift, and her feet were bare.

'Who are you?' he called out.

'You know who I am.'

'Say your name.'

A man appeared beside her, slipping his arm casually about her shoulders. Jackdaw gazed in amazement – it was John Joseph!

The sea grew cavernous as he reached the rock's foot

and pools of amethyst and jade appeared. Everywhere was the crashing of water and the smell of the ocean's magic breath.

'You know her name,' John Joseph called out.

With a cry Jackdaw threw his arms over his head and allowed the sea to close over him. He did not care if he never saw daylight again.

Yet after a few moments he surfaced once more and found that he was not at Hastings but swimming in the River Wey in the grounds of Sutton Place.

It was still high summer in his dream and a man leant over the river bank, almost on top of Jackdaw, to cool a bottle of champagne in the water. He was laughing overloudly and seemed a little drunk. Looking beyond him Jackdaw could see a host of people – women in short dresses with bandeaux about their heads, men in extraordinary striped jackets and light trousers, thronging the banks in droves.

Some of them had sat down to picnic – tablecloths covered with food and wine were everywhere – and some danced to music provided by a strange dark box with a horn attached to it.

'Too ripping, Lord Northcliffe,' said a girl with long legs, red lips and an ivory holder for what appeared to be small white cigars. 'Simply splendid.'

She looked out over the river, then shouted, 'I say, look there! I think somebody's fallen in.'

They both stared to where Jackdaw stood in the shallows. The man said, 'I can't see anybody.'

'No, neither can I now. Must be the bubbly.'

She shrieked with laughter and Lord Northcliffe loudly unpopped the champagne cork and poured her out another glass.

'What do you think of my home, eh?' he said, and with a nifty hand pinched her buttocks.

140

'Simply divine – all that lovely history. I say, Alfred – may I call you Alfred, I would be so thrilled? – is it haunted?'

A funny look came over Lord Northcliffe's face. 'Don't ask me that.'

'Why?'

'Because I am the only one who can see anything. Mollie my wife thinks I'm mad, I believe.'

'Well, I don't. I should simply *adore* to spend a night in a haunted house. May I?'

'By all means,' he said rather abruptly. 'But I'm afraid you won't find me about. I have insomnia.'

She frowned, rather puzzled. 'I don't follow, I'm afraid. Too silly of me, but . . .'

He gulped some champagne and said, 'I know it sounds ridiculous but I have a theory that it is the house that causes my sleeplessness. So every night I go to a bungalow on the Clandon estate. It's the only way I can get any shut-eye.'

'Good Heavens! What ghosts do you see? Surely not Anne Boleyn with her head tucked underneath her arm?'

'No, only a White Lady.'

'Ooh, how deliciously spooky.'

'She haunts the garden too – in Lady Weston's walk. You can smell her perfume when she walks past, feel the vacuum that she has created . . .'

His eyes were distant and staring and the girl said, 'Is that who she is then? Lady Weston?'

'Yes, I think so, damn her.'

He looked suddenly depressed and as if he was about to get into a morbid mood when a diversion was caused. One of the picnickers rose from her place and running to the river bank in quite the most extraordinary garb Jackdaw had ever laid eyes on – a thigh-length all in one black outfit which clung to her body and showed the lines of it quite distinctly – dived in head first.

She came to the surface exactly beside Jackdaw and looked straight at him as she rose from the depths. Then she put out her hand and touched him, quite casually, on the shoulder. Something about the feel of him – he did not know what – must have frightened her because she started to scream.

'My God,' shouted Northcliffe. 'Somebody's drowning.'

And he jumped, fully clothed, into the water. After a moment's contemplation his companion, giggling madly, did the same.

Jackdaw, for no apparent reason, could not bear to have them near him and started to swim away from where they threshed about like elephants at a water hole. But as he went he turned his head and saw Northcliffe look up and directly at him. It was such a melancholy stare, with terrible madness in its depths.

'White Lady, Grey Lady, long-dead Lancer,' Jackdaw heard him shout. 'Why do you all come to torture me? Why do you claim Sutton Place as yours . . . yours?'

His voice died away and Jackdaw rolled out of his chair and fell on to the floor, the brandy bottle still clutched tightly in his hand.

In the kitchens of Sutton Place, on that very same night, Cloverella sat dozing before the fire. It was midnight and the search parties were all out, for the Missus hadn't come home. She had gone riding before tea time and there had been no sign of her since.

At five o'clock the principal groom had organized a group but so far – though they were combing the forest inch by inch – there had been no trace. Cloverella had been called upon, along with the other kitchen servants, to provide nourishing soup and vittals for the rescue party. But though they had been feeding them for what seemed like all night, they had nothing to report. The whereabouts of Mrs Trevelyan remained a mystery.

Now she slumbered in a high wooden chair, warmed by the glow of the embers which reflected pinkly in her cheeks.

She dreamed that she stood in the courtyard of Sutton Place but that, once more, it was a quadrangle, closed in by a soaring and lofty Gate House. She looked towards the Middle Enter and saw, standing there, a red-headed man in Tudor dress; beside him a woman with dark hair and a closed secretive face.

She knew at once that they were Sir Henry Weston – son of Francis and Rose – and his wife Lady Dorothy Arundell. She knew also that she had entered the body of her ancestress, Cloverella the Witch.

She looked down at herself and saw that she was clad in a crimson shift and that black hair hung to her waist. She knew that she was powerful but that the knowledge of nature's secrets had not corrupted her soul.

'Cloverella,' said Sir Henry, 'you must make the rain come. You must end the drought. My lands will perish if you do not.'

'What do you say, Lady Dorothy?' she had answered. 'Shall I proceed?'

The dark brown eyes – almost the shade of mahogany – had turned towards her and Cloverella had read pain in their depths; pain at the misery her patron's family had suffered at the hands of Kings and Princes.

What a thread of blood ran between Lady Dorothy and Sir Henry! One's father dead upon the block accused of adultery with Queen Anne Boleyn; the other's – a friend of Francis Weston and created a Knight of the Bath with him at Anne's coronation – beheaded for joining the mighty Seymour faction: those who had

143

pushed their sister Jane into Anne Boleyn's place and had been the uncles of the boy-King, Edward VI.

'Yes,' Dorothy said slowly. 'Bring us easement, Cloverella.'

Dorothy had turned away then and buried her face in her hands. Cloverella had said, 'Look, Lady Dorothy. I will make it rain flowers upon you.'

She raised her arm towards the sky, one finger pointing upwards, and willed with all her might that rain might fall disguised as petals. And it had come! But in flakes the colour of blood. The crimson drops – as solid and heavy as snow – had started to swirl about them and the figures of Lady Dorothy and Sir Henry had grown faint in the blizzard.

'Help me,' Cloverella heard the Lady of the Manor cry. 'Help me with your magic power. For we are doomed and accursed – the Arundells and the Westons alike.'

'I will do all I can,' Cloverella had shouted. But even as she spoke she had felt herself vanishing – disappearing from sight – so that nothing was left upon the cobbles of the courtyard but a crimson robe and a crystalline rock that had fallen from the sky beside her.

Cloverella woke with a dreadful shout and clutched her shawl about her.

'Whatever is the matter?' said Job the under-gardener.

'Dreaming,' she answered. 'Dreaming funny things. Do you ever dream, Job?'

'Now and then. Of food mostly. Pass us that cold game pie.'

'Did Cloverella the Witch ever visit Sutton Place?'

'What?'

'It doesn't matter. Any sign of Mrs Trevelyan yet?'

'No. I reckon she be dead under a snow drift.'

'I don't think so,' answered Cloverella slowly. 'I reckon

she's tucked up somewhere nice and cosy and will be back with us before long.'

Job could not answer for chewing.

At Strawberry Hill nothing disturbed the night's quiet. J.J. and his penchant for maidservants had long since removed themselves to Navestock in Essex; while George – the only man to equal his brother's legendary wildness for miles about – lay soberly asleep for once, in the Holbein Room.

Similarly, in the Tribune, the Earl and Countess slumbered in their large bed beneath the walls of blue watered silk, and the three girls slept undisturbed in the big room overlooking the river. But Horatia was dreaming.

She dreamed that she was fully grown – a young woman – standing upon a big white rock that was not quite out at sea nor yet inshore. On the beach a young man – wearing of all ridiculous things the uniform of the Lancers – was walking towards her.

'Who are you?' he called.

'You know who I am.'

'Say your name.'

She was about to do so when another man, whom she had not seen sitting behind her, came and put his arm round her shoulders.

'I love you,' she said to him. 'Do you love me?'

For an answer he just smiled and this made her cry because her feelings for him were so intense.

'Do *you* love me?' she called out to the Lancer – but he had vanished. And when she turned round the man beside her had gone again.

She was alone, with all the misery that conveyed; desolated, isolated, she knew with bitterness the meaning of the word solitary.

The scene changed and she wandered amongst a great

145

crowd at an exhibition mounted in a palace of crystal. A jolly man with a large moustache had her by the elbow, firmly propelling her towards a refreshment hall.

'I say, Horatia,' he chortled, 'what a marvellous thing that you have consented to be my wife. Capital, quite capital. I must be the luckiest man here, what!'

She turned to look at him with a bleak and miserable eye.

'But I'm not going to marry you,' she said. 'You are *not* the bridegroom. Where are the other two?'

'They're dead,' he answered, 'both dead and gone. It's me or loneliness you know.'

And with that she woke up. A dark sticky patch lay on the sheet beneath her and she touched it with a wondering finger. In the silence of the night, telling her nothing of its miraculous approach or its primitive burgeoning within, the moon's cycle had come upon her for the first time. Womanhood, with all its pain and triumph and power, had begun its progression inside her.

In the dark hours before dawn Mrs Trevelyan came home to Sutton Place. She was in Mr Webbe Weston's trap, the pony driven by young Mr John Joseph himself. She was very cold and very tired and her riding habit was badly ripped. She had had, so they said, a nasty fall and had lain unconscious for several hours before Mr John Joseph found her.

But her maid, pouring jugs of hot water into the hip bath placed before the bedroom fire for her mistress, somehow felt that this was not true. For a smile played about Mrs Trevelyan's lips and she hummed a snatch of song.

'Tell me, Siddons,' she said, as she slipped first one and then the other of her slender legs into the violet scented water, 'are the Webbe Westons really fallen upon

146

hard times as it is rumoured? Or was Sutton Place merely too big for them?'

'I don't know, Mam,' the girl answered truthfully. 'It is said that the house has ruined them – but I don't know what they have in the bank. The family was certainly very rich once.'

'I see.' Mrs Trevelyan rubbed herself with some oil from a blue bottle. 'Where is Mr John Joseph now? Has he gone home?'

'No, Mam. He is in the kitchen with Cloverella and she is giving him some soup. I think he awaits a word from you.'

'Then he shall have one. When I am clean and in my dressing gown you may send him up for five minutes. I shall receive him in my sitting room. It would not be proper for him to see me in here.'

She glanced around the room, her eyes taking in the graceful hangings and the white draped four-poster.

'Very good, Mrs Trevelyan.'

'And Siddons . . .'

'Yes, Mam?'

'Send up some hot coffee when he comes – I would not like him to complain of my hospitality.'

She smiled secretively to herself and the maid bobbed a curtsey. She could not wait to go below stairs and report to Cloverella her innermost suspicions.

8

The birthday dawned very brightly and fine – hot, lazy and brilliant as any day of high summer should be. From very early morning the river had been swarming with activity – fish jumping up to feel the sun, ducks upending as they chewed the weed, heron flapping their wings and skimming low, eyes alert for prey.

And in Strawberry Hill the servants had also risen with the sun and set to work to make Horace Walpole's Gothic castle a gem in every way. Those items of the famous collection that could be dusted or washed had been painstakingly attended to; the Gallery had been swept to a shine and its silver polished; the blue and white striped paper and the deep blue glass of the Breakfast Room glowed with the use of myriad damp cloths. For today the Earl Waldegrave was to be fifty and a grand party had been planned.

From Navestock J.J. – now twenty-one and more handsome than ever – was to come; and jolly Uncle William and his wife were also to visit. Then there were to be friends and locals and one of the Earl's brother officers from the old Paris days. It was all very exciting.

Horatia and Annette, who had grown closer again since the cycle had started in Horry two years ago, had been up early as well; the elder girl putting cucumber and strawberry juice on her face and then carefully painting it with delicate powders and rouges. A young man was to visit and she was agog. The Earl's old friend Colonel Money was to bring his nineteen-year-old son – already a lieutenant in the Army.

'Do you think he'll be handsome?' Annette said to her sister, putting on a dress of blue muslin with wide sleeves and a pelerine of fine white lace.

'It's possible,' answered Horatia. 'But do you care? Wouldn't you rather he be witty?'

'I should like him to be both.'

'If he is you can reckon he'll already have a sweetheart.'

'That's true. Well, in that case, I'll go for the looks. I can always teach him clever things.'

Horatia laughed. She was still a little girl compared with Annette and was not wildly excited at the thought of a young officer coming to visit Strawberry Hill. In fact she considered it fractionally a nuisance that she must dress up in her best pink frock – a colour that had never really suited her – and take a good brush to the curls that tumbled almost to her waist. But still, it *was* her father's birthday and a formal luncheon was to be served in the Gallery and J.J. and George would be together again and bound to get up to some excellent japes.

A tap on the door revealed George himself dressed all in dark green with a flamboyant waistcoat and several dangling seals.

'J.J.'s carriage is coming up the drive,' he said. 'Shall we go and meet it?'

'You can,' answered Annette. 'I have not finished dressing. Do you like me in this blue, George? Or do you think I would be better in the peach silk?'

'No, the blue.' George was not really thinking, having one eye to the window to watch J.J.'s progress.

'Why?'

'The same shade as your eyes.'

This was patently untrue but it seemed to satisfy Annette, and George took Horatia by the hand and hurried out before his sister could delay him longer. In the distance, winding up from the entrance that led to

149

Twickenham village, J.J. – leaning out of the carriage window – was waving his high-crowned hat with enthusiasm. Horatia began to run towards him, followed by a noisily breathing Ida Anna, who had seen all the fun from the house. George came behind at a more respectable pace.

'Horry! Ida!' J.J. was calling. 'Come here you scallowags.'

He banged with his cane on the carriage roof and it came to a halt as he jumped out. He swung Ida Anna into the air and looked Horatia up and down appraisingly.

'You're growing up,' he said. 'I think you might make a Beauty yet.'

George came briskly to join them and Horry was struck yet again by the likeness between them. Though in fact two years separated them, they could have been twins.

'What have you been up to?' said George. 'How's Navestock?'

'One makes one's own fun.'

'Like that, eh?'

'Very much so.'

J.J. whispered something in George's ear and his brother rolled his eyes.

'You don't improve,' he said.

'No, thank God, I don't,' answered J.J.

Upstairs the Countess was watching this meeting from the window of the Tribune and she called out to the Earl, who was lying on the bed. 'J.J. has arrived. Now, there'll be no quarrels, will there?'

He did not answer, merely groaning slightly, and she turned to look at him rather sharply.

'James?'

'No, my dear,' he answered quietly, 'there'll be no quarrels. I don't feel up to it.'

She crossed over to him and said more gently, 'Are you quite well?'

'I've a touch of indigestion, that is all. It was probably last night's wild duck.'

'Oh! But you didn't eat much of it. Well, I hope the pain will pass. I wouldn't like you to be indisposed upon your birthday.'

'Don't fret yourself. You go down and see J.J. I shall follow shortly.'

Anne gave him a penetrating look but the Earl had closed his eyes, wincing a little. She hesitated a second in the doorway.

'Do try to rally, James. There are so *many* people coming. It just wouldn't do if you were not there.'

'I will join you very shortly, I promise.'

And he was true to his word. No sooner had the butler called out the name of the first guests to Anne who, flanked by her children, stood ready to receive them in the Library, than he walked in smartly to take his place beside her. He was very pale but still dashing with his almost grey hair and blue eyes bright and vivid in contrast.

'Father,' said J.J., when the non-family arrivals had been greeted, 'I am so pleased to see you. I have missed you.'

The Earl smiled quizzically. 'Missed the discipline I expect. How are you, J.J.? How does having your own establishment suit you?'

'Very well, Sir.'

'And the running of the estate? That is going smoothly?'

'Tolerably well, thank you, Sir.'

'Good, good.' The Earl put his hand to his chest with a little grimace.

'Anything wrong, Sir?'

'Just a touch of heartburn. Fetch me a glass of champagne, J.J. Maybe that will clear it.'

From the doorway the butler called out, 'Colonel Archibald Money and Lieutenant Archibald Money,' and despite his discomfort the Earl was amused to see his eldest daughter clutch Horatia's shoulder in a sudden flurry.

The two old campaigners from the Duke of Wellington's time greeted each other like brothers and it seemed to Anne, who was watching narrowly, that her husband had recovered himself. But at three o'clock when the guests – about eighty in all and packing Strawberry Hill to the very doors – trooped through, chattering and cheerful, to where the feast was spread out on a damask-draped trestle, he took his wife's arm.

'Are you still unwell, James?'

A light perspiration bedewed his upper lip and his skin was the colour of parchment.

'I don't seem to be able to shake off this malaise. After the repast I may just sit quietly with Archie Money. I doubt anybody would notice in the rout.'

He looked about him to where the assembled throng shoved and pushed cheerfully to get at the food.

'Nobody will miss me,' he said – and the words had a strange ring to them, sending a sudden inexplicable shiver down Anne's back.

But the glasses were being charged and raised in his direction and there was a general cry of, 'Happy Birthday to the Earl Waldegrave. Good luck to you, Sir,' and then a shout of, 'Three cheers.'

The Earl went to his place at the top of the huge high table and raised his goblet.

'I thank you all for your good wishes on my fiftieth birthday . . .'

He staggered a little and Anne heard somebody whisper, 'He's drunk.' She turned round to give a furious glare and thereby missed the hoarse whisper of 'Help me!' which escaped from the Earl's lips.

He seemed to recover himself, said, 'What a charade . . .', turned his eyes up to Heaven and dropped where he stood.

J.J. and George appeared to spring as one to his side and crouch beside him. Like Gemini they raised him together and J.J. put his ear on to the Earl's chest. There was a stunned silence in the Gallery, not one of the assembled guests even so much as coughing.

'Oh Christ!' said J.J. loudly. 'He's dead. His heart's stopped.'

The quiet was profound; still nobody moved a muscle. Then, without warning, the Countess put her head back – her white profile etched like a statue against the crimson curtains – and opened her mouth. The scream that came out was terrible; ghastly; inhuman.

'No,' she cried. 'No, no, no.'

She sprinted forward and threw herself on to the lifeless form that lay cradled in the arms of her two sons. Instantly panic broke out. Half the guests seemed to think it the right thing to crowd forward and see if they could help; the others decided it was best to leave and jammed the small doorway that led on to the corridor. More headed for the curved passage at the far end of the gallery that went to the Round Room.

A wave of high-pitched cries broke out interspersed with shouts, curses, and even a terrible and noisy fart. Not since George Montagu had come to see the Gallery in Walpole's day and had been 'in raptures and screams and hoops and hollas, and dances, and crossed himself a thousand times over' had there been such an exhibition at Strawberry Hill.

J.J. stood up, his eyes blazing, and threatened with his fists anybody who came near his father threatening to crush him, while George began to drag the body over towards the windows, Anne clinging to it and screaming all the while. Poor Annette burst into tears and did not even find comfort in the fact that young Lieutenant Money put his arms round her and held on tightly; whilst Horatia felt the room begin to spin round her, so bizarre and terrible was the situation. Ida Anna stood desolately, tiny fists grubbing at her eyes, in the centre of the surging wave of people, all moving in different directions at once and none of them caring if she was knocked flying.

In the midst of all the confusion one voice alone rang out.

'Run for the physician,' Uncle William was bellowing at the footman. 'Go on, at once. We might still save him.'

He heaved Anne, who clawed and hissed at him like a cat, off his brother's body and lifted the Earl unaided to where the fresh air came through an open shutter. Then he, with no knowledge at all of things medical, pumped with his hands on his brother's chest. But there was no response. The kingfisher eyes were glazed and fixed, the cheeks already streaking white.

'Oh God, God,' said William, breaking into sobs, 'How could this have happened? He was only fifty – and today at that – and a stranger to illness.'

J.J. and George looked at him, both with hot unrestrained tears running freely.

'I've heard of it,' said J.J. 'It is called a heart attack. The heart stops suddenly and violently. Men of his age are often victims, or so I've been told.'

'Well I've never known such a thing,' William answered. 'Is there no previous warning?'

'He thought he had indigestion,' said George. 'That must have been it.'

'Let's get the Gallery cleared for God's sake.' William's voice was urgent. 'There'll be a riot in a moment.'

J.J. jumped on to the table.

'Ladies, gentlemen,' he shouted. 'Please go home. There has been a fatality. The Earl Waldegrave is dead.'

The response to his plea was simply that everybody pushed harder in the doorways. If it had not been for the intercession of Colonel Money it seemed that everything was set for a miniature stampede.

'One at a time,' he bawled in voice military. 'Archie, man that far door. Everybody goes out single file, understood? If they refuse, you are at liberty to strike, is that clear?'

'Yes, Sir,' said the Lieutenant, letting go of Annette and executing a smart salute which seemed quite ludicrous in the circumstances yet at which nobody had the heart to laugh.

And somehow order was restored. Lieutenant Money, strong with importance, took his father at his word and threatened with look and gesture those who tried to push their way into the corridor; meanwhile George picked up the fainting ladies and carried them through to the Round Room, and J.J. took one of Horace Walpole's lacquered screens and placed it in front of the Earl's body.

Annette and Horatia, with no time to think about themselves, looked after the Countess who, in a little bundle of pain, had sunk on to the floor in a corner, and now howled like a vixen bereft of her fox. It was terrible to hear and it took all Horatia's courage to so much as lay a hand on her mother's shoulder as Anne gave way to the most bitter tears that can ever be wept.

Eventually, with Uncle William and his wife helping, to say nothing of Anne's personal and most beloved

155

servant, they managed to lift the Countess and take her to the Tribune where she broke free of them and ran round and round the room like a tragic and maddened animal. This most frightening sight sent Annette into an hysteric that was only cured by Lieutenant Money surprisingly showing steel and slapping her cheek.

The physician came at last, wiping his spectacles upon his sleeve, and four of them managed to hold Anne Waldegrave down while the medical man dropped some liquid into her throat from a phial. After this she was still and finally fell asleep, J.J. and George holding her hands and Horatia sitting at her feet.

'Oh poor Mama, poor Mama,' cried Annette to Archie Money. 'What will become of her?'

'Time heals most things,' he said sensibly.

He really was a pleasant young man, Uncle William thought, and very good for his eldest niece.

'Yes, but . . .' Annette was going on, 'she *needed* my father so much. You see, they fought every day.'

Archie stared astonished and she added, 'It was the thing that kept her going – the constant battle of wits. She loved him to distraction, yet could never forgive him for being born to the aristocracy when she was not. Oh dear, oh dear.'

She started to weep again and Archie took the opportunity of once more holding her closely in his arms. Horatia, meanwhile not listening to them, had slumped forward on her mother's bed and was almost asleep herself – yet could still hear whispering in the room.

'The Earl is being laid out now, Sir,' the butler was saying.

To which Uncle William replied, 'He must be put in the Library.'

'Yes Sir.' There was a shift in the balance of sound and

it was obvious that the servant spoke to someone else. 'Have you any further instructions, Lord Waldegrave?'

There was a moment's pause and Horatia opened her eyes. Uncle William, J.J. and George were staring at each other blankly.

'But . . .' said William.

'I meant the new Lord Waldegrave, Sir.'

And with that the butler gave a deferential bow in the direction of George who, with an odd expression of both fear and excitement upon his face, suddenly stood up.

'Yes, Hemsley,' he said. 'We shall retire to the Breakfast Room. See that several decanters are sent up, would you. And have the nursery maid help Lady Horatia to bed. That will be all at present.'

Then he turned and led the way out of the door. The new reign had begun at Strawberry Hill.

On the very same day the Earl died at Walpole's Gothic castle, the most beautiful party was being held at Sutton Place; so elegant and pretty was it, in fact, that some said it was the finest gathering seen at the mansion house that century. And as the year was 1835 and only the Webbe Westons and Mrs Trevelyan had been tenants of any note since 1800, it was very likely true.

Marguerite had had Sutton Place cleaned from rafter to cellar – except for the Chapel which was not her responsibility as it was still opened every Sunday for public worship. It was rumoured she had even had the lawn polished. Whether this was true or whether it was not, she had certainly hired the services of a small brass band who now sat on little gilt chairs, some distance from the house, playing every merry tune they had in their repertoire.

Elsewhere, many other small tables and chairs had been dotted about outside with the thought that, should the weather prove inclement, they could always be carried quickly into the Great Hall. But Mrs Trevelyan seemed to have organized even that. The same sun that had shone so brilliantly upon the Waldegraves now blessed the widow of Sutton Place; the sky was a perfect blue, the birds sang in time to the music – or so it seemed – and Mrs Trevelyan swayed amongst her guests beneath a shady hat and a parasol like a rose in bloom.

There were those unkinder souls amongst the ladies who asked – some silently and some aloud – whether this was the widow's equivalent of a coming-out ball; whether the grand display, with every eligible man in the County present, not to mention a great many from London as well, was Mrs Trevelyan's determined effort to gain herself a match before the year was out. And then there were those who equally said that young Mr Webbe Weston would offer immediately – if Mrs Trevelyan would but consent to hear him – and that he had been mad with love of her for the last two years. And then eyes turned towards the poor relations of Pomona House – as they were covertly known – and lorgnettes were raised and heads were nodded.

Certainly young John Joseph seemed none too happy as he strolled along the lawns, his sister Mary on his arm and Caroline and Matilda just behind: and his Mama – what a shame she always wore such drab and silly clothes! – looked ready to weep if anybody should so much as speak to her. However, boring Mr Webbe Weston – ill at ease in a frock coat and top hat – was obviously truculent, as if he knew full well he should be the host today and the house really en fête for him.

'They say he lost his money through an ancient curse,' commented Mrs Beltram with a snort.

'I'd say he lost it through sheer stupidity,' answered her sister Lady Hey, munching hard upon a fondant and

158

raising her eyeglass at the same time. 'Damn fool had a fortune when he inherited, frittered it all away.'

'Oh, hardly frittered, Gertrude. They poured money into the restoration of Sutton Place.'

'And a lot of good it did them! All they can do is look green about the gills with envy while their tenant queens it over the whole damn bunch of 'em.'

She waved a gloved hand at Mrs Trevelyan who was wending her way amongst her guests, being charming.

'She's a pretty girl.'

'Yes. And she wants a pretty man, too.'

'I've heard . . .' Lady Hey lowered her voice and leaned towards her sister's ear, 'that she is John Joseph's paramour.'

Mrs Beltram's lorgnette fell from her hand.

'But he is far too young for her! Why, he could almost be her son!'

'Oh, nothing will come of it. I dare say he is vigorous – and that will be the beginning and end of it as far as she is concerned.'

'You're speaking very frankly today, sister.'

'Getting too old to do much else. Good Heavens, there's that ghastly Huss woman. You remember, the skinny governess? She married old lecher Gunn when nobody else would have him.'

'She's looking quite well on it. How dee do, Lady Gunn? Very good weather for the rout, is it not?'

Miss Huss approached, rolling her eyes slightly.

'Good afternoon, Lady Hey, Mrs Beltram. May I sit with you a moment?'

'By all means. Have a cake.'

The erstwhile governess waved a feeble hand. 'No, thank you. Sir Roly and I dined quite fully today.'

She smirked for a second and Lady Hey said, 'Enjoying married life, are you?'

159

Lady Gunn coloured up. 'Er . . . yes.'

'Not with child yet?'

Lady Hey was old enough and distinguished enough to adopt the role of eccentric and yet keep her place in society.

'I believe so.' Lady Gunn looked profoundly uncomfortable as she spoke.

'Well, I'm blessed,' roared Lady Hey – while her sister made shushing sounds – 'who'd have thought Roly to have so much go! Well done, my dear.'

Lady Gunn looked round miserably and was never more pleased to see anyone than Mrs Trevelyan bearing down upon them with a sweet smile.

'What charming dresses,' she said. 'Lady Hey, you look most elegant.'

''Really? I thought myself a regular frump. There's no accounting, is there?'

'I must be on my way,' said Lady Gunn, rising. 'There's Sir Roly over there now, talking to Caroline Webbe Weston.'

'And giving her the eye, I shouldn't wonder,' said Lady Hey as Lady Gunn disappeared.

Mrs Beltram tut-tutted but Mrs Trevelyan merely smiled and said, 'Caroline has grown into the most beautiful of those three girls.'

'I hear she paints,' said Mrs Beltram.

'Yes, she's very good – in both oil and watercolour. Ah, here comes her brother.'

Lady Hey and Mrs Beltram exchanged a flicker of eyelids as John Joseph approached and bowed.

'Good afternoon, Lady Hey. Good afternoon, Mrs Beltram. I hope I find you both well.'

'I cannot complain at all for my age, thank you. I see you've grown a moustache, John Joseph. Very dashing – but it makes you look older.'

John Joseph appeared pleased.

'I wonder if I might speak with you, Mrs Trevelyan,' he said.

'But of course,' she answered, smiling.

John Joseph looked at his feet.

'Well . . . er . . . that is if Lady Hey has no objection, it is a little matter relating to the estate. It might be better said privately.'

Marguerite stood up. 'Ladies, will you forgive me? It is such a nuisance – but it is a fact. Business can intrude even on the merriest of days.'

She swept off, her full skirts wafting behind her, and John Joseph found himself hurrying to catch her up.

'Marguerite,' he said beneath his breath, 'this really is too bad.'

'What is?'

'You have not had a word for me all the afternoon. Every time I look at you you are laughing with some man or other.'

She stared at him icily.

'May I remind you that a great deal of organization has gone into this gathering and that it is the duty of a hostess to be with her guests. Don't be such a child, John Joseph.'

He looked back at her miserably. What gossip said about him was true – he was almost insane with passion for her. And the two years that he had been her lover and had so many times possessed her body – sometimes roughly, though she had always forgiven him for that – had made things a thousand times worse. For feasting made him hungrier: he was completely obsessed with the very idea of Marguerite Trevelyan, all thoughts of bettering himself or joining a foreign Army gone for nothing.

Now he said, 'So I am a child, am I? You did not seem to think so two nights ago.' But her answering frown had him cajoling and pleading. 'Don't be angry. I can't bear it. Oh, Marguerite, could we not be married and put an end to this hell?'

'You know that is out of the question. I am fifteen years your senior. We would be completely dropped by polite company.'

'Who cares about them? Marguerite, if you would consent to be my wife I could happily join the Austrian Army or the Spanish. You would be the leader of the field as an Army wife in either of those countries and Guildford society could go to Hell.'

Marguerite changed her expression to that of a sad, sweet smile.

'Oh, John Joseph, if only it could be. But your Mama and Papa would never forgive me.'

'They had their lives. Now I want mine. As far away as possible from Sutton Place – and with you beside me.'

He looked at her, his seascape eyes earnest and shining.

Marguerite's little laugh rang out. 'Why, here comes Lord Dawe. How are you today, my Lord? I was just telling our young friend what fun it is to arrange a garden party.'

Lord Dawe, who was seventy if a day and had a face like a walrus, gave a breathy laugh, revealing teeth as irregular as a mountain pass. His voice, however, was like cream as he said, 'I think it a splendid occasion, my dear. Would you organize such a rout for me? I have to entertain some fellow magistrates quite soon and since my beloved wife died I simply don't have the heart for that kind of thing.'

Marguerite dropped a little curtsey.

'It would be my pleasure, Lord Dawe. When do you plan to have this gathering?'

He offered his arm. 'Stroll with me, Mrs Trevelyan, and I'll tell you. Good day to you, Webbe Weston.'

He raised his silk hat to John Joseph who stood glaring furiously, unable to do a thing. Marguerite dropped another curtsey.

'Good day, John Joseph.'

'Mrs Trevelyan . . .'

'Yes?'

'May I speak with you later?'

She turned to look at him over her retreating shoulder.

'I may be a little too tired. If you could call tomorrow.'

He turned on his heel, giving only the most peremptory of bows, and walked towards the nearest table where he sat down, his arms folded and his chin on his hand.

'Want a cup of tea?' said Cloverella, appearing from nowhere. 'I'm serving maid in this part of the garden.'

'She's organized it like a military manoeuvre,' commented John Joseph bitterly.

Cloverella followed his eyes to where the figure of Marguerite – once again pushing mourning to its limits in a gown of lavender lace – swayed beneath her pink parasol on the arm of Lord Dawe.

'I should think she's very clever at that?'

'What do you mean?'

'Just what I say.' Cloverella grinned at him, her teeth an ivory flash in her nut-brown face.

'Cloverella, are you suggesting . . .'

'I'm suggesting nothing, John Joseph, except that you are going to seed and need a kick. Why, if I was a man I'd give you a thrashing.'

'Don't speak to me like that, Miss. You are only a serving girl here – old Blanchard's bastard. Just you remember that.'

Her hand flew to her mouth and she let out a cry. John Joseph had never seen the funny little creature weep before – but now tears trickled silently out of the corners of her eyes and into her mouth.

'You're a beast to say that to me. I've always been a good friend to you but now I swear that's at an end. I've a mind to put a spell on you, I truly have. You deserve all you get, John Joseph.'

'Cloverella, I'm sorry . . .'

But she had flounced off, her silver tea tray in her hand, her mob cap starting to work loose and fall down over her eyes.

In the distance the wretched young man espied his sisters hurrying towards him rather excitedly, in fact Mary – despite the elegance of the occasion – had broken into a delicate run.

'John Joseph,' she was calling, 'you will never guess what has happened.'

He rallied himself sufficiently to give a smile.

'What?'

'Amy has just come up from Pomona House with a message. General and Mrs Wardlaw and all three of the children have called unexpectedly and Father is asking Mrs Trevelyan if they might join us here at Sutton Place. Oh, John Joseph, Jackdaw is here!'

She was pink with pleasure.

'Don't get too excited. Mrs Trevelyan might say no and then we'll have to go home.'

'I don't care. It will just be so wonderful to see him – them – again.'

In the distance Mr Webbe Weston could be seen nodding at Mrs Trevelyan and she – still holding the arm of Lord Dawe – was nodding back and smiling.

'She's saying yes,' said Caroline. Her light blue eyes twinkled at her sister. 'There Mary, this day has been made perfect for you.'

In the distance the little band played a chugging version of 'Greensleeves' and Matilda in her best schoolmarm manner said, 'That was written for Anne Boleyn by

Henry VIII, you know – or so it is told. To think she walked these very lawns we tread now.'

Nobody answered her for a second as her brother and sisters, in their individual ways, thought about what she had said.

'Do you think she was truly wicked?' Mary asked at last.

'No.' This from Caroline. 'I think the King turned against her because she could not bear a son.'

'But our kinsman – Francis Weston, though one can hardly call him an ancestor – was beheaded because of her.'

'Perhaps he loved her,' said John Joseph. 'Perhaps he adored her so much that he would gladly have gone to the block for her.'

Caroline gave him a sharp look from beneath her darkened brows.

'I don't think so. I think he loved Rose, his wife. I think Francis was a little foolish courtier caught up in Henry VIII's great black web.'

Mary shivered. 'How nasty that sounds.'

'I think it was nasty. I think they were dangerous times. But then what times are not, pray?' Her light eyes ran over the distant form of Mrs Trevelyan and then slowly moved round to take in her brother. 'Anybody can make a total idiot of themselves in any century for a comely woman.'

John Joseph gave her a quick stare but Caroline seemed merely to be looking around her generally so he answered nothing.

Mary said, 'I do believe I can espy General Wardlaw over by the house. Is that he?'

Matilda screwed up her coffee-coloured eyes.

'Oh yes, it is. And there's Mrs Wardlaw. Good gracious, those officers can't be Jackdaw and Rob!'

165

But they were! Resplendent in their uniforms of the King's Dragoon Guards and the 9th Lancers, Robert and John Wardlaw – the elder taller than his brother by almost a foot – stood brightening the company of guests with their scarlet and blues.

'Goodness me,' chorused the Misses Webbe Weston. For the soldier brothers were without doubt at an age when the passing of years could do nothing but bring further compliment. The very notion of sagging flesh, thinning hair, rounding stomachs and slowing steps was, for Jackdaw and Rob, one that could not even be considered. They waited at the back entrance of Sutton Place looking about them like two young champions, melting hearts and creating flutters wherever they gazed.

Inside himself John Joseph felt sick; his soul wounded and angry with his personal failure. He detested the fact that his once great family had become destitute, had been forced to give up an ancient heritage and live like mice on their own estate. He detested even more that he had no decent living, was nothing but a grubby agent collecting rents and demanding dues. But most of all – bitter, bitter indeed because it was what he craved and yet would have so gladly put aside – he hated his dependence on Marguerite Trevelyan. He longed to shake off the sickness within him that laboured under the name of love.

So when he looked now at his old friends Jackdaw, and his brother Rob, despite his early fondness for them he felt envy and a desire to belittle. And he was the last to walk forward to greet them behind his running sisters.

He saw Caroline swing into Jackdaw's arms and, over the top of her head, John Joseph felt his friend's jewel eyes fix firmly on him.

'Oh God,' he thought, 'the bastard's reading my thoughts.'

166

But he managed a smile and a handshake.

'Jackdaw, what a surprise. And Rob too. Both on leave?'

'Yes. We've been together in the Cape Colony . . .'

'The Kaffir War?'

'Yes. So we've got some time off.'

'Jackdaw's so clever,' said his sister Violet, quite stunningly pretty with little black curls and a face shaped like a flower. 'He went all around amongst the savages speaking to them in their own tongue and disguised as a Spanish priest.'

'How cunning.' John Joseph's voice had the merest edge to it. 'And what of you, Rob? Are you a spy?'

Rob's big fair face cracked into a grin.

'Good Lord no. Just a fighting man. Haven't got the brains for anything else. Come on Jackdaw, let's go and pay our respects to our hostess. Excuse us a moment.'

They wandered off, after bowing to the three girls, in the direction of Mrs Trevelyan who was already engaged in conversation with the General and Helen; Lord Dawe had been abandoned at a tea table.

'You should see your face,' said Mary suddenly. 'Truly, John Joseph, you look as if you would like to kill Jackdaw and Rob. Whatever is the matter with you? You can't have fallen out with them. You've seen nothing of them since they joined up.'

'I think,' Matilda put in thoughtfully, 'that you should take a commission abroad, John Joseph. You have seemed so unhappy these last two years.'

Caroline's light pupils flicked over her brother.

'*Cherchez la femme,*' she said.

John Joseph rounded on her furiously.

'And what is that supposed to mean?'

'It means look for the lady, doesn't it?'

'What are you inferring?'

'That you're crossed in love, John Joseph. I believe there's a mysterious woman at the bottom of all your moods.'

'I don't have moods,' snapped her brother, furious, and stalked off towards the mansion house without uttering another word to anyone.

A side door in the East Wing was open and stepping inside John Joseph stood, in the sudden coolness, looking, on his right, at what had once been John Weston's library. The family books were still there – *his* books in truth – and he felt sick at heart yet again that he had been cheated of everything to which he had been born. With an impatient gesture he turned towards the room and marched into it.

Just for a fleeting second he had the impression that there was somebody there already. A skirt seemed to swish in the opposite doorway as a presence went out and he thought he saw a mane of silver hair. But when he looked again the room was empty. Taking a book from one of the shelves, he sat down.

He must have dropped off to sleep because when he woke once more the light was beginning to fade. Outside, Sutton Place was floating in a lavender mist as the haze of a summer evening shrouded the old amber brickwork. And now there *was* somebody with him because a voice spoke from a shadowy corner, making him start out of his skin.

'Do you know the legend of Sir Richard Weston's portrait?'

'Who are you?' he hissed, frightened, in reply.

'That doesn't matter. *Do you know the legend?*'

'No. I don't even know the portrait. Where is it?'

He stood up, deliberately craning his neck to see who was addressing him, but could make out little but a dark shape like that of a man – or perhaps a woman – in a voluminous black cloak.

'It hangs in the Long Gallery. It has been painted over. It now shows John baptizing Christ. You must have it restored.'

'How do you know this? Who are you?'

'A friend. Let me tell you about the portrait. It weeps – real tears – every May 17.'

'May 17?' John Joseph repeated uncomprehendingly.

'Yes. Does that date mean nothing to you?'

'No; no it doesn't.'

A terrible sense of panic was beginning to beset him and he longed to turn away but somehow could not leave that quiet, even voice that spoke neither loudly nor softly but on the same relentless and compulsive level.

'It was on May 17, 1521, that Sir Richard was granted the Manor of Sutton by Henry VIII; on May 17, 1536, his son Sir Francis went to the blade; on May 17, 1754, the Young Pretender came to Sutton Place and broke Melior Mary's heart. It is a wicked date in the history of the Manor of Sutton.'

'Is that the date on which Queen Edith laid the curse?'

'Who knows? It was so long ago, that its origins are buried in the mists of history. But May has always been great with weal and woe for the family of Weston. Be careful of it, my friend.'

'Who *are* you? Let me see your face.'

The cloaked figure shrank into itself. 'Come no closer.'

'Why? Are you afraid to let me see you?'

'I am afraid for *you*.'

John Joseph took a step forward.

'What do you want with me?' he said.

'To tell you to leave Sutton Place. Go away – and when you inherit – sell!'

John Joseph's arm went out, his fingers ready to clutch the cowl off the hooded figure.

'No,' it said.

Outside in the corridor a man's voice called, 'John Joseph? Where *are* you? Everybody's going home.'

He turned towards the door – and then back again. Where the figure had sat there was nothing but a blackbird; its bright eye anxious, its beak starkly yellow in the gloom. As John Joseph lunged towards it, it flew off, beating itself against the mullioned glass of the window.

'Oh God!' he said.

Even he – unclairvoyant though he might be – knew what a bird trapped in a room meant. It was a messenger of death, of doom, of ill-tidings.

'John Joseph,' the voice called again.

'I'm here, I'm just coming. I've been sleeping – and dreaming. God help me!' he added in a whisper.

That evening all the Wardlaw family sat down to dine with the Webbe Westons in Pomona House. The big round table was packed – just as it had been at that Christmas long ago when they had first met. And now the children were grown up – Violet and Caroline, aged fifteen and sixteen, being the youngest. The conversation was fast and unrestrained as befitted such an attractive gathering and Mr and Mrs Webbe Weston sat back thinking themselves, for once, quite the most elegant host and hostess.

'Of course the Kaffir Hordes were first-rate fighters,' the General was saying boringly. 'Quite unafraid for themselves and therefore a fierce and unrestrained enemy.'

He looked at Helen for her approval and she smiled at him. He was ageing a little now – grey of whisker and creased of eye – but he worshipped her more than ever,

170

as if she personified the passions of his youth and had become doubly precious to him.

'It was my first taste of action,' said Rob. 'I found it exciting.' He smiled his broad white-toothed smile. No two brothers could have been more unalike than he and Jackdaw yet they loved each other, for Jackdaw put his hand out and patted his brother's sleeve.

'Don't let those words deceive you,' he said. 'Rob was commended for gallantry.'

'I think it all splendid,' said Caroline. 'You must be very proud of your two sons, General Wardlaw. I can just imagine Jackdaw disguised as a Spanish priest.'

She laughed. She was very pretty indeed with her wheaten locks swept up in a knot of curls.

'Damn good,' rumbled Mr Webbe Weston. 'Fine boys. Envy that, Wardlaw.'

John Joseph, who had been looking miserable all the evening, stared at his plate and swallowed a mouthful of food without enjoyment.

'But John Joseph will turn up trumps, Father,' said Mary kindly – making the situation much, much worse. 'I'm sure he will join a foreign service and do extremely well.'

There was rather an uncomfortable silence.

'He will,' said Jackdaw. 'I feel it.'

'Not one of your ridiculous premonitions, I hope.'

It was the General speaking – but his words held a begrudging admiration. He had been forced over the years to acknowledge that his younger son was powerful in a way that he could not understand.

'Yes,' answered Jackdaw lightly. 'One of my premonitions.'

John Joseph looked up with a spark of interest. 'Oh? So what's going to happen to me?'

'I'll tell you later – a private consultation.'

171

Matilda, adjusting her brown shawl round her shoulders, said, 'Will you read all our futures, Jackdaw?'

'Not tonight. But I'll come over tomorrow if you like. We're staying at the Angel.'

'Oh yes please.' Mary's answer was a little too quick. She was twenty now and dying to be married and her feelings for Jackdaw had intensified on seeing him again.

'So your gift has returned?' It was John Joseph speaking slowly and almost reluctantly.

'I don't know – sometimes it is there and sometimes it isn't. I am not as afraid of it as I used to be.'

'And what does a bird trapped in a room mean?'

'A bird is death,' said Jackdaw. 'All folk tales tell us that.'

And later on when the ladies had retired and the General and Mr Webbe Weston sat plying Rob with questions about the Kaffir war, John Joseph and Jackdaw stepped outside into the summer night and spoke of it further.

About them was the smell of high season and in the pear tree of Pomona House a nightingale sang.

'I saw a bird in Sutton Place,' said John Joseph. 'I was dreaming. I thought it was a cloaked figure warning me against the curse. But when I woke up it was a trapped blackbird. What do you make of that?'

'I think you must get away from here.' Jackdaw gave one of his jerky bows in the direction of Sutton Place. 'She's dangerous, John Joseph. She's not what she appears. But you know that.'

'I don't understand what you are saying. If you are asking me if I am in love with Marguerite Trevelyan, the answer is yes. If she would have me I would marry her tomorrow.'

'But she won't have you,' said Jackdaw.

'No – she says I am too young for her.'

172

'Too young – or too poor,' answered Jackdaw beneath his breath.

'What was that?'

'Nothing important. John Joseph, I am going to take a turn about the parkland. I will see you tomorrow.'

He loosened the collar of his mess jacket and strode off into the darkness thoroughly bored with his friend's tedious love affair. But he had not gone more than a step or two into the night-scented air of the Home Park before a voice whispered into his ear, 'Good evening, Jackdaw.'

He whirled round and there was Cloverella giving him the sauciest grin imaginable beneath the flirtatious moon.

'Well, hello cousin,' he said. 'How have you fared while I've been at the wars?'

'Precious bad.' She fell into step beside him. 'I've had two years of Mrs Trevelyan – and that's enough to send anyone to an early grave.'

'I see she's got John Joseph gasping like a hooked fish.'

'As we predicted.'

'Yes; though we had no need for second sight to do it.'

She laughed and said, 'I'm tired of John Joseph. It's up to him to save his soul now. But what of your affairs – you're a full-grown man these days?'

'I would hope so. I've been two years in the Army.'

'That's not what I meant.'

She danced ahead of him into the moonlight. 'Did you ever hear tell of Giles the Fool?'

'The one who haunts the Chapel?'

'Yes. We heard him playing his tricks the night we found Sam Clopper.'

'I remember.'

'He died out here in the forest. And nobody ever found his body except – or so they say – that poor boy Matthew Banister who ran from Sutton Place when he discovered the true identity of Sibella Gage.'

'I know little about that.'

'I've only heard stories but they say that Melior Mary – who became an old maid and left Sutton Place to John Joseph's grandfather – was mad for love of him. And then again she was in love with the last of the Stuarts.'

'It sounds very complicated.'

'I believe it was. But anyway she was the one who destroyed Sutton Place.'

They had walked far enough now for the house to be visible through the trees and – in a most unearthly way – they heard Mrs Trevelyan's laugh ring out.

'Nobody will ever do good here,' said Cloverella. 'Not strangers nor family.'

'No.'

'It's cursed well and true.'

'That seems beyond doubt.'

They came to a halt, looking at the mansion dappled in the moonlight.

'I think I'll go and weave an enchantment,' said Cloverella. 'Go and talk to the tutelaries that Giles the Fool loved so well.'

'Tutelaries?'

'The fairies that look after families. Come on with me.'

An irrational feeling swept Jackdaw in that teasing, fickle light.

'Yes,' he said. 'To hell with it. Why not?'

'There speaks a true descendant of Dr Zachary.'

She was suddenly very close to him, her nut-brown cheek almost brushing against his as she sidled and laughed before him.

'You *are* a pretty thing,' he said.

'Do you want to kiss me – cousin-like?'

'No.'

'No?'

174

'Not as a cousin. Give me your lips as you would your other lovers.'

'What other lovers?'

'You know damn well – John Joseph, all of them.'

'Do you mean that?'

'Yes.'

For answer she kissed him full on the mouth, her little tongue flickering around like a butterfly.

'Shall I have you, Cloverella?'

'Here in the moonlight?'

'Yes, here.'

'In the very sight of Sutton Place?'

'Well perhaps,' said Jackdaw – and he laughed out loud – 'discreetly hidden behind a tree.'

And with that the two descendants of Norfolk's bastard son fell to grinning and chuckling and headed off, arms thrown about each other, into the darkness of the forest.

9

Out at sea – but not a quarter of a mile from the shore –
a mist lay waiting, white as an empty shroud. And the
passengers embarking on board glanced fearfully towards
it and then longingly back, over their shoulders, at the
mighty sweep of chalk cliff that represented England,
solidarity and things familiar. There was not one figure
swathed beneath bonnet and shawl, wrapped tightly
round in caped coat, or hugged into Army weatherproof
that did not, momentarily, wish itself off this vessel,
straining at its ropes like a morning greyhound.

Yet, despite this craving for home, feet pounded up
the gangplank like remorseless gunshot, the noise
drowned only by the rumble of engines as they made up
steam to take their cargo across the Channel to France.

Standing at the ship's rail John Joseph Webbe Weston
– twenty-two years old, notably handsome, and with
apparently everything in the world to live for – contem-
plated, just for a second, throwing himself overboard that
he might land head first on the granite quay below and
smash his brains out. And his sister Mary who, most
surprisingly, had boarded at his side, sobbed drily and
aloud, regardless of the fact that she was just twenty,
round of breast and possessed of a most kind disposition.

And as they set off – the engines booming and chuffing,
the people on the shore waving strips of handkerchief or
hats, the passengers shouting until the sound fell flat
against the density of fog – brother and sister clung to
each other and wept.

'She's done for me,' said John Joseph.

176

But Mary did not hear him and buried her face in his shoulder, not listening as she murmured, 'Jackdaw. Oh, Jackdaw.'

They were going; leaving England and Sutton Place and all the pain it had inflicted on them in their short lives.

Three weeks before they had watched from the back of Holy Trinity, Guildford – John Joseph dressed all in black and sombre as a crow – as Mrs Trevelyan, clad in violet from head to foot and swishing satin as she swayed up the aisle, had taken Lord Dawe for her husband. She had not caught their eye as she left the church on her bridegroom's arm and climbed into the brougham bearing his coat-of-arms. But just for a second, as John Joseph had swept off his hat and called loudly, 'God bless the bride,' her eyes had met those of brother and sister.

The gleam in them had been without mercy. She had fought her way from Fish Street to a title and she cared not a damn who had been trodden beneath in the climb. In fact she had almost sneered at the world as the carriage had whisked her off to Lord Dawe's great estate in Woking.

And as she had vanished from view, leaving the heir to Sutton Place hopelessly staring after the retreating wheels, from Mary Webbe Weston's trembling fingers had fallen a ball of paper that had once been a letter. She knew every word of it by heart. It said:

My dear Mary,
    I am writing to your parents and John Joseph by the same post but wanted to tell you personally that I am once more to be stationed abroad. The young Queen of Portugal – she has yet to see sixteen years – is widowed and all the world presses for her hand. It would seem that her many suitors require a translator and as the British Foreign Office wishes to maintain its interest – I am sure you will mentally add an exclamation mark as do I – I am to play Dan Cupid.

177

I enjoyed being with you all very much on my last leave – so did my mother and father, Rob and Violet. But sadly it seems to me that at least one year will pass, if not two, before I see Sutton Place again.

I know that when I return you will be married – one of my premonitions – and so, in one sense, I bid you adieu but eagerly await my meeting with a new member of your family. My fondest affection to you all,

Jackdaw.

She had wanted to die. Why did his ridiculous second sight not tell him that *she* loved him? And then came the horrible suspicion that perhaps it had – and that this was his way of ending her sad little hopes.

If only anger had followed in the wake of that thought. But it had not. If she could have but considered him silly, playing ridiculous Army games and trying to speak a hundred languages as if they were his native tongue. But she could not. He was the most sensitive man of her limited acquaintance; irresistibly gentle, irresistibly tough. A combination fascinating to any woman on earth. She adored him wildly and forever.

She had answered an advertisement in *The Times*: 'Gentleman residing in Paris, requires Companion for his two daughters, one aged three years, the other three months. Full staff kept, nurserymaid but no nanny. English household.'

She had replied instantly. If Jackdaw could leave the country for two years, then so could she. She would show him her mettle. And, as if fortune favoured her bravado, the answer from France had come by return offering her the post of paid Companion in the household of Mr Robert Anthony.

Mrs Webbe Weston had fallen into a prompt but elaborate swoon on hearing Mary's request to go abroad and it had only been the intervention of her father that had saved the day.

'Strange business. There 'tis. Nothing here. Girl's life.'

So Mary had accepted and arrangements had been finalized by letter. Miss Webbe Weston was to commence her employment on October 1, 1835, and passage out would be paid by her father. Passage home – should that prove necessary – by her employer. And that was how she came to be beside her brother, who stood so wretched, staring back towards England's fast-receding coastline with such a dire look in his eye.

Yet, even as she watched him, he braced himself. He had been made an utter fool by Marguerite Trevelyan, but still the blood of Westons – however thinly – flowed in him and Mary saw him square up his shoulders and deliberately turn his back on the past.

He was taking the most adventurous step of his hitherto uneventful life: he was going direct to Vienna, with no prior application to the Inhaber of a Regiment – which was the stipulation for Catholic gentlemen of extraction foreign to that of Austria – to join, or attempt to, that crack force of fighting men, the Imperial Army of the Emperor.

'Will you be happy?' Mary asked, lost in admiration for his resolve in the face of humiliation.

'I will endeavour. If all else fails I shall buy a house in Vienna where we may live, the four of us – grumpy old bachelor and his three spinster sisters.'

'Heaven forbid!'

'At least it would be better than rotting in the shadow of Sutton Place.'

'Oh yes – anything but that. Oh, John Joseph, is it the curse that has brought us to this?'

'Who knows.' He kicked irritably at a knot in the deck's planking. 'Who can ever know the truth about what is half legend and half supposition?'

'But if it *is* true – and *I* think it is – what of poor

179

Matilda and Caroline? You cannot be serious about a house for all of us to share?'

John Joseph tipped his sister's chin so that her eyes looked directly into his.

'Better that than dying slowly as slaves to an ageing mother.'

'But what will become of them really?'

'Caroline will secure herself a good match, have no fear. She has beauty and ability – and she knows how to use both.'

'You sound so bitter about women.'

'I shall be bitter until the moment I die. And yet, for all Marguerite has done, I still love her. I would have her back tomorrow if she would consent.'

'But what of your pride?'

'With her I have none.'

Mary turned to stare out to sea. 'At least I have that. I could never beg Jackdaw.'

'Then in that you are fortunate. Marguerite has made me a creature with no respect for his soul.'

Mary squeezed his hand.

'I pray that you will meet somebody some day. John Joseph, do you remember the dreams you used to have? When we first went to Sutton Place, and shared the nursery so long ago?'

'What of them?'

'Do you remember you dreamed of having a wife? You said she had red hair and that it was beautiful. May that not come true?'

'If it does then I am doomed.'

'Because part of the dream was of death on a battlefield?'

'Yes.'

Mary turned thoughtfully towards him. 'We must all die one day so you could say, by that token, that all of us are doomed. Perhaps to go in battle would be fine. Clean and brave and without lingering.'

'But it was not quite of that nature,' answered John Joseph quietly.

From somewhere deep in the ship a bell sounded.

'Come along. We are called to dine.' John Joseph proffered his arm. 'May I escort you below?'

'Only if you will propose a toast?'

'And what is that?'

'That John Joseph and Mary Webbe Weston may return from their journeyings in triumph.'

'I'll agree to that.'

He paused at the top of the steep steps that would lead them, jostling with the other passengers, into the quarters below deck.

'Mary . . .'

'Yes?'

'Is it better to love like the proverb – to the point of self-destruction – rather than not at all?'

Just for a moment she reminded him of the bossy little girl she once had been – for her mouth took on a firm, compressed look.

'I know nothing of the world, as you can vouch, but to me the answer can only be yes.'

'And why is that?'

'Because otherwise one may as well not have drawn first breath. What else can we give to life if it is not our fine feelings?'

'But those can be expressed through art and literature, surely?'

'But what would art and literature be without the pains and pleasure of love?'

For the first time in a long while a smile crept round John Joseph's mouth.

'You are a very astute young woman for all your sheltered upbringing.'

Mary laughed up at him suddenly.

'We are the legatees of Sutton Place, John Joseph. If it can give us nothing else beside its darker side, surely it can give us knowledge of old truths.'

'I'm glad you think as you do,' he said, linking his arm with hers. 'Without the benefit of wine let me say the following: here's to endeavour and a hostage to fortune; here's to a finger-snap in the Devil's nostril; here's to destiny – and the sweet, sweet blood of challenge.'

'And here's to winning against the chance.'

And with that the heir to Sutton Place and his sister plunged into the steamy depths of the cabins below to drink to their new lives and to good fortune.

10

The beginning of a new age – of an era that would see Britain take the great step from the Age of Elegance to the Age of Empire – began quietly enough.

In the hours just after dawn the Prime Minister, Lord Melbourne, went by closed carriage to Kensington Palace and there a little girl – under five feet tall and only one month past her eighteenth birthday – was awakened from her sleep. Putting a shawl over her nightgown she received him in an ante-room and he knelt to kiss her hand.

'The King is dead,' he said. 'Long live the Queen.'

She tried to look dignified but a big smile that showed all her teeth spread over her face. The days of her prison-like existence were over; the tyranny of her elders was at an end. And a few minutes later, after Melbourne had gone and when the Duchess of Kent – her mother – called out in her guttural German voice, 'Vikki, go back to bed,' the reply came, 'No Mother. I wish to watch *this* morning come up.' The rule of Her Majesty Queen Victoria had begun as it would continue.

In that very same morning, the British people – unaware of the change that had taken place during the night – rose from their beds and set about their various affairs.

Anne, the Countess Waldegrave, stared out over the green lawns of Strawberry Hill and sighed. Another dreary day avoiding a quarrel with George – who had run the family into hideous debt with his extravagance and wild living; another day of desperately missing the Earl; another day of wondering how on earth she was going to

183

marry off Annette – now aged nineteen – without a proper dowry, not to mention Horatia who had developed a shapely bust and could no longer be thought of as a child.

Another day when she would express her fears for the future of the girls out loud to her son. And another day when he would merely give his attractive grin and say, 'Don't worry, Mother. They're pretty; they can always go into the theatre, you know.'

'I can't think how you could speak so,' she would answer. 'They are your sisters – not common little nobodys.'

George would always laugh uproariously at that and say, 'The day that being the sister of the Earl Waldegrave cuts any ice in polite society is the day I'll know I'm getting old.'

Then Anne would stamp her foot and storm out of the room – just as she had done with his father before him. She considered it quite the most dreadful fate in the world to be a young widow with three unmarried daughters and two irresponsible sons.

And at Pomona House – though very far from being a widow, as Mr Webbe Weston ('Good health? Very! Daily riding. That's the trick') never had a day's illness – Mrs Webbe Weston had similar thoughts. She could hardly afford at present – should Matilda or Caroline be lucky enough to receive a proposal – to dress them for the wedding and give them a slice of cake afterwards, let alone the dowry. Since the departure of Mrs Trevelyan, Sutton Place had only had one tenant and now stood empty, so there wasn't even a month's rent to ease the situation. What a wretched affair it was, to be sure. She gave a deep sigh.

But there were, at least, two rays of sunshine. Mary, thankfully – and she felt guilty for thinking like that for

184

surely every mother should wish to dance at her daughter's wedding? – had spared them the expense and had married in France. Mr Robert Anthony, Miss Webbe Weston's employer, had turned out to be a widower of only thirty-five and within six months Mary had forgotten about her girlhood passion for Jackdaw and slipped his ring upon her finger.

And as for John Joseph – well, what a triumph! He had taken to the Army as if it had been what he wanted always.

'Which perhaps,' Mrs Webbe Weston thought, 'it might well be.'

Despite the fact that he had not applied beforehand he had been accepted into the Emperor's 3rd Light Dragoons and had – in the two years that had passed since he joined up – risen to the rank of Captain. He had justified his slow start completely. He was not twenty-four till next month and yet he was already an established officer and gentleman. He had more than caught up as a soldier of fortune.

In Hastings Helen Wardlaw had slightly similar thoughts to those of the two other mothers. Not that she had any money worries – the General's pay was more than enough to keep them in comfort and both Rob and Jackdaw were totally self-supporting. No, it was really about *how* her children were growing up that she was concerned. Or, to be perfectly honest with herself, it was how Jackdaw was developing. They had been so close when he was a child but from the time he had gone into the Army a type of inner privacy had grown in him – almost as if he were deliberately taking a step away from her.

He was not like other young men. He had never had a sweetheart – though she suspected that he was well favoured by the girls that followed the regiment – and somehow he had grown more and more introspective. He was like a man with a secret and she often wondered if he was looking for something hidden. She thought about the girl he had mentioned when he had been a little boy – the girl he had seen as a new-born baby. She had been called Polly, or something of that sort. Was he still thinking of her?

Helen got up from her chair and went downstairs to where Violet was practising the pianoforte. Seating herself on the stool by her daughter's side Helen said, 'Have you had a letter from Jackdaw recently, my love? The wretch has not written to me in a month.'

'Yes, Mama. He wrote from Portugal that he was off on quite the most secret of postings and could not even hint as to where. Did I not tell you?'

'No. What with that and Rob transferred to the Bengal Cavalry, I wonder if we shall see either of them this year.'

'Poor Mama. Do you miss your boys?'

'Of course I do.' Helen hugged the little dark-headed creature to her. 'But you are more than enough consolation, my dearest.'

Violet kissed her on the cheek and said, 'But none the less it is worrying about Jackdaw, isn't it?'

'Good Heavens,' said Mary. 'I have never seen anybody so divine. John Joseph, you are handsome enough to make a woman faint.'

She pushed her brother to arm's length, twirling him as if he were a Maypole. He was a vision in a uniform of light blue, frogged across the chest with gold and trimmed with black fur at the neck, wrist and borders. In the style of the Dragoons and Hussars the jacket was draped over his shoulder, only one arm being in the sleeve, the other hanging loose and casually, while his free hand rested lightly on the hilt of his sword. In the other he carried his shako – such an attractive style of headgear, Mary thought – gorgeously decorated with gold frogging and chains and topped by a cockade of tall black feathers.

'What a dash!' she breathed rapturously.

John Joseph clicked his heels and gave a military bow. He had not set eyes on his sister since he had escorted her into the home of Robert Anthony two years before. Now he was rather amused to see that she was huge with child and that her old habit of giving orders had returned, encouraged no doubt by the fact that she had her own establishment, complete with husband and two step-children. To say nothing of a houseful of servants.

'I am glad you approve.'

'You look better in every way.'

He had lost the hunted air which had come upon him during his affair with Marguerite. Now he stood up straight and looked around with a merry blue eye, while his skin was no longer pale but tanned and firm. He still sported a moustache which suited him enormously as he had grown up enough to carry it off stylishly.

'You wait till they see you in England. Mama will swoon over the sherry and Papa will say: "Well done. Real man. Heart bursting. Could weep."'

They both laughed and John Joseph said, 'How are they? I have had so few letters that I know little. What has happened to Sutton Place?'

'I believe it had one more tenant after Mrs Trevelyan – who has produced a child at *her* age, which everyone says cannot possibly be Lord Dawe's.'

John Joseph ground his teeth but made no reply and Mary went on, 'Caroline wrote to me that everyone believes it to be her coachman's – a great hulking brute who could impregnate a harem – but that Lord Dawe is

187

as pleased as punch and calls the wretch "Papa's little miracle".'

John Joseph looked fractionally sick and Mary, realizing rather suddenly how tactless she was being, changed the subject.

'But Sutton Place is empty again and in a terrible state, I believe.'

'And what of Cloverella?'

'She wandered off after you went away, apparently not saying goodbye to anybody, just taking her things and leaving. Old Blanchard thinks she may have gone back to Wiltshire to stay with her mother's people. A bit of a mystery altogether.'

'How strange.'

'Mama wondered if she could have been expecting a child. John Joseph, you may be frank with me. Could that have been possible?'

'Are you saying could I have been the father in such an event?'

'Please speak truly.'

'Then the answer is yes, Mary. Towards the end of the affaire – when Marguerite was refusing to see me – I *did* sport with Cloverella . . .'

'John Joseph!'

'There's no need to look shocked. I lost my virginity to her years ago, if you really want to know.'

'I don't think I *do* really want to know. Certain things are best left to the imagination.'

Her belly suddenly heaved as the child within her moved strenuously and John Joseph, patting it with his hand, said, 'Seems to be catching, doesn't it?'

They both shrieked with laughter – just as they used to in the nursery of Sutton Place – and it was on this scene that Robert Anthony walked in, not quite sure what face he ought to be wearing.

He was a stout, jolly young man with rather a squirrel-like appearance – bright of eye and inclined to dart about in fits and starts – and was an ideal husband for Mary, ignoring her when she was in a mood to give commands while spoiling her with sweetmeats and presents when she was kind. Seeing that all was well with her now he joined in the laughter heartily.

'Oh what merriment!' said Mary, wiping her eyes. 'But one shouldn't laugh really. Poor Cloverella. I do hope that the whole thing is a figment of Mama's imagination.'

'I'll try and find out when I get back,' said John Joseph. 'If it is what you said it was and I am what I think I could be . . .'

Robert Anthony looked thoroughly mystified at this point but nodded his head brightly none the less.

'. . . I really must do something to help her.'

Mary laughed again, clutching her enormous stomach.

'Spoken like a true officer. Oh, John Joseph, you are so *terribly* grown-up.'

That night she went into labour and swore, ever afterwards, that it was John Joseph's doing for 'setting her off'. A dear little boy was born – Robert Anthony's first son – and was named Robert John Joseph, partly to remind his mother of the happy reunion.

A few days later his uncle took the public stagecoach to Calais and embarked for England wondering a little about the wisdom of it all. So many memories – and now the possibility of his having fathered a child; but above all – mysterious and so empty and echoing – Sutton Place. As the boat went into the harbour at Dover he found himself more afraid than he had been at any time during the last two years.

On the evening that John Joseph landed in England, three trappers came into Quebec from Hudson Bay,

189

armed with their pelts. That they were villains, all three of them, was obvious from their appearance. For a start not one of them looked as if he had seen soap and water nor a razor in a six-month; and for a second there was something in the way they walked into the cut-throat inn of their choice that showed – even to the assembled company of thieves – that here were men not to be taken lightly.

The eldest, and the largest, must have been well over six feet and had a mass of tangled grey hair falling from a scarred and balding dome. The second had the face and colouring of a fox and grinning pointed teeth. And the youngest, who was smaller than the other two, had dark, jewel-bright eyes and an evil-looking knife shoved into his belt, the handle of which was scarcely ever out of his hand.

They spoke in French but the one or two words that they did use in English showed pronounced Canadian accents. And they talked to nobody but each other, sitting with their backs to the wall and looking the other patrons up and down as they did so.

Eventually a group of the regular guests had had enough to drink to give them courage and they crossed over. Leaning above the smallest one, their ringleader hissed in his ear, 'Why don't you leave while you're still alive?' The answer to which was a hand, the fingers like wire, shooting out and grasping the speaker's shoulder, while a whispered voice replied, 'I have come to see Monsieur Papineau. I was told that I could find him here.'

There was a pause and then another of the number said, 'What do you know of Papineau?'

For answer the smallest trapper snatched the cruel knife from his belt with such violence that every one of his questioners took an involuntary step back. But he merely reached beneath the table and hacked the rough string that held together his pelts. Then he threw down before them – amongst the candle grease and wine stains – a fur that made them gasp. It glowed sapphire blue in its depths and the springing coat shone soft as falling snow.

'*That* is my introduction to Papineau,' he said. 'That is for the cause. I say finish with British rule – let us shake off the Imperialist yoke for once and for all.'

'Lower your voice. You speak treason.'

The jewel-eyes of the trapper went hard.

'Then let treason be the order of the day. Take me to Papineau. I wish to swear the oath beneath the cap of liberty.'

In the pungent smell of the Quebec inn nobody breathed.

'Papineau?' somebody repeated. 'Oath of liberty? What are you talking about?'

The smallest of the three trappers leapt to his feet, the other two watching him from where they leaned back in their chairs. They gave the impression – despite their lolling posture – that if anyone had made a move in their companion's direction they would have slit his throat as soon as look at him.

'You know bloody well,' he growled. 'I have offered you the greatest pelt ever seen – if that is not good enough, then goodnight.'

He began to gather to him his string of furs.

'Wait,' said a woman's voice from the back.

'It's Marie,' somebody muttered in an undertone.

The trapper appeared not to have heard, continuing to put together his beautiful collection of skins, looking neither to right nor left.

'Wait a moment,' said the woman's voice again – and a

pale hand went out and touched the smallest trapper lightly on the arm.

What happened then was incredible. The girl stepped forward into the ring of brightness thrown by the guttering candles, her nimbus of red hair lighting up like a magic cloud. And out of the corner of his eye the trapper must have seen it, for he suddenly wheeled round and said, 'Horry?' in a completely different voice from the one he had just been using.

She frowned and answered in French, 'My name is Marie. Who are you?'

He took a second or two to collect himself.

'The Jackdaw.'

'The Jackdaw? That is not a proper name.'

'It is the name by which I am known. Are you going to take me to Papineau?

She moved forward so that she could see him closely and they stood for a moment only an inch or two apart, her eyes taking in every detail of his appearance, from the fur hat pulled down over his jet locks to the battered boots on his feet.

'Well?'

'How do I know that I can trust you?'

'And how do I know I can trust *you*?' he answered. 'You have too much beauty for your own good.'

She brought her lips up almost to touch his.

'You are a pompous fool,' she said. 'Come, I will take you to Papineau.'

The circle of patrons drew back as she led him by the hand down an ill-lit spiral staircase that fell steeply into the blackness beneath the bar. And he should have known, even from the familiar way she entered the small cave-like room and from the shock of red hair growing *en brosse* from the man seated at the table before them, that Papineau – arch-traitor in the eyes of the British

192

government and the man whose headquarters Jackdaw had at last penetrated – was her father.

'There is someone to see you,' she said – and walked away, leaving Jackdaw the spy to stare straight into the eyes of the man who was leading the Canadian revolution.

The field was perfect for painting – green as an emerald and packed with a rather jolly sheep herd of mixed colouring. Moreover, in the pasture beyond, a cluster of brown and white cows grazed beneath the shade of some rustling oaks. The triumph of England in high summer lit the land as if God Himself had been a landscape painter.

'Which He probably was,' said Caroline Webbe Weston to herself, irreverently imagining the Almighty in a battered straw hat and paint-stained coat attending to the Creation with a mass of brushes in one hand and a well-coloured palette in the other.

She smiled at the thought and hitching her skirt hauled herself and her easel over the stile, her dark brows pointing upwards beneath her wheat-white locks as she shielded her eyes from the sun and stared about her as to where would be the best place to set up her things.

Much to her surprise – and slight irritation – she saw that another painter had already got there ahead of her and had established his place in the key position, with a view of the cattle dimensionally behind that of the flock, making the picture one flowing harmonious whole.

She thought, 'That is quite the best angling I have ever seen. He cannot be some downright dauber.'

And never lacking in courage or confidence, Caroline – after casually arranging her stool and equipment – strolled up behind him.

The back of his neck caught her attention at once; it was, without doubt, the most intriguing she had ever set eyes on. Very brown and at the same time both vulnerable and masculine, the lively dark hair sprung in abundant growth half-way down its length.

'Hello,' he said, without looking up. 'Let me just capture that wayward calf and then I will introduce myself.'

Caroline laughed. His voice was light and without malice. She felt that he was someone with whom she could pleasantly argue for hours the theory of paint mixing.

'I'm Caroline Webbe Weston,' she said. 'From Pomona House in Sutton Park.'

He completed a brush stroke and looked up at her. His face was wonderful. Bright and animated with sparkling, vivid bluebell eyes.

He stood up and bowed.

'Francis Hicks, Miss Webbe Weston. Of St Bartholomew's, London. A medical student not a patient, perhaps I should add.'

She dropped a little curtsey – which was quite out of character for her, for Caroline said what she thought and did not bother over-much with the finer points of considered behaviour.

'Shall we paint together?' he went on. 'I have some terrible sandwiches – thick as an old hat – and very lukewarm wine.'

'And I have greenstuffs and fruit.'

'Which sounds very healthy. I am studying surgery and am quite *au fait* with ailments of the stomach caused by stuffing down an evil diet.'

He grinned, cat-like, and Caroline did not know whether to take him seriously or not.

'I should like that very much,' she said, as her Mama had taught her – and then burst, for no reason other than his comical face, into laughter.

'Then shall we sit side by side? I would not like to

think that I had deprived you of such a vista just because I saw it first.'

He was incorrigible – full of fun as a pink air balloon.

Caroline shot him a look from beneath her jet eyebrows.

'Very well, Mr Hicks. As long as you promise not to peer at me for hidden complaints.'

'I promise. Bring your traps over here – we'll catch the light while it is good.'

It was immense – the immediate feeling of harmony, of shared interest, of attraction that was tangible in the golden July sunshine. They painted for four hours without speaking and then stopped to lunch, Francis spreading an old rug upon the ground and setting out his humble sandwiches. Then lying back, putting his rough old hat – rather like that which Caroline had imagined for God – over his eyes.

'Do you know Surrey well?' she said. 'Do you live here?'

'No, in Henrietta Street just off Cavendish Square, more's the pity. I love the country.'

'Do you know Sutton Place?'

'I've heard of it, of course. A ruined old pile near Guildford, isn't it?'

She wrinkled her nose a fraction ruefully.

'I'll say it is. We own it – that is my family. But we can't afford to live there. We're as poor as chapel mice.'

Without really meaning to she shot him a look from her forget-me-not eyes.

'I'm not,' he said, quite matter-of-factly. 'My father died and left my brother and me a load of truly delightful cash. It's awfully nice, Caro – may I call you that?'

'Please do. Forgive me if I go quiet – I'm trying to imagine what it must be like to have a spare pound or two.'

'It's fun,' said Francis.

'Are there just the two of you – you and your brother?'

'Yes. He's eighteen years older than I am. I believe I came to my mother as an afterthought – as well as a terrible shock.'

Caroline laughed again. She could not remember ever having been happier in her life.

'I want to paint you – now,' he said suddenly. 'While the light is still good. Will you sit for me?'

'In my painting clothes?'

'Yes, just like that. Goddess of Summer – wheat-coloured hair, eyes like the sky, lips like sunshine roses.'

'It sounds very romantic.'

'You *are* very romantic,' said Francis Hicks. 'Now be quiet and don't fidget, there's a good girl.'

'I want to sneeze,' said Caroline.

'Well you can't.'

'I must. It's hay-fever.'

Francis just went 'um' because he had a brush firmly clenched between his teeth, but after Caroline had given two rather hearty snorts, he added 'Sshh!' After that there was a companionable silence.

Eventually Francis said, 'I've done as much as I can – the light is changing too fast. Will you sit for me again tomorrow?'

'Are you staying down here?'

'Yes, at the Angel in Guildford.'

Caroline hesitated.

'I don't know that I can. My brother is coming home on leave and is due any day; he's been away for two years in the Austrian Army.'

'Really? How fascinating. I've always been interested in what drives bright young Englishmen into foreign service.'

'I think he harboured ambitions for soldiering but

thought he might do better abroad because we're Catholics. That's one of the reasons anyway.'

'And the other? Or is that personal?'

Caroline pulled a face.

'He was crossed in love – and then of course he's the heir to the curse, which always unsettled him.'

'The curse of Sutton Place?'

'Yes. Have you heard of it?'

'Oh yes,' said Francis surprisingly. 'It has been discussed at my club – quite seriously I might add.'

Caroline stared at him, astonished.

'I hadn't realized it was so well known. Do you believe in it?'

Francis lowered his brush and looked at her over the top of the canvas.

'I am supposed to be a man of science. But the answer is still a categorical yes.'

'Yes?'

'I believe there is another dimension just outside the grasp of mankind.'

'Have you ever seen a ghost?'

'Unfortunately not. Come on let's pack up. The shadows are lengthening and your family will want you home for tea.'

'Will you walk back with me?'

'Of course I will.'

As they crossed the stile and plunged into the green and gold of that late afternoon, a flight of swallows curved up almost from their feet and raced through the heavens like arrows, while above them a blackbird trilled into such a glorious song that they felt he would burst his heart with the joy of it. The cattle that they had painted earlier began, as one, to plod towards the corner of the field, heads down and lowing in harmonious sound, knowing that milking time was not far off; and everywhere the shadows of the trees dappled the landscape with fingers of coolness.

'I shall ask your Mama for permission to call on you,' said Francis.

Caroline's light eyes smiled at him. 'I notice you do not ask me first.'

'Who needs pretension? Here, give me your hand.'

She intertwined her brown fingers with his, noticing how long and strong they were.

'I think you will be a good surgeon,' she said.

'I shall try.'

In the far distance the first glimpse of Sutton Place became visible.

'That's it,' said Caroline. 'Our fabled family home.'

'It looks peaceful enough.'

'Like a sleeping tiger.'

'Aptly put,' said Francis, and nodded.

They cut left and walked the long way round by Jacob's Well till at last Pomona House was only a few yards distant.

'May I present my compliments to your mother now . . . ?'

Francis's voice dwindled away as Caroline shouted across him, 'It can't be . . .' and then started to run.

A handsome figure in a blue uniform, frogged with gold, wheeled about and hurried towards her.

'It's my brother,' Caroline called over her shoulder. 'It's John Joseph back from Austria.'

Then she suddenly stopped in her tracks, taking in with her artist's eye the full splendour of the magnificent blue dragoon into whom John Joseph had turned. Almost simultaneously she and Francis said, 'You must sit for your portrait – dressed just like that.'

'So you wish to join our brotherhood?' said Papineau.

'Yes,' answered Jackdaw, throwing himself on to a rough chair and staring fixedly at the revolutionary.

'Why?'

'Because I believe in freedom.'

'Pfew!' Papineau made a noise of disgust. 'What is that supposed to mean? One man's freedom is another one's prison. You'll have to think of something a bit cleverer than that.'

'The British took Canada by conquest. They have no right here. Let us break free like the American colonies. If anything we should be allied with France.'

Papineau looked at him narrowly but made no further reply. Instead he shouted, 'Marie, bring us some wine.'

She came forward with a rough stone bottle and two glasses and once again the candles threw their light upon her. She was exquisite – fine boned and lean, her hair clouding crimson. She was as out of place in the dark and dirty room as an orchid in a graveyard. Jackdaw found it impossible to take his eyes off her.

'So,' said Papineau, pouring for himself and his visitor, 'you believe in the Republic of Canada.'

'I have already offered the sapphire pelt as proof of my good will. Does that not speak for itself?'

'Not necessarily.'

'What do you mean?'

'A rumour has reached my ears,' said Papineau, leaning back in his chair, 'a rumour that, if it is true, can only be described as alarming. I am told that a spy is infiltrating our group, a spy who takes many disguises. Sometimes he comes as a priest, sometimes as an Irishman, sometimes as a trapper. But one thing is consistent, his general description. He is dark, not very tall, and is believed to limp slightly. As you came in, my friend, I thought that I noticed these characteristics in you. Marie, over here!'

She disengaged herself from a shadow and stood at her father's side.

'Make him walk before you. Let us see if he limps.'

She met Jackdaw's eyes with a totally unreadable expression.

'Walk,' she said.

'To where?'

'To the other side of the room. Don't try to be clever. I have a pistol pointing between your shoulders.'

He felt the hardness of the barrel push against his jacket.

'It would seem I have no choice.'

'None at all. Move.'

Very slowly Jackdaw stood up, his eyes rapidly running over the room for a means of escape. There was nothing but the door, beyond which lay the spiral staircase leading up to the inn.

'There has been a mistake,' he said loudly. 'I am Louis Dubois, nicknamed the Jackdaw.'

'If you can prove that, then all will be well,' answered Papineau calmly.

Reluctantly, Jackdaw took a few paces forward. Right behind him he could feel Marie, her breath on the back of his neck. He thought he must be going a little mad for, at the same time as knowing that he was in the most grave danger of his life, he desired her, wanted desperately to make love to her. He had the wildest notion that she was the girl he had seen in his dreams but that somehow the name was wrong.

'Well?' said Papineau.

Marie hesitated.

'I don't know. I'm not sure. I don't think he does limp'.

Papineau sat up straight.

'Let me see for myself. Move aside, girl.'

Very slowly she did so and at the same moment her gun lowered – but whether by accident or design who could say. Jackdaw seized his chance. He hurled himself through the door and up the spiral stairs faster than he had ever moved in his life before. Behind him he heard Papineau shout, 'Shoot him. What's the matter with you?' But no sound rang out.

But the raised voice had alerted the patrons of the inn and Jackdaw fled up the stairs to a scene of incredible violence. The other two trappers – in reality Major Tom Rourke of the Grenadier Guards and Captain Thomas Snow of the 4th Foot – were on their feet and punching with all their might and as Jackdaw reached the top a loose and bloodied tooth shot past him like a pellet.

The sounds of crunching knuckles and winded groans were unbelievable and Jackdaw's voice shouting 'We're discovered' was crowned in the uproar.

He managed to crouch as a huge man went for him with a chair and dodged just in time to see it smash against the floor rather than on his head. But then came a man with an axe, blood running down the back of his hands, and bearing the most evil snarl. A side door opened somewhere and Jackdaw was whisked through it as the axe blade split the panels of wood. A second later and he would have been decapitated.

He knew without turning that he had been saved by Marie but as he whirled round he saw that she was hurrying back into the inn, a despairing expression on her face.

'Wait,' he shouted.

But she was gone and Jackdaw did the only sensible thing in the circumstances – he ran into the darkness as far away from the place as he could get, more afraid than he had ever been in his life before.

And the fear would not leave him for the knock on the hotel room door, the next day, set Jackdaw's heart racing.

None the less he called, 'Come in,' softly, at the same time taking out a pistol which he had hidden beneath his pillow.

The previous night he had run from the inn till exhausted and had finally slept in a disused workman's hut. But the following morning he had come to the Hotel Reine – a seedy establishment in the rough area of Quebec, yet the agreed rendezvous point should he, Major Rourke or Captain Snow ever get separated.

Then he had broken every rule that he had been taught in the Army. He had bribed a child to take a letter to Marie. Even as he had written his name Jackdaw had known the risk he was taking. Quebec swarmed with revolutionaries; the child might betray him – or even Marie herself – and if Papineau should happen upon the note, Jackdaw could start counting his days.

Now he pointed the pistol towards the door, supporting it with both hands.

'Come in,' he said again.

The door opened a crack and the urchin's dirty face appeared.

'I did it – I did it for you, M'sieur. Don't shoot. I gave it to her – to Marie.'

'Did anyone see you?'

'No. She was alone. Papineau was out.'

Jackdaw lowered the pistol. 'What did she say?'

'She gave me this.'

A grimy piece of paper in an equally grimy hand was thrust towards him. Jackdaw flicked his eyes over it, half his attention still on the boy and the open door behind him.

It simply said: 'I will be there by midnight. If I am not,

sail with the tide.' She had signed herself, rather formally, 'Marie Papineau'.

'Is that all right? Can I have the other half of the money? You did say.'

Jackdaw's hand suddenly shot out and grabbed the boy's collar, pulling the poor wretch so close that they were nose to nose.

'Did you betray me?' he hissed.

'No, M'sieur – honest.'

'If anything happens to me there are those who will come looking for you.'

The child gave a yelp of fright and wriggled in Jackdaw's grasp. He looked near to tears.

'I haven't done anything. Please let me go.'

Jackdaw went 'Humph', released the boy and reached in his pocket for a coin.

'There you are. Now be off. But no tricks, mind.'

'No, M'sieur.'

The boy scuttled away like a spider and Jackdaw was left to read the note again.

He had written to beg Marie to meet him at the Quay d'Orleans – one of the many harbours that dotted the banks of the great St Lawrence river; and from which, by means of a small charter boat, he intended to make his way to Newfoundland and there pick up one of the great trading vessels headed for England. He was in duty bound to wait till nightfall for Rourke and Snow and then, if they were still missing, proceed without them. Those were the instructions given to all officers serving in intelligence: if one's cover was destroyed, no brave attempts at saving companions; simply lie low and then head back quickly by the safest route possible.

He thought to himself that he must be mad to risk all by asking Marie to go with him – yet that clouding hair seemed so familiar. He felt almost certain she was the girl whose dream self he had loved for years – yet something was not right. But he pushed away the nagging doubt with the thought that she would probably refuse to come. Why should she give up everything for a man she had known barely an hour?

He fell asleep on that uncomfortable hotel bed and had the oddest dream. He dreamed that he walked along the sea front at Hastings with Helen, his mother. Beside him, on his left, trotted a man he did not know but whose round, jolly face grinned at him like an amiable moon.

'You really ought to wait,' said the jolly man – pointing vaguely in the direction of the castle.

'Yes,' said Helen, nodding anxiously. 'Do be patient, Jackdaw. You are getting so headstrong.'

'She's up there, you see,' the jolly man went on, totally ignoring Helen and waving his cane aloft again.

'Who?' said Jackdaw.

The man laughed uproariously.

'As if you didn't know,' he chortled.

'But I *don't* know.'

'Then look for yourself.'

Jackdaw peered and saw that standing on the battlements – reduced to a dot by the distance – was a Princess from a fairytale, or someone who resembled one. Yet there could be no mistaking the gleam of that autumn head beneath the high day sun.

'Marie,' he shouted.

Helen and the jolly man looked astounded but said nothing. The figure waved its hand.

'I'm coming,' called Jackdaw, trying to hurry forward but finding that his limp had grown suddenly worse and he could scarcely walk.

The figure blew a kiss and disappeared from view.

'Come soon!' she shouted over her departing shoulder.

'You see,' said the man.

'See what?'

Jackdaw was near to tears. He could hardly move an inch, his leg hurt him so much.

'English,' said the man triumphantly.

'Oh go away.' Jackdaw had suddenly lost his temper. 'Who are you anyway?'

'Hicks. Algernon Hicks. May I present my card?'

He did so, bowed – and vanished into thin air. And with a shout Jackdaw awoke to his dreary and dangerous surroundings and a mood of lurking depression.

'Oh, Mr Hicks,' said Mrs Webbe Weston, 'I don't know what to say. I mean you have not been formally introduced.'

Francis smiled disarmingly.

'No, Ma'am. I met your daughter in a field where we both were pursuing our hobby of painting in oils. But allow me to assure you of my bona fides. I am the son of the late Samuel Hicks, Esquire, and brother of the present Algernon Hicks – also Esquire. I am studying medicine at St Bartholomew's Hospital with the hope of ultimately taking up surgery.'

A faint gleam appeared behind Mrs Webbe Weston's vacuous eye. She had been a 'martyr to her health' – her own words – ever since they had moved to Pomona House.

'Oh – er – well, in that case . . . I would ask you to stay to supper that you might formally present yourself to my husband but . . . such difficult times you see . . .'

'Nonsense, Mother,' said Caroline roundly. 'Father brought in two large hares the other night. Could we not have those jugged?'

Mrs Webbe Weston made a feeble move and then groaned.

'It is when I try to stand suddenly you know, Mr Hicks.

I get this dreadful pain that shoots down into my ankles from my back. I often wonder what it could be.'

Francis stood up.

'If you might allow me just to examine your upper back, Ma'am. I am most interested in the orthopaedic skills. Miss Webbe Weston should stay in the room but if I could ask the Captain to step outside. It will only take a moment, I assure you.'

'Oh!' said Mrs Webbe Weston. 'But that would not be seemly. I mean here – in my sitting room!'

'It will not be necessary to remove more than your shawl. An experienced hand can feel bone through a blouse as light as the one you are wearing now – which does suit you most enormously, I really must add.'

Mrs Webbe Weston fluttered and over her head Caroline and John Joseph exchanged a wink.

'I'll go and look for Father,' he said. 'I've missed him rather a lot.'

Much as Mary had predicted Mr Webbe Weston scrubbed at his eyes with reddened knuckles.

'My son! Soldier, eh? By Jove. Choked in chest. Ha ha. Capital turn out. What?'

John Joseph felt enormously gratified. Funny old buffer his father might be, but a parent's praise and approbation is a unique part of every human need. How wretched to be treated with coldness in the face of one's best effort. But Mr Webbe Weston knew nothing of such fine cruelties and threw his arms round John Joseph, guffawing and sniffing with joy.

'Always knew. Needed to go. Get away. No good.'

'How is Sutton Place?'

'Rotting. Hopeless. No tenants. Fall one day. Good job.'

'I hear that Cloverella has left.'

'Yes. *En ceinte*. Father unknown. Ho ho.'

John Joseph swallowed and said, 'It could have been me, you know.'

It was the first time he had ever spoken to his father man to man but Mr Webbe Weston bellowed with laughter.

'Farm lads. Or Jackdaw.'

'Jackdaw?'

'Not half!'

'Then you think I need not worry too much?'

'Lord no. Wild oat. Manhood.'

They went back into the house and saw Mrs Webbe Weston pink in the cheeks with excitement.

'Oh, my dear, this is Mr Hicks – a new acquaintance of Caroline's. He is staying at the Angel and has diagnosed that I have a tired back – he is studying at St Bartholomew's.'

The resourceful Francis bowed to Mr Webbe Weston and said, 'How do you do, sir? I am here to pay my compliments to you and your wife in the hope that I might be allowed to call upon your daughter.' There was just the suspicion of a wink in his eye as he went on, 'The cure for your wife's condition is a little mild exercise. Too much lying on the sofa is not advantageous. Even a little gentle gardening could be in order.'

'Capital,' said Mr Webbe Weston. 'Capital. Ha ha ha. Call Matilda. Family together. Sherry Sir? I'm indulging.'

'Well, Mr Hicks, I can't say what a pleasure it is to make your acquaintance.'

Mrs Webbe Weston was radiant, already flushed with two large glasses of sweet lunchtime sherry and now the comforting thought that she had at least a week – if not perhaps a lifetime if her little scheme came to fruition – to talk of her ailments to a professional ear.

She smiled knowingly at her husband who chuffed into

his whiskers and cast his eyes appraisingly over Caroline, the youngest and by far the prettiest of his daughters.

'So you wish to take my little one sketching tomorrow?' she said.

Francis smiled. 'With your permission, Ma'am.'

'I'm afraid that I will not be able to act as chaperone. The sun, you know. But of course if Matilda were to accompany you . . .'

'And John Joseph,' Caroline put in. 'We are dying to paint him. Will you come, long lost brother?'

'No, not tomorrow. I'll pose for you another day. I have an assignation to keep.'

'Oh?' Caroline's dark brows rose in surprise.

'With Sutton Place. I must see it again. I believe I have a love-hate feeling for the place.'

Francis said, 'Perhaps we could all go. I've been longing to have a look at it ever since I first heard the legend.'

'Now that *is* a splendid notion. Would you paint it, Mr Hicks?'

'Let us make it a painting picnic,' said Caroline, 'all four of us. Matilda, what do you say?'

Matilda, who had grown extremely drab and dull since he had last seen her – or so John Joseph thought – answered, 'Well, I'm not terribly good.'

'Oh, don't be such a ninny. It is high time you went out more. Mother, you really must let her go and visit Mary in Paris. It would do her the world of good.'

Matilda swallowed and stared into her lap and John Joseph said, 'You are getting very bossy, Caroline. Just like Mary in the old days.'

Caroline toyed with the idea of being annoyed and decided against it and laughed instead.

'Yes, I probably am. But you see my ideas are always so terribly *good*.'

Francis Hicks shot a most affectionate glance from his sparkling eyes and rose to his feet.

'Then, if that is agreed by you, Mrs Webbe Weston, I shall meet the younger people tomorrow morning at Sutton Place. What time do you suggest, Miss Webbe Weston?'

'Ten o'clock – while the sun is still high.'

'Very well, ten o'clock it is.'

He bowed his way out and Caroline, as soon as he was out of earshot, hugged her knees to her chin and laughed.

'What are you so pleased about?' said Matilda, a trifle sourly.

'Because – though he doesn't yet know it – I am going to marry him and be as happy as a bird. Oh, to think of it! You may come and stay with me, Matilda, and do the season. Won't it be wonderful?'

'And what if he is not agreeable?'

'He will agree,' said Caroline firmly, 'to everything I suggest.'

Beneath his breath the fisherman sang an old French song as the boat nosed its way into the darkness and up the mighty St Lawrence towards the salty vastness of the Atlantic. And Jackdaw, gazing at the fast-fading lights of Quebec, experienced every kind of emotion. Above all he felt immense relief that he had got out of the place alive. But equally, and for the first time, he knew wild and unrestrained passion. He wanted to take the slim flame of a girl who now stood beside him and possess her until she cried for him to stop. He had never felt anything like it before.

'Why did you come?' he said now, putting his hand on the wonderful hair.

'Because I wanted to see you again.'

'And that is the only reason?'

She laughed in the darkness. 'Perhaps.'

Her voice was musical, soft – and she spoke French like a native.

'Marie – I know it sounds ridiculous, but I believe that I have known you always.'

For answer she only shivered and said, 'Shall we go into the cabin? I do not like to think of such things. It makes me cold.'

He put his arm round her waist.

'You will never be cold while I have strength to warm you.'

Her answer to the boyish protestation was to laugh and kiss him beneath the chin.

'You are whiskery,' she said. 'Go and shave yourself.'

'Is that all you can say when I desire you so much?'

'Yes, it is all I can say.'

But when he straightened up from the cracked china bowl and jug of cold water at which he had removed his six-month growth of beard, his heart nearly stopped in his chest. While his back was turned Marie had slipped into the cabin's solitary bunk and now lay gazing up at the shadows on the ceiling which danced together in the candle's guttering flame. In the faint light her hair glowed like a fire's heart spread round her fine-boned face.

Jackdaw could not speak. He felt that all his life had been leading up to this moment. He stood still, almost without breathing, taking stock of the past and the present which had now melded into one – or so it seemed.

'I have always loved you,' he said to Marie.

He was past thinking. It did not occur to him to question the fact that the family scene into which he had wandered through the time boundary of his silly green marble had been one typically English, and that Marie – who lay so gently in his bed – was the daughter of a French-Canadian revolutionary; he cared nothing that he

210

could face court martial for consorting with the enemy. He did not give a fig for his father's opinion – nor even Helen's – when they clapped eyes upon the girl whom he had already chosen to make his wife.

But now he could wait no more – his blood was on fire for her! He crossed over and sat for a moment beside her, burying his face in the sweet curve of her neck. But it was difficult to be gentle – he would know no peace until he had kissed every sweet part of her, felt the small high breasts warm beneath his hands.

With no further thought Jackdaw pinned her wrists like two butterflies and threw himself across her. There seemed to be a pause in time as the world went spinning and he thrust his shaft, hard and demanding, into the innermost secret of her body. Then after a moment's gasp from her, they began to move together in a glorious rhythm.

'Oh Marie, Marie,' he said in ecstasy as the warm fluid of his love flowed into his beloved, 'promise that you will never leave me. Not ever. Promise me.'

But in the darkness she could only murmur, 'God alone can give the answer to that.'

11

'To think,' said Lady Annette Waldegrave, twirling before a full-length mirror and poking her tongue out at her reflection, 'that I am twenty years old – today – and I haven't even one miserable suitor to my name. I declare I'm fated to be a decrepit old spinster.'

'You don't look decrepit,' answered Horatia.

'Well, I feel it.'

But what her sister said was true. Annette had inherited her mother's blonde hair and had increased the beauty of her moonstone eyes with clever painting. Had she but had a reasonably wealthy – or even respectable – brother she would have been married within a year of her eighteenth birthday.

'It's all George's fault,' Annette went on, putting the family complaint into words. 'If he weren't such a wretched rake we would have money and reputation and callers and gaiety.'

'He *is* giving a supper party for you.'

'Yes – and who will be the guests?' She ticked them off on her fingers. 'Mother, J.J., you, Ida Anna, and a handful of George's more boring friends – the others wouldn't be allowed within a mile of Strawberry Hill.'

'Well be thankful for small mercies.' Horatia stood up as she spoke. 'I've had no party given for me since I was eight.'

Annette did not relent.

'Well, you haven't come out yet. I have – well and truly.'

Horry crossed to the mirror and stood peering at her reflection.

'There isn't much hope for me then. Any dowry that's going will be settled on you. I think I'll elope with the first person who asks.'

She suddenly laughed and whirled Annette round by the waist. 'Cheer up – it won't be too bad. We're sure to find some poor being we can persuade into putting up with us. Do try to be jolly – you are supposed to on your birthday.'

Annette gave her a begrudging smile and – as she always did when she looked at Horatia these days – felt just the faintest tinge of envy. For the truth was that Annette was pretty but Horatia was superb. Lady Laura Waldegrave walked on earth again in her granddaughter.

The slanting mermaid eyes, swept by jet lashes, gazed at the world with a jade-clear gaze; while the lips – neither conventionally shaped nor full – curled into a little smile. The body had grown neither short nor tall, neither fat nor thin, but curved in and out like a pretty landscape. Her breasts were marvellous; round and full-nippled, rising firm and supple in her frame like those of an arrow-shooting goddess.

Yet with all these assets it was her hair, still, that was the most exquisite thing about her. She wore it loose to her shoulders, tumbling like a waterfall, and swirling and blazing in a glory of reds – for at the thickest part of it, nearest her neck, it was as dark as ripened damsons but on the other edge, where the tresses thinned, it burst into a nimbus of flame. No one who saw her had any doubt – at fifteen Horatia Elizabeth Waldegrave was the jewel of her generation.

Now Annette looked at her again.

'You *are* beautiful,' she said. 'I quite hate you for it.' But she shook her head and smiled as she spoke to show she did not mean it. 'Remember what I told you when we were young – the eldest girl *has* to marry first; that's the rule.'

Horry laughed.

'Shall we go to the Gallery? Maybe George will have done his duty and invited some proper eligibles.'

Annette rolled her eyes.

'Heaven forbid. The most I've a hope of is the stammering curate. The little thing who incessantly drops his napkin upon the floor and flushes like a beet as he stoops to pick it up.'

'Poor creature! He only does it to hide the fact he blushes whenever you speak.'

'That will make a fine basis for courtship, to be sure!'

'Annette, you are so cruel. You must stop it. I am quite determined that you will enjoy your brithday, come what may.'

They linked arms companionably at this, smiled at each other, and went from the bedroom – which they still shared with Ida Anna – into a corridor which led on to the Gallery. This late March evening it stood – as ornate and fabulous and extraordinary as ever – dappled by the light from a great fire which roared away in the marble fireplace, heavily carved with wood, and crowned overall with a portrait of Horace Walpole himself. Nobody else was about but the sound of feet coming up the stairs told the Waldegrave sisters that a guest had arrived and a second or so later J.J. appeared in the doorway, a glass already in his hand.

'My doves,' he said, 'how entrancing you look.' It was obvious he was extremely cheerful and very slightly drunk. 'I've brought you a present, Annette. Happy birthday.'

He fished in his trouser pocket and produced a sparkling diamond clasp – obviously worth a great deal more

214

than he could afford and probably won over the gaming table.

'How very, very kind of you,' she said, fastening it to the shoulder of her evening gown, and standing on tip-toe as she kissed him on the cheek.

He was still desperately handsome, despite the drawn appearance that his illness and drinking combined to give, and next month he would be twenty-five. He should, by rights – as the bastard son of the late Earl Waldegrave – have been on the list of every matchmaking Mama in society. But rumours of his financial difficulties – in fact the financial difficulties of the whole family – abounded. Indeed, Horatia felt rather sorry for him. She thought that he could not have started a courtship with a respectable girl even if he had so desired. But whether he did so or not was highly debatable; the wild living of him and George was spoken of with bated breath in polite circles.

As if he knew that his brother was there George came in a moment later and stood, his arm round J.J.'s shoulders, silently toasting him. Their twin-like looks were uncanny. Only the bluish glow of George's hair and the fact that he was an inch or so shorter differentiated them.

'Well,' said George without preamble, nudging J.J. violently in the ribs, 'how are we going to get Annette married off? Twenty today and no suitor. Tut, tut, tut.'

He shook his head and clucked like a hen and Horry saw her sister go pink with fury.

'What about the curate?' answered J.J. 'Once he grows out of his spots and blushing he should turn out quite well.'

'Y-e-s,' George was reflective. 'But could he rescue the family fortune?'

'Doubt it.' J.J.'s voice seemed choked with laughter. 'For that you need a great deal of *money*.'

He collapsed, slapping his thigh and wiping his eyes with his cuff.

'How dare you?' Annette looked as if she was going to explode. 'How can you speak of me so? I am your sister, not some – some . . . chattel; a nothing to be sold in the market place! How can you mention me and money in the same breath?'

'Why not?' said George hysterically. 'I should have thought you go very well together.'

Annette began to cry and J.J. calmed a little and said, 'Don't, my darling. We have been teasing you, that is all. We have a surprise and this is just a silly joke. Now dry your eyes and close them tightly.'

Annette shot Horatia a piteous look and her younger sister said, 'How can you be so cruel? You are behaving monstrously on her birthday.'

George stopped laughing.

'We're not really. Tidy her up, Horry. We really have got a surprise.'

'But is it a nice one?'

'Very, very nice.' There was a sound of more footsteps on the stairs. 'Hurry up. She really must not look wretched.'

The door opened and a dashing figure stood there, bowing in the direction of the two girls. The voice of the butler intoned pompously, 'Captain Archibald Money, my Lord.'

'Money,' said George, stressing the word so loudly that there was simply no way Annette and Horatia could have failed to see the joke, 'welcome once more to Strawberry Hill.'

Annette went first pale and then pink again and only stepped forward to drop her curtsey with Horatia's hand in the small of her back. Archie – who had not called

216

since the Earl's funeral three years before – raised her fingers to his lips.

'Lady Annette,' he said. 'I have been unable to visit you till now as I was posted to the Bengal Lancers just after the most unfortunate loss of your father. However, I have written to the Earl and also to your mother the Countess to request their permission to pay my addresses.'

Annette went scarlet and it was left to Horatia to say, 'Why on earth didn't you say so before? She had almost given up thinking about you.'

The March winds, which blew round Strawberry Hill the night of Annette's twentieth birthday, died away and the rainbow month of April, sweet with daffodil breezes, took their place.

From Paris the brilliant Viennese Johann Strauss I set sail for England to conduct at the birthday ball of Queen Victoria in her Coronation year; and from Vienna John Joseph also set out for London as military escort to Emperor Ferdinand's envoy at the great celebrations. And from his barracks in London Jackdaw went off to Buckingham Palace in the magic of a blossom-heavy May evening to act as official interpreter for the guests from all parts of the world who had come to bow the knee to the nineteen-year-old girl who now ruled England.

But neither John Joseph nor Jackdaw knew that the other old friend – bound to him by distant relationship and affinity which transcended ties of blood – was to be present at the glittering occasion when Maestro Strauss bowed before the tiny Queen and then raised his violin to his chin.

There was silence in that great ballroom as the first seductive notes of the solo fiddle poured out the joyous notes of the waltz to the little monarch. And when she finally raised her white-gloved hand and put it into that of Lord Melbourne, that he might lead the dancing with her, there was a rapturous round of applause before the ladies lifted their hems by the loops and joined in the dance with all that assembly of gallant gentlemen come to pay allegiance to their sweet and youthful sovereign on the anniversary of her birth.

But as Jackdaw – bright in his regimental scarlet but with a heart dark as pitch beneath his solitary gold medal – whirled in the Viennese waltz, he did not see that John Joseph, dancing with Countess Lamberg, was about to bump into him. And thus they met after three years – back to back, slightly out of breath – and not looking where they were going.

They both wheeled round to apologize and then stared at each other.

'Jackdaw? You here? I don't believe it!'

'John Joseph! This is incredible.'

They remembered common courtesy and bowed to their respective partners explaining – in a rather garbled manner – that they had run into a long-lost childhood friend and had forgotten themselves in the excitement. But as soon as the dance was ended they discreetly left the ballroom and went to one of the balconies overlooking the Palace gardens, that they might talk without interruption.

'How is this possible?' said John Joseph, offering a cigar to Jackdaw and then lighting his own.

'Very simple, for me. I went to Canada to penetrate a ring of revolutionary fanatics who were sowing the seeds of an uprising. An uprising which could have severed Canada from Britain like the American colonies. But my disguise was discovered and I had to pick my way back to England. I was given a medal for my efforts.'

He said this last sentence so bitterly that John Joseph

gave him a sharp look. In the light from the flambeaux that lit the gardens, together with the rising moon, he saw that his friend had changed. He looked older, haggard almost, his mouth set in a tough line, the jewel-bright eyes cynical and cold.

'And . . .?'

'And?'

'And what is the rest you have not told me? You look as if you have been to Hell. Were you captured and tortured?'

'No, I escaped – with help.'

'Oh?'

'You are determined to know, aren't you? Very well. I met a woman, I fell in love with her. I broke every rule there is and asked her to leave Canada with me. And because she cared for me she did so. She was Papineau the revolutionary's daughter – and when we reached Newfoundland to board a trading vessel her father had her killed. I came back from booking our passages and found her dead in bed. She had been strangled with one of my belts.'

He stopped short and a harsh sound escaped from him.

John Joseph put a hand on his friend's arm.

'What a terrible thing. Was the murderer ever caught?'

'No, he escaped like a rat in the night. But that it was her father's agent is sure, because he pinned a note to her chest which said, "This for consorting with the enemy. Death to all traitors."'

John Joseph shook his head. 'I don't know what to say.'

Jackdaw looked at him grimly. 'To make it even worse – if that's possible – I have the idea that she was my destined woman. That there will never be anybody else.'

'What do you mean?'

'I used to dream about her even when I was a child. I

used to dream about a girl with red hair. It was a recurring vision.'

'Funnily enough I have had the same experience,' said John Joseph slowly. 'It stopped after we left Sutton Place but while we were there I often dreamed that I died in a tent on a battlefield in the arms of a red-headed woman.'

Jackdaw had gone very quiet. In his mind's eye he was back at the Spanish court where he had acted as interpreter for the Queen Regent. He remembered how he had fallen asleep fully clothed, a brandy bottle clutched in his hand, and how he had dreamed. He saw again the great white rock and the girl standing on the top. And he remembered how a man had appeared and stood beside her and put his arm around her shoulders, and how astonished he had been to see it was John Joseph. Was it possible that this extraordinary thread was running through both their lives?

'I don't understand,' he said.

From behind them stole the sound of an enchanting waltz tune, filling the night with notes like drops of crystal.

'Don't understand what?' said John Joseph.

'I dreamt once that I saw you with such a woman. I must be getting confused. Perhaps Marie was not . . .'

'Don't think about it any more,' said John Joseph. 'Remember what your father used to tell you; too much dwelling on mysteries does you no good. Come along, we mustn't desert our duties. I am here as a member of the Austrian envoy's escort – and also a dancing partner for the wives.'

'No wife of your own yet?'

'No, nor likely to have. I was badly hurt once. I wouldn't like to go through it again in a hurry.'

Jackdaw laughed shortly. 'We're two of a kind.'

In the distance Countess Lamberg's voice could be

heard calling, 'Captain Webbe Weston, where are you? You are booked on my card and Her Majesty has requested Maestro Strauss's latest polka. I should not like to miss it.'

John Joseph was about to step in through the French windows when Jackdaw detained him a moment longer.

'How is Sutton Place?' he called. 'Are you going to see it on this visit?'

'No. I only have a few hours free, and those in London. But Caroline and her fiancé, Francis Hicks, are coming up to join me and we plan to visit a theatre. Will you come with us?'

'Hicks,' answered Jackdaw abstractedly. 'I seem to know that name. When is this?'

'In two days from now.'

'I shall try.'

'Your friend – when did she die?'

'Ten months ago.'

'Then give yourself time. They say it heals all things.'

The opening bars of the polka were beginning to gain momentum and partners were being taken. The Queen was smiling up at Lord Melbourne again and laughing with pure pleasure.

'I think she has a passion for him,' whispered John Joseph, behind his hand.

'Yes, I believe so,' answered Jackdaw.

'It's time she was married.'

'They are probably saying that about you and me.'

'Then let them. I intend to avoid it as long as possible.'

'Hear, hear,' said Jackdaw, and they stepped back into the ballroom.

A few days after the little Queen went to Westminster Abbey – on June 28, 1838 – to receive the monarch's crown, Caroline Webbe Weston went to Holy Trinity to receive the wedding ring of Francis Hicks, Esquire and medical student.

Despite all Mrs Webbe Weston's fears the occasion was a great success and afterwards thirty people sat down to breakfast at Pomona House. Mary came from Paris with her husband and four little children, two of her own and two belonging to Robert Anthony; and Matilda stood as bridesmaid, happy in the knowledge that afterwards she would return to Paris to live with her sister for a year.

John Joseph was not there but sent greetings from Vienna, busy as he was with his Army commitments. But though he was missed the occasion was made jovial by the reappearance of Cloverella outside the church, throwing rice beneath the bride's shoe and pressing a sprig of heather into her hand. She wore a scarlet dress, rather tattered, and was slightly muckier than anyone remembered her being three years ago. By her side stood a delightful little boy with a mass of dark hair, bright twinkling eyes, and a pair of dirty feet. She laughed when they asked his name, and said it was Jay, which some took to mean that he had been named after John Joseph and others after Jackdaw.

The breakfast over, a pianoforte, violin and cello played Strauss waltzes, polkas and galops in the drawing room and the guests – particularly Francis's hearty elder brother Algernon, who had stood up as best man – danced the night away, long after the newly-weds had left for their honeymoon in Scotland.

As dawn broke the last of the revellers took to their carriages and wended their way through Sutton Park and it was then that Algernon, having helped the family to see that all was secure for the night, made his farewells and went off on foot to walk to Guildford and the Angel Inn. He was neither drunk nor sober but in that merry state that lies in between and so it was, whistling a tune and dancing a little as he went, that he first clapped eyes on Sutton Place.

The sky behind it was streaked with scarlets and blues – all the bold brave military colours he loved so well – but it was the great black shape of the deserted mansion that arrested him, made him stop in his tracks and stand staring, his mouth slightly open in admiration.

Algernon Hicks was not over-stuffed with imagination – in fact he was not a quarter as bright as his sparkling younger brother – but something in his jolly soul stirred at this very first glimpse.

'By Jove,' he said, and whistled extra loudly; then jumped violently as somebody said in the darkness, 'Would you like to see inside?'

He peered nervously in that uncertain light, wondering if something that he would have termed suspect was taking place, but eventually his eyes picked out the gypsy girl Cloverella, sitting beneath an elm tree in her ragged scarlet frock, her child asleep at her side.

'Oh, it's you,' he said. 'Oughtn't you to be at home? I mean, after all, a woman on her own at this hour of the night – or should I say morning?'

'I haven't got a home yet,' she answered, standing up. 'I only arrived back yesterday – came for the wedding.'

'Oh! Well, that's not too good. With the little one to care for.'

He reached vaguely in the direction of his hip pocket and then realized that he had emptied most of his money out before the wedding ceremony and given it to the hotel for safe keeping.

'Dash!' he said.

He was like an enthusiastic dog; friendly and silly and terribly kind but altogether something of a bore. When he laughed it was like loud barking and when he was sad

223

his head seemed to go down and his face take on a whimpering look. If he got interested in something he bounded about as if he had been invited to go for a Walk; when he was deeply distressed he emitted a low growling sound.

Physically, too, he had a smack of the canine. Large ears that flattened in the wind; big, rather bolting eyes, that rolled piteously when he was in disgrace; and a general impression of oversized feet that splayed down upon the floor like scampering paws. It was needless to say that he had neither been mated nor sired pups.

'Well?' said Cloverella.

'Well what?'

'Do you want to see inside?'

'But dash it all, it's locked up, isn't it?'

'That doesn't matter. I know the way in. You must, Mr Hicks. You're meant to see Sutton Place in the dawning.'

His spine pricked at her words but his nose went up like a pointer's.

'Really? You're not talking fairy-talk, are you?' He boomed like a bassett.

'In a way. Sutton Place is lonely – all shut up like that. Come on, Mr Hicks. Put your hand in mine.'

He did so, not consciously aware of what was happening, so caught up was he with the wedding wine and the glory of the dawn.

'What about the baby?'

'Oh, I'll wake him. He should see it too. Come on Jay, my lovely son. Open your darling eyes and show Mr Hicks his house.'

'*My* house?'

'It will be one day. Now, ask no more questions. Just look – and listen.'

'Listen to what?'

'If you try hard enough the house will speak to you.'

Mr Hicks sniffed, setter-like, and together they crossed the park and went over what had once been the cobbles of the quadrangle.

From every side history *did* speak: its mystic voice breathed within his ear. He saw alabaster bricks, the initials R.W., the grinning cherubs above the door. He felt beneath his feet the path trodden by those who were now dust, yet whose names would never – could never – be erased from the records of England's vast story. He touched with his own blunt fingers the stones that had been put in place by craftsmen who would be remembered for nothing except this, this epic house, this great and awe-inspiring monument – Sutton Place.

Very quietly – and very reverently – in that glow of early morning, Mr Hicks drew breath. He knew, as others were to do after him, that he had been consumed with a kind of love.

'I simply can't bear it, George!' shouted the Countess Waldegrave, stamping her foot. 'I can't, can't, can't bear it any more.'

'Be quiet, Mother, for pity's sake.'

'No I won't. I've been quiet long enough. I've put up with enough. I've held my peace too long.'

And with that she poked her parasol viciously at the overflowing buttocks of a rather florid – and extremely naked – opera girl who lay nestled up close to George on the ottoman in the Gallery.

'It's not fair,' the Countess went on, bursting into tears. 'I come back from a meagre little holiday in the Isle of Wight – and what do I find? My home – and it is mine, George, because I came here with your father when you were a mere babe-in-arms – turned into nothing more nor less than a common brothel.'

'Look who's talking,' said the opera girl.

225

'I beg your pardon?'

'I've heard it said that you were no better than you should be.'

'That's enough,' said George.

'To whom did you address that remark?'

'Not to you, Mother.'

'Well it certainly couldn't have been addressed to me,' said the opera girl, 'because until you led me from the straight and narrow, my good Sir, I was a girl of virtue. It was your fault – and yours alone – that I find myself in the condition in which I am today.'

'And what condition would that be?'

'I am expecting a child, Lady Waldegrave, if you must know. And it is your son who is the father and responsible for my shame. But he won't get away with it. I intend to move into Strawberry Hill and stay here until he admits that I am the mother of his heir and marries me. As I think has happened to you once or twice, if rumour is to be believed.'

Anne went white to the lips. 'How dare you insult me in my own home!'

'Well, it's true, isn't it? You wouldn't be so straight-faced if it weren't.'

'George, do something. See this common harlot off the premises.'

For answer George, doing up the button flap of his trousers which was gaping wide to the world, rang a bell for the butler.

'You must go, Hetty,' he said.

'Go? Never!' She jumped off the sofa and began to put on her clothes in haste. 'I'm carrying your bastard in my belly. You won't get rid of me. I intend to stay here until justice is done.'

'Then in that case *I* shall go,' said Anne with dignity. 'I still have a small sum left to me by my husband – and I also have a great deal of pride. I shall open up the London house in Montagu Street, dilapidated though it might be. I would as soon paint it with my own hands than stay another moment under the same roof as this doxy. I shall tell the girls not to unpack.'

And with that she swept out and back into the travel-stained carriage, from which her daughters – aghast and staring – had not yet descended, and set off for London without even a turn of her determined head.

12

It was ready; players in place; opening gambit. The Master Chessplayer removed his gauntlet and laughed at a pawn. It was time for lives to be woven one with another, for balances to change, for existences to alter for ever.

So, quite simply, a set of events that would lead to an enormous culmination came about. Small people took – apparently – little decisions and the path of chance changed.

Francis Hicks, shaving cream smothering his chin and his voice altered by the contortion of his mouth, said to his brother Algernon, 'Shall we go to Hastings? It's depressing to spend August in London. Come on – don't be a stick. Say yes.'

'But what about Caroline? I mean, dash it, you're still on honeymoon – almost. She won't want me tagging along.'

Mr Hicks's eyes looked slightly sad, like a spaniel with whom nobody wanted to play.

'Rubbish. She'll want to paint you in your wide-awake, staring moodily out to sea.' Francis honed a cut-throat on a leather strop. 'And I shall portray you with a telescope, in jaunty pose. Come on, Algy – we're relying on you as a model.'

Algernon barked noisily. 'Then in that case . . .'

But his jollity was stopped by the entry of his sister-in-law. He leapt to his feet, sending a small table and an aspidistra flying.

'Oh, jingo! Dashed sorry, Caro . . .'

Mr Hicks crouched amongst the rubble, squashing some earth into the carpet with his knee.

'Don't worry, Algy. I'll see to it.'

Caroline knelt down beside him, giving Francis a little wink meanwhile. She was prettier than ever, blooming with marriage. Her husband laughed, negotiating the area around his lower lip.

'Caroline, we would like to go to Hastings – if that is agreeable to you. I thought a holiday by the sea might brace us all up.'

'Is Algy coming too?'

Mr Hicks – on all fours – looked apologetic.

'Not if I'm a nuisance.'

Caroline, looking at the broken pot plant, smiled as she put her arms round him and said, 'How could you ever be a nuisance, dearest Algy?'

Meanwhile that old sea dog William Waldegrave, younger brother of the late Earl and now Viscount Chewton as George had no heir – or none legitimate, that is – descended from his carriage and rapped on the door of Number 18, Montagu Street, London. He stood there, looking a little bluff and puffing his cheeks in and out, waiting for the maid to reply.

He had entered the Royal Navy as a midshipman and had risen to the rank of Captain, after which he had given up the sea for a short spell and tried his hand in the political arena. He had never been unhappier in his life and had been only too pleased to return to wind and wave as Captain of the *Seringapatam*.

Now, on being shown into his sister-in-law's sitting room, he said, as if issuing a naval command, 'Dammit, Anne, I've come to invite you and the girls for a short holiday at Hastings. At my expense. Too bad, this wretched argument with George. Elizabeth and I feel sorry about the whole thing – so, as we are going down with the children, why don't we make up a family party?'

Anne pondered for a second but she could not escape destiny's plan.

'Why, William,' she said, 'how very kind. Are you sure we would be no trouble to you?'

'None at all. We shall book a suite of rooms in The Swan and make merry. The sea's in m'blood and I always have a damned good time at Hastings.'

'Then in that case we would love to come.'

'Splendid. If we leave on Friday, does that give you enough time to prepare?'

'Yes. I like to make haste, it passes the days of waiting so much better.'

'Then I'll send Jenkins down ahead to make the arrangements.' He kissed her on the cheek. 'The carriage will call for you at ten o'clock. Goodbye till then.'

As soon as he was gone, swinging the cane – his naval hat tilted jauntily – Anne hurried from the room, calling out, 'Girls, girls! We are going to Hastings with Uncle William. It will be such a treat. I came from there, you know.'

She remembered, with a hint of a naughty smile, Miss Anne King who had finally captured the Earl Waldegrave long after J.J. had been born – and with George on the way. Wild, rapturous days – all gone now that deliciously wicked creature, her husband, had been taken from her. She sighed as she smoothed the little black cap upon her head.

At the same time, Jackdaw was coming smartly to the salute outside his London barracks. He had not been posted abroad since the Canadian affair and had been allowed to remain in London. But this was his final leave, and he was about to make his way, as fate decreed he must, to Number 5, Pelham Crescent, Hastings, to stay with the General and Helen, Violet and Rob.

The first to arrive at their destination were Caroline, Francis and Algernon Hicks. They had taken the public stage known as the Paragon – the Hastings direct railway line not yet being open – which they caught at the Belle Sauvage, Ludgate Hill. Their baggage, including Caroline's bonnet boxes, had been hoisted aloft and they had set off in good spirits, Algernon treading on only two people's feet as he bounded cheerfully into his place.

The Paragon entered Hastings by way of Eastbourne Street, turned into All Saints Street and came with a flourish beneath the arch and into the stable yard of the Castle Hotel. Not having booked in advance, Francis made enquiries as to rooms but was told that all were taken – due, perhaps, to the extremely fine weather and the great number of visitors in the town. He was recommended to try the Swan Hotel – where Princess Victoria had stayed upon her visit – and, with a small boy, scarcely visible and labouring along beneath their mound of baggage, the merry trio made their way on foot.

On arrival at The Swan they found it in a flurry; maidservants in mob caps scrubbing the stone steps and polishing the brass knockers, ostlers whisking round the stable yard with brooms; while traders, delivering piles of meat and vegetables to the kitchens, jostled fishermen who bartered their catch direct with the cook.

But on enquiring at the desk in a rather dim reception area, smelling deliciously of beeswax and bootblack and staffed by a pince-nezed figure that bobbed deferentially as it spoke, whether the Queen was expected, Francis was told no, only Viscount Chewton and a large part of his family.

'Then do you have any accommodation?'

'Oh yes, Sir.' Bob, bob. 'A large room with a view of the sea. And for your father – '

'Brother.'

'Beg pardon.' Bob. 'For your brother a smaller room adjoining. Not too good a view from that one, I'm afraid, Sir. Mostly that of the outer staircase.'

'Suit me fine,' said Algernon. 'I intend to be out on Walks most of the time anyway.'

'Then if you would follow me, Madam, Gentlemen.'

The rooms were inspected and agreed to. Bags and baggage were unpacked and, after a light luncheon had been taken, the weary travellers retired for an hour or so: Algy to sleep on his back, his hands in the air like inert paws; Francis and Caroline to make love deliciously in the afternoon, watching the little dapples of sunlight dancing upon their skin.

Round about the time they rose to promenade before dinner, Jackdaw descended from the Royal Regulator – which he had caught somewhat later that day at the Bolt-in-Tun, Fleet Street – and, as the coach dropped him at the Saxon Office in St Leonard's, made his way to Pelham Crescent on foot.

Everyone was waiting for him in the first-floor sitting room, where the bay windows showed the voluptuous view of sparkling aqua stretched on for ever, with no line of demarcation between it and a butterfly sky.

Jackdaw could not help but feast his eyes on such a dazzle. But when he finally came to look at his family he saw that they were, at last, growing older.

The General's whiskers curled like snowdrifts about his cheeks and Helen had two silver wings sweeping from her temples. She seemed to be even more fragile and it was with a sense of shock that Jackdaw realized his mother, whom he had always thought of as a girl, must be over forty.

Rob, tall and strong as ever, now had lines of experience about his eyes and Violet, pretty little thing, sat gazing at the floor and blushing at her thoughts – the very picture of a maiden in love.

The Wardlaw family greeted their second son with enthusiasm, only Helen noticing the bitterness that now lurked behind his gemstone eyes. In fact the General found Jackdaw improved – not so damned dreamy and more a man of the world. He also thought – guiltily – that nowadays Helen and Jackdaw had grown more distant.

The General stole a glance at his wife – even in the middle of embracing his son – and felt his heart quicken with the old familiar passions. He would never – could never – get over his uncontrollable love. He would die saying her name. But his mind was far away from inevitability as he said, 'I've booked a table for us to dine at The Swan tonight. Cook's night off and all that. How will that suit?'

He slapped his son on the back to show how pleased he was to see him.

'Splendid. Have I time to wash and change?'

'Of course, of course. Thought we might stroll there at about eight o'clock.'

But this was where the Master Chessman winked his eye. For as Jackdaw hurried up the curving staircase that rose through the very heart of the elegant terraced house, his built-up boot caught on a loosened rod and he crunched face downwards on to the stairs, badly twisting the ankle of his good leg.

'Bugger!' he said quite clearly, and heard a remonstrating, 'Jackdaw, you are not in the barracks now,' from his father in the room below.

But Rob had guessed that this was more than a stubbed

toe and came haring up the stairs to where his younger brother lay groaning.

'What's wrong?'

'I'm not sure – a sprain most likely. Damn it all – just at the start of my leave.'

'Never mind,' said Rob, waiting for no further explanation but picking him up as if he were still a small boy.

And that was how Jackdaw came to be lying with a cold compress about his foot and a packet of cigars hidden beneath his pillow as his family came to say their farewells, on their way to dine.

His mother, dressed in dove-grey satin with a sweep of matching feathers in her hair, kissed him on the cheek and said, 'Anna will look after you. We have laid up a tray and put a bottle of champagne in ice. Will you be all right?'

'Of course I will. Have a wonderful evening. I shall want to hear all about it tomorrow.'

They left the house saying, 'Poor Jackdaw,' but nevertheless rather looking forward to their little excursion to The Swan, which had become awfully merry for Assemblies, Balls and Dinners since the Queen's visit, as Princess Victoria, six years before.

But even their most extravagant hopes of a good time were to be exceeded. For as they stood in the hotel entrance where the pince-nezed figure bobbed and said, 'Of course, Sir. This way, General Wardlaw,' a voice behind them exclaimed, 'Good Heavens, it can't be! Cousin Helen, how wonderful to see you!'

And they turned round to see a vision with wheaten hair and jet brows dressed in the very latest Paris fashion and sporting not only a wedding ring but a gentleman on each arm.

'Caroline!' answered Helen. 'I don't believe it! Why, the last time I saw you you were . . .?'

'Fourteen or fifteen. It was at Sutton Place.'

'The day of Mrs Trevelyan's garden party.'

'Yes, that's right.' Caroline dropped a little curtsey and added rather demurely, 'But I am married now. Cousin Helen, General Wardlaw, Rob, Violet – may I present my husband, Francis Hicks? And my brother-in-law, Algernon.'

How-do-you-do's were exchanged, bobs and bows executed, and formal handshakes disposed of.

'Are you dining here?' said the General.

'We're staying, Sir,' answered Francis. 'In fact we intend to call on you tomorrow.'

The General huffed cheerfully into his whiskers.

'Then what do you say to making up a table? Fine chance to catch up with the news, eh?'

All the ladies were in agreement and Algernon shook his head enthusiastically and bounded about. So, after some negotiation with the bobbing figure, the General led the way into a plush red dining room decorated with marble pillars and little gold lamps, and took his place at the head of a hastily laid table for seven, with Helen on his right hand and Caroline on his left. Beside Caroline sat Rob and Violet and then the brothers Hicks.

But theirs was very far from being the largest party present. In the centre of the room a great damask-draped table, as yet unoccupied, lay gleaming with silver and crystal and waiting for a group of twelve.

They all stared at it and Francis – whom the Wardlaws considered a most personable young man – said, 'That must be for Viscount Chewton. He's staying here, you know, with a vast family party.'

'Chewton? Chewton?' reflected the General. 'That's the Waldegrave heir, isn't it? I was stationed in Paris with one of them – the sixth Earl I believe. Good heavens – forgive me ladies – but he was a rogue.'

'Really?' said Francis.

'Yes.' There was a suggestion of a wink in the General's eye. 'Tell you later, Hicks, over the port.'

Francis raised his eyebrows and Algernon went, 'Ho!' and looked knowledgeable.

But further thoughts as to the late Earl's misdeeds were prevented by the arrival of the menu and the agonizing decision between fruits of the sea, as only Hastings could offer them, or the succulent delights of game and meats. However, choices were finally made and the Wardlaws and the Hicks were just settling down to an appetizer of a dozen oysters each when once more their attention was distracted.

A grey-haired portly gentleman, who could only be the Viscount, was coming into the dining room with a simpering woman clinging to his arm. But it was not really at them that the gaze of the onlookers was directed, for behind him, in couples, walked four of the most striking females.

The eldest – presumably the mother of the other three – was very small, almost doll-like, and had a sweet little hairstyle swept up beneath a widow's lace cap. Despite the fact that she was nearing fifty her black evening gown revealed a neat and highly fashionable figure. And the very sight of it, as she walked past him to her chair, caused Algernon to gulp noisily and drop his oyster.

Beside the widow walked her counterpart but some thirty years younger, the only difference between the mother and her eldest girl being that the daughter had eyes of a vivid moonstone blue.

But after them, pretty as they were, followed a girl of quite outstanding beauty, although the great cloud of hair swirling about her shoulders told polite society that she was not yet seventeen. For it was at that age that

236

curls must be put up on top of the head if one wished to be respectable.

'By Jove,' said Rob involuntarily, as her eyes met his for a moment.

But she was merely glancing at him, and walked past and to her place in a flurry of satin and scent of moonlit Araby.

The fourth girl was little more than a child. Barely in her teens, she had pert bootbutton-eyed prettiness, but her rose-bud mouth had a sulky simper and Helen and Caroline immediately concluded she was thoroughly spoiled. Violet, however, could not find it in herself to have coherent thoughts about anyone – so dazzled and amazed was she by all the splendid company.

Behind the quartette of ladies came a medley of children of assorted age, size and sex, presumably the brood of Chewton himself.

'Hastings must be swarming with Waldegraves,' whispered Francis. But though Caroline smiled and nodded, Algernon merely stared mumchance at the averted back of the pretty widow, even allowing his delicious dinner – which he normally would have consumed with enthusiasm – to grow cold before him.

In fact the presence of Viscount Chewton's family at the top table had a somewhat subduing effect. None the less Helen and Caroline made gallant efforts and family gossip and news on both sides was exchanged.

'And what of dear Mary? And Matilda?'

'The former never happier – running a large household of children and servants.' Caroline's dark brows slanted upward with amusement. 'And as for Matilda, Mary writes that she has taken on a new lease of life in Paris. She has even stopped wearing brown and has been escorted to the opera by an eligible young Frenchman.'

'I am so pleased. And what of John Joseph?'

'He is stationed in the Hungarian part of the Empire at the moment. There is trouble there, you know.'

'Oh?' General Wardlaw was suddenly all attention. 'In what way?'

Caroline lowered her voice. 'The new Emperor of Austria, Ferdinand, is quite mad, so they say. He even finds it difficult to write his name. Prince Metternich virtually rules the country and the young Hungarian nobles are rumbling in their throats. They would break away given half a chance. So a large military presence is maintained to try to frighten them witless.'

Helen shook her head looking, just for a moment, as young and as girlish as she had when Caroline first met her.

'These boys, these boys – John Joseph, Jackdaw, Rob! I wonder if they are happy stationed so far from their homeland.'

To this Caroline replied firmly, 'Well, my brother is, for sure. He could not wait to put an ocean between himself and Sutton Place.'

'Because of the curse?'

'I believe so. He hates the place, yet is fearfully fascinated with it. But how is Jackdaw?'

'In Hastings and in bed at this very moment. He is on his final leave before a three-year stint in India – and, of all things, has sprained his ankle.' Now it was Helen's turn to speak softly. 'I am worried about him, Caro. Ever since his return from Canada he has been different. I think something terrible has happened to him.'

'Does he still possess his mystic gift?'

'I don't know. He has shut himself off. He is not the childhood friend you once knew.'

'We shall come and visit him tomorrow – Francis and I. My dear Algy – ' she looked at her brother-in-law fondly ' – is a little too enthusiastic for a sickroom.'

She and Helen smiled gently and, as if he knew they were talking about him, Algernon turned to look at them and said, 'By Jove, Mrs Wardlaw – this is a very fine town. My guide book – ' he waved a well-thumbed volume – 'says one of the prettiest in England. Think I'll take a Walk to Fairlight Glen tomorrow.'

Caroline answered firmly, 'A splendid idea, Algy. Francis and I are going to visit my cousin Jackdaw so you'll be left to make your own mischief.'

He chortled with delight.

'Well, I don't know about that – but I shall be quite all right, Caro. Always jolly happy exploring, you know.'

Time was slipping. At the garrison in Buda – which lay staring across the River Danube at the grim fortress of Pesth – John Joseph Webbe Weston was travelling in his sleep. He dreamed that he was in Sutton Place, standing there, alone, looking about the deserted Great Hall.

The voices of centuries rang out to him. He heard Francis Weston speak words of love to Rose Pickering; heard Anne Boleyn sing to her King; heard Melior Mary Weston exclaim upon the colour of a baby's eyes; heard Elizabeth the Queen greet Henry Weston and all the while look upon him shrewdly, wondering if he and she might have shared the same father.

He heard the stars singing, the comets burst forth. He heard the past and the present merge in a shrieking chorus. There was no day, there was no night. There was nothing but the total oneness of the universe. He was near the secret of life . . .

And then it all slipped from him – as it must if he was to stay sane upon the earth – and he was dreaming more calmly. He walked up the Grand Staircase to the Long Gallery and saw that it was still the Chapel. At the end of it, by the altar, the Bride awaited. The white of her veil a mist, the red of her hair mulled wine.

'Hurry,' she said, without turning her head. 'I am ready now. Find me.'

'Is it you?' he answered. 'You of whom I dream?'

'Yes,' she said. 'I am your fate – your past, your present, your future. Know me when you meet me. That is all I ask.'

'I have always known you.'

'But will you when the time comes?'

The vision faded. He was in Hungary once more, dreaming of everyday things – cannon and horses and the stirring unrest of a once great and powerful people. He heard the voice of a poet say, 'Continents and oceans lie at our feet, gold and silver, strong and vigorous hands, and a rich and powerful language – we possess all but concord and liberty.'

He awoke into a grey and chillsome summer morning to sniff upon the air the very essence of revolution's first breath. And he did not know at that moment which he hated more – this far-off country ready to tear itself to shreds, or the dreadful manor of Sutton with its curse of despair.

On that same morning, so grey and cold in Buda but so bright and fine over England's south coast, Algernon Hicks woke punctually at six o'clock and leapt out of bed. Throwing open his window he stuck his head right out, pointed his nose towards the sea and engaged upon a series of breathing exercises. He then rootled in a carpet bag, took from it a travelling chest expander and, standing back slightly, began flexing his muscles whilst emitting a series of high whistling sounds.

This done, he dressed in a short-skirted jacket, a pair of trousers strapped under the instep, a high-collared shirt and a spotted neckcloth which he affixed with a pin. Tucking his wide-awake – a low-crowned informal hat – beneath his arm he went down to the breakfast room.

There he ate vastly. Sausages, kidneys, an alarming amount of rashers and several eggs were pursued by hot and wholesome bread and many cups of tea. Then, having glanced rapidly over *The Times*, he gave the waiter a noisy message for Francis and Caroline and bounded out into the morning.

Everywhere gulls wheeled and dipped, shouting their astringent cries into the never-ending blue.

'Skawk,' Algy called back. 'Skawk, gully.'

A small urchin, observing him, tapped his forehead meaningfully but Mr Hicks, undeterred, turned his feet in the direction of the Vale of Ecclesbourne, swung his walking stick with the carved dog's head three times into the air and set off at an alarming rate.

The mile and a half to the fishponds was covered in no time and, pausing only to mop his brow in the considerable morning heat, Algy struck off across the fields towards the edge of the cliff. There he went through a little gate and on to a smooth terrace of grass at the cliff's very edge.

'Was it here?' he said aloud. 'Was it here that Duke William had Harold laid to rest, to be the guardian of land and sea?' He struck a dramatic pose. 'By command of the Duke, you rest here a King, O Harold. Aargh,' he added, clutching his throat.

Fortunately it was too early for other visitors and he went on, quite regardless, down a flight of steps to the Dripping Well. Having amused himself by dropping a pebble to ascertain its depths, he followed the path round the dell and found himself in a beautiful valley, the centre of which was known as Fairlight Glen.

Here Algy felt an overwhelming need to relieve himself

and – glancing most earnestly to both right and left and then decorously stepping behind a bush, though not a soul was in sight – he merrily imitated one of the several small waterfalls that bounded in the pretty stream.

Then, with a cheerful whistle, he went on up the brow of the hill to the cliff's summit, his heart pounding with shock as he arrived at the top only to find that someone had preceded him. A woman was sitting on the famous Lovers' Seat, gazing out to sea. Desperate, Algy's one thought was that he might have been observed communing with nature and he hung back fearfully, wondering whether he ought perhaps hastily to retreat.

But she made no stir and eventually Mr Hicks plucked up enough courage to clear his throat noisily, several times over, and then shout, 'Good morning. Sorry to startle you.'

She jumped violently and turned round. He saw to his amazement that it was the pretty widow who had so caught his eye at dinner the previous evening; the kinswoman of Viscount Chewton.

'Oh good gracious,' she said. 'I did not expect to see anyone else at this hour.'

'No, dashed early. Sorry! It is just that I enjoy a Walk while the day is still fresh.'

He twirled his wide-awake – which he had plucked from his head at first glimpse of her – by the brim.

'Sorry to disturb you. I'll go. Wouldn't like to get in the way.' He panted apologetically, his anxious face crumpled like a boxer dog's.

'Oh please don't do that on my account. It was just that I was lost in my thoughts. Pray take a seat and admire the view.'

'Really?' He bounced forward enthusiastically.

'Yes.' He gingerly took a seat at the far edge of the wooden bench. 'I'd better introduce myself. Hicks is the name.' He stood up again and made a bow. 'Algernon Hicks of Duke Street, London.'

'And I am Anne, the Countess Waldegrave.'

Algy became a little flustered and bowed several times, obviously debating whether or not to kiss her hand. He eventually decided against, sat down, and stared out towards the horizon, completely dumbstruck.

'I am staying here with my daughters,' Anne went on conversationally, ignoring the silence. 'My brother and sister-in-law have a suite at The Swan.'

'Yes, I saw you there last night.'

Anne stared at him in surprise.

'Really? I'm afraid I did not see you.'

'No,' said Algy, going a shade of tomato, 'I don't suppose you would. I am not very noticeable.'

As he was the clumsiest, largest-footed man the Countess had ever seen, this remark bordered on ridiculous, but she controlled herself and said, 'You are also a guest there?'

'Yes. With my brother and his bride. That's why I like to keep out of the way. They were recently married. I do not wish to be – *de trop*.'

'Of course not.'

She smiled at him politely and just for a second their eyes met. He thought her stunning, the fact that she was somewhat older than he not detracting from her charms a fraction. She, on the other hand, thought him laughable – but not unkindly so. If she had been asked to find a total contrast to the Earl she would have chosen this large and enthusiastic buffoon who clung so anxiously to his hat and walking stick as if his very life depended on them.

'Do you know Hastings well, Mr Hicks?' she asked at last, rather sorry for him.

'Can't say that I do, my Lady. I came here when I was

a child and once again as a young man. The second time was much more fun!'

'Oh?'

'Yes.' He had stopped being so anxious in his enthusiasm. 'My brother had been born then – he is eighteen years younger than I – and I spent the whole holiday making sandcastles for him and playing with a model schooner. It was glorious.'

'You have no children of your own? You are not married?'

Algernon went crimson.

'No. My mother died when Francis was five and shortly after that, my father. I brought my brother up, you see, and not many young ladies were interested in having him as well. One was, but I could not bring myself to care for her. She smelled so terribly of camphor.'

Anne pealed with laughter, putting her hand over her mouth.

'How terrible for you. I cannot think of a worse fate.'

Algy moved on the seat, delighted that the pretty Countess found him amusing.

'She was plain as well. Awesomely small of eye.'

Anne shrieked. 'You are so droll, Mr Hicks.'

'Really? My Lady, may I continue to talk to you?'

'But of course. Shall we stroll? I know Hastings very well for I was born here. My father was in the church – he is retired now though still very much alive – and became an Army chaplain. I went with him when he was promoted to Paris and it was there that I met my late husband, the Earl.'

Algy wondered briefly if this was one and the same as the sixth Earl, of whose daring exploits and wickedness General Wardlaw had spoken in such awed tones.

'But, alas, he died three years ago,' the Countess

continued, 'and so I come to visit my birthplace accompanied only by my unmarried daughters.'

She gave a wistful sigh and Algy straightened. He had never been more pleased than at this moment – learning that the little lady was definitely a widow. Not that he wished the late peer any harm, of course, but she was so obviously in need of protection.

Now he said, 'Yes. Loneliness can be a problem.'

Just for a moment he stopped his cheerful huffing and looked bleak and Anne – almost as if she was reading his thoughts – said, 'It must be a wrench for you now that your brother has married. Especially as you were both mother and father to him.'

Algy looked guilty and said, very fast, 'But Caroline is a wonderful girl and most kind to me. I really have gained a sister.'

'But it is never quite the same. They will inevitably be wanting to do things on their own.'

'Yes. But I knew it would happen one day. Francis is so different from me, you see. Quite a brilliant boy really – and very good-looking and humorous. I realized from the start that he would have no difficulty in finding a wife.'

Anne could not help but laugh at his long, sad face.

'Come, come, Mr Hicks,' she said, taking his arm without realizing it, 'you speak as if you are in your dotage. I warrant you could give me a year or two, yet – widowed though I might be – *I* have no intention of retiring from life. You must positively plan to go out and about.'

They had reached the bottom of the cliff path while they talked and the Countess said suddenly, 'Let us walk to Old Roar. We will just have time before luncheon – that is if you have no other engagement – for my daughters are busy all morning at Barry's Library with their aunt.'

Mr Hicks went very slightly pink, so pleased was he. He let out a word of acknowledgement that sounded to Anne incredibly like a bark and added, 'I would be honoured, my Lady.' Then he bowed – dropping his wide-awake in the process. Anne stooped to pick it up in order to hide her amusement. Very flustered, Algy crammed it down over his ears.

'And perhaps . . .' he said hesitantly.

'Yes?'

'Perhaps . . .' He stared at his shoes while Anne stood in polite silence. 'Perhaps afterwards, you – and your daughters of course – might join me for luncheon. If I don't presume.'

'That would be delightful,' answered the Countess, after only a moment's pause. 'Provided it would not inconvenience your brother and his wife.'

'They will not be there,' Mr Hicks replied firmly. 'They are out on a visit. You will be my guest alone, Lady Waldegrave. May I hope that you will join me?'

'It will be a pleasure, Mr Hicks,' said the Countess – with only the merest hint of laughter in her voice.

Two summer weeks passed in all the glory of high season and on the very last day of the Waldegrave family holiday Jackdaw managed, at last, to get a shoe upon his foot and walk out of doors with the aid of a cane. It was so warm that he wore only the lightest shirt and trousers and a jacket of white drill as he headed towards the sea front, breathing deeply as he went, and loving the salt and sun that lay in the air like the ocean's dew.

For no reason he felt ridiculously happy and yet, at the same time, something prickled at the back of his spine. The whole occasion was fraught with familiarity. He was sure that he had walked before along this very path, warmed by an identical sun. And equate it though he might with having lived in Hastings all his life, Fate's pull towards the inevitable told him otherwise.

Beside him walked Helen and behind him Rob and Violet, but he listened to none of them, concentrating, as he was, on this curious conviction. And then the dream-like feeling deepened. Coming towards him was a man with a round, amiable face, swinging a cane with a dog's head carved upon it.

Jackdaw's mind flashed back to the Hotel Reine in Quebec. With his inner eye he saw again the figure on the battlements of Hastings castle, heard himself shout, 'Marie!' and saw the incredulous expressions of both his mother and the jolly man. And he went cold. Without doubt this *was* the same man. The vision was coming true.

Jackdaw's thoughts went whirling – Marie was dead, an innocent slain because of her love for him – yet was what he suspected true? Was the girl he had dreamed of, the girl he had once stood beside when he travelled through time and space, somebody altogether different? He stopped in his tracks with the sheer import of the moment, disregarding his family's protests, and looked frantically about him.

And then he heard it. The high clip-clop of hooves, the rumble of carriage wheels. He knew the watershed of his life had come and he turned to meet his destiny.

The girl sat with her mother and sisters in an open landau, a parasol above her glowing head. She was dressed in white muslin and she turned to look at Jackdaw almost as soon as she drew level with him. He knew her at once and felt a moment's bitter anguish that Marie had been sacrificed because of his mistake. Because here, in this beautiful girl whose clear eyes stared into his, all doubt was laid aside.

The carriage passed by and began to turn inland, away

from Hastings and towards London. The dream came true once more – horrifyingly. He started to run after it – not giving a damn in Hell for the expressions on the faces of the passers-by, nor Helen's cry of 'Jackdaw!', nor the Hicks' startled stare.

'Stop,' he shouted. 'Please!'

The girl turned her head to look at him over her shoulder. Was that a hint of a smile about her lips? And then he fell. He lay, helpless, upon the ground, gazing to where the carriage turned right and out of his vision completely.

'Oh God,' he said, 'I can't lose her now.'

The jolly man crouched over him and lifted him up.

'Are you all right, old fellow?'

'Yes, yes. Thank you. Tell me, do you know the people in that carriage?'

The man went very slightly pink and answered, 'Yes, I do as a matter of fact. That was the Countess Waldegrave and her daughters.'

'Is one of them called Horry?'

'Are you referring to the Lady Horatia?'

'Yes,' said Jackdaw. 'I think – I am.'

13

Christmas Eve 1838! At Windsor Castle Lord Melbourne
and Queen Victoria came out of the Chapel, she – tiny
little thing – supporting herself on the arm of the great
statesman and smiling up at him. And watching the young
monarch as she and the Prime Minister exchanged this
merry glance, Lord Greville whispered to his wife, 'She is
in love with him, of course.'

Lady Greville was outraged.

'How can you say such a dreadful thing? He is almost
sixty and she not yet twenty.'

Greville smiled smoothly.

'Naturally she does not know it. And as for him – why,
he has an infinite capacity for loving without having
anything in the world to love. He was treated atrociously
by his wretched spouse and has never been moved since –
until now.'

Lady Greville thought of Lady Caroline Lamb – Melbourne's late wife – whose public pursuit of the poet
Byron had scandalized society and brought William
Lamb, as Melbourne had then been, to the brink of
despair.

'It would be as well in the circumstances,' Greville
went on, 'if Her Majesty were soon to renew acquaintanceship with her Cousin Albert.'

'That match would be much favoured by her family,'
Lady Greville agreed. 'And I, for one, would dearly love
the Queen to settle down. It is no good for a country to
have an unmarried monarch. It makes things too – light.'

'Yes,' answered Greville slowly. 'That state of affairs is potentially dangerous.'

He bowed as the Queen came closer.

'Look at little Vic now,' he whispered, 'she's blushing.'

'He makes her laugh too much,' came the reply. 'It doesn't do for a Queen to be too merry. It is the place of all women, even royal women, to guide family life.'

'Yes, my dear,' said Greville with a smile. 'I am sure she will do so when the time comes. Meanwhile I intend to wish her the compliments of the season. And I shall have a word about Prince Albert to ears that will be interested. I think things will be very different twelve months from now.'

'I sincerely hope so,' said Lady Greville as she dropped an extra low curtsey.

In London, in Henrietta Street, Cavendish Square, at exactly that moment, Caroline Hicks slanted her dark eyebrows upward as she stared in a final appraisal of her Christmas Eve dining table; red candles and white damask, Christmas roses and holly berries, mistletoe and crimson napkins. She thought of blood on snow and shivered, though half with pleasure.

'Is Madam satisfied?'

The butler sounded slightly anxious. It was important to him that this Christmas dinner – with noble company for guests – should be a notable success.

'Very satisfied, Rivers,' was Caroline's reply. 'And what of the menu?'

'For the first course, Madam, Veloute à la Reine,' said Rivers, clearing his throat, 'followed by Lobsters Bouchées. Then – at Madam's especial request – a light entrée of Sussex ham in champagne. Then for the main poultry, beside the Christmas turkey of course, there are quails in aspic, Pheasant Mandarin and a fresh young goose.'

Caroline smiled. 'As well as beef?'

'Yes Madam. And a saddle of mutton for those who wish it. And for dessert we have Charlotte Malakoff and Gooseberry Fool and, of course, a Christmas Pudding which I shall bring in *flambé*.'

'Together with a sideboard of cheese and fruit?' Caroline asked.

'And the '87 claret and the '84 hock – as the master ordered.'

Caroline turned and bit her lip nervously as Francis came into the room. 'I do hope it will be good enough for the Countess,' she said.

'It will be good enough for the Queen. Thank you, Rivers. That will be all.'

As the butler left the room Francis followed him into the hall and called up the stairs, 'Come along, Algy. Our guests are due in five minutes. Let us present a comfortable family scene in the drawing room.'

A muffled bark was heard, and after a second or two Mr Hicks himself padded round the bend of the staircase, wearing a smart black cutaway and new white shirt, but for all that seeming very ill at ease.

'*Courage, mon brave!*' said Francis – and winked at Caroline. Algy bridled and said, 'I don't know what you mean,' but further banter was prevented by the sound of carriage wheels drawing up in the street outside and Rivers appearing discreetly from nowhere.

Abruptly the trio scuttled into the drawing room. Caroline hastily picked up a book and the two men took up positions on either side of the marble fireplace.

From the doorway Rivers called out, 'The Right Honourable the Countess Waldegrave. And the Ladies Annette, Horatia and Ida Anna.'

251

Caroline dropped her book prettily and rose to her feet with a smile.

'My dear Countess, how very pleased I am to welcome you. May I wish you the season's greetings.'

'And to you, my dear. Thank you for inviting us to share your festivities.'

Behind her the Ladies Annette and Ida were demure in rose and buttercup but the Lady Horatia had gone against all decreed fashion and, despite her glowing hair, wore violet. The result was breathtaking – and even the disciplined Rivers stared slightly.

Algernon, meanwhile, was flushing from pale to puce, hopping from one foot to the other as if desperately anxious to leave the room. But the Countess would have none of it. She patted the sofa next to her and said, 'Thank you, Mr Hicks, for sending round Charles Dickens's latest novel. What a clever young man he is to be sure. Though I can't say I enjoyed the story as much as *The Pickwick Papers*. It is so depressing, where the other was so funny.'

Algy making a great effort, swallowed violently, and said, 'Yes.'

'That tragic boy – Oliver Twist,' the Countess went on. 'I shudder to think that there are children really living like that.'

'But there are, Ma'am,' answered Francis. 'The workhouses – and the thieves' kitchens – that Dickens writes of merely highlight the hypocrisy of our society.'

The Countess gave him a penetrating look, obviously wondering if he was in any way denigrating the aristocracy, and decided that he was not when Francis added, 'I frequently see the plight of the poor as a medical student and have not yet learned to regard them as so much flesh. Some of them wring me to the heart. We are all members of the same species after all.'

'Francis, I think you are getting too serious,' said Caroline.

'Yes, I am, my dear. I shall stop it, for here comes the sherry. Crisp or sweet, Lady Waldegrave?'

The conversation broke into three parts with the arrival of Rivers bearing the crystal-laden tray – the Countess and Algernon Hicks going more deeply into the merits of the youthful new author Dickens; Francis, Annette and Ida Anna discussing the sad fact that Lady Annette's betrothed, Major Money, still had another two years of duty in India, and Caroline finding herself face to face for the first time with Horatia Waldegrave.

The elder girl studied the younger intently. What spirit lay behind such a beautiful exterior? Was she vapid and stupid as were so many of her aristocratic contemporaries?

Very much as if she had read Caroline's thoughts, Horry said, 'It was kind of you to ask us to dine, Mrs Hicks. For all you knew we could have been the most boring creatures in the world.'

'Which you are obviously not.'

Horatia gave a little laugh. 'No. The Waldegraves have been called many things – but boring is not one of them.'

Caroline said nothing, merely giving an encouraging nod. Horatia went on, 'We are supposed to be a wild family, you know. And my brothers actually are! We girls are staid and respectable in comparison.'

'You don't look staid.'

'Nor too respectable either, I hope. There is nothing more dull than a conventional veneer, would you not agree?'

'I would – heartily. But I suppose I may grow decorous as middle-age catches me up.'

Horatia laughed again.

'I think decorum is something born in one, Mrs Hicks.

253

I felt sure when we first met in Hastings that the Hicks family had much in common with the Waldegraves.'

'You think so?'

Without meaning to, Caroline found her eyes straying to where Algy and the Countess sat side by side, heads rather close together. Horatia followed her gaze and also, apparently, her train of thought.

'Yes, *I* think so,' she said.

Caroline looked up sharply but Horatia would not be drawn any further and changed the subject. 'I do so admire your house. It is from the Regency period is it not?'

'Yes. Would you care to see over it? We have not been here very long and I am still at the stage of being in love with it.'

'I should like that very much.'

Horatia stood up and Caroline led the way, their departure almost unnoticed in the hub-bub of conversation and general sipping of sherry.

The house, Horatia discovered, like so many of its contemporaries built when the Prince Regent ruled England, was terraced and rose round a magnificent and curving staircase. Following Caroline upwards Horatia came to a first floor where there was a good-sized landing and two more reception rooms; one – or so it would seem from peeping in – Caroline's little sanctum and the other a library where Francis had a desk strewn with papers and several learned medical books.

But it was at neither of these that Horatia really looked. Instead she felt her attention drawn to a painting which hung – well-lit by an overhead candelabra – on the wall of the landing, dominating the area round it.

She had never seen anything quite like it. In the background stood a house, diminished almost to the size of a doll's by the clever use of perspective, but a fairy

254

house for all that, all aflower and aglow in the summer sunshine; two wings linking a Hall which, even in this minute detail, blazed with stained glass.

And because it stood so well in the background, the house seemed to float in the air, like a castle from legend. In fact the outlines were blurred and misty, giving the place, altogether, an ethereal and quite breathtaking quality.

In the foreground, made to look larger by the diminution of the mansion, stood a man, his face turned towards the artist but his dark blue eyes staring beyond. Horatia had a vivid impression of strong handsome features and a bold military uniform, of long brown hands gripping a sword hilt. She took a step closer to the painting and saw the signature, 'Francis Hicks, 1837.'

'Your husband painted this?'

'Yes.'

'Who is the subject?'

'My brother. He is a Captain in the Imperial Austrian Army. What do you think of it?'

Caroline was amused when Horatia answered, without shyness or artifice, 'I think he is the most handsome man I have ever seen. Quite remarkable really.'

The elder girl laughed gently, 'I meant the painting.'

'Oh! Oh, I see. It is very well done. The house has a magic look about it. Where is it?'

'Near Guildford. It is called Sutton Place and is our family seat, though none of us live there any more.'

'It looks quite old. Is it?'

'Tudor. Built by Sir Richard Weston, a courtier to Henry VIII.'

'You are descended from him?'

'No. His direct line died out. Our connection with the family is more than remote. In fact my grandfather John Webbe adopted the name Weston in order to inherit.'

'So you were born a Miss Webbe Weston? And your brother is presumably Captain Webbe Weston?' Horatia's eyes had returned to the picture and were taking in every detail.

'Yes. John Joseph is his name. I have another portrait of him in my snug, painted by myself. Would you like to see it?'

'If I may, please.'

They stepped into Caroline's little salon and there, flanked on one side by a portrait of Francis and on the other by that of a hearty-looking man in sensible gaiters together with a nondescript woman, hung a more conventional officer-and-gentleman type of picture. In this John Joseph again had a hand resting on the hilt of his sword but in the other held a shako – the name given to the squarish, plumed cap worn by the hussars and dragoons.

'Well?'

Horatia's hair glinted firelights as she whirled round to look at Caroline. 'I hope he is not married or promised.'

Caroline could not help smiling again, so infectious was Horatia's manner as she danced little glances in the direction of John Joseph's likeness.

'No, he is not. Why?'

'Because,' said the minx, '*I* have decided to marry him.'

'Lady Horatia!' said Caroline, half shocked, half amused. 'You are still very young. He is a full grown man.'

'Young girls,' answered Horatia matter-of-factly, 'have a habit of growing up, whereas men of your brother's age tend to stay the same for quite a few years.'

There was so much basic truth in this that Caroline could do nothing but shake her head as Francis's voice called from below, 'Caro, where are you? I believe Rivers wants a last-minute word with you.'

It was about the seating arrangements. It had been Caroline's original plan to put Francis at the head of the table and Algy at the foot but she had now done a rapid rearrangement so that her brother-in-law could sit on Lady Waldegrave's right. But – having smoothed out this minor problem – the meal itself went splendidly. The cook – Mrs Rivers – the skivvy and the extra girl had done their mistress proud. There had never been such a delicious spread at Number 7, Henrietta Street, and it was with praise ringing in her ears that Caroline eventually rose to lead the ladies to the drawing room while Francis and Algy smoked their cigars.

Algy, who had drunk far more than was customary for him, was very surprised, therefore, when after five minutes Francis suddenly rose from his seat, muttered something about having to see Rivers urgently and left the room. He was even more surprised when, a minute or two later, Caroline poked her head round the door, like a little serpent, and on seeing him sitting there rapidly withdrew it.

Chuffing somewhat to himself, Algy poured another glass of port. And it was then that the door opened again and Anne Waldegrave appeared in the entrance. Algy bounded to his feet but Anne said, 'Do sit down, Mr Hicks. I have only come in to look for the playing cards.'

'Are they *in* the dining room?' asked Algy, astonished.

'I don't know. Caroline has gone to see Rivers and for some reason did not ring for a maid.'

She looked as puzzled as Algy felt.

'Shall I help you look for them?'

'If you would, please.'

And that was how they came to be tugging at the door of the lower cupboard of the sideboard, and how Algy came to wrench the wooden knob off the door and fall backwards from a squatting position and thus find himself, at long last, at the Countess's feet.

'Oh Mr Hicks,' she said. 'Are you hurt?'

'No, I don't think so. Dash it, I am sorry. Must look an idiot down here.'

'Not at all. Here, let me help you up.'

She proffered her small hand and put her fingers in his and Algy felt his brain spin. He tried to pull himself upwards but the port wine told on him a little, and he slipped down once more. And then, suddenly, it was time for him to be rewarded for all the years of sacrifice; the years of bringing up his young brother on his own and making a good job of it. For, without the slightest bidding and not knowing quite why she did so, Anne, the Countess Waldegrave, bent over and kissed him lightly on the cheek.

Algy stared at her dumbly – and then, very tentatively, raised her fingers to his lips and gave a faltering but responsive salute. His look of adoration was so dog-like that there was no alternative for the Countess. She patted him on the head and then let her hand stay a second longer than it should have done.

'My Lady,' said Algy in a strangulated voice, somehow struggling into a kneeling position from where he lay. 'I . . . I . . .'

'Yes, Mr Hicks?'

'I know that we are of but recent acquaintance . . . not worthy at all . . . but if devotion . . . oh dear.'

'Algernon – I shall call you that and you really must address me as Anne – are you trying to ask me something?'

He nodded his head.

'What is it? Please do say.'

There was silence for a moment – and then the words came out.

'If you could see your way . . . I mean . . . I want to marry you, my Lady. Yes, by jingo, I do.'

'Then you shall.'

'What?'

'I care for you, you foolish man.'

'But why?' He was so genuinely surprised, he found he was able to speak.

'Because you are kind and endearing and I believe I can trust you with the welfare of my daughters – and indeed my own.'

'Oh yes, you may. You can be assured of that, my Lady . . . Anne . . .'

He said the words as if he was saying Queen.

'Then,' answered the Countess matter-of-factly, 'we are betrothed. You may kiss me.'

'By Jove,' said Algy – and did so.

Winter came severely but spring followed and one wet day in early February, when the crocuses were putting up their tremulous heads in the windswept squares of London, a pretty little wedding took place in St Mary's Church in the parish of Marylebone. The bride wore pale violet and was given away by her son, George, the Earl Waldegrave; in the front pew sat two of her beautiful daughters and her earliest indiscretion – J.J. – sober as a judge and accompanied by a pretty Jewish girl, who carried herself proudly and did not allow her escort to misbehave himself at all.

On the bridegroom's side of the church sat Caroline Hicks accompanied by Mr and Mrs Webbe Weston, who had made the excursion from Guildford by railway and felt frightfully daring. Francis Hicks was standing as the best man and the bride – who carried a posy of snowdrops – was attended by her eldest daughter, Lady Annette.

Mr Charlton the curate presided and the ceremony

proceeded well until the moment when he asked Anne to repeat the words that would bind her to Algy for ever. Just for a second, then, she hesitated, thinking back to the two occasions when she had been called upon to make those very same vows: the first a civil ceremony in Paris with George leaping in her womb and barely concealed by her flowing dress; the second Twickenham Church – the day after George's christening – when she had worn the Waldegrave wedding tiara and stood in the sunshine with the dashing Earl by her side, listening to the villagers cheering.

And now as she remembered she darted her eyes sideways to look at Algy. She had heard the old saying that both men and women go for the same type of partner when repeating their loves – but how patently untrue in her case. Beside her stood a faithful creature, pink with joy and jolly as a pup, so delighted was he with his first venture into matrimony. The Countess recalled with bitterness the reluctance of the Earl to marry Miss Anne King and how only the threat of two little bastards had shifted him. And thinking of this, as Algy turned to look at her enquiringly in the silence, she gave him a beautiful smile and made her vows in a clear voice.

Afterwards they all repaired in carriages to Henrietta Street where Rivers and the rest of the staff stood outside and cheered Mr and Mrs Algernon Hicks in. Then they sat down for the breakfast, the bride and groom at the head of the table with George on her right and the beautiful Jewish girl next to him. On the girl's other side sat J.J.

'Well, my dear,' said the Countess, at the very first opportunity, 'I am afraid I have not had the pleasure of your acquaintance. Pray introduce yourself.'

Very stylishly the girl – whose expression transformed

into that of a little coquette when she smiled – rose from her place and dropped a deep curtsey.

'Francis Braham, Lady Waldegrave. Forgive me for not speaking before – but you were otherwise engaged.'

A mischievous smile crossed her face – and everyone present thought how stunning she was.

'Braham . . .' said the Countess, frowning slightly.

'My father is John Braham the singer, my Lady.'

Anne's brow cleared and she said, 'How interesting to have such a distinguished parent.'

Everyone – even those unmusical – knew of Braham. The orphaned child of German Jews, he had sold pencils in the street in order to survive, but his singing in the synagogue had brought his great gift to the attention of Leoni and he had appeared at Covent Garden even before his voice had broken. Anne believed that the tenor had amassed a fortune but that this had now been lost over two unwise investments – the building of the St James's Theatre and the Colosseum in Regent's Park. She had heard it said that Braham had been forced back to the stage and concert-room by his debts and wondered what his daughter was doing with J.J. Or did Miss Braham not care for money – was social climbing alone sufficient attraction?

As Frances took her seat again she looked at Anne as if she could read her uncharitable thoughts, her huge dark eyes secretive and very slightly mocking. The Countess noticed that both J.J. and George turned to talk to her at once, and then laughed a good deal. It occurred to her rather sharply that the opera singer's daughter had done what she could not; both of the brothers were on their very best behaviour and J.J. was showing signs of being absolutely besotted.

'Well George,' said Anne. 'I hope you will invite me and your stepfather to Strawberry Hill soon.' She lowered her voice. 'I trust there is no one in residence other than yourself.'

'Nobody, Mother. Those days are over.'

He stole a look at Frances Braham's averted head, to where the lively black hair bounced over the creamy neck.

'I am very glad to hear it. I would like to think that we could be a united family once more.'

The Earl put his hand over his mother's.

'I would like that too. I will try to be a good son in future.'

'Long may it last!' thought Anne – and very slightly bowed her head to the beautiful Jewess. For all Miss Braham's tender age – Anne doubted whether she was yet eighteen – she was obviously a young woman of considerable influence.

But George had taken this as his cue to rise and propose the health of the bride and groom, to which Algernon made a noisy reply and Francis responded on behalf of all concerned. Then it was time for Anne to change into her travelling dress for the journey to Hastings, where she and Algy were to spend their honeymoon.

Annette and Caroline led the way upstairs, followed by Horatia and Ida Anna. But on the first-floor landing Horatia lingered a moment and turned back to stand on her own before the portrait of John Joseph and Sutton Place. The blue eyes of the sitter looked beyond her – unlike most paintings – and she climbed a stair or two to see if she could catch their glance. But it did not work – Francis Hicks had cleverly achieved the effect of someone gazing into the far distance, thinking his thoughts and caring not at all for the onlooker.

'Horatia,' said Caroline behind her, making her jump, 'what are you doing?'

'Renewing my acquaintanceship with your brother. How is he nowadays?'

'I have not heard recently. He is still stationed in Hungary, I believe.'

'When is he next home on leave?'

Caroline laughed. 'I don't know, you naughty thing. You are determined to meet him, aren't you?'

Somewhat to her surprise Horatia shook her head, the wonderful hair moving like silk.

'Not really. I would rather dream about him like this – brooding away in his portrait – than have him see me and be indifferent to my very existence.'

'I am sure he could never do that,' Caroline answered, looking at the superb profile turned towards her.

'Who can tell? Why *does* he look so sad, Caroline?'

'He was crossed in love some years ago – and then I think he worries about Sutton Place.'

'About the house? Why?'

'It carries an ancient curse – or so they say.'

'Really? How fascinating!'

'I suppose it is in a way. But not to the Lord of the Manor and his heir.'

'Who are your father and John Joseph!'

'Yes.'

Horatia turned to look back at the picture.

'Yes, I can see it now,' she said. 'The house looks so small there – but it isn't in reality, is it? Really it looms rather large.'

'It looms larger, my dear Horatia,' answered Caroline, 'than anything I have ever known.'

And with that she turned away and went back upstairs.

14

The months tumbled over themselves. The blustery little February when Anne Waldegrave had taken Algernon Hicks for husband turned into a boisterous blowy March. And then, all of a sudden, it was April and there were rainbows in the fields, arcing over showers and shadowing spring-legged lambs. And then summer came once more – and brought changes.

Queen Victoria, in accordance with the wishes of many, met her cousin again and wrote in her diary, 'Albert's beauty is most striking, and he is so amiable and unaffected – in short, very fascinating.'

And, round about this time, on May 25, 1839, John James Waldegrave, Esquire, married the beautiful Frances Braham and took her to stay at Strawberry Hill. Every bell in Twickenham rang to greet the bride and she ran from room to room crying out with delight.

'Strawberry is so beautiful,' she exclaimed. 'Oh please, George, may J.J. and I remain for a while? We will be no trouble.'

He kissed her hand, his lips lingering just a fraction too long.

'You shall have the best rooms,' he answered, 'and they shall be made so comfortable that you will never want to leave.'

Of the two soldiers there was news as well – though not as happy as that of the rest. John Joseph had returned to Vienna, where he threw himself constantly into the pursuit of pleasure – drinking, gambling and patronizing houses of ill repute. Despite the fact that he was still only twenty-seven years old, he seemed fired with a determination to burn himself out.

As for Jackdaw, he had become almost ascetic by comparison. His glimpse of Horatia Waldegrave in Hastings, in the summer of the previous year, had restored in him the old joy he had known before Marie's murder. He believed in destiny again, he believed in forces outside himself, he believed in the old wild magic of the house of FitzHoward. And now he sought to encourage it, hoping that one day it would lead him to where Horatia waited.

He had arrived in the Indian states in the autumn of 1838, and found that the prevailing unrest gave him great opportunity for freedom. Disguised as a horse-dealer he had picked his way through the mountain passes, talking to tribesmen, gathering information, learning the movements of troops. And also learning about himself.

Everywhere he came across old truths, ancient wisdoms, and his step to the study of Raja Yoga seemed pre-destined. He who was doubly heir to the family magic because of the true identity of his great-great-grandfather – something of which he had no inkling – began to train his mind on the path towards total development.

But while he led one life and John Joseph another, Mr Algernon Hicks and his wife and stepdaughters were preoccupied with the little practicalities of happy everyday existence.

They had closed up the house in Montagu Street after the wedding and moved into Algy's home in Duke Street which, large and extremely comfortable though it was, was none the less furnished in typical bachelor style. With money to spend at last Anne busied herself with total redecoration and furnishing, aided in everything by Annette and – to a lesser degree – Horatia; Ida Anna being too busy cheeking her governess to take a great deal of notice, other than ensuring that her room was of the maximum prettiness and luxury.

The advent of a new eighteen-year-old sister-in-law had excited them all and J.J. and Frances Braham had been invited to dinner several times so that the Hicks family might look over the half-Jewish girl who now stood on the edge of the aristocracy. They had not quite decided what they thought of her – but on one thing they were all agreed. Beneath all the beauty, the smiles, the winsome ways, lay a determination as strong as a man's.

'She will get everything she wants, that one. You mark my words,' said Anne to Algy, as she waved the girl and J.J. off in their carriage.

He nodded in agreement. He was occasionally capable of quite shrewd observation.

'She will always please men,' he said now. 'She is such a good listener.'

'I had not noticed that.'

'That is because you do not see her with a man's eyes.' Anne bridled very slightly and Algernon was suddenly all placation. 'Though nobody could even so much as look at her when you are there, my love,' he added over-heartily.

Anne laughed. 'You are learning new tricks, Algy – despite the proverb.'

He chortled merrily as they closed the front door behind them.

Christmas came again. This time George played host at Strawberry Hill with his sister-in-law Frances as the charming hostess. Caroline and Francis Hicks were included amongst the house guests, loving the miniature splendour of Strawberry Hill which Frances was renovating, though the three young people did not have enough money between them to meet the bills.

But nobody thought of that as 1840 dawned to ringing

266

bells – the sound doubly brave because of the Queen's personal happiness. Her betrothal to Prince Albert was announced.

And in the spring, when Algernon and Anne had been married a year and eight days, the Queen and her cousin went to the high altar, and then – after a glorious reception – on to a brief honeymoon at Windsor.

Lord Melbourne had been entirely forgotten as she wrote, 'Albert's excessive love and affection gave me a feeling of heavenly joy and happiness.' And the following evening she and the Prince gave a dinner party and the next night a dance, for both of which occasions he helped her put on her stockings! A month later the little Queen was pregnant and this, then, being the fashion, Caroline Hicks followed suit and by April, 1840, was able to stand appraisingly before a full-length mirror and see the tiniest rounding of her stomach.

Everyone thought of babies and as J.J. lay watching his wife undress in the river-dappled moonlight he called out to her, 'Will you give me a child, Frances?'

She turned to look at him, her thick black hair falling to her waist as she removed the last pin that held it in place.

'You know I will – but not yet. I want to see more of life, J.J. It is such fun here at Strawberry. Think of all the parties we have had.'

And it was true. Since their marriage they had spent scarcely any time at their own property in Essex, George having seen to it that the lives of the three of them at Strawberry Hill had been a frivolous and endless round. The fact that all the Waldegrave estates were mortgaged to the hilt and that daily calls from creditors were a common occurrence bothered them not at all.

Now J.J. turned restlessly away from her.

'It is different for you, Frances. You are strong. I have

had so many attacks recently that I feel the need to leave a child as my heritage.'

'How can you speak so? J.J. darling, the doctor has told you that epilepsy is not a fatal illness.'

'Bugger the doctor, I know how I feel! I want a child, Frances.'

'Well you can't have one yet.'

'Oh no?'

He got out of bed and stood stark naked before her, that same dangerous moonlight transforming him to a leering faun. Suddenly nervous, Frances clutched her dressing gown tightly around her. Sick though he might be J.J. still was stronger than she and Frances knew that none of the Waldegrave men was ever pleased by a woman's refusal.

'J.J., please don't look at me like that! I am tired.'

Once, many years before, in that very same room with its blue watered silk walls, the Earl Waldegrave had looked at the Countess in just such a manner. Now history repeated itself as his bastard son took a purposeful step towards his pretty bride.

She had a moment of rapid decision – to struggle or to play. As always with her, already so clever with the opposite sex that men constantly paid court to her regardless of her marriage, she chose correctly. She gave a thrilling little laugh and, neatly sidestepping, rushed past J.J. and out of the door, glancing back with a flutter of soot-dark lashes as she did so.

Then down the fantastic Gallery she sped, her bare feet scarcely touching the ground. J.J. rushed behind her, totally nude, chortling with laughter as it dawned on him that this was love play. She was ahead of him down the stairs – pausing only for a second to give him another deep look – before she had rushed out through the small cloister and into the garden. And there she spun round and round in the moonlight, her thin gown whirling out to reveal her long legs and naked hips.

At his window George felt faint. He was madly in love with his sister-in-law, coveted his brother's wife, and the sight of her twirling exotically was so exciting that he knew he must turn away. But somehow he could not. He watched, trembling and sick, as J.J. came out and lunged for her. He saw her look up at the windows, and stood back behind his curtain. Then he saw her tumble to the ground, curving her body upward as her husband – huge with desire – thrust into her almost violently.

George thought he would lose his reason as he saw the way she received J.J.'s shaft with a total lack of inhibition, pushing back and laughing with pleasure. He had never wanted anything as much as he wanted Frances then and to watch her reach her peak – calling out in frenzy – was more than he could stand. He turned away and fell on his bed in despair, blocking his ears against his brother's great groan of triumph.

But within three weeks that groan had turned to the death rattle. Frances and J.J. had returned to their London address – Number 38, Jermyn Street – only for him to grow mysteriously ill.

Returning from hat shopping in Bond Street, Frances had found her husband lying on the floor, apparently having an epileptic fit. But this time the fit had not gone away and – after J.J. had vomited violently – the pretty Jewess had sent for the doctor. He had made an examination, looked grave, muttered something about 'wild youth' and put the patient to bed.

The next day J.J. had seemed worse, hardly able to move a muscle of his face or body. The doctor had visited and gone and would visit again, but was not there, typically, when the end came. J.J. had lapsed into unconsciousness and Frances had suddenly heard his breathing rasp. Terrified, she had shot out of the house and banged frantically on a neighbour's door. Nobody in for three whole houses – but at number 30, in response to her cries and shouts, a man had popped his head out of an upstairs window.

'Help me! Help me!' she had screamed. 'My husband is dying.'

He had sprinted up the street with her and they had rushed up the stairs and into the bedroom just in time to see J.J. die. On his death certificate had been written 'Water in the head'. Frances was a widow at merely nineteen years of age.

Whether that scene of passion in the grounds of Strawberry Hill had been the triggering cause nobody could say, but Frances – heavy with guilt – could not catch George's eye. Nor could he look at her. He wondered the very same thing. And, added to the burden of what he had observed as an unwitting peeping Tom, was his lunatic love for her. His ghastly conflict of emotions was unbearable. For he was glad that she no longer had a husband, yet he grieved desperately for the brother who had been like his twin.

The two of them followed J.J.'s coffin dressed in starkest black. They did not speak to each other and yet something in the way in which her son touched her daughter-in-law's elbow gave the weeping Anne – supported on one side by Mr Hicks and on the other by Lady Annette – a sense of unease.

'Oh Algernon,' she said later that night, when she had stopped crying and had been given brandy and put to bed. 'I have this terrible feeling that George truly cares for Frances. I mean *cares*.'

Algy looked knowing. 'Yes, my dear, I think you are right.'

'But how dreadful! She is his brother's widow!'

'So nothing can come of it.'

The Countess stared at him a little blankly and Algy went on, 'Any kind of liaison between them is quite against the law. It is a prohibited relationship in the eyes of both the church and the state.'

Anne looked at him bleakly.

'I do hope George will be careful,' she said. 'Frances is so very . . . I don't know what the right word is.'

'Powerful,' said Algy slowly. 'That little girl is one of the most powerful people alive.'

'Oh dear,' said the Countess.

But what of Sutton Place, that had stood so forlorn for so long? Several tenants had lived there after the departure of Mrs Trevelyan and the last of these had disappeared one cold summer midnight with ten wagonloads of fine old oak furniture and paintings. The discovery had so upset Mr Webbe Weston that he had been seized with apoplexy and had been bedridden and speechless ever since.

Caroline came from London to look after her father, since Mrs Webbe Weston could do little else but weep. Yet this meant Caroline's separation from Francis who, having just qualified, was plunged into the full duties of a trainee surgeon and was quite unable to leave the hospital.

On September 29, Mr Webbe Weston took a turn for the worse, having had another kind of violent seizure. And by the strange law of coincidence, as he made a choking sound and clutched at his throat, George, the seventh Earl Waldegrave, and Mrs Frances Waldegrave clinked champagne glasses and laughed.

They were on their way to their wedding, having eloped to Scotland where the terms of the 1835 Marriage Act did not apply. The city of Edinburgh was warmed by a late autumn sun and the bride and groom had not a care in the world. The fact that George was to stand trial for assault, having beaten a policeman into a horribly injured state in a party with his rowdy friends, did not bother them at all. They had both achieved their crowning ambitions – George to possess Frances and she to enter the aristocracy. And as for poor J.J., why he had been laid in his grave almost half a year!

But at Pomona House the atmosphere was far from carefree as Mr Webbe Weston's condition worsened, his wife wept ineffectual tears and his daughter grew larger and larger with child. If it had not been for the intervention of Cloverella and her dear little boy the situation would have been unbearable. But, as it was, the nut-brown girl fetched and carried without a grumble and the little soul ran about helping, talking to Mr Webbe Weston in the funny language that only small children and the very old can understand.

But by October – still unable to leave her parents and yet almost at full term – Caroline took it upon herself to write to Mary, Matilda and John Joseph to come to their dying father's bedside. As George and Frances entered Strawberry Hill triumphantly as husband and wife, Caroline put the last strokes to the letters which spelled out the truth to her sisters and brother – there was no hope left.

But Mr Webbe Weston was to know one final happiness before he died. For Francis Hicks – on a flying visit to his father-in-law – found himself delivering his own baby son. Caroline, who had been ignoring acute backache all day so anxious was she about everyone else, had no idea at all that she was actually in labour until she let out a groan – even as she sipped a cup of tea – and said, 'Francis, I know this cannot be possible but I feel . . .'

She could not complete the sentence, so overwhelming

were her sensations. There was no time to fetch the midwife and doctor from Guildford; there was hardly time for Francis to shout at Cloverella to wash herself and come at once – for he had strong views on antisepticism, not altogether in tune with some of his fellow practitioners. There was just time to lift Caroline up and lay her on her bed and to soap himself up to the elbows before Francis guided the little body into the world.

As his gurgling son cried, so did he. Hardened medical student he might have been but the miracle was too great for him. Sweet, lively Francis had tears streaming down his face as he kissed Caroline's cheek and then set about making sure no infection could attack his wife or child.

Mrs Webbe Weston, who had been out for tea and missed the whole thing, burst into copious weeping again – fortunately Francis had by now controlled his emotion – and had to be revived with brandy. But it was on her husband that the effect was most profound. On seeing his new grandchild – the first to be born in England – he made a feeble attempt to sit up in bed. And when Francis had helped him and propped him on pillows, he spoke for the first time in four months.

'Fine . . . boy. Wonderful . . . news. Over . . . joyed. Good . . . bye.'

And later that night he died.

Mary and Matilda arrived from Paris the next morning – too late. But at least they took over the arrangements for the funeral. There was still no word from John Joseph so in the end Mr Webbe Weston was laid to rest without the final respects of his only son.

He came a week later, travel-stained and tired, and quite devastated that he had not been in time to see his father again. His regiment had been on manoeuvres outside Vienna and Caroline's letter had taken two weeks to catch up with him.

'Will you stay in the Army?' Mary had asked, when he had had time to settle down.

'Of course. What else is there?'

'You are the master of Sutton Place now.'

'I shall put the house in the hands of agents. The less I have to do with it the better.'

'You still hate it as much?'

'More if anything. It eats at me like a canker.'

'Why?'

'Guilt.'

'I don't understand you.'

John Joseph had turned away. 'It is very complex. I am guilty because the house is run down and robbed and pillaged through our neglect. And yet at the same time I could not bear to live there again. I have made a new life for myself away from it – as have you. And that is how I wish to remain.'

'John Joseph,' Mary had said in that old bossy way of hers, 'you must tell me the truth. Are you happy?'

'No. But I am not unhappy. I am nothing; in limbo.'

'But why, for Heaven's sake?'

'Because I died within – at the risk of sounding dramatic – on the day she married.'

'What?' Mary had exclaimed incredulously. 'You are still thinking of Marguerite Trevelyan? That trollop! You must be out of your mind.'

'I agree with you.'

'Why on earth don't you find yourself a wife and forget all about her?'

'I don't know.'

Mary's cheeks had gone pink with annoyance.

'Well,' she said, 'I have never heard anything so idiotic in all my life. I think you are an utter sop! I used to respect you, John Joseph, but this is too much. Do you remember how we drank to the future on board ship?

The words we said? And you have gone back on the whole thing. You might have made a new life physically – but in your mind you are still chained to her. Perhaps that is the way the curse of Sutton Place has struck you. By turning you into a total clown.'

And with that she had stamped her little foot, just as she had always done, and flounced from the room. And her fury with her brother had not stopped there. On the journey to London – to which the entire family were called for the reading of Mr Webbe Weston's will – she would not utter a word to him, nor in the solicitor's office. In fact it was not until they were all sitting down to a high tea, so famished were they with the stress of the past few weeks, that the ice thawed a fraction and she passed him a slice of ham.

But none the less the atmosphere was not easy and Caroline was quite relieved to hear the front door bell ring, signalling a visitor. Rivers entered the room deferentially.

'The Lady Horatia Waldegrave has called to see you, Madam,' he said.

'Oh good. Show her into the drawing room, would you, Rivers.'

But too late! In a flurry of bonnet ribbons and fur cape, her cheeks bright from the cold, Horatia stood in the doorway.

'Caroline, forgive me,' she said. 'I have just heard the news about your baby and I felt I had to . . .' She stopped short, her eyes widening and her mouth opening slightly as her attention was caught by John Joseph's rising from the table. 'Oh my goodness, it's the soldier of fortune,' she exclaimed.

They stood staring at one another in silence for what seemed like for ever but was, in reality, only a minute. He thinking her quite the most beautiful girl he had ever laid eyes on, terribly young and innocent and vulnerable, and regrettably of the upper class, so nobody he could seduce.

And something of his thoughts – however well trained he was in the social graces – must have shown because he saw Lady Horatia's pink cheeks deepen to rose. For she, unlike him, had fallen in love with John Joseph at first sight. She had been half way there anyway. But she had enough presence of mind, now, to bob him a little curtsey, look away, and finish her sentence to her hostess.

'I felt I must call and bring the baby a gift. But I had not realized the family was here so I will return another time.'

She turned to go but Caroline's voice cut across.

'No, Horatia, you must stay. We are only sitting down to tea. Please do join us.' Her eyes twinkled a little. 'There is a chair there by John Joseph. A place shall be set for you.'

Horry looked up and once again caught his eye. Despite her youth and inexperience she knew perfectly well that he was appraising her and her unconventional nature rose to the challenge at once.

'Very well,' she said, 'but I would prefer to sit next to you, Caro; then we may catch up with the news in an undertone. For I believe it is not polite to discuss babies at the tea table.'

She had scored. John Joseph looked minutely perturbed as all the ladies – except Mrs Webbe Weston who sniffed slightly – laughed. Horatia felt the thrill of her first verbal foray with a man and went on, 'Are you on a long leave, Captain Webbe Weston? If so I do hope you will recount your adventures in Foreign Parts to my Mama and stepfather. He is very interested in that kind of thing.'

'Saucy minx,' he thought but said out loud, 'Yes, Lady

Horatia, I am here for a month to settle my affairs. I will most certainly call.'

'Thank you,' she said gravely – and turned away to Caroline.

She did not look at John Joseph again – at least not whilst he was looking at her – and he found that this rather intriguing behaviour attracted more of his attention than he cared to admit.

Aware of his glance but fortunately with no idea of what was going through his mind, Horatia was concentrating on other things, saying quietly to Caroline, 'Tell me what you truly think. You can be perfectly honest.'

'About George and Frances?'

'Yes.'

Caroline paused a moment and Horatia put in, 'You will not offend me. You should hear what Mama has been saying.'

'In that case I will admit to you freely that I am shocked.'

'It is atrocious behaviour, is it not?'

'Atrocious. It is not so much that they evaded the law by marrying in Scotland – I find the law foolish on that point anyway, for after all they are not related by blood. No, what I find so terrible is that J.J. had only been dead five months.'

'Hardly cold in his grave, as they say.'

'Precisely.'

'Caroline, do you think there was any kind of attachment *before* J.J.'s death?'

'Does your mother think so?'

'She thinks that George was always madly in love with Frances but I heard her tell Algy that she did not believe the affair to have been adulterous.'

'No, I don't suppose it was. But he certainly stepped into his dead brother's shoes very promptly.'

'And into his bed I'll warrant. Frances must be very ruthless.'

'Perhaps we are being a little unkind,' Caroline answered thoughtfully. 'Maybe she was grief-stricken and sought consolation with the man who so closely resembled her dead husband.'

'I suppose there's some truth in everything we say. I only know, however, that I find it fractionally boring to have her as a permanent sister-in-law.'

Caroline laughed.

'Horatia, you are outrageous.' She lowered her voice to just above a whisper. 'What do you think of the portrait now that you have seen the reality?'

Horry smiled, looking directly at her hostess.

'The paintings do not do him justice. He is far more exciting in the flesh. But a terrible rake I should imagine.'

Caroline looked absolutely astonished.

'What makes you say that? I have always thought of him as rather correct.'

'I think that is his act for you. But didn't you tell me he was once jilted?'

'Well, hardly that. He was madly in love with a woman many years his senior. But still very beautiful, you understand me. I think she broke his heart by marrying some beastly old peer for money. Mary was telling me only today that he still pines for her.'

'None the less I reckon he plays the field.'

Caroline looked at Horatia, shaking her head. The days of what people were to think of later as Victorian attitudes had not yet begun. The Queen was too young and too happy to have time for moralizing. But, nevertheless, Horatia was still exceptional for her day. There were very few seventeen-year-old girls who would have dared be quite so forthright to their hostess. But this particular young woman regarded hypocrisy as the deadliest sin of all.

Now Caroline laughed and said, 'You are so refreshing! Will you stay and dine with us, Horatia? You are just what we need after the recent sadnesses.'

'But Mama is expecting me back.'

'Then we shall send the footman round with a note so that she need not worry. Will you stay? Then you can have plenty of time to play with little Charles before Nanny gets strict.'

'I would enjoy that very much,' said Horatia.

Tea at an end Mrs Webbe Weston, who was showing some signs of further weeping, was put to bed to await Francis's return from duty; she had great faith in her son-in-law's ability to cure all her ills. With their mother out of the way Mary and Matilda – who were returning to Paris on the following day – took a carriage to Bond Street anxious to catch the shops. And so it was that, after half an hour in the nursery admiring the new baby, Horatia came down the stairs and found John Joseph standing alone and staring up at his portrait – Sutton Place tiny in the background.

Without a second thought Horry went and stood beside him, aware once more of the dark blue eyes looking her up and down in a glance that she had seen George – and poor dead J.J. – give so often to women.

'The house looks insignificant,' she said without pre-amble, 'but Caroline tells me that it is not.'

'Oh? What did she tell you about it?'

'No more than that.'

They turned to look at each other. There was no artifice whatsoever between them. They were both products of backgrounds which had no room for that which was false or shallow.

'You are a very unusual child, Lady Horatia,' said John Joseph slowly.

'I suppose you use the word to put me in my place.'

'Not at all. I think to say someone is unusual is a compliment.'

'You are deliberately mistaking me, Captain Webbe Weston. I am seventeen and have actually left the tender mercies of my governess. It was the noun I questioned.'

He looked away. 'Would you like to know about the house?'

'Very much.'

'It falls beneath the spell of an ancient curse.'

'Really? Who laid it?'

'A Queen of England. Very long ago. Her name was Edith and she was a niece by marriage of King Knut.'

'Why did she do it?'

A small smile twitched at the corners of John Joseph's mouth and the seascape eyes held a slightly mocking look.

'I think she had had an argument with her husband. And you know what women are like for revenge.'

'No,' answered Horatia, shaking her head so that the great mass of curls – thrust to the top of her head now that she was too old for hair upon her shoulders – rippled like warming wine. 'No, I don't know what women are like. My brothers do – did – but I have no idea.'

'You are quick with your replies, are you not?'

'Am I? Captain Webbe Weston, please stop teasing me. I would much rather hear about the cursed house than enter the verbal lists with you.'

He laughed aloud. 'What an amazing character! Very well then. The house was cursed in 1048 to know death, madness and despair: with particular reference to the heir. A manor house was built there by the Bassett family in the reign of King John – previous Lords of the Manor had all met untimely ends – and then they, the Bassetts, were all wiped out. After that it passed through many hands – each time bringing with it its wretched legacy – until it was given to Sir Richard Weston, a courtier of Henry VIII, by the King himself.'

'Caroline said he built the present house.'

'Yes. It must have been marvellous then. Alive with people and noise and smelling of food on spits and mulled toddy.'

His mouth drew down in a hard line and Horatia said, 'Why should that sadden you, the fact that it was once happy?'

'Because I find it obscene that something once so beautiful should now be desolated.'

'What caused its ruin?'

'The curse really. None of the Westons had any luck there – they were even forced to leave during the Civil War.'

'Really?'

'Yes. It is said that Charles I visited the house secretly during that time and the ghost of Anne Boleyn – who can only be seen by royalty – appeared to him.'

Horatia shivered. 'How dark!'

John Joseph smiled. 'Very dark, Lady Horatia. Anyway the line eventually dwindled down to one solitary woman – Melior Mary Weston – who, legend has it, went mad there and let the house fall into decay around her.'

'And she did not marry?'

'No. Despite having beauty and a fortune she let it all go for love – or rather for lack of it.'

'How sad!'

'Yes.'

Horatia knew by this one monosyllable that his sister had been right, that he still had strong feelings for some woman somewhere.

'Well, I suppose she preferred that to marriage with the wrong person,' she answered.

'Yes.'

'Which was her decision to make, though not the right one in my opinion.'

He looked at her questioningly and she went on, 'I would rather marry some jolly old soul with whom I could amble on than shut myself up in a rotting palace and wait for death.'

'How colourfully put!'

'You do not agree?'

'I have not given the matter a great deal of thought. Anyway, Miss Weston had family connections – though not those of blood – with my grandfather, John Webbe. And she left him the estate on the proviso he adopt the name Weston. So here we are – the Webbe Westons of Sutton Place.'

'Unaffected by the curse?'

John Joseph gave a bitter laugh. 'On the contrary – there are more subtle ways of ruining people than actually killing them. And that is what happened to my father. He was ruined in the true sense of the word.'

'He lost all his money?'

'Every penny. Sutton Place bled him white. Two hundred thousand pounds' worth of timber had to be sold from Sutton Forest; Melior Street and Weston Street were also sold – to say nothing of Webbe Street – and finally we had to let the house itself. Only one tenant served it well – ' John Joseph had turned to stare through the window at the lamps throwing fuzzy comets of light into the winter-dark streets of London ' – and after she left it was robbed and pillaged by everyone who stayed there. Furniture, books, paintings – they have all been taken from under our noses.'

'And what are *you* going to do?'

282

'Put it in the hands of London agents, economize and try to bring the property round.'

'Not sell?'

'I don't know yet. It may come to that.'

Into the sudden silence between them came all the thousand and one little noises of a family house going about its business. From the upstairs nursery baby Charles Hicks started to cry, this sound followed by the cooing of Caroline's voice and Nanny going to fetch something to placate him. From the bedroom above them Mrs Webbe Weston let out a deep sigh and there was the thud of a book dropping upon the floor; while from the living room came the noise of someone putting coal upon the fire. Outside carriage wheels turned and Francis's cheerful voice could be heard as he hummed a tune while River's measured tread crossed the hall to open the front door for his master. To complete this cameo of domestic bliss a smell of roasting pork, of sage and onions and apple sauce, came wafting up the stairs to assure the household that a delicious meal awaited them when all their little tasks were done.

'This is a happy home, is it not?' said Horatia.

'Very.'

'Could it not be done for Sutton Place, this lovely, warm homemaking?'

'No. It is too big and too sad.'

'But it was like that in Sir Richard Weston's day.'

'That was before its memories came.'

'I could make it happy again,' said Horatia.

John Joseph turned away from the window and looked at her in total astonishment. One of her curls had fallen down and clung to her neck giving her a slightly dishevelled look. But despite that she was still quite the most beautiful girl he had ever seen.

'What do you mean?'

'What I say.'

To his amazement she took a step forward and put her hand on his arm.

'I want to marry you, Captain Webbe Weston. I really am quite sure I should because I love you so much.'

He did not answer. His distant memory was stirring and he saw in his mind's eye the ghastly battlefield and himself as a dying soldier: the recurring nightmare of childhood. And he saw too – quite distinctly – the hair of the woman who had sat beside him; the hair like foxfire in autumn; the hair of Lady Horatia Waldegrave.

'What are you saying?' he asked abruptly, rudely almost.

'That I fell in love with you at first sight. Don't scoff! Romeo and Juliet did so.'

'That was in a play.'

'But based on truth.'

He was struck dumb as the madcap girl fell on one knee before him.

'Hurry up with your answer; Francis will be in in a minute. Captain Webbe Weston, will you accept my proposal of marriage?'

At last he laughed, cracking forward in a guffaw.

'Get up at once,' he said.

'No, I will not. John Joseph, will you marry me?'

'No, Lady Horatia,' answered the owner of Sutton Place. 'I most certainly will not.'

15

On the January night that the new master of Sutton Place went to say farewell to his inheritance, a great frost gripped the land. The trees stood white beneath a sky that glistened with stars, brilliant as gems in the dark torrent of blackness, and the land was hard under a moon that glittered like a gypsy's brooch. Everywhere was the listening hush of winter, as even the fox kept to his lair, and the only sound was the crunch of wheels on ice as John Joseph's closed carriage made its way slowly up the drive, the coachman wrapped in a dozen scarves and gauntleted to the wrist to keep away the cold.

They had left Guildford at six, partly through the owner's whim to see the mansion house in darkness and partly to keep his promise to call on the widowed Lady Gunn, formerly Miss Huss the desperate governess. But now John Joseph regretted the idea as the horse's hooves slipped on the little wooden bridge that crossed the frozen River Wey.

Yet seeing that icy trickle made him think back to when, all those years ago, he had lost his virginity on the shores of that very river and he smiled to himself at the memory of sweet, naked Cloverella. And then he thought of how he had raped Marguerite Trevelyan on just such a winter's night; of how she, too, had been naked beneath her riding habit.

He turned to stare restlessly out of the window, looking to where the trees clawed at the night with their white splintery fingers. What a great and wonderful forest this had been when the Saxon Kings hunted the lands – before the curse had even been uttered. But now the place had been decimated by the selling off of wood to meet the debts of the Webbe Westons. He twitched with irritation. What a wretched affair! And then, unbidden, the face of Horatia Waldegrave came to his mind: that glorious and unconventional child. What a pity that she was so young – and not to be compared with Marguerite.

The carriage rounded a bend in the drive and there, ahead of him and slightly to his left, loomed the vast and unrelenting shape of Sutton Place, its windows dark and sightless. All the old feelings came back – fear, hatred, guilt. And yet there was a certain grim pride in it all, that he owned a part of English history.

Before the Middle Enter, on the cobbles of what had once been the quadrangle, a large and blazing bonfire had been built and as the carriage approached John Joseph was able to see the weirdly leaping shadows light up the terracotta brick of Sir Richard Weston's manor house. And then as he came even nearer he stared in astonishment. For there, in that strange and magic light, Cloverella and her son were dancing barefoot to the accompaniment of her flute.

He watched, astounded, as two pairs of little feet stamped and jumped as if they had gone back to another age. What a sweet scene to have stumbled across – and yet the roaring flames and the fact that Cloverella came from witches' stock made John Joseph shiver. Had an ancestress of hers met her death in such a blaze?

Now, to break the spell, he called out through the carriage window, 'Cloverella! Hey, Cloverella! It's me, John Joseph.'

She looked up and waved her arm, continuing the dance but pointing out to Jay that the master had come back to Sutton Place. And he, not yet five years old, gave a gruff little bow and then stood still respectfully. John

Joseph could not take his eyes from the child, wondering if this was his bastard or if Jackdaw was responsible.

But as the carriage came to a halt and he approached on foot, he found there were no real clues in the child's appearance. For Jay's eyes were the colour of hazelnuts, as were his mother's, and his hair was thick and dark. Yet was there a hint of the fine Webbe Weston nose? And yet surely that smile was Jackdaw's?

Totally confused he looked at Cloverella but she merely shrugged her shoulders and laughed.

'I'm not telling.'

'But if he's mine I want to know.'

'Jay belongs to himself, Master. Now, will you step inside for some beer?'

'Yes. Though not for long. Just enough time to talk to you about the future.'

Cloverella gave a rather irritating smile.

'I think the future is going to take care of itself.'

'And what is that supposed to mean?'

'Nothing in particular, Sir,' she answered, as if she really meant 'Everything'.

They had stepped through the Middle Enter and were standing in the darkness of the Great Hall. Outside the blazing bonfire cast light upon the stained glass windows which glowed first ruby, then midnight, then gold. Escutcheons old as time flared into momentary brightness and the Westons' crest – the Saracen's head – appeared suddenly vivid, sticking out its tongue.

'It looks almost merry,' said John Joseph.

'That's why I lit the fire. To give the new master a welcome. And somehow I thought you would be bringing a bride here with you.'

'Cloverella, what are you talking about?'

'Oh, I just had this feeling that you had met the right one at last.'

'You and Jackdaw do nothing but have feelings. Don't you ever think things out? How could I have met anybody? I've been in London settling my father's affairs and putting Sutton Place into the hands of agents.'

'Well, there are women in London, aren't there?'

John Joseph could make no reply to this and he rather crossly followed Cloverella across the Hall and off to the left.

'I've lit a fire in the Library and brought some ale up from the cellar. I'll light the candles. You sit down and make yourself comfortable. Come here, Jay. Go into your nest, my darling.'

She had put a quilt and pillow by the hearth and, waving his hand to John Joseph, the little boy snuggled into it and closed his eyes.

'He often sleeps there. It's the warmest spot.'

John Joseph fished into his pocket.

'Here, Cloverella, for God's sake get him some clothes and shoes. He looks such a little rag-bag. If he *were* mine, I wouldn't like to think . . .'

'Oh don't worry, Master. He doesn't go short of the important things. He has hot food and plenty. And he has love and kisses. Ragged trousers don't really count.'

'Well they do to me. Here, take it.'

'Thank you.' She put the guinea on the mantel shelf, pouring John Joseph some beer at the same time. 'Now what are your instructions about the house?'

'I would like you to stay on as caretaker. Of course the agents will send down a representative to take an inventory . . .'

'What's that?'

'A list of all the items in the place so that the tenants won't steal. More than they have already, that is.'

His eyes went rapidly round the shelves of the Library and he added, 'Half the books seem to be missing.'

288

'They are. I reckon each tenant – with the exception of Lady Dawe – has helped himself to a few.'

'It's disgraceful,' said John Joseph, abruptly rising from his seat and starting to pace the floor. 'I really ought to sell the wretched place and be done with all this letting and pilfering.'

'Then why don't you?'

'I don't know.' He stopped short in front of her. 'I once had a dream in this very room, Cloverella. A dream in which death came to me disguised as a bird. It told me that there was a hidden portrait of Sir Richard Weston in the Chapel. It also told me to sell Sutton Place when the inheritance was mine. But now that it is, I hesitate.'

'Why? No good luck has ever come to anyone here.'

'I know that. Do you think I don't believe in the curse? It is just that I find it so difficult to let places – and people – go.'

And what he said was true. He had been born when the sign of Cancer the Crab had held ascendency in the heavens and, like all those governed by that symbol, John Joseph Webbe Weston had almost to be at the point of death to release his claw.

'Yes,' answered Cloverella, 'I realize that – but I think you should put aside sentiment and think of the future.' She added just a shade too casually, 'They say Lord Dawe is looking very old these days.'

John Joseph gave her a penetrating look.

'Are you trying to tell me that one day soon Marguerite will be free?'

Cloverella stooped to put a log on the fire, her back turned completely.

'How many years is it since you have seen her?' she asked in a muffled voice.

'Five.'

'Then I wish you joy,' said the witch girl, standing up

and wiping her palms on her skirt. 'I meant you to look to the *real* future. You are a fool to yourself, John Joseph. I regret that you were ever my lover. I dislike the thought of consorting with clowns.'

An angry flush had come into John Joseph's cheeks as he said, 'Cloverella, every argument we have had has been over her. From where I stand you seem a jealous shrew.'

'Then I am sorry that we shall part on bad terms once more – but part we must. I shall care for your mansion house, Sir, if you still wish me to do so. But let me say this to you.' She took a step forward and stared straight into his eyes. 'Sometimes destiny shows you the path. No, more than that, tries to guide you upon the right way, for there are always two roads open. But if you refuse the one that is meant – then God help you. You will have to strive hard to come back to that same point.'

'I don't believe you,' answered her employer. 'I believe that I am master of my own fate, that I can bring circumstances round by my own endeavour.'

'Then I can only put my blessing upon you and hope that no evil befalls. Goodnight, Sir.'

And with that she left the room leaving John Joseph alone with the sleeping child. He stood staring into the flames for a long moment and then bent down gently to look into Jay's face. Beneath his scrutiny the little boy stirred and woke, quite unafraid to find himself alone with a stranger.

'Jay?' said John Joseph.

'Yes Sir?'

The boy yawned and stretched, putting his arms over his head.

'Did your mother ever tell you your father's name?'

'No, I don't think so, Sir. Why, are you Papa?'

Before he could stop himself John Joseph had echoed, 'No, I don't think so.'

'Oh dear,' said the boy, 'I would like you to be.'

'Do you miss a father then?'

'No. But I don't want you to go.'

'Don't worry, Jay,' said John Joseph as he stood upright and picked up his greatcoat, 'I'll be back to play with you. In fact I shall try to come back every year.'

The innocent child smiled up at him, unaware that the only thought in the mind of the master of Sutton Place was that Marguerite Dawe might soon be widowed and free to receive his courtship.

And outside the warmth of the bonfire was nothing to the crackling fire of his heart. He rubbed his hands together cheerfully, full of plans and hope. He would resign his commission, restore Sutton Place and have the woman he worshipped at his side. John Joseph's imagination had not progressed a jot in all the years he had been away; his vision as narrow as that of a man in a tunnel; his soul as empty as a worn-out cockle shell. He did not deserve help.

But, quite unknown to him, Cloverella had finally tired of the situation. Very rarely in her life did she practise the arts which had been passed down in her family from Cloverella the Witch. But now she knew that the time was right for her to assume power. She also knew that to misuse this power would mean, in the end, that she must pay the penalty.

But now she thought only of what had to be done. From virgin beeswax her fingers formed a female image which she crowned with a scrap of human hair, picked up from Lady Dawe's private pew in St John's, Woking. Then, from a tin hastily slipped into her dress, she withdrew five of John Joseph's hairs taken from the collar of his greatcoat when she had helped him off with it.

291

Then she moulded a male doll and put John Joseph's hair to its head. A look of triumph crossed her face. From inside an old book she produced a folded slip of paper within which lay a full lock of one of Marguerite's curls. Cloverella smiled. She had cut it off while her mistress dozed, all those years ago when Mrs Trevelyan had ruled Sutton Place. Like her famous ancestress before her Cloverella had been taught always to collect the hair of one who might prove to be an enemy.

Now, saying aloud, 'The heart of John Joseph Webbe Weston,' she made a small wax heart and, while it was still warm, pressed the lock of hair into it. She marked it with John Joseph's initials and pinned it on to the male figure. Then she said, 'Evohe! Met in lust, part in loathing,' and plucked from the now solidified heart one of the hairs.

The spell was nearly over. She cried out again, 'Evohe! Evohe! When all is gone, then so dies love.'

She bowed before the images and opening a small casket put that of John Joseph inside. Then she picked up the wax Lady Dawe and walked with her across the Great Hall and back into the library.

Jay slept as peacefully as when she had last seen him, a golden guinea – which John Joseph had obviously left for the child alone to have – clutched in his grubby fist. Cloverella bent to kiss him and then stood gazing into the fire, passing the waxen dolly from hand to hand. Eventually she thought better of destroying Marguerite entirely and put the likeness outside the kitchen door with some rubbish.

'Get you out,' she said, 'vanquished and gone. Sutton Place and its master have no further need of you – and never will so long as he lives.'

* * *

'What's the matter, John Joseph? You look a trifle pale.'

Lady Gunn bent forward solicitously, spilling her port as she did so. The erstwhile Miss Huss had taken to imbibing in widowhood and dreaming the fevered dreams of her youth – those in which she loitered for military men – in a haze of drink.

She had, in the manner of the true drunkard, grown immensely thin with age and this, coupled with her flat chest and bony hips, gave her a sexless air. It could have been man or woman who sat swathed in black satin, a black lace cap upon its head, nodding away at the poor Captain, who dabbed at his moustache nervously with a linen handkerchief.

'It's nothing, Miss . . . Lady Gunn. A slight pain, that is all.'

'Have another port,' came the response – and a generous helping for both him and the hermaphrodite followed forthwith.

It was just at that moment Cloverella had drawn the first hair from the heart of the wax dolly; a ritual she would repeat weekly until every strand of the curl had gone. And John Joseph had felt it as a physical pull at the very strings of his heart.

'It was *so* sad the loss of your poor dear father. I was *so* overcome at the funeral. I am *so* sorry that I could not take my leave of you.'

As Lady Gunn had been carried out unconscious – presumably having been well fortified against the cold before her arrival – John Joseph could not help a twitch of the lips.

'Ah the old days,' she went on, not pausing for more than a quick swig at her glass. 'Do you remember that terrible Christmas when Sam Clopper went missing? And to think he was found all that while later. Do you know several people have written that tale since – a child playing hide-and-seek in an old oak chest – just as if they had thought of it themselves?'

'No, I didn't know.'

'Well, they have. It is incredible how these stories get round. I was told the other day whilst playing whist that young Mr Dickens – have you read *Nicholas Nickleby*, so funny and yet so stark? – has heard the story of poor Miss Melior Mary Weston and was most impressed with it.'

'Really?'

'Yes.' Lady Gunn finished her glass. She was a brilliant conversationalist when in her cups. Out of them she had a tendency to be morose. 'And I am quite sure that just such a character – an old woman who locks herself up in her house and allows it to decay around her – will appear in a novel of his one of these days.'

'Good gracious,' said John Joseph.

He was not really interested. All sorts of ideas were beginning to flood through his mind; the need to get back to the Angel Inn before the frost made the roads impassable being paramount. Then thoughts that he had not had since he sailed for Europe; worries that his life was drifting by, that he would be twenty-eight this year and still preferred the company of loose women, that he had not really got his future into any kind of shape other than that of Captain in a foreign army. He shifted in his chair restlessly.

'Not in any further pain, dear John Joseph?'

Lady Gunn's hair beneath its widow's cap appeared to have slipped sideways and he realized with horror that it was a vast wig.

'No. But I really must be taking my leave. The roads were very bad getting here. Will you forgive me?'

'No I won't, she said, lurching up archly. 'You don't come and see me often enough, you naughty boy.'

He detected a glint in her eye which had him backing nervously to the door.

'A fault that shall be rectified. I will call whenever I am in England.' He clicked his heels and bowed, military style. 'Goodbye, dear Lady.'

She raised her glass of port, which was miraculously once more full to the brim.

'I drink to you, my gallant Captain. I knew that you would be an Army man when I watched you play with your tin soldiers. Adieu, adieu.'

She struggled to kiss him but the effort was too great and she fell back into her chair.

'Goodbye, Lady Gunn. I may see you in a year's time if all goes well.'

But this idea – though sincerely meant – was not destined to come about, for as soon as he arrived in Vienna he received a posting to Poland.

So when, later that year, Horatia Waldegrave asked, 'Do you hear a great deal from John Joseph?' his sister Caroline replied, 'No, he has been sent to Cracau. There is insurrection there, you know.'

'And when is there not in the Austro-Hungarian Empire? It seems far too big to control,' was the rather sad reply.

'Too big and too uneasy. There will be terrible bloodshed one of these days.'

'Don't speak of it,' said the younger girl, very solemn. 'I would not like to think of your brother in danger. It quite puts me into gloom.'

Caroline laughed.

'Well, we can't have that on Annette's wedding day. Let me change the subject and say how beautiful your dress is.'

For at last poor Annette – who seemed to have been betrothed for ever – had achieved her dearest wish and actually married Archibald Money, now promoted to Colonel and grown slightly pompous.

The ceremony had been in St James's, Westminster, with all the family there, Algernon and the Dowager Duchess – the rather elderly title bestowed on Anne now that George had married Frances Waldegrave – George and Frances themselves, she only just twenty but already with a knowledgeable look in her pretty eyes, and Caroline and Francis Hicks. The Ladies Horatia and Ida Anna had walked behind the bride as her attendants, wearing dresses of ice blue and rose pink respectively, and with wreaths of flowers in their hair.

Afterwards everyone had stood upon the steps for a daguerrotype image to be struck. Then they had proceeded to Webb's Hotel in King Street, Covent Garden, for the breakfast. And it was here, with Lady Horatia seated opposite Caroline, that the conversation between the two of them had taken place.

'Thank you. Annette wanted us both in pink but I refused.'

She laughed and shook her foxfire hair, swept on top of her head in a mass of curls, and the shades of damson that grew nearest to her neck were visible for a moment. Caroline caught herself thinking that her brother must be a total fool not to have fallen in love with Horatia. For she was quite sure – though neither of them had said a word to her – that something had passed between them.

She sighed to herself. What was it about John Joseph that made him so detached? She hoped that Mary was wrong, that he did not still nurse a passion for the wretched Lady Dawe. Aloud she said, more forthrightly than she had intended, 'Are you fond of John Joseph, Horatia?' The girl coloured up. 'Yes – but it is not reciprocated. He thinks me a babe-in-arms. A silly nursery goose not fit to leave its governess.'

'But he is only ten years older than you are!'

'In his eyes it could be a hundred!'

'Then if I were you I would forget all about him. There must be scores of young men just longing to throw their hearts at your feet.'

'That sounds horrible – and extremely messy!'

Caroline laughed. 'You know perfectly well what I mean. Did you ever meet John Wardlaw?'

'Who?'

'A distant relative of mine who lives in Hastings – that is when he is not stationed abroad with the Army, which he practically always is. He was so smitten with the sight of you driving along when you were there on holiday that he ran after your carriage and fell down. It caused a mild sensation. Do you remember?'

Horatia grinned. 'I remember something. I heard somebody shout but never saw properly who it was. We were all terribly flattered and wondered which one of us had taken his fancy.'

'Well it was you.'

'I'm delighted.'

'He's in India now: a kind of spy for the military.'

'How exciting! Will he come back?'

'One day I suppose. His brother has returned to get married. In fact both Jackdaw's . . .'

'Jackdaw?'

'That's his nickname. John Wardlaw – Jackdaw. Both his brother and his sister Violet are to be married in the spring. This is quite the year of the wedding.'

Horatia counted on her fingers. 'Annette, Jackdaw's brother and sister – anybody else?'

'Yes, thank God. My funny middle sister Matilda has got herself a proposal at last. She is to wed her French beau in Paris in the summer and Francis and I are going.'

'Will John Joseph be there?'

'If he can get leave from his Polish tour. But if he does so it will mean that he cannot return to England this year.'

Horatia looked momentarily sad before her mermaid eyes brightened.

'But he will be back one day,' she said.

'Yes,' answered Caroline slowly, 'one of these days the master must return to Sutton Place.'

The manor house changed with the seasons; the moulded alabaster grew white and crisp in the spring time, the brickwork glowed rose as the warmth came back to the land.

And it was with Strawberry Hill gleaming in the same summer sunshine that the Earl and Countess Waldegrave were taken away to prison. 'The Waldegrave Outrage' had caught up with him at last.

The savage beating of the policeman had taken place before his marriage – during Derby Week – when he and the rowdy Waterford set had lurched back from Kingston Fair. But it had taken a year, while the press cried out for justice, for him to come to trial. The sentence of six months' detention in the Queen's Bench and a fine of £200 seemed only fitting.

Yet it had surprised many that Frances had decided to take up residence with her husband.

'She must be made of steel,' said Anne to Algernon, putting down her copy of *The Times*. 'I don't know whether I admire her or not.'

'You must,' he said, his wise face on. 'She is the most determined character of the age – of any age probably.'

'Yes, but Algy, that doesn't mean I have to *like* her.'

'No. *Do* you like her?'

'Definitely not. I think she is determined to climb high

and has used my sons – both my sons – as her ladder rungs. Unscrupulous little bitch.'

'None the less we must go and visit them tomorrow. And afterwards perhaps we might take a train into the country.'

'To anywhere in particular?'

'I thought perhaps Woking, Guildford way.' He looked decidedly like a retriever. 'There's a great house there I want to show you. It belongs to that young man John Joseph – Caroline's brother. I was very taken with it when I first saw it.'

Anne picked up her newspaper again. 'Very well, my dear. What is it called?'

'Sutton Place. I feel quite sure that you are going to like it, Anne.'

'No doubt, no doubt,' she said from the depths of *The Times*.

And with that they fell into silence and the manor house was temporarily forgotten.

16

The world had never been more beautiful, England had never been more beautiful, London had never been more beautiful! And the very act of getting on to a train – hissing and puffing and smelling like dragon's breath – had never been more exciting. Or, at least, that was how it seemed to Major John Wardlaw – smart as paint in his uniform of the 9th Lancers, his mistrust of the railway system finally at an end. In fact he leapt on to the York-bound train with such alacrity that he almost sent a charming young woman flying and she, all blushes, hardly knew where to put herself with such a dashing and rather attractively limping Army man escorting her to her seat.

But any hopes she might have had of striking up a conversation were dashed when, first of all, he picked up Charles Dickens's latest book – *The Old Curiosity Shop* – and then, tiring of that, stared out of the window as if his eyes could never get enough of the scurrying landscape and that spring morning in 1842.

'You have returned from abroad?' she ventured.

'Yes, three years in India. I had forgotten England in a way. Forgotten just how fresh the countryside can be.'

'It *is* very pretty,' she said, staring to where cherry trees formed an arch of snowflake under bridal white clouds in a bluebell sky.

'It's glorious,' he said. 'I hope I am never posted again.'

'Are you journeying far?'

'York – then on to Scarborough. To see my grandfather.'

But there the embryonic dialogue broke down and he

took to looking out of the window again, eating up the changing scenery, his eyes growing more and more entranced with every turn of the wheel. The young lady sighed, gave up and turned to a copy of *The Romany's Heirloom* which seemed to be more promising.

And so it was, with only the sound of churning wheels and spitting steam to disturb him, that Jackdaw took stock of himself. He looked back on his life, sitting there in that railway carriage, and thought of everything that had brought him to this point.

He remembered, first of all, his childhood; his fear of disappointing his father; his short leg and built-up shoes; his second sight.

Then he thought of the boy; that grasp of other languages within a week of study, comparable only to the lifting of a veil; the meeting with John Joseph and his instant love for him – not sexual but brotherly, worshipping a heroic figure. Next he remembered dawning manhood: the loss of innocence with the Misses Fitz; Mary Webbe Weston's infatuation and Mrs Trevelyan's hatred; Cloverella's gypsy mouth on his.

But most of all he remembered Horatia, each little vision of her cherished and taken out like a favourite jewel from a casket. And he thought finally of seeing her at Hastings – and making a fool of himself.

The train entered a tunnel and Jackdaw closed his eyes. He was at peace, his only regret that he had tried at one point to suppress his inherited gift. India – glad though he had been to leave it – had taught him much of the way of psychic development. It would take a lifetime to grasp the true concept of Raja Yoga – the royal path to perfection of the spirit – and he had studied for only three brief years. But he had entered, through its means, the threshold of awareness.

And now he knew that with this – this journey to

Yorkshire's wild cliffs – he would come one step nearer the truth. For not only his grandfather had sent for him but also his great-uncle and aunt. The three magic children of the house of FitzHoward – ancient as they were – were together in England and ready to receive him.

He thought back to what he knew of them, Pernel, Jacob and James; the grandchildren of the great rake Joseph Gage and direct descendants of Zachary Howard, son of the Duke of Norfolk by a Romany girl, and astrologer to the court of Henry VIII.

That they were vastly old was undeniably true. He calculated that Pernel, his great-aunt, must be ninety-four and his grandfather Jacob and his twin brother James at least ninety-one. That they had all been born in Spain, to which country Joseph Gage had gone as a mercenary when he had lost his fortune in the collapse of the Mississippi Company, was also true. What was not quite clear was how Jacob – a Colonel in the Spanish Army – had managed to get himself an English peerage from George III, when the family was known as a rabble bunch of Jacobites.

The accepted version was that he had brought about a trading treaty between England and Spain, but the truth remained shrouded in mystery. Whatever the reason, Jacob had settled in England – in Dorset – with another home set high on the cliffs above Scarborough. From time to time his brother and sister would make the unlikely journey from Castile to Yorkshire, sending for members of their family. Then the trio would disperse and there would be no further reunion for several years.

Jackdaw knew of their powers, had been told by his mother that they had inherited their grandmother Sibella's gift. And now he sat in the train, gazing out over England's sweetly changing face, and looking forward to the visit that lay ahead, and asking the magic trio what they knew of the mysteries of life.

Before making his way to Jacob Gage's gracious house, perched on the clifftop like a temple, Jackdaw strode out along the rocky path to where the ruins of a huge castle straddled a headland dividing two of the most magnificent bays in the world. Everywhere was sweep upon sweep of blue; vast skyscapes stretched down to a cobalt thread that lay along the horizon like a tinker's ribbon. Far away from the shore the white froth of the distant waves glinted azurine, and inland, where the beautiful sand curved like double horseshoes, drops of sparkling aqua played upon the sea's edge. There seemed no other colour anywhere, only the cornfield sweep of the beaches breaking the pattern, to show that the world had not vanished into the sky.

Jackdaw drew breath. In the vast concept in which he found himself standing it was not difficult to sense that unseen forces were at work and that soon he would learn of things too powerful for him to fully understand.

And so he changed for dinner that night in a state of considerable excitement. He had never seen the three magic children together – or if he had he could not remember the occasion – and when he entered the drawing room he stopped and stared in wonderment.

Pernel sat very upright in a high-backed chair, her hands clasped upon an ebony cane, her mass of white hair swept up on her head and adorned with three black ostrich feathers. On her fingers she wore jet rings and her dress was of black taffeta, the only colour about her being a diamond brooch as big as a plum. This seemed to have a life of its own, and gleamed and winked a thousand million rainbows without her so much as breathing.

She saw Jackdaw's fascinated gaze, chuckled and said,

'That was left to me by Joseph Gage. It once belonged to the Infanta. I see that you like it.'

Remembering himself Jackdaw bowed very deeply and then went forward to kiss her hand.

On either side of her chair stood the twin brothers – his grandfather and great-uncle. He had heard it said by Helen that when they were children only their mother Sarah could tell them apart, and now he could truly believe it. For his grandfather stood doubled before him. Two old men, white-haired but still with clear grape-bright blue eyes unwearied by time, gazed at him from identical faces.

'Grandfather?' he said uncertainly and the one on the left laughed.

'Jackdaw, how are you? You met your aunt and uncle when you were very small but I feel sure you do not remember, so let me introduce you again. Pernel my dear, may I present your great-nephew? James, this is Jackdaw.'

Jackdaw bowed once more and offered his arm to Pernel as the trio rose and went into the dining room. She walked very stiffly and slowly but never faltered in her steps. Like the twins' he found her eyes quite amazing, lucent as water and not wrinkled or pouched in any way.

'I see you like me as well as my brooch,' she said. 'You must come and visit me in Spain. I believe you are fluent in Spanish.'

'Yes I am.'

'Then we shall speak it at dinner tonight that we may be more private before the servants.'

And with that she switched languages effortlessly.

They spoke of everything – of the political scene; of Prince Albert's influence on the Queen; of the theatre; of the family and Violet's first baby. But they said not a word of the gift in which they knew they all shared until the meal was ended and they had withdrawn into Jacob's private sanctum. Here a servant drew the heavy velvet drapery and logs were stacked on a fire that had been lit against the sharp spring night.

Then, at last, Jacob said, 'Jackdaw, you have guessed already that we have summoned you for a purpose.'

He thought, 'So it's coming at last,' and prayed that he would be equal to them, that their old power would not overwhelm him utterly.

'Yes, Sir.'

'Then sit down, my child.'

'Here,' Pernel put in, 'on this stool by my feet.'

He did as he was told and felt his great-aunt lay her hand upon his shoulder. The contact was electric. A current passed through her fingers into his frame. He felt fear combine with his desire for knowledge.

Most unexpectedly then, Uncle James, instead of telling him anything, said, 'Speak to us of Karma.'

Jackdaw gaped at them. He had come to them for truth and now they were asking *him*.

His grandfather read his thoughts and put in, 'Wisdom must be shared, Jackdaw. That is the law of the universe. Tell us what you learned in India of death and life.'

'Sir, only that they are a continuing process – like the march of the seasons.'

'With many lives within the framework of the whole?'

'Yes. And each step, each part of the path, governed by Karmic law.'

'Tell us,' said Pernel.

In Jackdaw's eyes they were transformed. He did not know what mystery was at work in that room overlooking the great cliffs of Scarborough – that landscape surely scooped by a god – but to him the old people were young again. He sat in his grandfather's study with three contemporaries; all four of them black of hair and bright of eye and talking of the mystery of the universe as sister and brothers all. Quietly he spoke.

'Basically it is cause and effect. The Law of Karma is that we initiate events through our actions – for good or for evil – that we reap as we sow.'

'But it is far more complex than that, surely?'

'Yes,' said Jackdaw, 'it is very complex. It is believed that we are only now, in this life, living out causes that we set into motion in other lives. Do you agree with the theory, Grandfather?'

'To a certain extent. But I do not believe in inevitability. We are given a choice of courses – and therefore of end results as well.'

'I am sure that is so,' said Uncle James. 'There are two paths for everyone, all the time.'

'And the Life Force governs all?' This from Jackdaw.

'We are all part of it: we come from it, we return to it. It is omnipotent.'

'And those with our gift. What is their function?'

'To be allowed to glimpse, as through a tear in a blindfold, something of the pattern of destiny.'

They were all silent, thinking how complex were the stepping stones of existence, the only sound the roar of the wind that had come up suddenly from the sea.

'So why have you sent for me?' said Jackdaw slowly. 'What part is it you wish me to play?'

They all turned to look at him simultaneously, three pairs of eyes regarding him unblinkingly.

Then Jacob Gage said quietly, 'It is not yet the right time for you to seek your soulmate.'

'What?' He looked at them, his jaw dropping.

'We know about her,' said Pernel. 'You have dreamed of her always and you have seen her only once.'

Her nephew's astonished silence spoke for him, and his

grandfather went on, 'If you find her now – and she is not far away – another soul will never see the truth. It will perish not knowing fulfilment.'

Jackdaw remained silent and Jacob went on, 'Somebody close to you – it is not meant at this time that you know who it is – is condemned by fate. But it is your part to assist his earthly development. It is destined, Jackdaw, that you take no positive action to find the woman you love. All I can do is assure you that she *will* come to you when it is the right time for her to do so.'

An unenlightened young man – a young man brought up, as Jackdaw had been, in the rough and tumble of the British Army – might have scoffed at this, might have come out with silly statements about his life and to Hell with the rest. But Jackdaw listened carefully.

'So I must let what will be, be?'

'That is the right choice for you at present.'

'I shall do what is decreed.' He bowed to his three magic relatives and laughed suddenly, breaking the mood. His great-aunt saw him through a woman's eyes and thought how attractive he was. And they all drew even closer together, that the descendants of Dr Zachary might speak of secrets until the dawn had come up over the wild bays of Scarborough, streaking the blue void with strands of coral and flame.

'I have here, ladies and gentlemen, the silver bell carved with masks with which Pope Clement VII cursed the caterpillars. Now what am I offered for this rarity? Do I hear fifty pounds? Fifty pounds yes. Sixty pounds? Seventy pounds? Thank you, Madam . . .'

The auctioneer's voice slipped into its familiar drawl as hands popped up like corks and the twentieth day of 'the Most distinguished Gem that has ever Adorned the Annals of Auctions' commenced with a flourish. The

307

Gallery in Strawberry Hill had been a saleroom for over two weeks now, while Horace Walpole's collection went under the hammer amidst a blaze of strong reaction both in the press and privately.

Anne thought it quite dreadful, a blow to the Waldegrave honour, but George had simply shrugged his shoulders. He had been released from prison the previous November, his send-off tumultuous, his home-coming greeted with cheering and fireworks. And then he had announced his intention of selling up the treasured collection, leaving Strawberry Hill and going abroad. By his side stood Frances, getting prettier and prettier and cleverer and cleverer.

'*She's* behind it!' Anne had said furiously to Algernon. 'That minx, that scheming witch. What does she care about her heritage? Why, her father sold pencils outside the synagogue to keep himself from starving. What price the English aristocracy to her?'

Algy's brow had furrowed like a mastiff's.

'You must be careful what you say, my dear. There are many who would resent that remark.'

'I can't help that.' Anne's voice had broken in a sob. 'Since Frances Braham's arrival on the scene there has been nothing but trouble. J.J.'s death, George's imprisonment – and now this!'

Algy pondered the wisdom of pointing out that Frances had hardly been responsible for the first two, but decided against it after a glance at Anne's face. Instead he said, very mildly, '*The Times* declares that the collection is worthless.'

And indeed it had. Not only that. Parodies of the catalogue – which had sold out eight editions – were changing hands amidst much jocularity, offering, as it did, such items as a pimple from the nose of Oliver Cromwell, a pip from the Garden of Eden's apple and the bridge of the fiddle which Nero had scraped whilst Rome burned.

Now Anne, who had had enough of all of it, rounded on him.

'Very easy for a newspaper to say. Our kinsman Horace Walpole made it his lifetime's work.'

And she had been proud, when she had been mistress of Strawberry Hill, to show her visitors the curious accumulation of pictures, portraits, watercolours, gems, swords, urns, statues, china, vases, books, manuscripts, muskets, medals, coins, tapestries, rings, clocks – in fact all the sundry bric-à-brac of a compulsive hoarder's obsession.

But everything had not been rubbish and to dismiss the collection, as *The Times* had done, was both silly and unfair. For amidst the rummage could be found Holbein's portrait of Katharine of Aragon; Cardinal Wolsey's red hat; a missal with miniatures by Raphael; a contemporary bust of Caligula; Alexander Pope's copy of Homer; and rare and precious manuscripts.

And now the sale was into its third week – with a fourth envisaged – and 25,000 people had already attended. The British Museum had bid for the finest manuscripts, coins and prints, and Buckingham Palace itself had acquired the collection of tracts.

'Ladies and gentlemen,' said Mr George Robins, the auctioneer from Covent Garden, 'I have here a fan of ostrich feathers, the base being filled with butterfly wings. It is said that this fan once belonged to the Empress of Russia and was given to the Lady Laura Waldegrave by an unknown admirer, supposedly a Venetian nobleman. The fan is not part of Walpole's collection as such but was added to it after the death of Lady Laura. Now, do I hear fifty pounds?'

'Yes,' said Anne, who was sitting defiantly in the front row, clutching her catalogue in a kid-gloved hand.

'Fifty pounds from the Dowager Countess Waldegrave. Any advance? Thank you, Sir.'

The bidding had started in earnest and Frances and George, unobserved at the back of the Gallery, stood stock still. Outside a carriage waited to take them to Dover, for tonight they were crossing to France and a new life. They had already made £20,000 from the sale of their kinsman's memorabilia and Mr Robins believed that the sum realized might well reach £35,000. And as far as George was concerned his ancestral home could fall to the ground, for he had paid off the worst of his debts, had married his brother's widow, and there was nothing left for him in England.

He half turned his back now but Frances pulled him round.

'Your mother is going to be beaten,' she whispered. 'Her opponent represents a private collector, and will go to two hundred pounds.'

'Let Mr Hicks buy it for her then.'

'George, how can you be so cruel? We are unpopular enough as it is.'

'Any advance on two hundred pounds?' said Mr Robins. 'Do I hear two hundred and ten pounds? No? For the first time then, at two hundred pounds, the fan of Lady Laura Waldegrave. For the . . .'

'Two hundred and ten pounds,' said Frances clearly.

'Two hundred and ten pounds to the Countess Waldegrave. Any advance on that? Do I hear any advance?'

Four heads turned and Frances found herself the subject of four, quite different, angry glances: Anne's haughty and proud, telling Frances, with a look, that she was a parvenu little Jew; Mr Hicks's canine and snarling; Horatia's glacial, flashing like emeralds on ice; Ida Anna's

310

insolent and cheeky, her bootbutton gaze hard as nails as she actually mouthed the word 'Bitch'.

'No? Then for the first time, going at two hundred and ten pounds . . .'

Frances saw Mr Hicks go to raise his arm and the Dowager Countess lay her gloved hand upon it and shake her head.

'. . . sold to the Countess Waldegrave. The next item . . .'

But the Hicks family was not staying for any more. With a mighty swish of her skirt Anne had risen from her gilt chair and was making her way to the door, past the very spot where her husband had died at her feet. They drew level with Frances and George, who stood trapped in the entrance, unable to move without rudeness bordering on insult.

Anne's chin went into the air at an angle of ninety degrees and it seemed almost as if she would cut her son and daughter-in-law had not Mr Hicks barked, 'Anne, goodbyes are in order, I think.'

For the first time George felt a sneaking admiration for the stepfather he considered an absolute bumbling idiot, and he made him a small bow.

'Goodbye, Sir.'

'Goodbye, my Lord.' Algy was always terribly formal with George.

'Goodbye, Mother.'

Anne's chin lowered again and she gave her son a very penetrating glance from eyes that were still a rare shade of blue.

'Goodbye George. Goodbye Frances. I hope that you will find happiness in Europe.'

She stood very straight and proud as she said this and the atmosphere was knife-like. George caught himself wishing that things could have been different, that he could have been different, that he had not enjoyed drinking and gambling and fighting quite as much as he did. But, most of all, he wished that he had not loved his brother's widow so desperately that he had permanently blacked his name in England by an illegal marriage to her.

'I hope that you will be happy too,' he said inadequately.

Horatia stepped forward looking very beautiful in a simple summer dress of muslin.

'Will we hear from you?' she asked.

'Yes, we will write,' said Frances. She added very softly indeed, 'I bought that fan for your mother. Will you see that she gets it on her birthday?'

Unsaid thoughts hung between them; thoughts of each other's beauty and wit, thoughts of whether they could ever really like one another, thoughts that one of them had already had two husbands and the other none at all.

Horatia brushed her cool lips against Frances's cheek. 'Thank you,' she whispered.

'Well I,' said Ida, 'will be glad to see the back of you both.'

'How dare you!' shouted her mother furiously, because it was very much what she would like to have said herself. 'It is not your place to speak like that. I've a mind to take the strap to you.'

'Then do so. It would be worth it just to have seen *her* face.'

'Come on, Frances,' said George, 'this is no place for us.'

She smiled, a trifle wistfully.

'No,' she said, 'I don't think it is.'

And with that she turned and got into the waiting carriage without a backward glance. As George jumped in beside her and the coachman cracked his whip, the

312

auctioneer's voice could be heard from inside Strawberry Hill: 'Going, going, gone.'

'Oh dear,' sighed Anne, 'nothing will ever be the same again. Poor Strawberry Hill, poor Sutton Place. Is it the fate of both of them to be ruined?'

'I doubt it,' said Mr Hicks jollily. 'Something usually turns up.'

Despite the fact that it was six o'clock in the morning and Vienna was still suffused with that roseate glow brought only by the first hour of summer daylight, the entire population seemed to be on the move. Carriages bustled, street-cleaning carts sprayed, horsemen rode past and large and old-fashioned coaches trundled busily towards the city gates. Flower girls thronged everywhere, offering their fresh-picked blooms to carriage folk and riders alike, and cheeking the newspaper boys who sold their wares with cheerful shouts.

And the general flow of all this equipage and excitement was to the royal palace itself – the Schönbrunn – which stood, like Versailles, outside the city, backed by the hills and fronted by an enormous courtyard, in the centre of which a great fountain leapt in a million rainbows towards the sun.

For today was one of great celebration – the Emperor's official birthday. In fact even now, even as everyone – all washed and shining and smart – made their way to the Investiture that began the proceedings, a twenty-one-gun salute was fired to wake those Viennese who were still in their beds.

All the soldiers – including those members of the 3rd Light Dragoons who were to receive an honour – rode together. And as these military men crashed into the vast court before the palace, their horses' hooves echoing and re-echoing a million times, there had never been such a dazzle and sparkle of breastplate, such a jingling and ringing of spur, such a rattle of sword hilt, on such a fine summer morning. It was a sight to soften the most cynical heart, to see the Emperor's troops come to his palace in their pride and glory, and all aglow in the early sunshine.

In their midst – and picked only for their extreme loyalty to the Empire – rode the English soldiers of fortune, that band of Catholic gentlemen who had chosen a foreign Army where they might make a career for themselves rather than the frustrations of English military life. And amongst them, handsome, world-weary, but still fractionally moved by the greatness of the occasion, rode Captain John Joseph Webbe Weston to receive the honour of Knight of the Order of Malta for his part in keeping the uneasy country in a state of peace.

He was in a strange mood, half of him elated and another half quite miserable and wretched that he had absolutely no one of his own to sit in the gallery of the Throne Room and watch him be dubbed by ancient sword. He felt a million miles from home and lonely as a gypsy.

As always, when he thought of England, his thoughts went to Marguerite and then veered straight off again. It had been a strange thing but more and more – noticeably since his last leave at home – he had found himself hardly able to remember what she looked like. And more and more strongly had come to him the thought that perhaps he had been obsessed by the *idea* of her rather than by her herself.

Another strange thing had been the way Lady Horatia Waldegrave kept coming into his mind. He had found himself more than once – in fact very frequently – picturing her as she had dropped on one knee before him and proposed marriage. Of course, he had treated it as a

314

joke. The only thing to do in the circumstances. But none the less . . .

He caught himself – even here, even outside this magnificent palace the area of which covered a square mile – thinking about her; remembering the way her hair glowed; recalling her little habit of wrinkling up her nose when she was in earnest; the way her eyes sparkled like gem stones, like lake water, like . . .

'Captain Webbe Watson?'

He started violently and found himself looking down into the face of his Austrian sergeant.

'Yes Lutz?'

'Time to dismount, Sir. The procession is forming up. I'll take your horse, Sir.'

'Very good.'

John Joseph swung out of the saddle and saw that the rest of his fellow officers were already marching to the end of a mighty queue – in which stood at least eight hundred people – stretching from the doors of the Schönbrunn right across the courtyard and into the distance. At its head were Princes, at its foot foreigners, all of them intent on seeing the crazy Emperor celebrate his anniversary and perform his duties as best he could.

'If only *she* were here,' thought John Joseph – but his mental picture of Marguerite, swaying through the crowd beneath her pink parasol, faded. Try as he would he could only picture Horry, dressed in green and smiling like a mermaid.

It was two hours before the huge doors finally closed behind the last man, and the hundreds of feet had walked the quarter-mile corridor and found their way into the Throne Room. Everywhere, as they went, were flowers and palm trees; reflecting in the thousand mirrors, woven into the arches and round the pillars, hanging in garlands from the balconies. John Joseph, who had been in the palace many times on duty, had never seen it more festive and could not help but wonder what caprice had taken the Emperor today.

That the monarch suffered from epilepsy was, the Captain knew, without doubt; that he was actually idiotic was dubious. The best that could be said was that intellectually Ferdinand was simple, the worst that he was raving mad. At first his fitness to succeed his father had been questioned, and now Prince Metternich – who had supported the Emperor's succession at the time – virtually ruled Austria and Hungary through what was, in practice, a council of regency.

Poor child-like Ferdinand. He could write his name only with difficulty and yet he was the figurehead to an Empire rivalled by that of Britain alone. While his ministers decided the fate of millions of subjects, he played in the gardens of his palaces. But it was for his wife, the unsuspecting Princess Anna Caroline of Savoy, that John Joseph felt far more sorry.

The Emperor was obviously quite incapable of consummating the marriage. Terrible tales of the wedding night were told to this day, reminding the Captain of the legend of the curse of Sutton Place – of the tortured and unconsummated love between King Edward the Confessor and his bride Edith.

'What a terrible fate,' John Joseph thought – and unbidden came the idea that it was high time he married and produced a son, followed by the notion that he would only be siring another heir to the curse. He wondered if this was the way it had manifested on him – by forcing him into the role of self-imposed exile.

But further melancholy thoughts of this nature were arrested by a wild fanfare of trumpets. Everyone rose to his feet – the recipients of honours from small gilt chairs placed in the body of the Throne Room, the onlookers in

316

the balcony above. This was followed by a great drum roll and, glancing up, John Joseph saw that Maestro Strauss had been called to the palace to conduct the music for today's ceremony: the black hair and fiery eyes that had earned him the nickname the Moor just visible over the railed musicians' gallery. At a passionate move of Strauss's arms the orchestra launched into the national anthem and it was to this accompaniment that the Emperor made his entrance.

The reason for the palm trees was immediately obvious, for with his dress uniform – which he had obviously been forced to wear – he carried a pith helmet of the type worn in Africa. This, as soon as the music had ceased playing, he solemnly put on his head. John Joseph felt the hysteria of sheer tension come upon him and was quite sure that he would crack with laughter if he so much as caught anyone's glance. He gazed fixedly at the toes of his boots, the bright polish reflecting his moustache and his eyes creasing at the corners. For the third time that morning he thought of Horatia and was only thankful that she was *not* there, for he would never have been able to resist her impish grin.

'My subjects,' said the Emperor, 'my Princes, my Dukes, my toy soldiers – sit down if you will.'

He gave them a smile totally without malice. For all his stupidity he was perfectly harmless and had earned himself the nickname of 'the Kindly'.

Now he said, 'Let my birthday – let *all* my birthdays – begin.'

And with that Maestro Strauss struck up a waltz.

The Investiture took four hours, the Emperor constantly wandering off the dais on which the thrones were raised. Sometimes he would vanish for as much as ten minutes and come back with a mouth full of biscuits. At other times the interval would be shorter – presumably

317

he was relieving himself – and he would trot back looking more cheerful. Meanwhile the poor recipients, without the benefit of such luxuries, suffered manfully and could hardly await their call to the ante-room in which they were allowed to sit just before they received their honour.

'My God,' said Wingfield, a fellow English officer, coming back from the jakes, 'I thought I was going to burst. How did you fare, Webbe Weston?'

'I tried mathematical problems to keep my mind off it. What an ordeal!'

'I suppose it's worth it. Your family here to watch?'

'No, they're all in England. Yours?'

'My wife lives here. We're in the married quarters. Dashed comfortable. I suppose you'll be trying them some day.'

'Yes,' said John Joseph slowly, 'I suppose so.'

But it was his call. From the doorway the major domo was shouting out, 'Captain John Joseph Webbe Weston of the 3rd Light Dragoons, Your Majesty.'

John Joseph drew himself up to full height, put his shoulders back and walked with measured tread – every inch an Englishman and proud of it – to the foot of the crazy old Emperor's throne.

'Well, my boy,' said Ferdinand, ignoring the aide-de-camp who was whispering in his ear, 'and what are you here for, eh?'

'I am to receive the Knighthood of the Order of Malta, Your Majesty.'

'Are you? Well, well! And what have you done to deserve that?'

'I have been serving with the occupying force in Cracau, Sir, and before that in Pesth.'

'Pesth? Is that across the Danube from Buda?'

'Yes, Sir.'

The Emperor looked delighted, as if he had just been given top marks in a geography examination.

'You see, I know more than they think.'

'Yes, Sir.'

'You remind me of a tin soldier I have. I am very fond of my English soldiers, you know. Will you come and play battles with me?'

John Joseph looked up into the simpleton's kind blue eyes. He remembered his own little regiment, with which he had played at Sutton Place. He thought of Jackdaw, of his sister Mary, of all the people with whom endless games of Battle and Beat Boney had been executed.

'I should enjoy that, Your Majesty.'

'Would you? Would you really? A wistful expression crossed the Emperor's face. 'But I don't suppose they'll let you. Will you try to ignore them?'

'I won't listen,' said the Captain. 'I shall come if I may, Sir.'

'Then tonight. After the birthday ball. Is that agreed?'

'It is,' answered John Joseph – and for no reason kissed the warm old hand that was extended towards him.

'For that I shall knight you.'

And with that mad Emperor Ferdinand of Austria and Hungary raised the sword of state, gasping as he did so, tapped John Joseph on both shoulders and said, 'Arise a Knight of Malta, my little English soldier.'

Then he gave a charming smile – and winked one of his eyes.

Part Two

17

Time blurred, slipped sideways and passed. Five whole years went by – for some fast, scampering times; always Christmas, always Easter, always New Year; for others the monotony of week in, week out, dragging like a leaden weight. Yet it was the same time-span for them all. And that was part of the mystery; some saw life as rushing along, others felt it a daily monotony of never-ending length.

But to the two inanimate objects so deeply involved in the link between the Webbe Westons, the Waldegraves and the Wardlaws, change came gradually. Sutton Place – so beautiful and proud when Richard Weston laid a great carpet beneath the feet of Henry VIII – slipped with each melancholy falling brick into shabbiness. While Strawberry Hill – Horace Walpole's little jewel – grew wretchedly more dilapidated and deserted. 'A place intrinsically more paltry does not exist' was the opinion of a writer on a tour of the Thames in 1845.

But what of the people? They whose lives had become joined within the boundaries of destiny? How had they fared in five years? Had they moved any nearer to the places they must adopt before End Game?

Of the Webbe Westons, small change. John Joseph serving his adopted country like a true soldier; not posing too many questions, obeying orders, turning his brain into a machine, not asking his soul about the rights of another's death put into his hands. Of the girls – Mary, Matilda, Caroline – children, children, children. Yet Mary was too bossy, Matilda too sensitive, Caroline too clever, to become mere reproductive machines with no thoughts of their own.

And of the Wardlaws, what? Helen and the General – now that deep middle age lay upon them both – were becoming as one. She always the adored, the more aloof, the brighter, had at last seen the boring and conventional man for what he really was: kind, attentive, prepared to die for her instantly should the order be given. With the change of her life, she mellowed. Began to love as she never had before. And at last he was rewarded for the years of worship and felt himself totally at one with her; the children all gone, only he and she to stare out of the window of 5 Pelham Crescent into the wild sweet blue of an evening seascape.

And of Rob, Jackdaw, Violet? The first named to rise ever upward in the British Army, to become a family man and know the joy of stability. For Jackdaw, the wonder of enlightenment to set against the nagging of his heart. He had been patient for five years yet with no sign of the crystal beauty, the wondrous joy, that only Horatia could bring. And for little Violet – motherhood again. But this time with a closed mind in its wake. Nothing for her but warm pink bodies, nurseries with night lights, waiting for a husband to come home. No thought, no quest – but just as happy for all that.

But finally what of the Waldegraves – the Earls of Strawberry Hill – who had chosen to fly in convention's face and live their lives to each full second, regardless of public opinion? How had they fared in the sweep of Fate's avenue?

Of Anne, the Dowager Countess, and Mr Hicks – family happiness. He, who had never asked anything of life except a good Walk and a pat upon his willing head, had found contentment with that brittle little lady who had overcome a bastard child, a shot-gun wedding, a naughty husband, two infant deaths, the death of two adult sons – for George had recently died, leaving Frances a widow again – and the ruin of the home she had once loved.

And her three beautiful daughters? Annette of the moonstone gaze delighted in producing children for Archibald Money; delighted in her status as Colonel's lady; delighted in getting away from all the mad, bad days and living now in a tidy house with a tidy mind.

And of beautiful Horatia, the jewel of her generation? Had she married well and wisely, without thought or care for the dictates of her true heart? No, of course not. She preferred to sit, warm as a sun rose, and wait for the moment when either her great love would come to her or she would forget all about him and find that some other young man was as sweet and loving as she.

And that is how they were all positioned when destiny called the tune once more. When the wheel of fortune opened up to them the paths that each might follow.

The first thing to happen was the return of John Joseph – who had not been on leave to England for five years, so bad was the situation in the Empire. The next was that Frances – funny little half-Jewish Frances – walked round the ruinous Strawberry Hill and thought, 'I cannot, I *must* not let this fall to the ground.' The third was that Horatia turned down her latest proposal of marriage. So there they were – ready.

And again, the first to act was John Joseph. He got on a train bound from Dover to London and then boarded another train to Woking. It was Sunday morning and, without even so much as leaving his baggage in a nearby hotel, he took a hansom cab to St John's Church. There he sat in the back pew watching for the arrival of Lady Dawe.

Cloverella, forewarned of his visit by letter, had, that

very morning, drawn the last hair from the waxen heart of his image, and now sat back to await events, Jay playing at her feet.

Horatia, meanwhile, got up on the same day, had a small Sunday breakfast and went walking with Ida Anna – she whose bootbutton gaze had grown sharper with every passing year – in the lush green splendour of St James's Park. And after a while, walking correctly along beneath their shady, wide-brimmed bonnets, the sisters were caught up by their mother and stepfather. Then the quartet took a leisurely walk – there being plenty of time before luncheon – to the home of Caroline and Francis Hicks. It was a serene day. It was warm April, it was 1847. The young Queen – now a happily married mother of five children – ruled a Britain that had never been greater, never basked in greater glory of Empire, of strength, of everyone in their accorded place. To them it seemed like paradise – except for the aching of Horatia's heart.

Yet over luncheon Caroline said, 'He's back, you know. My brother, John Joseph. After a five-year tour of duty. What a time away!'

Anne asked, 'Will he stay here now?

And Caroline answered, 'No, he sees no future for himself unless he remains in the Austrian service. Poor John Joseph, he is trying so hard to bring the property round.'

At that Mr Hicks had boomed, 'I love Sutton Place. I really do. I wouldn't mind living there, you know.'

There had been one of those tiny, very important, frozen silences and then Francis had said, 'Why don't you? I believe it's up for leasing at the moment. I think that would be a splendid idea.'

Algy had puffed and said, 'What about it, Anne?'

And very surprisingly she had answered, 'I am bored

with London and close quarters. Why don't you investigate, my dear?'

Another little wheel had just started to circle in infinity.

At that very same moment – service being late in St John's – John Joseph was watching Marguerite Dawe, the woman who had been his *idée fixe* for what seemed like for ever, taking her place in the family pew. She was a widow again, dressed from head to foot in black taffeta, with a feathered black hat swathed over one eye. She was as beautiful as always, though time had taken its natural toll with a fine tracery of lacy lines now clearly visible on her cheeks and at her eyes. Beside her sat a boy of ten or eleven, the younger Lord Dawe. The boy sired by the coachman if Mary's gossip were to be believed. But if his father were truly base-born, nothing of it showed in him. He sat ramrod straight, having handed his mother into her seat, his eyes to the front, his cap upon his knees. Every last inch of him breathing aristocracy and breeding. He was an admirable young person.

John Joseph sat quite still and looked at the two of them – his mistress and her fair-haired son. And it was then that he knew – with an awful lurch in his stomach which told him an era had just ended – that he had been mistaken. That he had wasted twelve years of his life in a dream; that Marguerite meant nothing to him – and never had. That lust had blinded his eyes and he – foolish, idiotic, unrelinquishing he – had never been in love at all.

He rose to sing a hymn with legs that were weak beneath him. He felt then that he was incapable of emotion, that he was an empty vessel only able to sound in the theatre of war, merely capable of taking hired women. His soul plunged into desolation, there in God's house. He loathed himself, he abhorred the wasted years – and then Marguerite very slowly turned to look at him.

Whether she had recognized something of that light

baritone voice singing behind her, whether she instinctively felt his presence, he was never to know. All he could say was that they were suddenly in full eye contact, pupil staring into pupil, with no pretence at manners or averted gaze. Quite openly and boldly, there in church, they stared one another out.

After an age, in which he grew cold as death and she – with all her years of training – masked her feelings, she allowed a faint smile to hover round her lips. He gaped at her all the more. Where was his response? Had he been frozen to the marrow? A million questions danced in his brain as he realized he was indifferent to whether she laughed or frowned, lived or died. Feeling himself a man of straw he made her a formal bow, then turned where he was and – with the congregation in full voice looking at him as if he had just turned lunatic – strode from the place without looking back.

He had wasted his life on a falsehood. He had as much sense as that sweet mad Emperor with whom he played war games. Knowing what he must do, John Joseph got into the cab that still waited at the church gate and directed the driver to Woking station.

In the gentle afternoon that followed the tearful April morning Horatia strolled with her family back to Duke Street, half listening to her mother and stepfather discussing – with growing excitement and belief – the possibility of renting the manor house in Surrey that John Joseph once had told her was cursed. But she could not concentrate on anything – not their excited talk, nor the blueness of the sky, nor the children playing in the park, nor the military men in their scarlet-and-golds. All she could think of was one soldier in particular. For the man who had captured her wild little heart was back in England.

She knew – for sure and without any gypsy gift – that

he would come and see her. Felt she still had a chance of his loving her, for surely Caroline would have said something had he been betrothed or his affections engaged elsewhere. And this made her so happy, so bright, that she ran home ahead of the others and arrived glowing and panting to whirl in past the butler and straight into her mother's reception room, hardly noticing the card that lay on the silver tray in the hall.

That John Joseph was sitting there, very correct and upright, his hands resting on the hilt of his sword, tilted straight before him, was in some ways the biggest shock she had ever had – and in others no surprise at all. He stood up and bowed as she came in, staring at her as if he had never seen her before.

'Lady Horatia,' he said. 'I was just passing and thought I would present my compliments.'

The lie was transparent, hanging in the room about his head.

'Oh,' she said, feeling an utter fool, 'oh! My goodness, I can't think it has really been five years. You haven't changed.'

'*You* have,' he said. 'I did not think that you could grow more beautiful – but I was wrong.'

There was a silence during which they regarded one another properly for the very first time. She saw him – as it were – stripped. Gone the military fineness and bravura and in their place, visibly, a saddish man, a man who had been driven into situations he did not relish. But also a determined man. For there was a look in John Joseph's eye that Horatia had never seen before. A look that excited her beyond words.

He saw beauty – and rare beauty at that. A beauty made possible by the illumination from within. For Horatia had taken the best of the Waldegraves – their brand

of courage, their lack of convention, their scorn of hypocrisy – and had developed into an unusual woman; a
woman who could be fiercely loyal to those she liked on
one hand, and yet, on the other, would not bother to
cross the room to speak if she did not.

The pause continued until John Joseph said eventually,
'You know why I am here, don't you?'

She pulled her bonnet from her head and threw it on
to a chair, one of the blue ribbons trailing for a moment
between her fingers.

She did not answer him directly but said instead, 'I had
not quite thought it would be like this. I imagined there
would be courtship, lovemaking even.'

'I don't have time,' he said bluntly. 'I have eight weeks
in England – and that only granted because I have served
five years without leave long enough to return home.'

Outside a blackbird trilled a song of springtime
revisited.

'This is not very romantic,' said Horatia – and then
suddenly laughed. The day seemed to grow even brighter
and, after a moment, John Joseph found he had to smile.

'You wretch,' he said, 'you haven't changed a bit.'

'Why are you not on one knee?' she answered. 'I knelt
for you.'

In the hall could be heard the sound of the butler
opening the front door to Lady Waldegrave, Mr Hicks
and Ida Anna.

'May I take you to dine tonight?' John Joseph said
without moving. 'Perhaps your Mama will permit now
that we are engaged to be married.'

'This,' said Horatia, 'is quite the worst proposal I have
ever endured. I have a very strong mind to say no – and
be damned to the fact that I love you so much.'

The words thrilled him, inadequate character that he
felt himself to be.

'Do you love me?' he said. 'Like that? Very much?'

'You know I do. Why, I would die in battle for you.'

The words had a chilling ring, reminding him suddenly and vividly of his childhood dream.

'Do *you* love *me*?' she asked.

He looked at her and knew that he did not, knew that he was incapable of anything more than self-delusion. For twelve years he had yearned for Marguerite – only to find cold ashes in his mouth. He was aware now, and terribly so, that such powerful emotion was beyond him.

He hesitated in his reply and was saved by the opening of the door. The Dowager Countess stood framed in the opening, her astonished face gazing at them. John Joseph forestalled anything sharp she might have had to say by clicking his heels and giving an extremely formal bow.

'Madam,' he said, 'I have come here to pay my addresses to the Lady Horatia. I wonder whether I might speak to you and Mr Hicks privately.'

'Good gracious,' said Anne, totally knocked off her balance and behaving with utter lack of decorum. 'Are you proposing to my daughter?'

John Joseph looked faintly surprised at this uninhibited response but answered, 'Yes, Lady Waldegrave, I am.'

'Well, thank goodness for that,' said Anne roundly. 'The little wretch has been pining for you for years. I quite thought I was going to have a fully fledged spinster on my hands.'

And with those words the betrothal of John Joseph Webbe Weston and Lady Horatia Waldegrave was formally begun.

That night they were allowed to go out alone, despite the rigid rule of chaperoning. Mr Hicks – leaping about enthusiastically – had opened champagne and lent them his smartest carriage, and then they were given permission to go to the theatre and follow this with dinner, providing that Horatia was returned home by midnight. In view of everything John Joseph considered the arrangement lenient.

'It is only that they fear I will turn into a pumpkin should twelve o'clock strike,' said Horatia, and laughed, leaning back against the plush upholstery of the brougham.

'And will you?'

'Very probably.'

Her profile was lit momentarily by a street lamp as she said this and John Joseph revelled, then, in his new-found position.

'You're delightful, Horatia,' he said, and raised her fingers to his lips.

She had chosen apple green for her betrothal night, the material swished and frilled into a full skirt, the bodice swathed tightly over her high and pretty breasts. And as she moved a musky scent came from her hair and skin, filling his senses with old familiar urges. He slipped his arm round her waist, letting his hand cup – just for a second – her bosom.

'I'm innocent,' she said in the darkness, 'quite.'

'I had hoped so.'

'Don't be predictable,' came the sharp retort. 'It is merely that nobody asked me – and anyway I have had scant opportunity. My brothers – poor dead things. . .' her voice went very quiet but after a moment regained its usual tone '. . . sowed wild oats everywhere, but we girls were watched like crown jewels.'

'That is how it should be.'

He was being deliberately pompous and he smiled to himself. She nudged him crossly.

'I am not so sure that we will make a match,' she said.

'Horry, I am teasing you. You are a scamp. A prim

woman would not do for me, for how would she put up with life in a foreign country, serving a foreign Emperor?' He added as an afterthought, 'Do you speak German?'

'Not a word – but I shall quickly learn.' She paused, then said, 'You won't leave me behind when you go to the front, will you?'

'There is no front at the moment – there is no war. But no, you shall accompany me when I go to the garrison towns. That is if you wish. Many Army wives prefer to remain behind in Vienna where there are shops and theatres and Johann Strauss.'

'I shall go with you. I do not see much point in marrying you if I stay away.'

'And you really do want to? Marry me, that is.'

She turned into his arms for answer. They had never kissed before, not even a formal greeting on the cheek, and John Joseph was surprised by the way she parted her lips beneath his. She was a natural mistress, a courtesan, a wanton.

She clung to him breathlessly as their mouths drew apart, a little afraid of what she had discovered in herself.

'Do you love me?' she asked. 'You did not answer before.'

Once again he hesitated.

'I sense that you do not.'

'Horatia, to be blunt, I am not sure what love really is. I thought I knew, until recently. But now I realize I know nothing. Only that there is something lacking in me.'

'But you have mistresses.'

It was a statement, that was all. There was no hint of criticism in her voice or attitude.

'How did you know that?'

'By the way you hold me. John Joseph, can I ask you one thing?'

'What is it?'

'Do you intend to be faithful to me – love or no love?'

'Yes,' he answered, 'utterly. There is no reason for marriage otherwise.'

'Then in that case I will teach you to love me by some daring plan.'

He laughed. 'I would put nothing past you,' he said.

The letter, in handwriting simultaneously familiar and strange, was brought by Jackdaw's batman just as the Major was hurrying from his room to attend Church parade and was left, lying on a silver tray until the following day. It was with both shock and delight, therefore, that he saw at breakfast that John Joseph was not only to be married but wanted him to act as best man.

'. . . a wonderful girl,' he read, 'whom I have known slightly for some years. She is actually a connection of Caroline's through marriage.'

No name given, Jackdaw noticed – and felt a first faint prick of apprehension.

'So,' he read on, 'it would be a great privilege and pleasure if you could see your way to acting as my best man. Because of the shortness of my leave the wedding will take place three weeks from now, on Friday, May 17 . . .'

Why did that date strike a chord?

'. . . and my fiancée and I . . .' still no name '. . . will be staying in Guildford with my mother to establish residency. There is to be a Catholic ceremony in the Chapel at Sutton Place, as well as an Anglican at St Nicholas. If you could, therefore, address your reply to St Catherine's Hill, Guildford, I would be most obliged.'

'Well, well, well,' Jackdaw thought, 'after all this time. I wonder what finally persuaded him away from Lady Dawe.'

Despite his pleasure something was amiss, he knew it.

And yet even his heightened perception could not – or would not – tell him what it was. He picked up the letter again.

'. . . great family reunion. I have written to your parents and to Rob and Violet to invite them. I intend to use the Great Hall in Sutton Place for the breakfast. Also the house itself as a place for overnight guests, so if you can get a short leave, so much the better. With very great affection, Your friend, John Joseph.'

So his boyhood hero was to become a married man. And Sutton Place, which had known so many brides and grooms in its long and strange history, was to see the sole heir – the last of the Webbe Westons – take his first step to continuing the line.

Jackdaw pushed the remainder of his breakfast aside and lit a cigar – a luxury he occasionally allowed himself at this hour of the day. Leaning back in his chair he began to puzzle out why the date May 17 seemed significant. And then it came to him in a flash – the recurring date! The date when greatest evil fell on the house of Weston and its kin. John Joseph himself had told him the story years ago. On May 17, 1521, Sir Richard Weston had been granted the Manor of Sutton by Henry VIII and had gone on to build the mansion house; on May 17, 1536, his son Francis had been executed for high treason, accused of adultery with Queen Anne Boleyn; on May 17, 1754, the Young Pretender had come to Sutton Place and taken Melior Mary Weston on the first step to madness. It was a sinister pattern.

He wondered if his friend realized and knew at once that he did not. The date had been picked in haste, probably the day when the ministers of both Catholic and Anglican churches could perform the ceremony. Then Jackdaw thought about warning him. And promptly realized how foolish he would sound. Best to remain silent.

He went to his desk, picked up a pen and wrote in a bold, flowing hand.

My dear Friend,

May I say how honoured and delighted I shall be to act as your best man. It seems so many years since I have seen you but I cannot think of a more splendid way of meeting again. I look forward not only to the grand family reunion but to being presented to your bride. (I have to be formal as you omitted to tell me her name.)

I shall arrive in Guildford on May 16, and after taking a room at The Angel will come straight to St Catherine's Hill to receive your instructions. Until then be assured of my every good wish to you both.

Yours,

Jackdaw.

He sealed the envelope and rang for his batman.

'Yes, Major Wardlaw?'

'Put this in the post, would you, Jenks.'

'Yes, Sir.'

'And, Jenks . . .'

'Yes, Sir?'

'I shall need my dress uniform cleaned and ready for a wedding soon.'

'Yes, Sir. What date, Sir?'

'May 17, damn it.'

'Sir?'

'Nothing. Just that I wish the bridegroom had chosen any other day of the year but that.'

'Not very lucky, Sir?'

'No,' answered Jackdaw slowly, 'not very lucky for those connected with that wretched house. Thank you, Jenks. That will be all.'

18

'Oh dear,' said Mrs Webbe Weston, leaning briefly out of the window and turning the palm of her hand towards the sky, 'I believe it's going to rain. Oh it mustn't, it really can't. All those guests! Oh dear.'

Family weddings, family funerals and family births were always a great strain to her; part of which was the uncontrollable role played by the weather. Would it be too hot for the ladies, might the bride faint clean away; would the baby shiver at the font and catch a fatal bout of bronchitis; could the earth of the graveside slip in the wet and feet slide precariously over the newly-dead? All serious matters to be watched with eyes cast above to look for portents.

And tonight was no exception. With Number 6 St Catherine's Hill – the small terraced house she had taken since her husband's death – packed to the doors, a downpour started, casting a faint gloom over what should have been a jolly party. For everybody had come a very long way and relished not at all the thought of a soaking on the wedding day.

Little Violet Wardlaw – looking no older now that she was Mrs Bertram Berkeley – had travelled the farthest of the home-based guests, undertaking the journey from Shropshire unaccompanied, for Bertie did not believe in children being left totally in the charge of servants. But Mary and Matilda had travelled from Paris and brought their husbands with them, having no such worries about leaving their broods. Caroline, on the other hand, had brought all three of hers, and Francis as well, and was occupying an entire suite at The Angel. On the floor above them were staying Mr Hicks and Lady Waldegrave.

Mrs Webbe Weston sighed with stress. Uncle Thomas Monington – her late husband's brother – and his family were due to arrive first thing on the following morning, and Jackdaw Wardlaw was coming on the last train and was to be picked up at Woking by John Joseph.

Organizing their sleeping quarters had been a nightmare, as The Angel was packed with Hickses and had no room for anybody else, but fortunately Sutton Place was reasonably fresh – old Blanchard and Cloverella having rounded up the remaining half dozen estate workers for a scrubbing party – and the bridegroom and best man were to spend the night there.

Mary and Matilda and their respective partners had a small bedroom each at St Catherine's Hill and Mrs Webbe Weston had put the Ladies Horatia and Ida Anna into the third. In desperation she had decided to take the servant's attic bed for herself and put the girl on a shakedown in front of the fire. All very trying for a widow woman. But at least there was no supper to worry about as Mr Hicks was giving a grand dinner at The Angel, to which every member of the wedding party had been invited.

So it was with a sense of relief that the bridegroom's mother heard Mr Hicks's three carriages – he had brought all of them from London to ferry the guests – arrive outside the front door. And it was with a type of curiosity that, having been handed into the leading carriage, followed closely by Ida Anna, she saw her son kiss Lady Horatia's hand and observed the bridal pair look at one another in silence. She wondered, with all of her funny boring little brain at work, what they were thinking.

If only she could have guessed that both were merely reacting – feeling in a dream, unreal. Everything – for

338

the pair of them – had happened so fast that both were aware they were marrying a stranger.

'I will see you in half an hour,' John Joseph said. 'I'll take the small carriage to Woking and collect Jackdaw. Then we will come straight to The Angel.'

Horatia blushed very slightly in the darkness, knowing full well that this was the same Jackdaw who had pursued her carriage in Hastings years ago and fallen flat in his attempt to make her stop.

'I can't wait to see him,' she replied – with only the merest hint of anxiety.

'Oh God!' said Jackdaw. 'This can't be happening to me!'

But it was. In the downpour that was drenching London and the Home Counties a carthorse had slipped in the wet and the brewer's dray it was pulling had overturned, slewing barrels all over the road.

'Sorry, Sir,' said the driver of the hansom cab. 'We'll have to take another way round. Never get through here in a month of Sundays. Hope you've plenty of time for your train.'

'I'm afraid I haven't. I've only just come off duty.'

'Well, I'll do my best.'

But it wasn't quite good enough and Jackdaw limped on to the platform just in time to see the last train to Woking steam away. His old mistrust of the railway system reasserted itself and he swore imaginatively. Then, being a sensible Army man, he made his way to the one and only telegraph office in London and sent a message down the system that was still in its infancy – less than ten years old. Samuel Morse had begun it all with a demonstration to the Franklin Institute and now there was a key in London with sounders in most major towns. Jackdaw knew, as he booked himself into a room in a nearby railway hotel, that his message – in the original

339

Morse code – would now be tapping out to the sounder in Guildford and would be taken by special delivery direct to John Joseph at The Angel before the soup course had even been cleared away.

And so it was.

'A telegram,' said Mrs Webbe Weston – and fainted.

As she plunged forward, narrowly missing her bowl, there was a fuss and diversion and the opening of the envelope was delayed a few moments. But when it was finally torn, John Joseph smiled.

'Missed train owing to carthorse stop,' he read. 'Will go straight to Sutton Place tomorrow stop. Don't proceed without me. Signed Jackdaw.'

'He's missed the train,' he said aloud. 'He'll join us in the morning.'

Mrs Webbe Weston groaned feebly and said, 'Who's dead?' without opening her eyes.

'Jackdaw's missed the train, that's all, Mother.'

'Died in pain?' said the silly creature, and lost consciousness once more.

They had to take her home after this and the dinner party broke up somewhat earlier than anticipated.

And so it was – as had often happened in the past, though not one of them had been aware of it – John Joseph, Horatia and Jackdaw all dreamed upon the same night.

The first to do so – being the first into bed – was Jackdaw. He dreamed to begin with that he woke up. There in the hotel bedroom, a shaft of moonlight full upon them, were the three magic children, who stared at him without saying a word. He got out of bed and went to stand before them, bowing low. He noticed that they all wore black and that each had a mourning ring upon the index finger.

Pernel noticed his gaze and said, 'You will not see us

340

again in this life, Jackdaw. It is time – and we will none of us survive the other two by more than a month. You, of all people, know how fortunate this is.'

He nodded his head and his grandfather spoke.

'Jackdaw, your most testing experience is about to begin. Do not break faith.'

Jackdaw said, very simply, 'Am I to meet her at last?'

'You will gain and lose everything – but in the loss is the gain. Do you understand?'

'Yes.'

'You must do nothing to break the law of destiny.'

'I understand.'

'Here,' said Uncle James, 'is a present for you. Do you remember this?'

He held his hand out, his jet ring flashing a million sparkles in the moonlight. Drawing closer, Jackdaw saw that there was no colour in the trio at all – they were entirely made up of shades of black and white.

'What is it?'

'Look. Look closely.'

The pale hand unclenched its fingers and there, lying in the palm, was a little green sphere.

'My marble!' said Jackdaw. 'My funny old marble. I travelled through time with that once. Where did you find it?'

'That is not important. What *is* important is that you do not lose it again. It can help you to understand yet more than you do now.'

The magic three were beginning to fade even as he watched them.

'Don't go! Give me your blessing before you do.'

'Go in peace, Jackdaw; grow in wisdom. That is our wish for you.'

'God bless the souls of the magic children,' he said.

They were gone. There was nothing but the sparse

hotel bedroom, the small hard bed – and the twinkling green sphere in his hand.

Even as Jackdaw moved towards wakefulness, Horatia walked – in her sleeping mind – down a long and graceful beach. She had been there once before in her dreams but still did not know where it was. Above her – and slightly to her right – rose a crescent of houses, perched on the side of a hill. In their midst was a colonnaded chapel from which bells were chiming out 'Haste to the Wedding'.

Two men walked with her down the beach but she could not see their faces – and yet she had her arms linked with them both.

'Are we going to the wedding?' she asked.

'Only two of us can do that,' answered one.

'Which two? Am I allowed to go?'

'You can always go – because you are the Bride.'

She laughed but the other one said, 'It is true. You will be well loved, Horatia Waldegrave.'

And with that the man holding her left arm broke free and ran towards the sea. She watched helplessly as he plunged into the waves and swam off towards the horizon.

'Will he come back?' she said.

But to her horror the second man had started to walk rapidly away from her and she stood alone. She remembered in this dream another – the great, fast-flowing river, the sense of total desolation. She knew just such bewilderment and despair before she moved into a lighter level of consciousness and began to sleep more peacefully.

And for John Joseph, bedding down in the chamber known as Sir John Rogers's room, sleeping and waking became horribly intertwined as he dreamed that Giles the Fool was walking in the Chapel that had once been the Long Gallery. He heard, in his sleep, the rattle of the jester's stick against the wall, the sad sobs of anguish.

342

And he woke to find that it was reality – something *was* moving in that part of the house.

He got out of bed very crossly indeed, convinced that Jay was up and about and being naughty. But when he crossed the Great Hall the pricking of his spine told him that the atmosphere was loaded with fear and that no little boy could cause such tension.

None the less he called the child's name as he proceeded up the Great Staircase. There was no reply – only a deep and unnerving silence coming from the very heart of the house.

'Jay?' he called again.

And then ahead of him were a million whispers, a million shadows, in one deep sad sob.

'Giles, damn you,' John Joseph shouted, suddenly furious, 'why are you weeping? Don't you know joy from sadness? I am getting married tomorrow – today. There is happiness in Sutton Place again. What's the matter with you?'

The shadows danced wildly over the walls as the Lord of the Manor of Sutton lunged forward in search of the jester long dead; Giles, who had served Sir Richard the builder until he – the Fool – had died of a cancerous growth. But then John Joseph's attention was attracted by something on the wall. He drew nearer until he stood directly before the small, crude painting. It showed John the Baptist – wild of hair, mad of eye and half naked – immersed to the waist in a grey-watered river. Before him stood Christ – again an unusual concept; black-haired, dark-eyed, a young preaching Rabbi.

But it was not at the realistic approach of the artist that John Joseph now stared; instead he looked at two trickles of water that welled down the canvas unchecked. His mind went back twelve years. He sat in the library of Sutton Place and heard a voice speak to him out of the shadows. He heard again that thin reed say, 'Do you know the legend of Sir Richard Weston's portrait?' Heard himself reply in the negative and heard the voice go on, 'It hangs in the Long Gallery. It shows John baptizing Christ.'

John Joseph's heart began to beat wildly as he picked up a piece of plate from the altar and attacked the rotting canvas. The paint fell away in large damp flakes. Beneath, John Joseph could dimly perceive something black. He struck at the canvas harder, holding the candle tree above his head to give more light. And then he saw it – the portrait of a man in black, white-ruffed, and skull-capped; two widely spaced eyes gazing out.

But to his immense horror he saw that those eyes wept. He put out his finger and licked the substance that fell upon it. He tasted salt beneath his tongue.

'Oh Christ!' said John Joseph. 'Oh Christ! Oh Christ! Why?'

He sank into a corner, his knees to his chin and his eyes staring wildly, trying to remember the rest of that terrible conversation before Death had turned into a bird, as legend decreed it must.

And then it came to him: the date. May 17, the day on which the portrait of Sir Richard Weston wept. Of all the terrible and grim coincidences he had chosen the blackest day in the history of Sutton Place for his marriage to Horatia Waldegrave. John Joseph leaned back against the wall at that, and cried on the dawning of his wedding day.

Jackdaw awoke abruptly as the first finger of dawn crooked and beckoned over the grey of London's skies. For a good minute he did not know where he was. Then he remembered. The poor carthorse splaying its feet in

the cut through to Waterloo; the barrels tipping everywhere; the missed train.

But most vividly he remembered his dream of the night
before: the farewell from the Gage children – the progeny
of Garnet who had known no magic himself yet whose
daughter and twin sons had spread their wisdom in the
world for nearly one hundred years.

He felt beneath his pillow. Very much as he had
expected, the green marble was there. The dream had
been too real, too disturbing, to be just a figment. He
smiled to himself and got out of bed, putting the sphere
into his overnight bag. It did not seem blasphemous that
it should snuggle in safety beside his shaving brush.

Having washed and scraped his chin, Jackdaw put on
his dress uniform and, his bill settled, hastened to the
station. The train for Woking was huffing and chuffing at
the platform like a steam-powered Algernon Hicks and
he jumped aboard and was out of London within minutes.
And then it was easy. A hansom cab from Woking direct
to the great gates of Sutton Place itself.

It was still only eight thirty in the morning as they
swung open before him, outlined against a sky that
threatened to rain but yet withheld its cruel drops from
the people below.

As always, whenever Jackdaw saw the house after an
interval, it took him by surprise. Of its many moods,
reflected so accurately by its amber brickwork, it had
today its fresh look, as if it had been built only fifty
years. The stones round the doorway, newly washed by
last night's downpour, blazoned the initials of the builder
for all the world to see. R.W. and the tun – the rebus on
Weston.

And, as the Middle Enter was opened for him by Old
Blanchard – once a postillion to Mr Webbe Weston senior
– Jackdaw glimpsed the transitory change in the Great

Hall. The gloomy place, shut away and neglected for so many years, blossomed like a hot-house. Sheaf upon sheaf of flowers decorated the trestle tables, three in all, set out for the wedding feast. And to add to their fresh-smelling sweetness there were sprays of tumbling ivy, woven hard around with forget-me-not and cornflowers and blue varieties of which he did not even know the names. Somebody with great skill had transformed Sir Richard Weston's dining hall into what it must have been when Francis – first heir to the manor of Sutton – had married his childhood sweetheart.

Now Major John Wardlaw took a step within and felt something of all the brides and grooms who had trodden the place before. How many weddings, how many consummations, how many conceptions, how many births, had gone into the great and wonderful history of Sutton Place? And, again, his magic gift brushed something of the old happiness upon him and he rushed up the West Staircase calling out, 'John Joseph! John Joseph! I'm here – Jackdaw!'

His friend, clad over all in the uniform of Captain of the 3rd Light Dragoons of His Imperial Majesty the Emperor of Austria, and wearing about his neck a riband bearing the cross of the Knight of the Order of Malta, appeared in the doorway and called out, 'Jackdaw, thank God you're here!'

Immediately there was rapport between them; the old ways, the boyhood friendships, revived at a glance, so that there was no hesitancy when John Joseph said abruptly, 'You realize what the date is?'

And there was no silliness on the part of Jackdaw as he answered, 'Yes.'

'It just didn't occur to me!'

'Well, so be it.'

'What do you mean?'

'What I say.' Jackdaw climbed the stairs and drew level with his friend. 'It is chance, a coincidence, a mistake. That is how you must regard it.'

'But Jackdaw – my dear old friend, how are you? – it has *happened*. I have somehow managed, quite blindly, to pick the accursed day.'

'John Joseph, leave it to work itself out. You can only worsen the situation by adding negative thoughts.'

The Captain smiled for the first time. 'You are right – as always.'

'Then are we bound for St Nicholas?'

'Yes. Horatia and the wedding party meet us there at ten o'clock.'

'Horatia?' said Jackdaw – and his jewel eyes grew shuttered with the secrecy of his thoughts.

It was very still in the old church; all the incense of three hundred years melding into one aromatic whole to heighten the senses of those who sat in the congregation. Even the old uncles, William – the Earl Waldegrave now that George had died without issue – nodding quietly to himself; and Thomas Monington for once smiling and benevolent in the haze.

Everyone was at readiness: the bridegroom and best man dressed to the hilt, the bridesmaid bright-eyed in the porch, the Reverend William Pearson, Prayer Book well in hand, all with one purpose. All waiting for the moment when Lady Horatia Waldegrave would sweep up in her carriage, accompanied by her stepfather, Mr Hicks, and descend at the doors of St Nicholas, Guildford.

The organ, throbbing out chords of melodious nothingness in the background, was part of the somnolent atmosphere until it suddenly played a solitary, high, clear note at which the cheerful carillon of bells in the steeple was hushed.

'She's here,' hissed everyone, with enough volume to send a whirlpool whisper running from font to altar rail and back. There was a murmur of voices in the porch – the vicar saying, 'How dee do?'; Ida Anna piping, 'You look lovely.' And then the music changed.

Jackdaw knew, of course. Knew, even before he had turned his head, that destiny had taken its inevitable twist and that Horatia Waldegrave, whom he had always loved but never met, stood behind him in a great cascade of swirling satin and organza ruffles, her veil of silk tulle held in place by the Waldegrave tiara.

As he turned, so did John Joseph, and they stood together staring at the bride who made her way slowly up the aisle, holding the arm of her stepfather and looking modestly – and most uncharacteristically – at the ground.

Aware of his lapse of manners, Jackdaw moved his head, but Horatia must have sensed this because she suddenly looked up. Very briefly their eyes met. They brimmed recognition at each other and then, quite deliberately, she turned her gaze to John Joseph who now stood, every inch a soldier, his face correctly and stalwartly turned towards the altar.

In that moment Jackdaw was aware of everything: knew that she knew him – but really did not. Knew that she was full of love for her bridegroom and that this was what was meant by his gaining everything – and losing all. He had found his soulmate at last but she was going to another man.

In the silence that followed, the opening words of the marriage ceremony were spoken and within minutes, or so it seemed to him, Jackdaw passed John Joseph the gold ring that was to bind Horatia to his greatest friend.

And then how the organ cried out! With merry shout it told all the world that the master of Sutton Place and his bride were coming out into the fresh clean morning and heading for the mansion house that had belonged to his kinsfolk for over three hundred years.

As the gates swung open the lodge keeper and his family waved their caps and kerchiefs before the carriage bearing the bride and groom. And further up the drive, at the point where the little bridge crossed the River Wey, an enormous daisy chain had been hung from one post to the other, completely barring the way. The only four children left on the estate – Jay and three of the other Blanchards – stood there demanding toll from Horatia.

And she was not found wanting. John Joseph had warned her the night before and inside her reticule was crammed a sticky bag of sweets.

'God bless you, Missus,' said Jay, in his funny, touchingly gruff little voice. 'God bless you, Master.'

He made a jerky bow and John Joseph saw that the child – probably for the first time in its life – was wearing an enormous pair of lace-up boots.

The daisy chain was removed and the cavalcade of carriages – a dozen in all – swept on up the drive and clattered into the courtyard, only to see that more guests had arrived and were standing before the open Middle Enter, waving and cheering. Horatia simply could not believe that Frances – her double sister-in-law, dressed in starkest widow's weeds – was there on the arm of a very redoubtable and very elderly gentleman who, quite clearly, was old enough to be her father but whose feelings were far from paternal.

And romance was in the air not only for the Widow Waldegrave, for also present – very *grande dame* and eccentric – was Uncle William's second wife, Mrs Sarah Milward of Hastings, standing with General and the Hon Helen Wardlaw. The sight of Frances prompted Horatia to whisper, 'I think there may be another Waldegrave bride soon.

John Joseph glanced at the newcomers from the carriage window as Old Blanchard lowered the step and came to a shaky salute. And it was thus that he caught Cloverella's eye.

She was dressed in crimson from head to foot, her frock sweeping the cobbles below, a gold-threaded shawl about her shoulders and gold ribbons tying up her brown hair. And he saw that she held something in her hand and was looking at it, smiling and winking, and then looking back at John Joseph.

'Welcome to the bride of Sutton Place,' she called out in a loud clear voice and, as Horatia set her satin-pumped foot on the ground, Cloverella made an extravagant gesture. The witch girl knelt on the stones, picked up the hem of the bridal gown and kissed it. Then from the pocket of her dress she produced her flute and a silver ring with a green eye worked into its flat broad surface.

'Wear this, my Lady,' she said, 'and no ill-luck will visit thee.'

It was hideous, quite the most monstrous gift with which a bride could be presented. None the less Horatia slipped it on next to her wedding band and, bending over, helped Cloverella up and kissed her on both cheeks.

'Ladies and gentlemen,' said John Joseph, 'there are refreshments within. The second ceremony will take place in half an hour.'

'And I shall pipe in the happy couple,' added Cloverella.

Once again she muttered something to the thing she carried in her hand and, for a fleeting second, John Joseph thought he caught a glimpse of a waxen doll. But when he looked again he saw there was nothing and knew he must be mistaken. Not even Cloverella would bring such a heathenish thing to a wedding.

Meanwhile Jay, who had removed his boots, came running up the drive with the other children, and a wonderfully natural thing occurred. Jackdaw, quite forgetting the occasion, caught his first glimpse of the child whose parentage was so doubtful and, turning to John Joseph, raised his eyebrows. The bridegroom, also forgetting himself, shrugged his shoulders and shook his head. Then they grinned at one another like naughty boys who had once gone in for a night of education with the Misses Fitz. They were in total harmony. Jackdaw would never, could never, do a thing to harm his friend.

But oh how he loved the bride! Everything about her, now that he had seen her closely, enraptured him. Her immense physical beauty, her unconventional approach to life, her utter fearlessness . . .

He closed his mind, deliberately shuttered it off, and listened to the notes of Cloverella's flute as Jay, dancing barefoot around his mother, caught the coins that the jovial wedding guests threw to him. Then he watched as they processed into the Great Hall before the Roman Catholic ceremony began in what had once been the great Long Gallery of Sutton Place.

An hour later it was all over; John Joseph and Horatia had been married twice and had been pronounced man and wife by vicar, priest and registrar. Their two wedding certificates had been signed: the Anglican by Lady Waldegrave, Uncle Thomas Monington, Mr Hicks and John Fearon, a school friend of John Joseph's; the Catholic simply by Algernon and Uncle Thomas. The same wedding band had been slipped on her finger, passed by Jackdaw – dying for love, and saying not a word.

It was time for the wedding breakfast. On the top table sat Uncle William and Mrs Milward, pretty little Frances with her elderly suitor, who turned out to be George Granville Harcourt, not only Member of Parliament for Oxfordshire but a wealthy widower into the bargain. And, of course, the Dowager Countess and Mr Hicks, the latter very fine in a black morning coat, white frilly shirt and black and white spotted cravat.

Toasts were drunk in champagne, feasts were made of lobster, game birds, and various pies, with cheeses and a dozen different desserts; while those on the lower table – the Blanchards, Cloverella, the lodge keeper and all the children – drank strong ale.

At length John Joseph rose to make his speech. In the pocket of her dress Cloverella turned the waxen image of him. She was determined to use all her power to make him love Horatia. She had vanquished Marguerite Dawe and now she summoned all the old forces of magic into play.

Cloverella did not know the meaning of jealousy. To her all was natural. The taking of a lover, the passing on to another, was merely the re-echoing of seasons. In that sense she was amoral – and yet she was the most highly principled of them all. She would never do a deliberately harmful thing. She believed in the old religion; she believed in nature taking its true and purposeful course.

Now she listened and smiled as John Joseph said, 'My Lord, my Ladies, ladies and gentlemen – I thank you all so much for being here today. I promise you that though Horatia and I will be, in a week's time, some distance from you, we will never be apart from you in our thoughts. I thank you for both coming to our wedding – or should I say weddings? – and coming here, to Sutton Place, to toast our health.

'I know that I am the luckiest man in the world and I promise to serve Horatia as she deserves. In other words, with all the loyalty of which I am capable. May I ask the assembled company to rise as I give you the toast: my beautiful bride – Horatia Webbe Weston.'

Anne Waldegrave Hicks patted at her eyes and Frances snuggled, smilingly, into the arm of Mr Harcourt. Mrs Milward, on the other hand, shouted out very loudly, 'Good for you, Sir. I wish there were more bridegrooms of your ilk.' And from the lower table Cloverella called, 'Here's long life and happiness to the pair. What say you?'

Everybody pledged their cup, rising to their feet to do so. And Jackdaw drained his glass with the rest. He wished them that – long life, happiness, everything they could desire.

As dusk fell the guests left Sutton Place. Flambeaux were lit and thrust into holders to show the revellers their way and it was then that Mr Hicks, happy and bouncing, said to his wife, 'By jingo, Anne, the deed is done.' And in reply to her enquiry explained, 'We're to live in Sutton Place. I'm going to sign the agreement with the agents on Monday. We will take over as soon as John Joseph and Horatia leave for Austria. What do you think?'

Looking up at the great house – into which four Strawberry Hills could have fitted quite easily – the Dowager Countess shivered visibly.

'Do you not think it might be too large for us? After all, there will only be you and me and Ida Anna.'

Her husband looked anxious, bearing the expression that always made her want to pat him.

'Well, in that case, my dearest . . .'

'No, Algy. I am only being foolish. I know you fell in love with the place years ago.'

He beamed merrily. 'Yes, at Francis's wedding to be precise. But I would not wish to foist my caprice on you.'

Behind them the house – with John Joseph and Horatia

framed in the Middle Enter, waving goodbye to the guests – vanished as they rounded the bend in the drive.

'It will be all right, Algy. It will help John Joseph – and so Horatia too – and I know it will please you. Pray proceed.'

'Very well, sweetheart. I shall.'

And with that they fell into silence and stared out of the carriage windows to where the sapphire sky glowed blue over Sutton Forest.

And it was at that same sky that the bridal couple gazed as Old Blanchard shot home the bolts on the huge door and bade them good night, before they quietly took each other's hand and, in their wedding clothes, walked up the smaller staircase to the chamber at the back of the house which had once belonged to Melior Mary Weston. Here Cloverella and the gardener had excelled themselves. It seemed that there were a thousand white blossoms in the room – though in reality it was probably barely a hundred – and the old four poster bed had been hung with new lace curtains, woven round with satin ribbons.

'How beautiful,' said Horatia.

'Like you – it befits you.'

'John Joseph,' said his bride, 'I am afraid.'

'Don't be,' he answered. 'Come here and sit with me on the sofa.'

'I have heard some women say – though never my mother – that they must bear men's appetites.'

Her bridegroom laughed out loud at that.

'Some women may forbear – but not you, Horatia. Not you, my wild fox. You were born to know love's great fierce beauty.'

Then he would say no more, gathering her into his arms and kissing her mouth and her neck until, at last, she grew languorous. Then, after a while, he moved her gently closer to him, and unfastened the white dress, letting his lips run down to the now naked nipples, down to the perfect breasts, the roundest and firmest and finest he had ever seen.

He was ready for her – hard and strong and more than able to initiate her to womanhood. But he was too kind to hurry her. Instead he coaxed her to her feet, so that the dress swathed down, mermaid-like, to her ankles and she stood there in her shift, the bridal veil still upon her head. Then he, too, stood up and slowly removed her stockings, her veiling; every last thing she had on.

Now at last he saw her – one glorious curve following upon another, a constant harmony from neck to shoulder to breast, waist and hip.

'You are so beautiful, Horatia,' he said. 'Stay like that in the firelight.'

And as she watched him, he undressed too, and she saw that he was the opposite of herself; muscular, powerful and with a great shaft that both horrified and fascinated her.

'Come to bed,' he said. 'I promise not to hurt you.'

But he did – he could not help it! As he claimed the most secret part of her body for his, she could have cried out at the strength of his thrusting. But, at last, the pain ended and there came a faint throbbing between her thighs which seemed to grow in intensity and insistence.

Hearing her gasp John Joseph moved relentlessly, pinioning her where she would have escaped him.

'Don't be afraid,' he said again.

And her shout of ecstasy was his reward as the bride of Sutton Place tasted passion – raw and sweet and unashamed – upon her sweat-beaded and newly-awakened body.

19

The packet boat had become a blob on the horizon and a summer shower had blown in from the sea before Jackdaw finally turned away from the quayside, wet through. To say he was sick at heart would have minimized how he was feeling. He had not cried for years; not since Marie had been killed. But now he wept like a child.

Climbing up the gangplank, going away from him on to the steamer that ran regularly between England and France, had been John Joseph and Horatia. And Jackdaw had felt that this was the end, that he would never see his childhood friend again.

The sense of foreboding had been unbearable, and Horatia's face, framed in a ribbon-trimmed bonnet, had not helped at all. Jackdaw was more in love with her than ever, if such a thing were possible; sick with guilt at the force of his feelings for his great friend's bride.

And then John Joseph had hurried back down the gangplank – out of earshot of Horatia, who stood at the top waving – and had clasped Jackdaw to him, embracing him on both cheeks in the Austrian manner.

'If anything happens to me,' he had said, 'you will care for her, won't you?'

Jackdaw had been unable to reply, merely staring at his friend aghast.

'Who can tell what lies ahead?' John Joseph had continued. 'With the Empire in such upheaval God knows how long we can hold out without fighting. Listen. My will is with my solicitors in London. I have left everything to her – Sutton Place, everything.'

Jackdaw was still unable to speak.

'Do you remember once, at the Queen's birthday ball, how we spoke of a dream I had – a dream in which I died on a battlefield in the arms of a girl with red hair?'

'And I told you that I, too, used to dream of her?' Jackdaw had found his voice at last.

'Yes. I wonder what it means. But I do know one thing – the curse of Sutton Place has not done with me yet.'

Jackdaw's strength had returned. 'I told you on your wedding day to ignore the date. I tell you again, now, to fight off evil. The path of destiny is not inevitable, John Joseph.'

But at that point the ship's bell had rung and there had been a call of 'All ashore, who are going ashore.' It was too late. The friends must part.

'. . . so you see, Horatia, there is to be no mention of the unrest in Hungary, or anything like that. No war talk, in other words.'

'No,' said his bride. 'John Joseph, are you *really* sure that this is the correct thing to wear?'

Her husband's eyes flickered over her as they sat side by side in the carriage taking them to the royal palace of Schönbrunn. He thought he had never seen her more enchanting and supposed that it must be marriage – or perhaps the bed-magic that they had found together – that made her smile so radiantly.

So instead of answering her question he asked another.

'Are you happy, Horatia?'

'I will be when you fall in love with me.'

'But I *do* love you.'

Horatia gave an impatient little move.

'You are fond of me – as you would be of a lap dog. But I am *not* a dog, John Joseph.'

357

'No, you are a foxfire vixen! I could ravish you here and now.'

She laughed and pushed him away.

'Stop it. I look enough of a rag-bag as it is. Are you *sure* that this is the right sort of thing to wear for meeting the Emperor?'

'Yes!'

He had come to the married quarters they occupied together in Vienna's heart, to find the bedroom a sea of clothes and Horatia – arrayed in a very formal cloth-of-gold gown – preening before a cheval mirror. He had looked at her astonished and she had exclaimed, 'Oh, isn't it exciting! A message has come from the palace. The Emperor has sent for us to go to him. Something about an evening of card play. I had no idea that you were on such intimate terms with him. Mother will be thrilled.'

John Joseph had laughed and thrown his tunic on to a chair, stripping off his shirt that he might go and wash.

'I am afraid it isn't quite like that, Horry.'

'What do you mean?'

'When I told you that the Emperor was simple, childish, I was not exaggerating. Mentally he is about eight years old and has great difficulty signing his name. Prince Metternich rules the Empire, make no mistake about it.'

'Then are we not going to the palace after all?'

'We are going – but not for cards. The invitation really means to play soldiers.'

Horatia looked stunned. 'Play soldiers! With a King!'

'Yes, why not?' John Joseph seemed slightly put out. 'His favourite is a tin soldier with my name, and in his battle room – he has a whole turret devoted to model battlefields – I lead the Austrian Army against everyone from Attila the Hun to Napoleon Bonaparte. I have just savagely routed Genghis Khan!'

Horatia shook her head in disbelief. 'I don't know what to say! It would be funny if it were not so pathetic.'

'What is pathetic about it? He is perfectly happy in his private world. I love the Emperor. He is kinder than the brilliant plotters who surround him, I can assure you. I often feel I would like to join him permanently.'

He turned and poured some hot water into a basin, busily splashing himself and lathering his chin.

'Do you not wish me to come? I would hate to spoil your play.' Horatia felt quite unreasonably jealous.

'It would be hardly wise to disobey a royal command.' John Joseph pulled a slight face as he negotiated the razor round his chin. 'But I could make some excuse if you feel that you would hate it.'

He sounded so off-hand that Horatia wondered then – thinking that her husband had more fondness for the Emperor than herself – whether she could ever make John Joseph fall in love with her. She felt a moment of total desolation – standing there in her golden gown and watching the man she had married, but hardly knew, busy at his ablutions with his back turned.

She sighed. 'You know I will come if I am welcome. But if you feel me to be an intruder, then leave me behind I beg you.'

John Joseph was amazed. He had never thought to hear Horatia get so hurt over anything. He dabbed his face with a towel.

'Horry, I didn't mean . . .'

'Please don't say it. You must think me made of poor stuff that I would not feel sympathy for a harmless old fool. That I could love him as you do is a different matter. I give love deeply, John Joseph, or I do not give it at all. Perhaps I have learned something from you in the last respect.'

For no particular reason, at this final and stinging part

of her remark, John Joseph felt a strange constriction in his chest. It was a sensation that normally he would have associated with anger, which was hardly the case at present. In fact he felt abnormally guilty that he could have upset his wife so greatly.

'Sweetheart, forgive me. I did not mean to offend. Please come with me to meet the Emperor – he will be so unhappy if you do not. Before I left for England he would pretend that the English soldier might come back with a bride. I beg you not to disappoint him – and me.'

Once again the strange constriction – and obviously a softening of his features, for Horatia, after observing him narrowly for a moment or two, gave a half-hearted smile.

'Very well – to please him.'

His desire to hug her overcame him and he held her closely to his damp chest.

'But change your beautiful dress, darling. The Emperor plays like a little boy – kneeling on the floor. Wear something that will not be spoiled.'

And though she shook her head over it she agreed to put on a simple muslin gown and chip bonnet to meet His Imperial Majesty Ferdinand, monarch of Austria, Hungary and the rest of the vast Slav empire.

None the less, as the carriage turned into the huge space of the courtyard and she saw a palace equalled only by Versailles, she quailed once more.

'John Joseph, are you sure this silly gown will do? I feel like a milkmaid.'

'And look like a rustic Princess. Be patient, dearest.'

'Why the Hell,' he thought, 'do those words catch at my throat? And why oh why does the turn of her head, the set of her chin, the glance of her eye, affect me so damnably much?'

But he could not spare the time to follow the path down which his ideas were leading. Bewigged flunkeys in powder-blue livery were flinging open the carriage doors and letting down the steps. And Horatia – her eyes iced jade with the excitement of it all – was setting her pumped toe on to the first step of the palace. Behind her hastened John Joseph, smart as a peacock in his frogging and furbelows – an Austrian Captain to the manner born.

The march down the magnificent corridors – a distance only just beneath a mile – was a revelation to Horatia. But nothing ever again would make such an impact as the moment when a pair of golden doors – worked all over with cupids and open-winged swans – was thrown open and a major domo, banging a cane three times upon the ground, called, 'Captain John Joseph and the Lady Horatia Webbe Weston, your Imperial Majesty' – and nothing happened.

They both stood there – English officer and aristocratic wife – peering into the magnificence of a state drawing room in deadly silence and breathing hardly at all until, finally, John Joseph whispered, 'Sir?' And then from somewhere – apparently the back of a velvet sofa with fanciful griffin feet – a voice whispered back, 'Psst!'

The major domo and John Joseph exchanged a glance. Then the servant said, very loudly, 'Will that be all, Imperial Majesty?'

'Psst,' came the reply again. 'Are you there, English soldier?'

John Joseph took a step forward. 'Yes Sir. And my wife.'

A nose bearing a large pair of pince-nez appeared briefly round the corner of the seat and then withdrew again.

'If she is pretty then you may bring her forward.'

The major domo said in an entirely different tone of voice, 'Shall I leave you, Sir?'

He spoke to John Joseph, who answered, 'Yes, it will

361

be quite all right. My wife and I will go in two hours. If the carriage could be waiting.'

'Very good, Sir. Any trouble at all, just pull the bell.'

At these words Horatia looked decidedly nervous but John Joseph, propelling her firmly by the elbow, took the initial steps on her behalf and went into the drawing room.

Horry gazed about at splendour. In a large and magnificent fireplace, supported on either side by marble mermen carved in quite superlative detail, a fire of logs the size of tree trunks leapt and crackled against any chill that might intrude the ancient palace that night. While on the mantel shelf above she stared at a million reflections. Ice glass pendants dipped from a central stalk, winking and blinking in the candlelit room to blaze the eyes and remove the unsuspecting soul to Arctic-land.

Above the fireplace, resplendent in silks, in brocades, in starch-stiff collars and high-cheeked ruffs, hung the long-dead ancestors of the house of Hapsburg. A dozen Kings and several insipid Queens looked down upon the carpet brought from Turkey in its prime and spun by four master weavers. It glowed red from its heart: the red of a dragon's fearful eye, a lover's pulsing blood; the red of a gypsy's swirling dress.

The colour was consuming, catching Horatia's breath as she stood there, nervous and unsure, but for all that not afraid of the funny little Emperor who knelt behind the sofa, thinking himself hidden and yet revealed a hundred times in the fifty glancing mirrors that lined the walls, reflecting countless rooms with countless mirrors and countless little monarchs crouching on all fours.

There was another protracted silence and then Horatia could keep quiet no longer.

'Peep-oh!' she called out. 'I can see you!'

The pince-nez rose from behind the sofa and dodged

back again as she looked. In response she dropped to her knees behind a great winged chair. John Joseph stood shaking his head and smiling. 'Sir, you may only play this for a few minutes,' he said. 'We have come to see the soldiers.'

But the Emperor had different plans and Horatia watched his many reflections circle the furniture and creep up behind her. She spun round and found herself looking into the kindliest eyes, the sort of light blue that is most common amongst those of limited reasoning.

'Peep-oh!' she said again. 'You're out! I've caught you.'

The Emperor gave a sweet smile.

'You've brought me a doll,' he said. 'English soldier, you have brought me a doll for the house. Isn't it pretty! Can I give it sugar plums?'

And with that he delved into his pocket and, taking out a rather dusty delicacy, popped it into Horatia's mouth before anybody could say a word.

'Imperial Majesty,' said John Joseph, crossing over to them and helping first the Emperor and then Horatia to their feet. 'May I present my wife?'

He bowed. Following his example, Horatia dropped a court curtsey as she had been taught by her mother years before – skirts wide, knees steady, arms to the side and slightly behind, face looking to the floor.

'It moves,' said the Emperor, clapping his hands. 'Does it sing and dance too?'

'Yes, Sir.'

'And what is it called, this little wife doll?'

'Horatia, Sir. Lady Horatia Webbe Weston.'

The Emperor skipped a few steps, nimble with ecstasy.

'It is beautiful,' he said. 'Come on, Lady, I am going to show you my battle tower.'

As he spoke no English and Horatia hardly any German, John Joseph found himself translating, so it was easy for him to say, 'You are not afraid, are you?' without Ferdinand's being aware of a thing.

'Not at all. I like him.'

'He loves you. Look, he wants you to dance.'

The Emperor had switched the starting mechanism of a wall-hung polyphon which now began to tinkle out a Strauss waltz. With a curtsey – small and bobbing this time – Horry began to circle round him, but the Emperor called out, 'No, no, no. English soldier, you are to dance with her. Wife dolls should not dance on their own.'

His eyes assumed a sudden cunning clarity.

'If you let them do that,' he added, 'other tin soldiers will come and take them away. So be careful.'

'I will, Sir,' answered John Joseph – and gave his wife a formal bow.

It was just as the Dowager Countess had feared; the Hicks family and their staff from the London home in Duke Street seemed to vanish into Sutton Place completely. Not one of them, not even Anne in her heyday, had ever lived in a mansion so huge, so awe-inspiring, or quite so shadowy, and the effect was frightening: subdued voices and scurrying feet down long dark passages became a way of life.

To add to Lady Waldegrave's problems, trouble had broken out on their very first night there. Aided by a depressed-looking Jackdaw, the Hicks' family servants had finally succeeded in getting all the furniture off the carts and through the Middle Enter. Then, after a scratch luncheon, following which the Major had returned to London, it had been Anne's task to oversee the disposition of the bedrooms. She had put the staff in various small rooms in the West Wing, with views out over the courtyard, and had chosen for herself and Algernon a room at the far end of the wing; a room that looked out over glorious parkland and was equivalent in position to the windows at the furthest point of the Long Gallery, now the Chapel. She had been told by Cloverella that this had been the apartment in which Marguerite Trevelyan had slept during her tenancy. And it was, certainly, that in the best state of repair and decoration.

For Ida Anna, Anne had chosen a room that had once been Lady Weston's apple loft but which, when Melior Mary had been a girl, had been conveted into two bedrooms – one for the heiress, the other for her adopted sister, Sheila.

'These shall be your bedroom and dressing room,' the Dowager Countess had said, and her daughter had squealed and run about excitedly.

But that night when the entire household – quite exhausted after moving day – had retired early to bed, there had been a piercing scream and Ida Anna, in bare feet, had come pounding the length of the West Wing corridor, thrown open her mother's door and jumped headlong on to the bed, violently frightening Algy who was lying asleep on his back, his hands in the air.

'Good God, child,' Anne had cried, sitting bolt upright and fumbling to light the oil lamp, 'whatever is the matter? Are you ill?'

'No, no,' the girl had whimpered, 'but there is something in my room. A ghost, a white lady. I saw her standing in the moonlight and watching me.'

And no amount of persuading, or cajoling, and no cups of soothing milk, could tempt Ida Anna back in there. She insisted on spending the rest of the night in her mother's bed, Algy trundling off sleepily to a guest room.

Next day the Dowager Countess had moved her tearful daughter into a smaller and less attractive place known, by tradition, as Sir John Rogers's chamber. And that, for the while, had been the end of the affair.

Caroline and Francis had come down for a few days and had stayed in the converted apple loft, apparently seeing nothing. And after that it had remained empty, waiting for guests.

And these there had been in plenty. In a feverish attempt to make Sutton Place seem inhabited, Anne had invited everybody – almost anybody – to view her new home and stay a night or two. A type of continuing house party began with which Algy, after a while, grew rather bored, and started to escape by taking himself off on Walks. He bought a pair of spaniels called Polly and Anthus – he thought this terribly droll and laughed about it excessively – and could be seen striding out in knickerbockers and stout shoes, in the general direction of Sutton Forest.

Meanwhile Anne busied herself with the inconsequentialities of occupying a time in which there was nothing really to do, and soon became involved with a scheme to marry off Ida Anna, who was now twenty-one and a thorough little pest.

It was decided, therefore, that on July 11 – the minx's birthday – a grand dinner party and dance would be given, with every eligible man of whom the Dowager Countess could think being invited from far and near. A guest list was drawn up, one of the names at the head of which was Major John Wardlaw. It occurred to Anne, the more she thought about it, that he could be no more than thirty, and that it was high time he was settled. In fact the more she mused the better she liked the idea. She wrote to him forthwith and invited him to stay for as long as his Army duties would permit. His reply came back promptly that he would be delighted.

This answer gave Anne food for thought and she

wondered, sitting at her writing desk in her study – a room that had once been Elizabeth Weston's saloon – whether the Major did, in fact, have a sneaking fancy for Ida Anna. She had never noticed anything that could lead to this conclusion, but he always seemed most happy to come to Sutton Place. If anyone had told her then that Jackdaw was in love with her middle daughter and even being with her family brought him vicarious pleasure she would have gazed at them in utter astonishment.

The appointed day came and from the afternoon on a stream of carriages bearing the house guests came through the great gates and up the drive. The first to arrive were Uncle William and Mrs Milward – as everyone still thought of her – and his eldest son William, Viscount Chewton. This cousin of Ida Anna's was in the Scots Fusilier Guards, unmarried, and a definite candidate for a husband. Uncle William's second son, the Honourable George, was also there and, at twenty-two, another possibility. In the carriage behind followed a great many of the Waldegrave girls – Uncle William's daughters – also on the look-out for husbands. It was going to be a vigorous occasion, Anne thought.

The arrival of Caroline and Francis Hicks, Annette and Archie Money and Frances with George Granville Harcourt – now betrothed and cooing like two love birds – completed the family. But the line-up of eligibles was impressive. Mr Harcourt had brought with him the Earl of Selborne – young and handsome and a joy to any Mama's heart; and there were six landowners' sons from round about and two unmarried clerics. Not to mention a surgeon friend of Francis's and Major John Wardlaw himself.

It had been Anne's intention to use the Great Hall as the centre of activity and accordingly the West Musicians' Gallery had been opened up, decorated with potted palms, and now had a six-piece string ensemble going at Strauss waltzes as if their fee depended upon the volume of sound. The use of plants and ferns had also been extended to the Great Hall and the panelled dining room, where fifty places had been laid at the vast table, sparkled with crystal and silver. To add to the hot-house effect banks of flowers were everywhere and little gilt chairs had been placed at random for those who wished to sit out. All this grandeur was crowned by a massive chandelier, hanging from the Great Hall's vaulted ceiling, and winking reflections of two hundred candles in its fluted glass pendants.

'Well, my dear?' said Anne to Algy, as she started down the West Staircase arrayed in burgundy velvet and looking nothing like her fifty-eight years.

'Wonderful, my darling. You have excelled yourself. It is an occasion fit for a Princess.'

'Let us hope it is an occasion fit for a betrothal, that is all.'

Algy barked incomprehensibly and patted her hand.

Jackdaw, hearing the dinner gong sound, made his way to the top of the staircase to find himself amongst a press of people, all forming into pairs to go down to dine. He offered his hand to Lady Laura Waldegrave who inclined her head and accepted it. At the head of the line – just behind her uncle and her sister-in-law, Frances – Ida Anna walked triumphantly, partnered by young Lord Selborne and pleased as punch with herself. Jackdaw shook his head and grinned. Disguised as a birthday ball this might be but he had not seen such a marriage-go-round in an age.

He glanced at Lady Laura sideways, saw a remote resemblance to Horatia in her – they were first cousins – and felt his heart quicken. As if she read his thoughts the young woman said, 'You are a friend of my cousin's husband, aren't you?'

'You mean Captain Webbe Weston?'

'Yes. Do you hear from him? I often wonder how Horatia is getting on. I wouldn't change places with her for a fortune.'

Realizing that this might sound insulting to John Joseph, Lady Laura added hastily, 'Nothing against her husband, you understand. It is merely that one cannot pick up a newspaper without reading of the deteriorating situation in the Austrian Empire. *The Times* is predicting revolution within a twelve-month. I must say I do not envy her.'

'I believe she loves him very much and wants to be at his side,' Jackdaw answered slowly.

'She obviously must. I think she is excessively brave. But then she was always a strange little girl.'

'Strange?'

'Unconventional. I remember her saying to me once that she wanted to marry a soldier and go to battles with him. I thought her quite tomboyish.'

'Well, she has married the soldier. Let us hope there are no battles to follow, that is all.'

'There will be,' said Lady Laura shortly. 'A mad Emperor cannot hold together an Empire of that size, mark my words.'

Jackdaw would have liked to go on speaking with her but found his place card on the table next to that of Ida Anna on his left, and Mrs Clyde, a wealthy farmer's widow, on his right. Ida Anna being far too preoccupied with Lord Selborne to give him so much as a word, Jackdaw found himself totally engaged with the widow, who turned out to be as stupid as Laura had been clever. She was small, fair, and considered herself exceptionally attractive to men. Furthermore, someone had once told her that her personality sparkled and she had from then on spent her time relentlessly living up to this description. She interspersed her sentences with merry and meaningless laughs and much batting of her bright eyes. It was irritating beyond measure, but she thought it witty to pick holes in every other woman present.

'Such a lovely colour the Dowager Countess is wearing.' Giggle, giggle. 'I would not wear it myself though – so fattening. Not that I need worry about that at my age of course.'

She was about thirty but looked a great deal less.

'Ah!' said Jackdaw, wishing she would talk to the man on her right instead.

Mrs Clyde did not take the hint.

'But I suppose when one is really mature,' she went on 'it doesn't matter what one looks like.'

Jackdaw was furious.

'Better by far, surely,' he said, 'to have maturity and wisdom and a certain style than be a perpetual child with an empty head.'

And with that Jackdaw leant across the table to talk to Mrs Milward about Hastings.

It took two hours for the seven-course meal to be served – a tribute to Anne's organization and the brilliance of her kitchen staff. And so it was at about nine o'clock that evening that the guests finally repaired into the Great Hall for dancing. The ensemble – who had had a fortifying break – were now back in the Gallery and playing a jolly polka for all they were worth. Amidst much gay applause Anne and Mr Hicks, followed closely by the birthday girl and the dashing young Earl, led the dancing off.

Jackdaw, having whirled with Lady Elizabeth Waldegrave, saw Mrs Clyde – grinning archly and making little beckoning motions – heading in his direction. Pretending not to see he took the only escape route immediately available. Turning, he went up the Great Staircase and into the Chapel, vanishing from her view.

Though the music here was louder, the back of the Musicians' Gallery being so close at hand, none the less the sound was deadened instantly by the extraordinary atmosphere the Chapel conjured. What had once been Sir Richard Weston's pride and joy – one of the longest Galleries in England – now mouldered in dampness, decay and obscurity; the beautiful windows closely shaded by interweaving tendrils and foliage of ivy.

With a shudder Jackdaw saw that the oak chest in which Sam Clopper had met his death was still in the same place, a fact he had not noticed on Horatia's wedding day, his eyes being constantly on the bride. But now he walked resolutely past it and into the lumber room which lay behind the altar.

When Melior Mary had committed the sin of turning the Gallery into a place of worship, the far windows – the windows from which so many of the Weston family had scanned the parkland for riders bearing news – had been converted into boarded-in louvres. In fact in one of them a bell now hung to call in the faithful, so far had the desecration gone.

With a sound of impatience Jackdaw heaved at the loathsome shutter which eventually gave way with a groaning of hinges. In the summer dusk he looked out over the Home Park and, to his right, the forest. He saw, with eager eyes, the view that had been gazed on so fondly for over three hundred years by the Westons and their descendants.

And then, as he leaned forward to see more clearly, he felt something hard in the pocket of his dress uniform. He put his hand in and drew out the green marble.

'I didn't know you were there,' he said aloud.

Just as he had done years before, when he had seen

Horatia and her family playing on the river bank, he raised it to his eye and peered into the convolutions and spirals that formed its magic heart. And then he slowly lowered it. The earth spun for a second or two as he did so and he grabbed at the shutter to steady himself. But it was no longer there. Neither it nor the bell was anywhere in sight.

With a cry Jackdaw wheeled round. The Chapel had gone too. He stood in a Long Gallery alive with candle-light and blazing fires, the walls hung with glorious paintings and tapestries, a thick carpet running down its centre. Of the Sutton Place he had come to visit that night there was not a sign.

While he stood there, staring, quite unable to move, a figure appeared at the opposite end of the Gallery. It was a woman and, peering, Jackdaw could see that she was wearing an evening gown of the classical type so popular in the early eighteen hundreds. It appeared that he had stepped backward in time. And yet something was not quite right, though Jackdaw, try as he might, could not think what it was.

He watched as she came nearer to him, looking at everything closely as if she were in charge of the appearance of the place. Then he saw her start violently as she caught sight of him.

'Oh good Heavens,' she exclaimed, 'you made me jump! I thought you were a ghost. How did you manage to finish ahead of everybody else? I thought they were still on the liqueurs.'

He made no reply and she went on, 'Never mind. Now that you *are* here you can make yourself useful. By the way, I'm Cynthia – Cyn for short.'

Jackdaw made a jerky bow. 'Wardlaw. John Wardlaw.'

She looked thoughtful. 'I don't remember that name on the guest list. Are you a friend of George's?'

'Yes.'

'Oh I see. Well, would you be an angel and stand at the top of the stairs and make sure they all troop in? If the first ones gawp at the paintings nobody will be able to move.' She paused, looking him up and down. 'Adore the costume. Did you get it at Nathans?'

'No, it's mine,' answered Jackdaw.

He did not know what to think. The girl's dress was that of the time of Waterloo but her manner seemed so strange. And, as far as he could recollect, old John Webbe Weston, John Joseph's grandfather, had lived in Sutton Place in the early years of the century and there had been nobody called George or Cynthia then.

But the girl had him firmly by the arm and was propelling him forward to the top of the Great Staircase. Looking down Jackdaw saw that a throng of people was coming through the small hall – presumably from the dining room – into the Great Hall. He saw hussars, dragoons, cavalry officers; in fact he even thought he glimpsed the Duke of Wellington himself.

'What's the date?' he managed to ask.

Cyn looked at him very oddly. 'June 17, the Eve of Waterloo. Don't you get it?'

But the first people were coming up the stairs: a very beautiful girl in a dress like that worn by Napoleon's consort, an old Field Marshal, a matron in a cashmere shawl and pearl-hung turban. They stopped on drawing level with Jackdaw and the girl said, 'Well! Whose little friend are you? Say, Cynthia, where have you been hiding him? Hello there!'

And she slipped her arm through Jackdaw's in the most friendly way possible. His one thought was that he must get away and look once more into the marble. But there seemed to be no chance for the new arrival went on, 'I'm Penny. Lucky Penny. Who are you?'

373

'Jackdaw.'

'Really? Isn't that cute. I just adore it.' Her voice had a twanging accent that he associated with the Americas. 'Say, are you here on your own?'

'Very much so,' he answered – and could not help a wry smile.

'Then in that case shall we dance a little later on?'

'It would be a pleasure.'

He gave a formal bow and Penny said, 'You're really something, d'you know that?'

She moved on leaving him to stand, statue-like, trying to avoid conversation, as about a hundred people, laughing and chattering, went past him on their way into the Long Gallery.

He was totally bewildered. He could not think why the Eve of Waterloo should be celebrated here in Sutton Place. Nothing made sense to him. And then he realized what was wrong. At the time of Waterloo the Gallery had still been a Chapel, full of rot and mould. He must have gone forward to some kind of pageant. That was the only possible explanation.

And then, as if to confirm his suspicions, a man appeared in the Great Hall dressed differently from all the others. A black cutaway tail coat and black trousers seemed, with a white shirt and white bow tie, to form some kind of evening dress. Yet, despite the fact that his clothes were so dull, he was obviously the most important person there.

'Gee,' said a voice in Jackdaw's ear, 'there's old man Getty now. You'd never think he was so damn rich, would you?'

It was Penny, smiling to herself and giving the Major an appraising glance as she did so.

'Who is he?'

She stared at him in astonishment. 'Paul Getty – our

host, the owner of Sutton Place. The richest man in the world. How come you're here and don't know him?'

'I've been abroad,' said Jackdaw hastily.

'But *everyone* has heard of Paul Getty.'

'Not where I was.' He looked round desperately for an excuse to get away but she firmly linked her arm through his.

'Oh no you don't. I know that shifty expression. We're going to have a dance and you're going to tell me a whole lot more about yourself.'

She steered him down the West Staircase and into the Great Hall to where a band – blowing trumpets and making the most dreadful noise in Jackdaw's opinion – was providing music for dancing. On the way down they passed Paul Getty going in the opposite direction, his horse-face bearing a look of resignation. It struck Jackdaw at once that the man disliked social gatherings but felt obliged to entertain from time to time. None the less he nodded his head at them both politely and Penny gushed, 'Wonderful party, Mr Getty. How clever to reconstruct the Eve of Waterloo. Just look at this wonderful Major. Doesn't he just take the part?'

Getty nodded without enthusiasm, then somebody said, 'Smile,' and a brilliant light flashed in Jackdaw's face.

'Great!' said Penny. 'One of those new Polaroid cameras. Can I have the print? Mr Getty, me – and the mystery man. Should be good.'

The momentary distraction was enough. Bowing very briefly and saying, 'Excuse me,' Jackdaw pushed his way through the dancers – who were throwing themselves about to the words 'One o'clock, two o'clock, three o'clock, rock' – and hurried into the small hall. There he turned into a short passageway, which was new to him, and through a door which led into a close dark room.

375

Startled, he heard a voice – but it came from a box in the corner which gave out moving, speaking pictures.

At any other time he would have stopped to examine it but now he dared not hesitate. From not far away he heard Penny's voice calling out, 'I don't believe it! This is incredible! There's only me and Mr Getty on this photograph! What the Hell's going on? I'm scared. You don't think . . .?'

He raised the marble to his eye and turned every effort of concentration on to Ida Anna's birthday ball. Once more he passed through a world of green convolutes, saw stalactites and stalagmites of emerald ice – and then nothing.

A voice said in his ear, 'Oh there you are! It was very naughty of you to play that game. I had kept this dance for you.'

He opened his eyes to find that none of it had happened at all. He was looking straight up into the face of Mrs Clyde, who was leaning over his chair where he sat, obviously just woken from sleep, in the butler's pantry.

'What am I doing *here*?' he muttered, knowing he sounded utterly stupid.

'You must have hidden after going into the small hall just now.'

'Just now? You saw me do that?'

'Oh yes – we all did.'

Jackdaw stared aghast and Mrs Clyde went on, 'You were up in the Chapel for an age and then you came down and crossed the Great Hall where we were dancing and went through the archway, presumably into here.' She looked at him closely. 'You look very pale. Is anything wrong?'

'No, nothing,' said Jackdaw quietly. 'I have just had the dream of a lifetime, that is all.'

Midnight! But no ordinary chiming of twelve from the steeple of the great church in whose protective shadow nestled Dommayer's casino. For this was New Year's Eve, 1847; the last year in which Europe under the rule of the old guard was to know peace. Revolution and change were everywhere. For the new moneyed class – factory owners of the Industrial Revolution – was rising to challenge the privileged ranks of the aristocracy. And, to add to this, nationalism was the word stirring on the lips of the oppressed. A deadly combination, poised to erupt like a time-bomb before another year would see its way out.

But as John Joseph and Horatia waltzed the night away to the music of Johann Strauss II – a revolution within that family was making the son more famous than the father – they did not allow themselves to think of it. He held her close to him, enraptured by her beautiful face, wondering why he liked her company so much, why he had grown so accustomed to her presence. He supposed that this was natural in marriage – and yet conversations with his fellow officers led him to believe he was perhaps fortunate.

It never occurred to the poor fool, who considered himself so hard with women, that he was falling wildly in love with her. That the little pleasures he got from watching her laugh, or smile – or even stamp her foot – were microcosms of the most powerful emotion in the world. He had no idea that the reason why making love to her gave more fulfilment than ever before was, quite simply, because he adored her. The woman he had married for the sake of marriage, at a moment of total disillusionment, had captured his heart without his even being aware of it.

But he was, at the exact moment when the clocks and churches rang in 1848 – which was to become known,

377

when the history books were written, as the Year of Revolutions – only sublimely happy that his wife was to accompany him when he and his regiment were moved out to Hungary the next day. For Louis Kossuth who had started life as a brilliant Hungarian advocate, publishing a secret nationalist newspaper, was now demanding independence for his nation – and Vienna was responding with troops.

'Are you glad I am to be with you?' said Horatia, reading his thoughts.

'Never more so. Most of the wives have elected to stay behind in Vienna.'

'But I am not "most of the wives".'

'You tell me that? You are a million times more beautiful and clever and brave than the best one of them.'

She laughed, snuggling a little closer. 'You sound very prejudiced.'

'Perhaps. I think you will hate Pesth though – the town is very old and charming but the heart has gone out of it.'

'Do *you* hate it?'

'Yes and no. I lived in the garrison before, which was depressing. But at least we will be in married quarters.'

'I think that is the only reason you married me – to improve your accommodation.'

He laughed down at her, his eyes lit by sun.

'You have guessed . . .'

'Don't tease me so!'

She suddenly looked very young and vulnerable and rather bleak, and for no reason at all that he could fathom his heart lurched. With a sudden change of face he said, 'Horry, do you regret marrying me?'

'I only regret that I am not cleverer.' Refusing to say another word she dropped a curtsey to the Colonel, who stood bowing in front of her, and whirled away into the dance before her husband could think of a suitable reply.

20

Just before first light the dream came, as clear and distinct as it had been twenty years earlier at Sutton Place. He heard again the moans of the dying, the whistle and pound of mortar, the scream of horses; saw himself as a dead man, Horatia at his side. But this time there was a difference, for he dreamt that he was a boy in the old nursery and that he was dreaming the sequence as once he had used to – a dream within a dream.

So vivid was the impression that when he woke and saw the outline of a tent, the rising sun filling it with warm pink light, he was startled and afraid, wondering where he was. And then he remembered. He and Horatia – along with the entire regiment that had been stationed in Pesth – were in retreat. The long-feared revolution had taken place. There was civil war in the Austrian Empire.

It had started in March with an uprising in Vienna of the 'young gentlemen of the University' and had ended with the overthrow of the glittering Imperial government. The capital had fallen into the hands of rebels. And at this signal revolution had broken out everywhere. By September 28 – a week ago, John Joseph recalled with a shudder – Hungary had been ready to declare war.

A tactical withdrawal from Pesth had been ordered and the gates of Buda closed and cannon mounted on the city walls as the National Guard and the Honvods had tried to storm the ramparts of their sister city. The ghastly day had culminated in the murder of Count Lamberg, the Austrian Commander-in-Chief. As his mutilated body had been borne past on scythes the Emperor's 3rd Light Dragoons on foot and horseback – the regimental wives in carriages – had hastily retreated from the city, their destination uncertain.

And now they were encamped on their way to join the force of Jelacic, the *Ban* – or leader – of Croatia, wherever that force might be. For there had been no time or opportunity to communicate with other recalled regiments and each detachment was heading for the Austrian frontier on its own initiative, harassed as it went by bands of Hungarian troops.

And thinking about these hunting packs made John Joseph wake thoroughly and sit up in his rough camp bed and look across to the other in which Horatia lay asleep. Except that she was not there and the thing that he had taken to be her was her blanket pushed back into a roll.

'Horry?' His voice sounded muffled in the taut canvas. 'Horry, where are you?'

But to call was ridiculous for the tent was small and he would have seen at once if she had been within. He swung out of bed, reaching for his jacket – he had slept in his shirt and trousers in case they were attacked during the night – and pulling his boots on at the same time.

Outside the dawn had turned from pink and was streaking the sky orange over the sleeping encampment, the glow from the wood fires almost the same colour. It matched, too, the hair of the young sentry who came to full salute as the Captain approached.

'Sir?'

'Good morning. Have you seen my wife?'

John Joseph spoke in German and the youth answered immediately, 'Oh yes, Sir. She said she wanted to exercise Lùlie and went off with her about half an hour ago.'

John Joseph gave a grim smile. 'Here we are in the

middle of a war and all Horatia can think about is taking the dog for a walk. Which way did she go?'

The sentry pointed east. 'Towards the dawn. She said it looked exciting.'

'Good God! She knows there are raiding parties about. Why didn't you stop her?'

'Sir, I did warn her it might not be very wise.'

'I'll have you on court martial if anything has happened – and the bloody dog as well!'

'Yes, Sir.'

'I wish I had never given her the wretched thing.'

But he had! Last Christmas just before the regiment had marched out of Vienna for Pesth. It had been in the window of a pet shop – a papillon with a hopefully wagging plumed tail and kind face. He had hidden it in his pocket on Christmas morning and Horry had been told to put her hand in with her eyes closed. She had squealed with delight as the jolly pink tongue had licked her fingers by way of seasonal greeting and the new pet had been named Lulie – short for Lucille – straight away. After that it had gone with them everywhere and during the withdrawal from Pesth it had been tucked firmly under Horatia's arm.

And now it may well have got her into grave danger. As John Joseph ran to where the horses were tethered, taking one that had already been saddled, he had never been more frightened. He had never expeienced such a wild pounding of his heart, nor such a lurching in his stomach.

And that was how love came to the Master of Sutton Place – the man who had of recent years believed himself incapable of such emotion: painfully fast, forced out by the fear that he might never see Horatia alive again.

And it urged him on to wildness. Calling out, 'If I am not back in ten minutes raise the alarm,' he galloped out of the camp as if pursued by Hell's children, shouting, 'Horatia, where are you?' in a voice hoarse with emotion. For now he had realized at long last that he *was* in love, he was abrim with it. Longing to hold his wife closely and tell her the things she had always wanted to hear, and he had been foolish enough not to say.

He prayed fiercely and aloud. 'Holy Mary, Mother of God, please let Horatia be safe. Don't let me lose her now that I have just found her.'

The countryside in which he found himself matched his mood; the soaring mountains the heights of his love, the wooded valley his secret thoughts, the broad river his flowing desire. And it was to cross this river, negotiating a precarious bridge, that he went now, doubting even as he did so. For surely Horatia could not have come this way across such rotting planks? Yet he was heading due east into the morning, as he was told she had done.

The crack of a bullet over his head made him crouch in the saddle but his horse – not his usual mount – shied badly, its feet slipping on the ancient wood. He kicked his heels into its sides, forcing the frightened animal to hurry across to the other bank and into the shelter of some trees. Here he reined in, looking about him cautiously and removing his pistol from its holster. Everything was very quiet and so, in the stillness, he started violently, wheeling round to stare straight down the muzzle of a musket, as a voice behind him said, 'Put your hands in the air, Captain. I am about to take you prisoner-of-war.' There, obviously itching to shoot him but not quite daring, stood a red-mantled Magyar renegade, armed with every conceivable kind of weapon – and carrying across his saddle Horatia's dog leash.

'Algy,' sighed the Dowager Countess.
  'Yes, my dear?'

'I feel so worried about my daughters.'

'Why is that, my dear?'

Anne sighed again, a fraction impatiently. 'You know why. Annette has lost her baby, Horry is involved in that ghastly war and Ida Anna has done nothing but moon ever since Laura married the Earl.'

Anne still had not forgiven her niece for using Ida Anna's birthday ball to secure for herself one of the best matches of the season by ensnaring the young Earl of Selborne. And from right beneath Ida Anna's nose to boot. It simply had not been fair in view of the fact that the birthday girl had come out empty-handed.

'It's not right to have so much worry,' the Countess sighed now. 'I have had a life of constant anxiety as far as my children are concerned.'

She was obviously in a mood to feel sorry for herself but, as the remark was patently true, Algy lowered his newspaper and prepared to listen.

'First J.J.'s death and then George's. Neither affecting *dear* Frances, who must be tying poor old Harcourt into knots with thirty-six years between them. And now so much worry over the girls.'

Algy cocked his head sympathetically. He still considered himself the luckiest man in the world to have married her, despite her tendency to grumble.

'I do truly think that if Ida Anna goes on like this she might end up an old maid.'

'Oh, surely not!'

'I think it more than likely. Young men are not what they used to be, Algy. So many *strange* people are around these days. A girl's choice is very limited. So I suppose I should be thankful that I have got two of them off my hands. Though it is so sad that Horatia married a member of a foreign Army. Oh dear!' She sighed again.

'Don't worry, my dear,' said Algy, reading her thoughts

correctly. 'I am sure that the Austrian Army wives will be quite safe and that law and order will be restored soon. There is no possibility whatsoever of Horatia's being in any danger.'

'I do hope not,' said the Countess. 'I really do hope not.'

'What have you done with my wife?' John Joseph shouted, totally disregarding the fact that he was now surrounded by six villainous-looking members of the opposing Army, one of whom held a knife-point to his throat. 'Speak up, damn you. Where is Lady Horatia?'

'Be quiet, Englishman,' came the answer. 'We don't know what you're talking about.'

'You've got her dog leash. I saw it myself. What have you done with her?'

There was a burst of laughter.

'Oh is *that* your wife? The red-headed one? Well, the Major rather liked her and is questioning her personally.'

The obvious *double entendre* threw John Joseph into a frenzy and he punched his immediate captor in the stomach, doubling the man up in agony. This was followed by a smashing of flying fists and two Hungarians were knocked senseless before the Captain disappeared beneath a heap of fighting men, blood coming from his mouth and nose.

'I'll kill the lot of you if she is harmed,' he gasped from the floor.

'Love her then?' asked one of them with a laugh.

'Yes,' said John Joseph, 'yes I do, by God. More than I've ever loved anybody in my life.'

'Oh, why did you have to tell me now?' asked Horatia from the doorway. 'I had always hoped it would be a more romantic setting than this. Oh, John Joseph, do you really?'

384

'I adore you,' he said – and lost consciousness.

'I am the happiest woman in the entire world,' she announced to her astonished captors. 'Oh, thank you for making it happen – all of you.'

And with that she planted a kiss on the cheek of the most evil-looking soldier of the lot and danced round the room with joy.

'The English are mad,' said the Major. 'All quite mad. But none the less it is touching. Lock them up together, Kosser. It is going to be a long war for them.'

'Nonsense,' said Horatia firmly. 'We shall be released in no time, just you wait and see.'

'I can't bear it,' said Anne with a sob, dropping the telegram on to the floor.

Algy, coming in from a Walk with Polly and Anthus and smelling of heath and heather and damp, hurried forward to catch her as she fell, half fainting, into a chair. They were in the Great Hall of Sutton Place and outside it was raining, the water lashing on to the stained glass windows and running down in blurred snakes of colour and the dull day throwing pools of gloom into the shadowy corners.

'Is it *very* bad news?' asked Mr Hicks apprehensively.

'Read it for yourself.'

He stooped and picked up the crumpled paper, smoothing it out and whining very slightly under his breath.

'Thank God,' he said, having scanned the contents.

'Thank God?'

'That they are captured – and nothing worse. I feared something more serious.'

'But Algy – dearest Algy – might they not be in danger at the hands of their captors?'

'I doubt that very much. I should think, my sweetheart, that they are in the safest place of all.'

'No,' said Horatia, 'it is app-ell, not app-fell. Try again.'

'Appfell,' replied her pupil, a surly-looking Austrian soldier of sixteen.

Horatia sighed. 'I don't seem to be making any headway,' she said to John Joseph in English.

'No,' he answered absently, busy at his journal which he was quite determined he would keep until either the war was over or they were released. 'No, my darling.'

He looked up at her very fondly indeed, his dark blue eyes taking on the warmth that was never far from them these days, for he had never been happier in his life. To him this time in captivity was like heaven on earth. Because although he and Horatia – plus the ever-faithful Lulie – had been brought back to the grim garrison of Carlsburg, in company with several hundred other prisoners-of-war, and despite crowded conditions and poor food, he was with his beloved almost every minute of the day.

Now John Joseph said, still in English, 'I think it is not so much your teaching as the fact that he is stupid.'

He smiled and nodded his head at the soldier as if he were paying him a compliment and Horatia said, half seriously. 'You shouldn't do that – perhaps he understands more than we think.'

'Appfell,' said the soldier, and at that both John Joseph and Horatia burst out laughing, joined, after a minute, by the youth himself saying, 'Good yoke – ya?'

'Very good joke,' said Horatia. 'But I think that is enough for today. You can have another lesson tomorrow.'

Then she smiled, just as she remembered her governess doing in the schoolroom at Strawberry Hill.

'Don't be too kind to him,' said John Joseph. 'I think half your pupils are in love with you.'

And it was probably true, for this was how the Captain's

386

wife had organized herself during captivity; by teaching English to her fellow prisoners. She had picked up the German language rather well and – aided by a battered dictionary – found it fairly easy to pass on the basic grammar of her native tongue to German speakers.

'But if I didn't teach I would go mad. My darling, this is not the liveliest fortress, is it?'

John Joseph put down his pen. 'Come here and sit on my lap. No, not you too, Lulie – you stay over there. Has anyone ever told you that you are not only the most beautiful but also the funniest girl in the world? Is there any such thing as a lively fortress?'

She pretended to frown. 'Well, I don't know. I have never really made a study of it. Perhaps there are fortresses where music plays from morning till night and people are jolly and laughing.'

'Well,' said John Joseph, 'you are right – there is just one. It is called Fort Frolic and it is hidden in a dark wood in the heart of Bavaria.'

Horatia cuddled on his knee like a little girl and looked up at him.

'There, every day, they dance and sing and play amusing games. And they dress up in marvellous clothes,' John Joseph went on.

'Who are *they*?'

'*They* are people who have been kind and good and tried hard and that is their reward – to go to Fort Frolic and live in the sunshine.'

'This is a very moralistic tale,' said Horatia. 'Are you sure they don't get bored?'

'No, they never get bored. They love it. Just like I love being here with you.'

'But don't you miss the Army?'

'Not at all. It is simply a means to an end for me. It saved me from being a pauper but maybe, if I work hard,

I can one day resign my commission and take you back to Sutton Place to live.'

'Would you want that?'

'No, not really.' John Joseph's face took on a grim expression. 'The place has never done my kinfolk any good, as you well know. But I do not feel these days that the curse has caught me up after all.' He was smiling again.

'Because of me?'

He gave her a kiss on the end of her nose. 'Yes, because of you, my darling. And for another reason too.'

'And what is that?'

'I believe that that dream in which I die on the battlefield can never come true. You see – and don't think me a coward for saying this, because I fear no man – I shall be locked away here until the war is ended. I am safe, Horatia, as are you.'

She flung her arms around his neck. 'Thank God for it. If I should lose you, my darling, I would lose the whole world.'

John Joseph stood her on her feet and crossed over to the window, Lulie trotting by his side. Through the bars he could see out, across the walls of the garrison, to an autumn landscape sweeping down to the river and across to where the town of Carlsburg gleamed in the brilliant November light. The trees were alive with the glowing colours of Eastern spice: cinnamon, nutmeg, saffron and paprika flamed from every leaf, interspersed with curry and clove. Everywhere nature seemed on fire as the great winter solstice took its first hold upon the land.

'The world is so beautiful,' he said, his back turned so that his face was unreadable. 'I would hate to leave it before I had run my course. But if I do, Horatia – ' He turned to look at her. 'No, don't say anything. If I do I want you to make me one promise.'

'And what is that?' she said, longing to touch him but afraid to move.

'You are not to stay alone. I would not like to think of your beauty unloved and uncherished. The role of lonely old woman is not for you.'

'But how could I love anyone else?'

'You will if you are meant to. Now stop frowning. Come here and stand beside me and let me tell you a story about the Autocrat of Carlsburg who lived in that tower you can see in the distance.'

He pointed and she went to him and they were in total harmony again on that cold and beautiful autumn afternoon.

Christmas in Sutton Place! And everybody, apart from the children, thoroughly miserable. Europe had endured one of the worst years in history; monarchs had been deposed; governments had gone down; nothing would ever be the same again. Only the British nation seemed to be secure; that is if one turned a blind eye to the political agitators – as Mr Hicks thought of them – called Chartists. They whose roots were in the London Working Men's Association and the central tradition of British radicalism. And they who called for justice for the working classes and spoke of the rights of freeborn Englishmen.

But their name was not mentioned during the festive season of 1848 as the children crowded around a Christmas tree – an innovation of the Prince Consort's from Germany – which the Dowager Countess had had raised in the Great Hall. Caroline's three boys and two little girls picked up their presents eagerly. And Annette's eldest son, young Archibald, punched his brother George, so eager was he to be first there. But not the presence of all the children in the world – and there were only nine –

could have consoled Anne. She could think of nothing but Horatia – and John Joseph of course – in some bitingly cold prison, with little to eat and no presents or fun.

In fact, so sad was she that she had wrapped them little gifts and put them away in a drawer against the day when the dreadful war would be over and they would come home to Sutton Place.

'Things will be better now that mad King Ferdinand has been deposed and Vienna has fallen to the Imperial Army again,' said Algernon comfortingly as he carved the turkey.

'I always felt rather sorry for him,' answered Caroline. 'John Joseph wrote that he was very kind and merely simple-minded. No real menace to anybody.'

'A simple-minded Emperor is always a menace,' reported Francis Hicks roundly. He had become a very good surgeon and equally confident in his opinions.

'I suppose you're right,' Caroline sighed. 'I wonder what the new one will achieve. After all he is only eighteen and succeeding at a most treacherous time.'

'He will bring the war to an end, you see,' said Algy, smiling at Anne. 'I have every confidence in young Franz Josef.'

'I pray he will,' answered the Countess. 'I pray that this time next year we will have darling Horatia – and John Joseph, of course – back with us once more. If only she had married a British Army man.' She felt Caroline's gaze on her and hastily added, 'Of course John Joseph is a perfect husband and son-in-law. It is just that I hate the thought of my girl in a prison cell.'

Caroline would like to have retorted that it was not the first time a Waldegrave had been behind bars, but she bit her tongue. It was no good raking up the past – and it was no good speaking ill of poor George who, like his brother, had died so sadly and so young.

So she said instead, 'I hear that Frances is considering restoring Strawberry Hill.'

'Yes,' answered Anne, 'and so I should think. It was she and George who stripped it and abandoned it in the first place. But Heaven alone knows if the scheme will ever come off. It is probably just one of her ideas.'

Her dislike of her ex-daughter-in-law had grown stronger with the passing years and now she added spitefully, 'It is said that old Mr Harcourt is thoroughly annoyed by the constant parties Frances insists on giving in his home. I do declare that she imagines herself one of the rising political hostesses of the day.'

Nobody quite knew how to answer – for it was all perfectly true. The parties at Mr Harcourt's house, Nuneham Park, were spoken of as the liveliest and gayest there were. And Frances's penchant for private theatricals and her insistence on acting some wretched piece called 'Honeymoon' over and over again had become something of a joke in the family.

Now Algy said mildly, 'It is her home too,' and was rewarded with a viperish look from his wife.

There was another slight pause and then Ida Anna's voice broke the silence.

'I heard Giles weeping in the Chapel last night,' she announced gloomily. 'There's bound to be a disaster in the family. It's supposed to be a sign of that.'

Her stepfather looked cross as a pug.

'Really!' he said. 'There are youngsters present! Mind what you say, young lady.'

Her bootbutton eyes narrowed to pebbles but she made no reply, merely tossing her head disdainfully. However, Caroline's eldest son Charles – now eight years old and as bright as his parents – said, 'Who is Giles?'

Nobody answered and after a moment his father – who had extremely progressive views on child care and did not believe the dictum that they should be seen and not heard – said, 'He is supposedly the ghost of a jester.'

'Ghost?' chorused all the bigger children together, while little Emily – Caroline's youngest but one – said, 'What is a ghost, Papa?'

Francis, realizing he had taken on more than he could cope with, said airily, 'A kind of fairy.'

'That's not what I've heard,' muttered Charles – but an icy look from Caroline reduced him to silence.

But afterwards when all had been cleared away and the family had withdrawn to the Music Room – a grand title for a place where once Sir Richard Weston's lads had slept – he whispered to his brother Frederick, the next in age to himself, 'A ghost is the spirit of a dead person come back to walk the earth.'

'I know. I heard at school,' came the reply.

'Then shall we hunt for Giles tonight? Charters Minor – the spotty one in my form – went on a ghost hunt in an old abbey once and saw a headless monk.'

Frederick went a little white and gulped but, none the less, said, 'All right. Shall we ask Archie and George to come?'

'No. They're always fighting. They'll spoil everything.'

'I just thought . . .'

'No. Listen, Mama is looking at us so we'd better be quiet. I'll meet you at midnight in the Great Hall. It's a nuisance that I'm sharing a room with Archie but he snores like a pig so I doubt he'll wake up.'

'All right.'

'And don't go to sleep and miss it.'

Frederick, looking pale but determined, answered, 'Don't you either.'

And that was how, when cards and music were finally

finished on that Christmas Day of 1848, two small boys, aided by the light from flickering candles, came to be creeping, in their bare feet, up the East Staircase to the Chapel which had once been a Long Gallery.

In their ears were the hundred and one noises made by a sleeping house. From before the dying fire in the Library – into which the brothers could peep if they looked back through the banisters – Polly and Anthus sighed dog sighs and everywhere timbers groaned and creaked as they cooled and settled. The huge grandfather clock in the Great Hall chimed a quarter and then resumed its sonorous tick, while somewhere a little carriage clock – a few seconds slow – tinkled a response. And from somewhere else above them, a floorboard moved as if a person had just walked.

They both jumped violently and Frederick said, 'What was that?' But Charles only went 'Shush,' and continued his stealthy stalking.

Before them lay the Chapel, lit by a frosty moon, shafts of silver light falling on to the floor at regular intervals from the ivy-clad windows. And in one of these shafts a man, wearing a thick shirt of some material like cambric and dark-coloured trousers, tied round the legs with criss-cross string to his knees, sat grinning at them. His face was so reassuring, so crinkled and jolly, and his eyes so twinkling, that he was not in the least frightening. And Charles – knowing perfectly well from Charters Minor that ghosts either wore white sheets or had no heads – was quite the reverse of frightened and walked boldly up to him.

'Who are you?' he said.

By way of response the man rose to his feet and executed a nimble cartwheel.

'I say,' said Frederick, coming up to them, 'that was jolly good. I wish I could do that.'

'It's easy, young Sir,' answered the man with a bow, his voice slightly accented, reminding Charles of some gypsies he had once heard. 'Look.'

He did it again and then fell to the ground in a rolling ball, his hands round his ankles and his head tucked into his chest.

'Gracious,' said Charles, clapping. 'Can you do any more?'

'Sit you there, young masters, and I will give you a show. Would you like that?'

'Yes please.'

They sat down on two of the Chapel chairs, side by side in their nightshirts, and watched a display of tumbling that took their breath away. Regardless of obstacles the man traversed the length of the Gallery with a series of leaps, jumps and falls that had them gasping. He finished with a high split jump, landing on one knee before them.

'I always ended like that,' he panted. 'Least I always did for Francis and Catherine.'

'Who?'

'Francis and Catherine Weston. They used to live here, long ago.'

'Oh,' said Charles, who had little knowledge of Sutton Place's history, other than that it had been inherited by his great-grandfather. 'Did you live here too?'

'I still do,' answered the man, grinning like a split pumpkin, 'in a way.'

'We haven't seen you,' ventured Frederick.

'Not many people do. They hear me sometimes though as I go round and about.' The boys looked slightly nonplussed by this and the man added, 'But I wanted to tumble for you – as it's Christmas and all. Now I think you had better go back to bed. It's very cold.'

It was – freezingly so, though the boys had not noticed it in their enjoyment.

'Yes, we will,' said Charles. He held out his hand, 'Well, thank you . . . what did you say your name was?'

'I didn't, young Sir. I didn't. Now goodnight to ye.' He bowed before them.

'Goodnight then.'

They began to go, a little awkwardly, glancing back at him over their shoulders. He stood watching them, his great smiling beaming face aglow, until the moment they turned to wave from the top of the stairs and he had vanished.

'I wonder how he got out,' said Frederick.

'There's another entrance to the Chapel at the far end – the one used by the public.'

'Oh! Nice, wasn't he? I wonder who he is. Jolly good at tumbling, didn't you think?'

'Yes. Pity he came in a way though.'

'What do you mean?'

'Well, no ghost would have dared appear with him threshing about.'

'That's true. Oh, well! See you in the morning, then.'

'Yes. Goodnight Frederick.'

'Goodnight Charles.'

And with that the two little boys went back to bed without another thought.

After that Christmas came a winter so severe that every country in Europe seemed to have moved back to the Ice Age. The vast rooms of Sutton Place became unheatable – nowhere was it quite so freezing as in the fortress of Carlsburg. Every night John Joseph and Horatia would share a narrow pallet, lying fully dressed and clutching each other to keep out the cold, the dog at their feet. But often one would wake, without the other, and shiver – the only warmth they had that of their love.

Yet of the physical expression of this love there was

little, as until the first week of February they had shared their cell-like room with an old Austrian soldier. But then he had died of pneumonia and in the brief privacy that followed John Joseph held Horatia – as naked as they both dared in that temperature – and kissed her beautiful mouth and breasts, his shaft at last where it had longed to be for weeks.

They had feasted on this lovemaking, aware that at any time another occupant might be found for the now empty bunk. And then one early morning, just as they had moved apart, and were in the light sleep that followed total fulfilment, they heard the bolts on their door draw back. But instead of the new occupant they expected, a guard stood there, grinning broadly, and saying in German, 'Come along, Missus, you'd better put your clothes on.'

His eyes ran up and down Horatia's body and she drew her shift to her chin.

'Why?' said John Joseph angrily, adding, 'If you stare at my wife like that I'll knock your bloody head off.'

The guard ignored him and continued to grin. 'The General-in-Chief is here and wants you to translate for him,' he said to Horatia.

'But I don't speak Hungarian.'

'That doesn't matter – he wants you. Now hurry up!'

John Joseph began to leap out of bed but Horatia put her hand out.

'I'll be all right. Don't worry.'

But as she marched the long stone corridors, hearing her footsteps echoing as if someone was behind her, she was not so sure. It went through her mind, quite without reason, that she might be going out to meet her death. And, as she had heard happened to dying people, her life flashed before her. She saw lazy river days at Strawberry Hill; she saw her father dropping at his birthday party;

she saw her poor dead brothers – and then she stopped herself.

Horatia Webbe Weston straightened her back, brushed her eyes with the back of her hand and refused to think such grim thoughts. Instead she said to the guard, 'Be so good as to tell me about the General.'

'He has just arrived, Missus. He's a very big high-up – but I don't know much more except that his name is Klapka and he is a Magyar.'

'But why does he want me?'

The guard winked his eye. 'He saw you out exercising your dog, Missus, and said you would be the very person to translate for him.'

'Well, translating is all he will get,' muttered Horatia.

'Eh?'

'Nothing.'

They had reached the end of the corridor and stopped before an oak door, heavy with hinges. The guard gave a deferential knock and a voice said, 'Come.'

At first Horatia could see nothing in the high-vaulted room, bedecked with regimental banners and antlered stags' heads and obviously, at one time, the mess of the officers who served the garrison. But then the clouds of cigar smoke that filled the air with rich-smelling wisps parted a little and she saw that, behind a desk, the back of a tall chair was turned towards her. From the chair a pair of muddied riding boots stuck out, and a hand which held the potent cheroot – and which, she also noticed, was bedecked by a large gold ring bearing an eagle's head.

'You may go,' said a disembodied voice in Hungarian.

'Yes, Sir.'

The guard executed a rapid salute, banged his feet on the floor and marched out, closing the door behind him. Just before he went, he caught Horatia's eye and leered.

It was then that Horatia realized she was not alone with the General because, from the shadowed recess by the window, the fortress Commandant stepped forward and said in Hungarian, 'Would you like me to leave also, General Klapka?'

'No, my dear fellow, that will not be necessary. But I must look at the English lady close to – I forget myself.'

The chair swivelled round to reveal the General richly, if somewhat dustily, apparelled in scarlet, his medals glinting upon his chest. Horatia saw black whiskers and moustaches and long dark hair – a typical Magyar noble.

He rose to his feet and bowed and said in German, 'My English is very poor, Madam, but as you can hear I command the German tongue. Perhaps you, with your knowledge of both, would help me to communicate with other English prisoners.'

Relief! He genuinely wanted a translator. Horatia gave him a brilliant smile and then regretted it as he advanced towards her with his bright eyes twinkling.

'Well, well, well,' he said. 'You *are* pretty, aren't you? I can see that I am going to enjoy travelling with you.'

'Travelling?'

'But of course. I cannot stay here more than twenty-four hours. I am at the front, my dear young lady, and you are about to accompany me – in your official capacity, of course!'

The Commandant gave a short gasp as Horatia said in English – and swearing for the very first time in her life – 'Oh no I'm bloody well not.'

The General advanced to within an inch of her and stared right into her eyes, his pupils almost touching hers.

'Oh yes, you bloody well are,' he whispered.

It was Jackdaw!

21

To end that cruel winter came a snowfall, dropping from a sky as grey as Arctic sealskin, and hiding beneath its white nun veil all the flowers that trembled with rebirth in the dark ground below. But then, when the flakes had melted, the sun at last showed his great face and burst through in a warm roseate mist. At this the crocuses flowered with the snowdrops, lambs were born and gambolled in the English meadows and the waters of the Danube threw off the last vestiges of ice and sparkled blue and deep as any Italian lake. All of Europe lay beneath a sky as wild and fine as a meadow of flowering violets. Everyone knew then that the ordeal was over, that spring had come to give them new life, that the earth had survived and had been born again.

In the crisp early morning air Mr Hicks's sensibly gaitered legs swung out as he headed through the Home Park with Polly and Anthus nuzzling and muzzling amongst the roots behind him. And Anne, well booted and dressed in serge, was only a step or two away with Ida Anna, who grumbled about the muddy terrain and wondered how long it would be until luncheon. But for all that the youngest Waldegrave was happy, glad to know a letter from the War Office in Vienna had arrived to say her sister and her brother-in-law had been released from captivity and that John Joseph had been able to rejoin his regiment. Not that she had thought a great deal about Horatia and her husband, too preoccupied was she these days with the worrying notion that she might be 'on the shelf'. Oh horrid and sickening phrase! For after all she was twenty-three now and men were not springing up in abundance, to put it mildly. She blamed it all on Sutton Place. For who would call there, to that haunted old pile?

And thinking these thoughts made her sigh aloud and say, 'Do you think I could stay in Vienna with Horatia, Mama? I hear it is the gayest capital in Europe.'

'It *was*,' answered Anne, 'but it has been in the hands of revolutionaries so goodness knows what has taken place. But, perhaps, when this dreadful war is over, a trip to Europe might do you good. After all, there are a lot of young Englishmen in the Austrian Army and I am sure John Joseph knows many of them.'

'But when *will* the war be over?'

'Your stepfather believes that it should be any time now.'

'How strange it is,' said Ida Anna, apparently changing the subject but not really doing so, 'that some women have three husbands and others have none.'

'Are you thinking of Frances?'

'Yes.'

'There is nothing strange about that,' answered her mother with pursed lips. 'She knows how to *please* men.'

'What do you mean?'

'That I cannot tell you,' said Anne, observing the strict conduct of the times.

'Well, why can't I do it? Please men, I mean?'

Anne looked a little flustered and said, 'We really ought to be getting back now. Come along, my dear. I am sure you are hungry.'

But Ida Anna's bootbutton eyes held a wondering gaze and she made a mental note to ask Cloverella what to do to be pleasing. For, after all, if her mother would not talk about it it was bound to be interesting.

But her attention was distracted when she got home by

the arrival of another letter – this one from Horatia herself.

Dear Mother, Stepfather and Ida Anna (it read),

How pleased I am to be able to tell you that John Joseph and I are back in Vienna, which has been badly bombarded but other than that has not changed a great deal. I cannot say too much about our two miraculous releases from custody – after all, the war is still on and certain things, by law, must not be stated in writing. However, the stories will certainly interest and amuse you when you *do* hear, which will be when we eventually get home on leave. Oh wonderful, wonderful thought!

Meanwhile we are both very well and very happy and you must not worry about us at all. We leave to rejoin the regiment on Monday and hope and pray that it will not be too long now before the wretched war is over and we can settle down to family life.

Our dearest love to you all,

Horatia.

'Settle down to family life, eh?' said Algy, guffawing a little.

Anne gave him a very reproving glance because Ida Anna was staring avidly. But inside she was overjoyed. Grandchildren were always welcome – and this one! In view of Horatia's ordeal the little mite would be doubly loved when it finally chose to appear.

'I can't wait for the hostilities to cease,' she said now, a small buzz of excitement blurring her voice. 'Oh Algy, when do you think it will be?'

'Within the next six months, my dear. I am certain of it.'

And he was right! As the family sat down to breakfast one summer morning in a room overlooking the gardens of Sutton Place, Algy rustled his copy of *The Times*, cleared his throat importantly, and said, 'Listen to this.'

The Dowager Countess and her daughter looked at

him expectantly and he went on, 'Vienna, August 18, from Our Own Correspondent. It is a somewhat singular circumstance that I should, on the Emperor's birthday (he is nineteen), have to inform you that the Hungarian war may be considered as nearly concluded.'

He could read no more. Anne had burst into tears and Ida Anna was about to follow suit.

'There, there, my dear,' he said, patting his wife's hand and looking kind. 'No need to cry. They'll be safe now.'

'Oh I hope so,' she said, 'I really do hope so. Algy, are you sure?'

'Of course. Fighting will be confined to little pockets of resistance, that's all. Just small skirmishes – and localized at that. There is nothing further to worry about.'

But despite her brave attempt at a smile there was still an anxious look in the Countess's eye.

'I will not be happy until they are both safely home,' she said. 'Not until the Master has set foot once more in Sutton Place and we can laugh at ancient curses.'

Algy put his head on one side.

'The ancient curse?' he said. 'Yes, I must admit I had forgotten about that. Never mind, my dear. It can't affect John Joseph now.'

'But I thought this was a mere pocket of resistance,' said Horatia, 'not a vast citadel armed to the teeth.'

'You're exaggerating again,' answered John Joseph, smiling. 'It is a fortress, that is all. They can hold out for no longer than a week. Now that General Gorgey has surrendered to the Russians, Klapka will lay down his arms and bring his troops out with their hands in the air. You'll see.'

They smiled at each other. As always when the name of General Klapka was mentioned they remembered Jackdaw's brilliant impersonation of the Commander, aided by nothing more than a passing physical resemblance. Remembered too how he had forged the General's signature on their papers and led them out into the darkness and away from the garrison of Carlsburg. It had been nothing short of a miracle that he had gone undetected. Yet he had appeared to enjoy himself, lighting cigar after cigar, and pulling a terrible face for the Commandant's benefit when Horatia had insisted that she would scream non-stop if her husband and dog were not to accompany them.

How he had kissed her then. She could feel it even now, even after five months. His mouth so hard and demanding, his body taut with tension. It had been difficult to realize that it was all an act – which it must have been. Yet still the kisses had rained upon her mouth one after the other and she had gazed astonished at his expression of ecstasy. She had thought him quite the most brilliant actor she had ever seen as he held her against his pounding heartbeat and buried his lips in the sea of her hair.

He had murmured in her ear then too. Something that had sounded like 'I have always loved you', but could not, of course, have been so. But, regardless of what it really was, the Commandant had been amused by his superior's behaviour and had seen them off with a wink.

'What about the husband?' he had said, with a jerk of his head in the direction of John Joseph.

'Oh, I'm sure we shall find a job for him,' Jackdaw had answered with a knowing laugh.

And that had been that. They had escaped captivity where dozens had failed, rescued by the daring of the Captain's boyhood friend.

He had left them at the border, heading off towards Russian lines in search, so he said, of the Czarevitch himself. They had watched his black horse plunging off into the night aware that now they were to find their way back to the Austrian force single-handed. But their freedom had lasted hours only. At dawn the next day they had been picked up once more by Hungarian troops and within a few days were back in Carlsburg.

But this time English diplomatic channels had opened and it was only a week before Mr Colquhoun – the Consul in Bucharest – had arrived to take Horatia away.

'But what about my husband, Mr Colquhoun? We don't want to be separated.'

The Consul had adjusted his monocle and cleared his throat.

'Lady Horatia, there is nothing I can do. Though he is a British subject he is also a member of the Austrian forces. I have been instructed by the Foreign Office to lead you – and you alone – to freedom.'

John Joseph had stood up. 'Horatia, you must go. Mr Colquhoun has his orders. Take Lulie and wait for me in Vienna. The Austrian troops are so near – that's right, isn't it, Mr Colquhoun? – that Carlsburg will fall to them any day. I should be with you in a month. Now don't argue.'

Mr Colquhoun bowed. He was the perfect English diplomat – about forty, going grey and with an air that most would describe as distinguished.

Now he said, 'Captain Webbe Weston is correct, my Lady. Carlsburg is right in the line of the Austrian advance. Your separation should only be brief. Now I will withdraw for a minute so that you may make your farewells.'

John Joseph and Horatia had said nothing when he had gone – exchanging one kiss which spoke more than anything they could ever have put into words. Then she turned away, Lulie under her arm, and went through the cell door without looking back. The idyll was over. They could never be quite so close again.

Eight weeks later he had walked through the door of their married quarters in the capital, very thin and haggard, but smiling with joy to see her. They had one night together before John Joseph by command – and Horatia by choice – had gone to rejoin the regiment. The Hungarians were on the point of defeat and every man was needed to drive home the victory thrust. Within hours they were heading for the fortress of Comorn, Lulie left behind to be cared for in Vienna.

And now the great citadel lay before them, straddling the banks of the Danube in all its impenetrable might. A catch of familiarity came to John Joseph's throat. Was this the place he had seen so often in that strange and terrible dream?

'Are you all right?' Horatia's voice interrupted his thoughts.

'Yes, why?'

'You seem a little shaken. Is it the size of the place?'

'Frankly, yes. I had expected nothing like this.'

They stared in silence to where the fortress – or rather the various parts that went to make it up – shone in the August sunshine. It was a brilliant construction, spanning as it did the entire river. On the right bank stood the Sandberg – a smaller fort protected by ten blockhouses. These had been put up in such a way that they protected the whole of the complex and, furthermore, must be taken successively. Behind the Sandberg lay the Danube fortification, bearing bomb-proof casements and space for two thousand men. These two armouries – known as the Palatinal works and stretching 18,000 feet – must fall to the Emperor's troops before the inner or actual fortress, which stood on the left bank, could even be approached.

'It's impossible,' said Horatia – and then went silent for fear of a rebuke as an Austrian Major rode past. She should not really have been at Comorn at all, only a few Army wives and camp followers being allowed near the mighty garrison before the final bitter blow that must be dealt to it in order to end the war.

'I hope to God we don't have to starve it out,' came John Joseph's answer. 'Look at that island beyond. It's one swarm of mosquitoes. If we are to stay here any time we will all be down with sickness and you, young woman, will be sent straight back to Vienna.'

'And if there is fighting?'

'There is no chance of that at the moment. It will need seventy-five thousand men to storm the place.'

'Then I shall stay as long as you will let me.'

He took her hand and kissed it. He felt so much love that tears sprang into his eyes.

'Horatia,' he said, 'if Comorn should finish me, I want you to stay a friend of Jackdaw's. He is a remarkable man, as you well know, and could help you more than anybody else.'

She was silent, thinking about what he had just said, the words spinning in her mind like tops but not really making any sense.

'I don't want you to speak of it,' she said eventually. 'Nothing can happen to you. I won't let it.'

He smiled a little sadly.

'I think there is a saying, "What will be, will be." You are a soldier's wife and must face facts. If I die, Horatia, Sutton Place is willed to you until you remarry. When that happens it will pass to Uncle Thomas Monington but I have settled on you a thousand pounds a year for life. That should leave you comfortable enough to make the match of your choice.'

'Stop it,' she said, 'stop it, stop it, stop it.' The hot

tears rushed down her cheeks and fell, splashing on to his outstretched hand. 'You are never to speak of it again. I can't bear it.'

'Very well,' he answered. 'But, whatever the outcome of Comorn, remember that I love you and will until my dying moment.'

'Which I pray is after mine,' was all she would answer as she walked her horse away from his and on towards the huge encampment that stretched along the banks of the Danube as far as the eye could see.

By the light of the full August moon Cloverella and Jay danced in a fairy ring, moving in a spiral, in to the centre and out again. The name of the pattern was 'Troy Town' and its origins were ancient – the shape of the dance supposing to represent the maze which resembled the walls of Troy. While they danced they sang, loudly and clearly, worshipping nature and the old magic in their special way.

But, for once, their usually high spirits flagged fast and it was with a sigh that Cloverella finally sat down, offering her twelve-year-old son a pull at both a stone bottle of wine, which she had brought with her, and a clay pipe which she had placed in her pocket.

Yet after a few moments' puffing Jay broke the silence, saying in a voice squeaking with the changes in his body from boyhood to manhood, 'Is something going to happen? Are you dancing Troy Town to see into mysteries?'

His mother sighed once more.

'Yes I am. All is not well here, Jay. The curse is awakening, my dear.'

He looked stricken. 'I thought so.' His voice went down an octave and he sounded momentarily full grown. 'Is it to strike the Master?'

'I don't know – perhaps. Would you be sad if it did?'

'Of course I would.' He was a child again, protesting and indignant. 'How could you ask me that?'

'No offence, no offence,' said Cloverella, puffing her pipe hard. 'I just wondered how close you felt to him.'

'Why, is he my father then?'

She smiled but said nothing, and the child went on, 'Or is it Major Wardlaw?'

Cloverella laughed, her white teeth gleaming in her nut-brown face. 'Do you really want to know?'

'Of course I do.'

'Then come here.'

And with that she leant across and started to whisper into her son's grimy little ear.

'. . . to crown the horrors of this war a pestilence was raging in the camps with such virulence that Prince Paskiewitsch states . . .'

Mr Hicks's voice – reading from *The Times* newspaper – died away.

'Yes?' said Anne.

He looked at her, his eyes like saucers behind his pince-nez.

'. . . that five thousand men of the Russian Army had been attacked by cholera in three days.'

'Well, thank God it is the Russian and not the Austrian,' she said after a short pause.

Unspoken thoughts hung in the air between them. Thoughts that the Russians and the Austrians had joined forces against Hungary and that camp sites were shared and epidemics were no respecters of nationality.

'It is here too,' said Algy, after a while. '*The Times* reports six hundred and eighty-six dead to date in the British Isles.'

'If only we knew where Horatia – and dear John

Joseph, of course – are. There has been no word since that one letter.'

Algy took his pince-nez off and rubbed the top of his nose.

'I expect we will hear something soon,' he said.

And to that Anne could make no answer.

September – and the time for all to be gathered in. Everywhere harvest festival; curling loaves, crispy apples, sheaves of corn and bright-eyed choristers. Voices raised up and up from spire and weather vane, thanking the Lord for providing the richness of the land. And on the banks of the Danube voices raised up and up from tent and canvas, asking the Lord how He could give so much suffering.

Because in that ridiculous last-ditch stand embodied by the fortress of Comorn, nobody could possibly win. Nobody, that is, except some foolish men of war whose pride it was to stand before others and orate meaningless words about victory and patriotism, feeling their own thin blood stir with the clichés and worn-out phrases which meant so much to them and nothing at all to mankind.

For on both sides – Austrian and Hungarian alike – there was agony of spirit. Within the fortress General Klapka felt his health deteriorate, leaving him too tired to argue with the Hussars and the Honvods who would rather have seen the walls of Comorn fall in ruins around them than surrender to the Emperor's Army. And beyond those walls, in the Austrian encampment, now swollen in number to 73,000 men – including a Russian corps of 18,000 – 10,000 soldiers lay stricken either with cholera or malignant fever. The Army of both factions was dying on its feet.

And in Vienna – to underline the futility of all this sacrifice – Prince Radetsky made his Victor Ludorum entry into a city transformed. For, in his honour – and he, poor man, knew little of the agony of Comorn – shawls, curtains, carpets, petticoats and every kind of flag imaginable had been hung from the balconies and windows of the houses beneath which he must pass on his triumphal journey to the Emperor's palace, the Hofburg. With Strauss's especially composed Radetsky March ringing in his ears, the Prince knelt before the Emperor and was crowned with a laurel wreath for bringing the Hungarian war to its close. It would appear that the last siege of all had been entirely forgotten.

But there – there on the banks of the great blue river that swept Europe's heart – everyone in the Austrian camp waited breathlessly for Vienna's instructions. Horatia had watched General Haynsu arrive and depart on the same day, mortified that the terms of surrender offered by those who occupied the fort were so hard.

And then, while the capital danced in celebration at the end of hostilities, the order came. It was to be a full siege. The Hungarians would be starved out if it took the Emperor's Army a year. But all of them – from Franz Josef down to the newest and rawest recruit – had reckoned without one thing. From the pilgrim route that lay between India and Mecca an insidious enemy had crept unseen to attack the people of Europe. Cholera stalked at Comorn.

September! Death of the year. The sun like blood as it rose over the damson river; corn stubble bones in the afternoon; the sky at evening a crimson shroud. It was a time for endings, for farewells, for breaking hearts.

He knew, of course. The Master of Sutton Place knew for sure that the wheel was slowing, that the circle was almost complete; felt with such agony of soul that his days with Horatia were drawing to a close. He would have given anything in the world, when he finally understood his destiny, to escape it.

But he could not and he did what he thought best, knowing that time was slipping away from them both. He gave his love to Horatia with such an open heart, with such generosity of his evolved and kindly spirit, that he wrapped her in a shawl of happiness. She walked amongst the sick and the dying, assisting the Army surgeons, almost lightheartedly. It was not that she was shallow, or did not care, it was simply that she knew herself to be cherished and protected by the strongest force in the world. And then, quite suddenly and most cruelly, it was taken from her.

John Joseph grew sick one afternoon and within three hours could not move from his bed. Horatia ran the length of the camp to fetch the nearest surgeon – too wild-eyed to cry – but when the doctor came back with her she sobbed for a moment or two.

'It's cholera,' he said briefly. 'Don't give your husband water, it will dilute the body salts even further.'

'But he's begging for it.'

'Then just a sip. No more. You must be cruel to be kind.'

'Oh God help me!'

'Perhaps He will. Start praying.' Harsh short words hiding a caring heart grown tired.

'Thank you. May I send for you if there is any change?'

'Of course. Keep him warm. It is all you can do.'

After he had gone Horatia sat down beside the bed and gazed with great tenderness at the man with whose portrait she had fallen in love, remembering John Joseph at the front of it now, staring into the distance; in the background, dwarfed but omnipresent, Sutton Place.

And looking into her husband's face, purplish and wrinkled with fever, and watching helpless as he endured

411

the agonizing cramps, she realized that the poor man had never had a chance. That he had been heir to a curse which had brought destruction, in one form or another, to all connected with it.

Already Horatia felt isolated, alone, at the bedrock of her existence. Outside the tent the noise of mortar shot, where the cannon pounded at the impenetrable walls of the fortress, reminded her vaguely that she sat in the midst of a vast Army. But to her there was nothing in the world but herself and the dying man who lay beside her. Regardless of all infection laws she lifted him up into her arms.

Very much to her surprise he opened his eyes.

'Horry?' His voice was weak and husky.

'Yes, darling?'

'Will I be missed?'

She could not answer for a moment, not quite understanding.

'Do I leave behind a good memory?' he persisted.

She knew then what he meant. He was anxious that people – not just herself – should remember him with affection.

'A wonderful memory, my darling. Everyone loves you so – especially me.'

Her voice broke into a sob and, putting her head against his chest, she bitterly wept.

'No, no.' The words were scarcely above a whisper. 'You must not . . .' The rest of the sentence was lost to her.

'Don't talk, my darling. Save your strength.'

His body went into a spasm of agony.

'Let me go,' he said.

Horatia looked at him astonished. He was asking her to loose her loving hold upon him, asking her to let him slip away.

'Is that what you want?' she whispered.

'Yes. I am a ship becalmed. Oh, blow up a wind and lift this hulk off to the land where the mermaids sulk.'

He was in delirium, of course, but how beautiful the words! Very gently Horry lowered him to the bed and watched him leave her. And then her heart fragmented into a million pieces and she wept until she fell asleep, all dirty face and tousled hair lying beside her sweet-love-gone.

But he who had died in the dawning came back briefly to speak to her once more. She heard his voice say, 'Leave Sutton Place, Horry. Leave that accursed house.'

It was a dream, of course. He had been dead since day-break.

A winter queen stood beside the grave of a black knight later that day. They put him in without ceremony, without coffin, with nothing but the Austrian flag and fifty of his fellow men for companionship. Over the mass grave a Catholic priest chanted and sprinkled holy water while, from the depths of her black cloak, Horatia drew a bunch of rowan berries – all she had been able to find in the sparse country around Comorn – and threw it in with white fingers. The dark earth closed over the glistening red – and with that, with that last gesture of love, John Joseph vanished from her sight. The Master of Sutton Place was gone for ever.

22

It seemed to the Dowager Countess, as the clouds of steam from the departing London train separated dramatically, that she had never really seen Horatia before. A solitary black figure – gauntly thin and walking with measured steps, a slow sad dog plodding behind it – appeared through the vapour coming towards her down the platform, its white face drawn, its hands thrust into gloves to protect them from the chill November wind.

'Horatia!' called her mother. 'We're here, darling.'

The figure made no response but continued its steady progress.

'Can she hear us?' whispered Anne to Mr Hicks.

'Yes, my dear. I think she is in a state of shock. You will have to treat her very gently.'

'Oh my God,' said her mother, starting to cry. 'My poor little girl.'

'Anne!' Mr Hicks was terse. 'Stop it at once. Weeping will do no good at all. You have to be a tower of strength to her now. Control yourself.'

He had never been so fierce with his wife, so distraught was he at the pathetic sight of his stepdaughter wending her way. He remembered how beautiful she had been when he had seen her first in the Swan Hotel at Hastings, how her presence had been a flash of splendour amongst ordinary mortals. And his faithful old heart was heavy within him to see the icy ghost of what had once been Horatia Elizabeth Waldegrave, the jewel of her generation.

He stepped forward, pushing past Anne in his haste.

'Horatia, my dear,' he said. 'Welcome home.'

She was like a shadow in his arms, so skeletal and frail had she become.

'Oh, Stepfather,' she said, 'I am very glad to be here at last.'

The Countess bustled up, acting the part of her life.

'I'm so happy to see you, my love,' she said. 'We have all been very anxious. Sutton Place will be far the brighter now that you have come back.'

'Sutton Place!' answered Horatia, giving a grim laugh.

Over the top of her head Algy and the Countess stared at one another with misgiving. Yet on the way back the widow seemed controlled enough. That was until the moment when the gates swung open before her and the lodge keeper came to a salute, calling out, 'Welcome back, my Lady.'

Then she said bitterly, 'Welcome back! To what? An empty house. *His* house.'

Very gently Anne said, 'But darling, it is your home now.'

'Much good may it do me. I will spend as little time here as possible.'

'But sweetheart, surely you will live with us? Where will you go to on your own?'

'I don't know and care nothing, so long as it is away from this cursed place.'

Anne would have said more but behind Horatia Algy put his finger to his lips and the rest of the journey up the drive was conducted in silence.

For once Ida Anna's thoughts were on somebody other than herself and she greeted her sister very sweetly indeed. But it was from Cloverella, of course, that the most dramatic gesture came. She appeared in the doorway wearing a travelling cloak, Jay – carrying a bundle and an old carpet bag – beside her.

'Here Missus,' she said, 'take my hand.'

Horatia did so and felt something warm and sticky. Looking down she saw that blood oozed between her closed fingers.

'That is the gypsy's way of swearing fealty. I am your bond woman from now till the end of my life. If ever you need me, my Lady, call to my likeness.'

She passed Horatia something wrapped in brown paper.

'Keep it like that until you need me. And when the day comes unwrap the image and say to it, "Cloverella, thou must come to me."'

Almost blindly Horatia took the parcel.

'Are you going away then?'

'Aye, my Lady. The change in Jay's body has come about. Now he must travel and learn if he is to be a great man.'

'A great man,' echoed Horatia and the ghost of a smile played about her mouth that such a little ragamuffin could be described in those terms. 'Have you enough money for that, Cloverella?'

'Enough for the two of us, Missus. We shall not be forced to beg.'

Horatia fished in her reticule and brought out a golden guinea and a white handkerchief.

'These were in the Captain's pocket when he died. I would like you to have them.' She added hastily, 'The handkerchief has been boiled and disinfected; it cannot carry the infection.'

Cloverella handed both to Jay, who bowed his head very solemnly. Just for a fleeting second he reminded Horatia vividly of someone but the memory of whom had gone before the thought could form in her brain.

'Then I shall say farewell, my Lady. Never forget that I will come if you call me.'

416

The widow took the girl into her arms. 'Thank you for your friendship,' she said.

Cloverella kissed Horatia's hand. 'Long life and good luck to the Lady of the Manor.'

And with that she and Jay began to walk away from the house and down the drive towards the gates. At the bend after which they would be lost to sight, they turned to wave – two brilliant figures. Then in a flash of scarlet petticoat, a merry flute tune and a scamper of little bare feet they were gone.

Horatia turned in through the door of the mansion house with a sinking heart.

'I never thought I would inherit you so,' she said aloud to it. 'With my true love cold in the ground before he had run his allotted course. Be damned if I won't get rid of you; sell you – and do away with your evil influence for ever!'

The stones re-echoed her voice as the first threads of darkness fell on that raw and cheerless November afternoon.

In her own little sitting room, beneath the officer-and-gentleman portrait she had painted of her brother John Joseph only twelve years before, but which – with him dead and buried in an unmarked mass grave on foreign soil – now seemed more like a hundred, Caroline Hicks sat opening her morning post. A very pretty woman, her face was spoiled at that moment by a deep frown which turned into a grimace of misery and finally tears as she read and re-read the letter in her hand.

'Francis!' she called eventually, springing to her feet. 'Francis, where are you?'

From above in his dressing room came an answering shout and she ran up the flight of stairs and along a short passage, bursting in without pausing.

'Whatever is the matter?' he said. 'Caroline, you're crying. What's happened?'

'Two awful letters have come,' she sobbed, rushing into his arms just as she had when they were first married. 'The first from Anne saying that Horatia is in a dreadful state – thin and gaunt and withdrawn from life. But the second even worse.'

'What is it?'

'It came from Helen Wardlaw. She and the General are heartbroken – Jackdaw has been posted missing, believed dead.'

'But I thought that bloody damned business had ended!'

The eminent surgeon that Francis had become very rarely swore in case he inadvertently did so before the respectful medical students, but this was too much for him. His tragic brother-in-law had died ten days ago before Comorn surrendered to the Austrian Army – what a futile waste of a life! – and now to hear that Jackdaw had been sacrificed just as hostilities had ceased!

'Did Helen give any details?'

'Yes. Apparently he went off to translate for the Czarevitch himself but went missing behind the Russian lines after a Magyar attack. Oh Francis, Francis, it is all too painful.'

She began to sob again – not just for Jackdaw but for her brother as well and for her sweet sister-in-law brought so low with anguish. Her husband looked grim. He thought of the years he had spent learning so painstakingly to repair human bodies – and then thought how one battle alone could put those bodies beyond his care.

'The politicians who wage war are senile and crazed,' he said. 'Sometimes I despair for mankind.'

Caroline wiped her eyes. 'Anne also wrote to ask if Horry could stay with us. Sutton Place seems to be

making her worse and it is felt that she would be better
with you keeping an eye on her, dearest.'

'Of course, of course. Does she know about Jackdaw
yet?'

Caroline paled. 'I don't know. I doubt it. Of course
she hardly knew him, even though he was John Joseph's
best man, but still she had the most intriguing introduction
to him. Do you remember it?'

'Do you mean when he ran after her carriage, shouting
and making an idiot of himself?'

'Yes. He must have been absolutely smitten with her.'

Lovely, clever Francis fixed his wife with a bluebell
glance that had grown no less sparkling over the years.

'I don't think he's ever stopped, poor man,' he said.

'Francis! How would you know that?'

'By the way he looked at her on her wedding day. I
would never have said this to you, Caroline, while either
of the poor souls were alive – but two bridegrooms stood
at the altar that day.'

'Did Horatia know?'

'No, I don't think so. She has never had eyes for
anyone but John Joseph.'

'You're right.' Caroline shook her head slowly. 'She
fell in love with his portrait when she was little more than
a child. Poor, poor creature – how *can* she be feeling
without him?'

'Like a ship floating in a sea of pain.'

'Will she recover?'

'Oh yes,' said Francis. 'The human psyche repairs itself
without realizing it is doing so. Even the most grievous
death cannot be mourned for ever. Sweet memory will
take its place and eventually happiness, of a different
kind to the one before, comes back.'

'I have told you often,' answered Caroline, hugging

him, 'you are a very wise man – and I love you. Will you try and help Horatia?'

'I will do my best,' said Francis.

On the night before she left Sutton Place to stay with the Hickses, John Joseph's widow had a wild bad dream. She stood on that long curving beach, so familiar from other dreams, and saw again the chapel set beneath the hill. But on this occasion its door was wide and open, and she – even though afraid to do so – felt herself drawn within. There was something sinister about the place this time, for solemn music from an invisible source was playing and big candles threw their flickering light on stained glass saints and dying martyrs.

To her horror she saw that two coffins stood in front of the altar, an order of black-cowled monks mutely guarding them. And even while she watched in terror, two of the monks lifted the lids and beckoned her forward to pay her last respects. She had known then – in that distant way in which sleeping thoughts come – that it would be better by far if she did not look. But the monks were coming forward – their quiet most menacing – to escort her.

One bowed his head, saying, 'It is your duty, Lady Horatia.' He seemed faceless, his voice coming from the all-concealing cowl.

Most reluctantly Horatia walked up the aisle and stood at the foot of the left-hand coffin. From there she could see a pair of military boots and a flash of blue uniform within the white satin interior. It was John Joseph.

She did not want to look on his face, could hardly bear the thought, but some terrible compulsion forced her forwards. She leaned on the coffin's edge and peered within, giving a cry of horror as she did so. For it was not her husband's body that lay there but his ivory bones.

420

Skeletal hands were crossed upon a uniformed chest that bore the Cross of a Knight of Malta, while his shako adorned a sombrely grinning skull.

She turned away and in her haste almost fell upon the coffin that stood to the right of John Joseph's. It rattled on its plinth and she was forced to grip it to stop herself falling. With equal horror she saw that this one was empty, that it waited for its occupant.

She wondered then if it was intended for her, if she was meant to have died with her husband and never returned to Sutton Place. But then the name plate on the propped-up lid caught her eye. She bent to read it and in the flickering light saw, 'Major John Wardlaw, 1817–1849. Rest in Peace.'

She started to cry hysterically at that and was still doing so when she woke up – drenched in sweat and shaking from head to foot. It was Ida Anna who came running to her, a shawl around her shoulders and her feet bare and cold.

'Oh Horry darling, what is it?'

'A nightmare. A dreadful one. Ida Anna, I dreamt that John Wardlaw was dead as well as John Joseph.'

Her sister looked stricken. She had never quite recovered from Anne's matchmaking plans in which Jackdaw had figured so prominently.

'Oh dear, I hope it isn't an omen!'

'So do I. He risked his life to come and get John Joseph and me out of captivity. If he had been discovered he would have been shot instantly. I would hate any ill to befall him.'

They sat in silence for a moment or two, each of them thinking of their jewel-eyed friend. Horatia remembering, with the very smallest blush, the way he had played the part of General Klapka and kissed her so hard and so deeply. Ida Anna recalling that strange time at her

421

birthday ball when he had been found asleep in the butler's pantry, not knowing where he was.

Then, to hide the fact that her cheeks were growing pinker and pinker, Horatia crossed to the window. Drawing back the curtains she gazed out to where stars danced in silver clusters around others of sapphire and milk, and low in the sky, a moon, thin and new, glistened with frost.

It was bitterly cold, even the little pools on the gravel walkway reflecting moonshine on the sheet ice that was forming on their surface, and from somewhere in the park the hoot of an owl added voice to the bitter scene.

With her back turned to her sister, Horatia said, 'John Joseph told me to seek him out, you know. Said that he could help me.'

'Jackdaw you mean?'

'Yes.'

Ida Anna padded over to her on freezing feet.

'You only had a dream, Horry. Perhaps Jackdaw *is* alive and well. Perhaps we are being foolish.'

Horatia turned and smiled at her, noticing how the hard little face had taken on a soft and loving expression.

'Do you remember when you were a little girl and you used to call yourself the favouritest baby in all the land?'

Her sister shuddered. 'Yes. How you must all have hated me.'

'We did. But you have made up for it now.'

The sisters hugged each other in the cold.

'Get back into bed,' said Ida Anna. 'I'll stay with you if you like.'

'I wish you would.'

And they got in together so that Horatia, in her sleep, felt the warmth of another body and this time dreamed that John Joseph was alive and with her once more.

But the next morning, fastening her black coat about

her and putting a black bonnet over her hair, she stopped to look at herself in the mirror. She was ugly thin, bony and hard, her face pinched and white, her mouth a line of misery. Round the beautiful eyes were circles of darkness and her foxfire hair had become that of a vixen exhausted by the savagery of the hunt. It lay dull and flat, hanging about her shoulders where once it had bounced. At barely twenty-six Horatia Waldegrave looked tired of life.

Ida Anna, Mr Hicks and the Countess were all at Woking station to see her off to London but once on the train a terrible feeling of isolation swept her. She wondered how she could possibly face the rest of her life alone, how she could exist without companionship and love. Then Horatia thought that if Jackdaw was alive, if that terrible dream had just been a figment of her imagination, he might help her to gain peace. John Joseph had told her that his friend studied old truths and wisdom. Perhaps, then, he might teach her to live with loneliness.

The train entered a tunnel and Horatia closed her eyes, trying to conjure behind her lids the image of her husband as he had been on their wedding day. But somehow his face would not come to her and she could only remember Jackdaw turning round and staring at her from the altar as if, as far as he was concerned, she was the source of all light.

She was too numb and too hurt to think – as a woman in full possession of her wits would have quickly done – that he obviously loved her. That he had kissed her as Jackdaw and not a member of the Hungarian high command, that he had never stopped caring for her from the second he had first seen her in her carriage at Hastings. And long before then – though that was something she would never know.

Instead she prayed most innocently – there with her

423

eyes closed – that her husband's friend was still alive, that they might speak of John Joseph together and share dear and cherished memories. But the second that she set foot on the platform at Waterloo station she knew that this was not so. One look at Caroline's set face was enough. Horatia was not even to be granted the consolation of Jackdaw's friendship.

She said without preamble – even before hugging Caroline – 'It's Jackdaw, isn't it? He's been killed.'

'Yes,' answered her sister-in-law. 'I'm afraid so. Helen says they've given up hope of his being found. There is to be a memorial service for him at St Mary-in-the-Castle, Hastings, later this week. Did she write to tell you?'

'No,' answered Horatia. 'But I know. You see, I have seen his coffin.'

The rest of her words were drowned in such uncontrollable weeping that it never did occur to Caroline to ask what this strange remark could possibly mean, but this did not stop her recounting the words to Francis that evening.

'She is having morbid fantasies. Caroline, I would strongly advise against her going to that service.'

'But she is insisting. Francis, surely you could give her some kind of opiate. And anyway you will be there.'

'I can't stop her taking an hysteric.'

'Oh she won't do that,' answered his wife. 'She is too proud. She would feel that she was letting both of them down – both John Joseph and Jackdaw.'

But none the less, despite the draught that Francis had given her, and despite the fact that her brother and sister-in-law were sitting on either side of her in the carriage, virtually holding her up between them, Horatia went dramatically white to the lips as the equipage turned into Pelham Crescent.

'Are you feeling ill?' asked her brother-in-law, very brisk and professional, not daring to be kind.

'No, no,' she murmured, dabbing at her mouth with a handkerchief. 'It's nothing – just a moment's faintness.

But her head reeled. She had recognized the chapel instantly. All those strange dreams where she had wandered the long beach or the headland, always with the same two shadowy men and always seeing a church that nestled beneath the cliffs. Obviously that had been a glimpse into the future; for now here was Jackdaw's memorial service, which could so well have been that of John Joseph, being held in the very place. The circle had just clicked into position, the pattern of her destiny was clear.

And yet – was it? For as she set foot within the building which had once been St Mary's Chapel but which had since 1828, when the church had opened for public worship, been called St Mary-in-the-Castle, Horatia's heart suddenly lifted.

It was inexplicable. The beauty of the place – cut in a semi-circle into the very heart of the great cliffs – could not account for the sudden uprush of spirits. Nor could the substance that Francis had given her, for that – so he had said – would make her quieter, calmer.

As Horatia sat in one of the church's huge galleries, all of which rested on a ledge in the cliff, she grew more and more uplifted. Her eyes, taking in the coat-of-arms of William IV over the clock and the large marble font – fed by a spring of never-failing water that issued from the cliff itself and which flowed into a little grotto covered in greenery – began to resume some of their old sparkle. And as the preacher took his place in the pulpit, she leaned forward almost expectantly, her chin cupped in her hand.

'Dearly beloved,' began the sonorous voice, 'we are

gathered here together today to honour the memory of one of the sons of the town of Hastings – Major John Wardlaw – cut down in the prime of his sky-blue youth . . .'

It was then that Horatia turned to Caroline and said, quite loudly and distinctly, 'Oh no, I don't think so. I really don't think that is true,' before she fainted completely away at her sister-in-law's feet.

And before she fell into unconsciousness she smiled. For quite distinctly, right into her ear, she had heard John Joseph whisper, 'Horatia, have faith. Jackdaw lives, my darling. I promise you he lives.'

23

'No,' said Uncle Thomas Monington. 'No, Lady Horatia. I simply won't agree to it. Sutton Place is to remain in the family and that, as far as I am concerned, is that.'

'But, Sir . . .'

'But me no buts if you please. The terms of your late husband's will are quite clear. Sutton Place was left to you until you marry again or die. Upon either of those events the house and estate become mine for life. However, as you know, if you remarry your husband granted you a jointure or allowance of one thousand pounds a year payable from the estate . . .'

'But Uncle Thomas, why can't we break the entail? You already have Sarnesfield Court and no heir. What do you want with Sutton Place? Why can't I sell the house and divide the money with you?'

'No!' he answered loudly, giving Horatia a look that could only be described as poisonous.

He was a horrid old man, long and spindly like a ginger spider. He had, in his youth, had orange hair but this had now turned pepper and salt, and his freckles, in sympathy, had merged into a whole giving him a leathery aspect. From his nose – the nostrils of which moved rapidly like bellows – descended great light hairs and his hands, covered with whiskers, constantly shook. His teeth, patently false, seemed ill-fitting in a mouth which salivated vastly as he spoke. Horatia hated him and wished him on the moon.

But it was not just his disgusting appearance that repelled her; his nature too, was scuttling and furtive.

Even in childhood, realizing that his elder brother – John Joseph's late father, whom Thomas resembled not at all – would inherit the Manor of Sutton, he had set about wooing his ancient kinswoman Anne Monington. He had been the little angel who had fetched and carried her salts and her gloves, who had exercised her ghastly dogs and who had given her sweet-smelling, hand-picked posies. His concern had not gone unrewarded. At a very early age he had inherited Sarnesfield Court in Hereford on the condition that he adopt Miss Monington's name.

It struck Horatia as strange that both John Joseph's grandfather and uncle had inherited vast estates from maiden ladies with the condition of a name change. Old John Webbe had added Weston and been rewarded with Sutton Place from mad Miss Melior Mary; his son Thomas had dropped Webbe Weston in favour of Monington and had acquired Sarnesfield Court, where he had lived as a gentleman ever since he had been twenty-one, and seemed now equally determined to see Sutton Place remain in the Webbe Weston family, though he himself had not a single child.

Horatia tried again. 'But why, Sir?'

'It was clearly your late husband's intention – ' he never said John Joseph's name ' – for you to live in Sutton Place in the event of his death and manage it as it should be managed. It seems to me – to put it very bluntly indeed, Lady Horatia – that you have flouted his wishes at every turn. But in this one respect, as a named heir, I can overrule you – and overrule you I will.'

He sneered triumphantly and Horatia had an overwhelming urge to hit him in the face. She was on the point of telling him John Joseph's last words – if they had, in truth, been his last words and not just a dream – but bit her tongue. Why should she discuss with this soulless wretch the innermost secrets of her heart? Instead she stood up and said, 'You may think what you wish, Mr Monington. I have my private reasons for not wishing to live in Sutton Place – and I also have my private reasons for wishing to dispose of the Estate.'

He sneered again, his face bending like india-rubber as he did so.

'Surely – ' A fountain of saliva went splashing in the sunlight. 'Surely you do not believe the story of an ancient curse? I would have thought a woman of your background would have known better. But then of course there is no accounting for female fancies.'

Horatia looked him squarely in his runny blue eye.

'As a matter of fact I do believe the legend and – though I have no intention of discussing him with you – so did John Joseph. He always wished to put as much distance between himself and the manor as possible. Therefore, as you have been frank with me, I shall be frank with you. Though you may thwart me so far as selling Sutton Place is concerned, where I choose to live is none of your affair. So I shall say good day to you, Mr Monington, and inform you that I intend to stay here in Leamington and leave Sutton Place as it is – rented by my mother and stepfather.'

His leathery face contorted like a mask and he stood hissing into his teeth for a moment. Then a totally unreadable expression crossed his eyes and he said, more lightly, 'Do you know your late husband's first cousin? My nephew Francis Salvin, I mean.'

Horatia stared at him blankly and answered, 'Of course. I know him and his family well. Why?'

'I thought of inviting him to Sarnesfield Court – and you as well. You see I am *not* without an heir, Horatia. Sutton Place will pass to him when you and I have finished with it.'

429

She could think of nothing more intelligent to say than, 'Oh!'

Mr Monington's whole tone had altered and he looked as near to pleasant as was possible for him.

'Then I shall ask my wife to issue an invitation shortly. You may count on it. Good day to you, Horatia.'

And with a bend of his scrawny body he was gone, leaving his niece by marriage staring after him and wondering what the rapid change in his tactics could possibly signify. Perhaps he thought Cousin Francis could soften the blow now that her plan to dispose of the manor house had been finally thwarted.

Horatia sighed, shook her head, and picking up two dog leads called for Lulie and Porter – the terrier pup Francis Salvin had raised for her. Then, pulling a shawl about her shoulders, she stepped out into the afternoon.

It was May. Everywhere blossom swirled in the air as a warm west wind shook the laden branches and sent pearl-white clouds scurrying across a sky blue as harebells. And borne on that breeze she heard the murmuring sounds of early summer; the bumble of bees blending melodiously with the cuckoo's distant voice.

Horatia's spirits, dampened enormously by Uncle Thomas Monington, lifted again. Everything had happened to her over the past eighteen months just as Francis Hicks had predicted, though she – sweet thing, playing with her dogs in the sunshine – had hardly been aware of it. At last she had found herself able to think about John Joseph without crying, and was able once more to take an interest in her surroundings. She had begun to enjoy living again and – despite dreadful opposition from her mother – had rented a house in Leamington which she now occupied with only a small staff for company.

But one thing had been a bitter blow. She realized, now that so long a time had passed since anyone had heard from Jackdaw, that she had had an hallucination in St Mary-in-the-Castle – brought on, no doubt, by the opiate Francis had administered.

She could have sworn, at the last second before she fainted, that John Joseph's spirit had stood beside her and spoken within her inner ear. But she had been wrong. Jackdaw was dead and she would never see him again.

Not that she lacked male company. Mr Colquhoun – the English Consul in Bucharest who had released her from her second imprisonment in Carlsburg – had called on her in Leamington. And then, for a year had passed since her husband's death as polite behaviour decreed, he had polished his monocle, dropped on one knee before her and told her that he had fallen in love with her at first sight. Even there, in that horrid place, and with the Captain right beside her.

'You were the prettiest thing I'd ever seen,' he had said.

Horatia had refused him, of course. But Mr Colquhoun was made of stern diplomatic stuff and had returned in December to continue his courtship. He had then taken great exception to the presence of Cousin Francis Salvin, who was there on a Christmas visit with his sister; decided that Francis was also pursuing Lady Horatia and had refused to call further.

The widow had giggled helplessly when Mr Colquhoun's letter had arrived. That anyone could take Cousin Francis seriously seemed, to her, quite beyond the bounds of possibility. Not that he was bad-looking – though inclined to put on weight; it was simply that he was so hearty and hale, the absolute epitome of an English country gentleman. His conversation centred mainly on hawking, cormorants and birds in general – on all of which he was an authority – or otherwise killing something. He had always, without fail, just been fox hunting, or shooting a pig, or bagging game birds.

But Horatia liked him for all that. He was kind and affable and in some ways artistic. He had done a lifelike and compassionate sketch of Lulie – plumed tail wagging again now that her ordeal in the war was over – when Horatia had stayed with his family in the Pennines. And he also excelled at burning pictures into wood – his favourites being dogs' heads, of course.

With his strangely mixed nature – cruel sportsman, bird lover and artistic soul – he reminded Horatia of a great gruff bear; fishing with his paw, dancing for children, lying on his back in the sun. It would also seem – with his total lack of interest in the ladies – that this particular bear did not require a mate.

Thinking about him now made Horatia smile and she hummed a tune into the May breeze. Then she thought, 'I must ask John Joseph . . .' and pulled herself up short. She had done it a million times since he had died; her brain a fraction of a second late in giving her the correct information. She had been going to enquire of her husband whether Cousin Francis reminded him of a cuddly bear too. And she had also been going to ask what to do about Uncle Thomas Monington and the future of Sutton Place. But then if John Joseph had been alive the future of Sutton Place would not have been in question – and Uncle Thomas Monington would have had no say in the matter whatsoever.

'So you see, my dear Countess, this matter concerns me greatly and I do not come here today in a spirit of interference but in one of anxiety – and if I may so phrase it, caring.'

Uncle Thomas Monington and the Dowager Countess Waldegrave sat in one of the smaller drawing rooms of

Sutton Place looking out to the distant orchards from which the sweet smell of blossom blew towards them on a light west wind.

'I'm sorry . . .?'

She stared at him a little blankly, wondering what he was trying to say to her. She hardly knew the man at all, having seen him only once since Horatia's wedding, but now, sitting opposite him in the sunshine, finding him rather nasty. He leant forward a little to speak again and sprayed so much that she recoiled. From somewhere in the back of the room Mr Hicks made a curious sound.

'I have obviously not made myself clear, dear lady.' Uncle Thomas flashed his false teeth. 'I have been to Leamington recently and seen the Lady Horatia. We had a friendly chat indeed – though she did have some foolish notion of selling Sutton Place which, of course, she cannot do because of the entail. However, it seemed to me – without wishing to alarm you in any way whatsoever, my dear Countess – that your daughter has been on her own too long. It is sad, but the Lady actually admits to disliking Sutton Place, and I feel it would be of great benefit to her if she were to marry again.'

He paused for dramatic effect and Anne gazed at him.

'And into the Webbe Weston family.'

There was a stunned silence and then the Countess said, 'But she is already a Webbe Weston. What do you mean, Mr Monington?'

'I mean, Madam, that with one neat stroke all Lady Horatia's problems could be solved. And that stroke is – ' he cleared his throat ' – marriage with my nephew and heir Francis Salvin.'

'Good gracious!' said Anne. 'What does Horatia feel about all this? Does she like the gentleman?'

Mr Monington sprayed furiously. 'They spent last Christmas together, Madam. Need one say more?'

'I spent last Christmas with my brother,' growled Mr Hicks from the back of the room. 'But I have no intention of marrying him.'

Uncle Thomas gave a most reproving stare and the Countess said, 'Algy, there is no need for frivolity. That was a silly remark. I am quite sure that Mr Monington has Horatia's best interests at heart.'

Mr Monington gave a repellent smile.

'Oh dear, dear lady – how wise you are! Such a match would not only end Lady Horatia's tragic widowhood, but also secure the future of Sutton Place for ever.'

Anne looked thoughtful. 'I must confess that she has written little of Mr Salvin in her letters to me – except to say that she found him amusing.'

Uncle Thomas pressed his fingertips together ecstatically and Algy – who was in a very strange mood that morning – said, 'Well, that *is* good news. At least she can laugh as she hands over her inheritance.'

Mr Monington looked very pained, which was really quite the most frightening sight, while Anne rose from her seat and paced back and forth.

'I am not sure, Sir, that my daughter is seriously entertaining the idea of remarriage. She has already turned down one extremely good offer from Mr Colquhoun, the English Consul in Bucharest.'

'Possibly because her affections were engaged elsewhere.'

'She never hinted such.'

The Countess stopped pacing, ignoring her husband who was grimacing in the background, and turning to face Mr Monington, who rose from his chair like a skeleton on wires, said, 'Very well, Sir. I shall do my part. I shall invite Mr Salvin to Sutton Place when Horatia is here. After that the matter is in the hands of fate, would you not agree?'

'Indeed, Countess, indeed.'

He brushed the back of her hand with his spongy lips.

'After all,' thought Anne, enduring the moist salute with fortitude, 'if Horatia does not like him there is always Ida Anna.'

Inside the trap the beautiful arctic fox struggled helplessly, its legs – unbroken but yet caught in the wicked netting – tearing again and again as it tried to fight its way back to freedom. But what a glorious sight it was, even in the wretched cage. A crystal being in a land of silver – with a pluming tail of snow, muzzle of glittering white, and eyes lakes of fierce and lonely purity.

The trapper could not kill it. He crouched over the small and primitive prison and saw it turn to look at him. There was blood on that lovely fur; red as poppies in frost. He put out his hand to touch it, knowing that the glacier teeth could not reach him.

'Come, my friend,' he said. 'Go free. It is not my intention to harm you.'

He cut the harsh twine with his knife, glancing over his shoulder as he did so to make sure he was unobserved.

Just for a moment victor and captive stared one another out. There was everything in that glance; gratitude, love, triumph – and envy.

'How I wish I were you,' said the captive. 'How I wish I could run into that great and silent forest and out beyond the vast peaks.'

The fox made no reply but paused a second longer, the flow from its wounded flesh running towards the captive in a brook of scarlet.

'What are you saying to me? That my time will come? That one day I will run wild again?'

The fox tilted its head back and howled to its fellows in the pine trees. Then it put out its tongue and licked the hand of the trapper before it turned and ran superbly over the snow and away into the ice-bright Siberian morning.

At dusk Sutton Place seemed to grow in size – or so Horatia Webbe Weston always thought. Wings grew longer in shadow and the Great Hall would rear against a sky suffused with the mulberry glow of a dying sun. But fascinating as this was, Horatia did not care for the illusion, thinking the house big and omnipotent enough. In fact she had found herself disliking Sutton Place more than ever on this visit to her mother and stepfather, wishing that Cousin Francis had not come to stay at the same time as she, and that she could cut the visit short and return to the friendly world of Leamington.

But that would have been the height of bad manners, for Francis was as enthusiastic over the house as she was opposed, marching about and exclaiming aloud at all the wonders. Quite as she imagined a bear would investigate a honey-pot. And this made her smile, for who could be in the company of such boyish enthusiasm and not have some of it rub off on them?

'A truly fine old Baronial Hall,' he was saying now. 'Simply capital. By Jove, Lady Horatia, how I would like to have seen it in its former magnificence. I think it must have been an evil hour when my grandfather pulled down the tower and gateway.'

'But they were in a ruinous state.'

'None the less, I believe that the past should be preserved when at all possible. In my opinion – ' he lowered his voice ' – he must have had the mentality of a Goth, as did Oliver Cromwell.'

She laughed out loud. 'Oh, Cousin Francis! You look so serious when you talk like that.'

He seemed gratified at her smile but went on, 'I *am*

436

serious. Why if Sutton Place were mine I would wish to see it restored. That is if I had the money to do so.'

Horatia sighed. 'Not something that is in the greatest plenitude in the Webbe Weston family, I fear.'

Cousin Francis laughed gustily. 'There may be ways, Lady Horatia. There may be ways.'

She looked at him blankly. 'What do you mean?'

But he would not say, simply contenting himself with putting his finger to the side of his nose and making a mysterious face.

'If you are thinking that I could sell it and break the entail then cease to do so. Uncle Thomas Monington is violently against any such scheme.'

Looking very sheepish Cousin Francis said, 'Let us not discuss it any further. I shall change the topic. Are you looking forward to visiting the Great Exhibition?'

Horatia smiled at him. 'Of course I am. It is a day that nothing could spoil.'

'Absolutely.'

But the cousins by marriage had reckoned without one thing. June 27, 1851 – the day when they had arranged to visit the miraculous display situated in Hyde Park and housed in a vast glass and iron conservatory – was the date of a heatwave. Even on the train, Horatia, Ida Anna and Cousin Annie, garbed as they were in many-flounced skirts maintained by at least a dozen petticoats, began to wilt.

And once there Horatia found that the tropical atmosphere lent the whole thing a dream-like quality. In fact she could half recollect having dreamt at some time that she had been at just such a place with just such a hearty man.

But nothing – be it heat or vision – could detract from the glittering palace of crystal dominating the landscape and housing within its wondrous structure naves and transepts, concert halls and choir halls, to say nothing of all the rare and beautiful things transported from every part of the Empire and Britain itself.

'The Prince Consort has triumphed,' said Cousin Francis importantly. 'This far surpasses my expectations. His words have come true – a living picture of the stage of development at which mankind has arrived.'

Horatia slipped her gloved hand through his arm – he really was such a kind and loveable bear. And he was so pleased at her doing this that he was all smiles when, most unexpectedly – while staring at a case containing a stuffed and mounted Indian tiger – they ran into the entire Hicks family.

'This truly is well met,' said Caroline, shooting Mr Salvin an enquiring look from beneath jet brows. 'Shall we remain as one great party?'

They all thought it a splendid idea and, after seeing as much as they possibly could in an afternoon, the family repaired to Soyers Restaurant to dine.

And it was then, while everyone else was busy with the menu and the two women had a moment of privacy, that Caroline leant across the table and said, 'Horatia, are you going to marry that man?'

Her sister-in-law's astonished expression was enough to answer her question but she went on, 'Because I am sure he intends to marry you.'

'Good Heavens, Caro, what makes you say that?'

'I think he likes you a great deal – and also it would be neat.'

'Neat?'

'It would tie up the Sutton Place inheritance, would it not?'

'But he is already the heir – after Uncle False-Teeth Monington.'

Caroline did not smile. 'There might be more to it than

438

that. Remember John Joseph left you an allowance of a thousand pounds a year in the event of your remarriage.'

'But that would come from the Sutton Place estate. Caroline, that doesn't make sense.'

'We shall see,' said her sister-in-law enigmatically and changed the subject by asking, 'Do you remember the first time you saw Jackdaw?'

'At Hastings? How could I ever forget.'

'I dreamt I relived that scene the other night. Horatia, I think he is still alive.'

John Joseph's widow went pale. 'What makes you say that?'

'Just a feeling. You had it once, too, in St Mary-in-the-Castle.'

'Yes, but I was wrong. Nobody could disappear without trace for this length of time.'

'I'm not so sure. I am very full of premonition at the moment. And part of it is that you should not marry Mr Salvin.'

'Oh, don't be so silly,' said Horatia, more loudly than she had intended. 'Nothing could be further from his mind.'

But there she was wrong, for three days later, as they were walking through the Great Hall, he suddenly said, 'I have so great a taste for all that is ancient that I feel I must declare myself here. Horatia, will you do me the great honour of becoming my wife?'

She pealed with laughter, dropping her book and clutching at her sides in the most unladylike manner. Mr Salvin, looking exceedingly huffy, said, 'And may I ask, pray, exactly what it is that you find so amusing?'

'Things ancient,' she chortled, indicating herself.

'What? Oh! Oh I see!'

Cousin Francis began to laugh too, roaring about in an excess of relieved emotion.

After a while they grew calmer and Horatia in a quiet voice said, 'Yes.'

'What?'

'Yes, you old grizzly. Listen, Cousin Francis – I don't love you but I do think you are fun to be with. Is that good enough?'

'Good gracious, I should say so. Horatia, this is my first love affair – '

'Hardly that.'

'No. I mean yes. But I really will try to make you happy. I will do my best.'

He sank to one knee, putting a hand over his heart to denote sincerity.

'I know that no one can ever replace your lost love, Horatia. But if you could look on me as a different love – then I won't have to bear too much comparison.'

His voice trailed away and Horatia hugged him with all her might.

'Whoever said comparisons are odious was right. Everyone has his own special place – and so have you, dearest Cousin Francis. And I can assure you it is deep in my affection.'

But there she lied, for he was like a brother to her. And she – loving, warm, wonderful Horatia – could no more have settled for that than have hurt her good dog Lulie, who had borne so much hardship with her.

That night – that very night – of June 30, 1851, the trapper caught a sable in his snare. It was quite dead when he found it but, for all that, he gazed on it with sorrow. He was not a killer by inclination, pressed into the role by forces he could not control. But as he skinned it he touched the pelt with a type of love and thought of the woman to whom, one day, he would present it. This was the only thing that kept him alive. And when he was told, 'Well done, seventy-two. You have been chosen to go to the Amur-Ussuri to hunt the great tiger,' he smiled. He knew then that Fate had moved at last. That in that bleak and remote spot, where the great tiger ran loose-limbed over the sparkling ice, it would be impossible to check the captive's every move. That he could, as the vast and terrible darkness descended, slip away and head for the Manchurian border – and there, out! Out on the old Cathay trading route, out on one of the ships bound westwards, out to freedom – and to see, once again, the woman for whom he had sacrificed everything.

As soon as she had become betrothed, as soon as poor Cousin Francis began to take her about as his fiancée, Horatia knew she had done the wrong thing. Not only her head but the constant knot of anxiety that tightened her heart told her she could never be Francis's wife. It was terrible to be always ill at ease despite the amazing round of pleasure he organized for her – picture galleries, circus at the Hippodrome, Madam Tussaud's, theatre visits, a fish and champagne supper at Greenwich, the Zoological Gardens – to say nothing of driving out in the jaunting car.

And this, of course, made her guilty. She could not bear the poor wretch to go out of his way to entertain her – though naturally all such jollifications were attended by a host of chaperones, in particular Ida Anna – while she, Horatia, had to pretend all the while to be light-hearted. In a way it was torture. Smiling up at him with one thought in her mind: how she could get out of the situation without causing too much pain. She had always hated hypocrisy and now here she was – the arch hyp-ocrite. She did not know which way to turn.

Yet all the time she was aware of funny old Algy – her dearly beloved and dogged stepfather – watching her with a brilliant eye. She felt that if the family had been different – if he had been her blood father instead of skating the narrow line of a parent brought in by marriage alone – then he would have spoken to her privately. Told her that she must not proceed. But as it was he merely looked, as if he could convey in a glance all the misgivings in his kind and faithful old soul.

And then came Portsmouth! Final and unendurable: Francis wanted to take her away on holiday. Naturally they would be accompanied by Ida Anna, his sister Annie, his friend Mr Cox and young Charles and Frederick Hicks – but none the less the enforced intimacy was more than Horatia could bear. She was absolutely determined she must tell him the truth before they went.

But there was no chance. Ida Anna – thrilled at the thought of continuing her excursions – was so full of excitement that to have called off the trip would have been cruel. Horatia believed then that she would never escape, that she would be drawn into marriage like dust into a suction brush, that it was her fate to see those merry moustaches and hear that cheerful voice every morning of her life. She was daunted and speechless at the prospect. Had she really lost her great love to replace it with this?

But Francis was obviously not in the least worried, not a shadow of what she was thinking brushing off on him. For, on their arriving at Portsmouth, after a long train journey, his first remark in the hotel was, 'I say, what a *severe* tea. By Jove, that reminds me of nursery days. How I like to see a good spread.'

And Horatia – looking round hopefully to see if somebody would catch her eye and grin with her – was amazed to see that the others were falling on the hams, jellies and cakes with relish. That it was only she who thought it a bit childish and would have preferred something lighter.

And then she felt herself a total prig and was unhappier than ever.

'I'm jolly well going to write to Captain Blackwood,' Francis was announcing. 'He commands the *Victory*, you know. I met him on the Moors some years ago and wondered if he might show us round.'

'I believe it is open to the public anyway,' answered Mr Cox – a thin tall young man with beady eyes.

'Is it?'

'Yes – provided they're not foreigners, of course.'

'Of course,' murmured everyone – except Horatia.

But the next day brought a happening which made her realize finally that she must break her engagement to Francis, whatever the cost. It dawned squally and dull, a fact that made all the ladies want to stay on dry land. But despite this, Salvin and Cox insisted on hiring a vessel to visit various ships moored in the harbour. With a great deal of lifting of tiered petticoats and careful placing of well-gartered legs, Horatia, Ida Anna and Annie managed to get aboard the rocking rowing boat and find themselves heading out towards the *Victory* across the grey and lapping waves.

But the whole excursion turned out to be embarrassing. Captain Blackwood appeared tremendously busy and hardly able to spare Mr Salvin the time of day, so the party made a tour of the vessel on their own, Francis pointing out with relish the spot where the hero of Trafalgar had fallen and died, and the brass plates bearing the motto, 'England expects every man to do his duty.'

'Immortal Nelson,' he kept repeating, his hat clutched across his breast in respect.

'Indeed,' said Ida Anna. 'Are we going back to the hotel now?'

'No, not yet. We have to see the *Excellent* first. You'll

like that, Lady Ida. It is the training ship. You'll see sword and gun exercise there.'

'Oh good.' Ida Anna's hard little eyes lit up at the thought of handsome sailors leaping about with swords. 'Are we going directly?'

'Yes.'

The noise was appalling, cannons and guns firing from the ship as if Trafalgar was, in act, being relived. Horatia felt she was going to faint, so oppressive was the whole atmosphere. And then it happened! An optical illusion, of course, but she distinctly saw a mirage of John Joseph reflected in one of the *Excellent*'s brightly polished brass fittings. She leant over the rail, her head spinning with shock, and then he spoke in her inner ear, just as he had done at St Mary-in-the-Castle.

'What are you doing, you foolish girl? Jackdaw lives. I told you before. You must . . .'

The voice faded away as Francis appeared at her elbow, anxious and worried and quite terrifyingly kind.

'Horatia, dearest! Whatever is it? You've gone pale as death!'

'A terrible headache. Let me go back, Francis. The noise is too much for me.'

He looked fractionally put out – and she prayed that he was not going to offer to accompany her.

'I shall be perfectly all right on my own. I must not spoil the party. Just let me go back and lie down for a while. I will soon recover if I am left to myself.'

She could see that he was dying to stay and was overwhelmed with relief when he said, 'Very well, if you are sure. We will be back as soon as we can. Forgive my leaving you but I am so anxious to see all the finest British oak in the building department.'

'Of course.'

She permitted him to half carry her into the rowing

boat and waved a handkerchief in farewell. Then she put her hands over her ears, trying to shut out every sound but that strange inner voice. But it had gone. Then Horatia knew for sure what she must do. There was only one person to whom she could turn for advice. Cloverella must come again to Sutton Place.

It had always been the tradition of the Westons to watch for visiting riders from the windows of the Long Gallery or, less comfortably, the Gatehouse. But now, of course, with the mansion house so changed this was no longer possible. The Gatehouse had gone, the Long Gallery was the Chapel. Only from the bedroom that had once belonged to the relentless Marguerite Trevelyan could one have an unsurpassed view out over the Home Park and beyond. But as this room now belonged to her mother and stepfather Horatia could find small excuse for loitering there daily. Instead she contented herself with listening for the sound of Cloverella's flute – for she felt sure that it was by this means the gypsy girl would announce her arrival.

It had seemed a terrible thing to do; to take the waxen image from its wrappings and see it for the first time, its head all bound up with Cloverella's own black locks. It had been even worse laying the thing upon her bed and saying to it, 'Cloverella, thou must come to me.'

Afterwards she had hidden it away again, wondering if she had done something awful and ungodly: telling herself that she was meddling in things that she did not under-stand. But there was no help for it – she had to ask someone about Jackdaw. And also how she could get rid of Francis without ill feeling: a thing she had still not had the courage to do. She felt that if she was not helped soon her nerves would begin to crack beneath the strain of uncertainty and falsehood.

She thought, then, that Mr Salvin would never go away from Sutton Place. And, indeed, they had been back from their holiday twelve days before he finally announced, at the breakfast table, that he was off that morning to London, where he was meeting Uncle Thomas Monington.

'Good,' said Mr Hicks, lowering his newspaper and staring fixedly through his pince-nez. 'That should clear the air.'

'What do you mean by that, Sir?' asked Francis, looking rather startled.

'What I say. I am sure Mr Monington will have very definite views on your future, Francis.'

And with that he refused to be drawn further, disappearing behind *The Times* as if it were a shield.

By ten o'clock Francis had left and the mansion house seemed still at last. Algernon and Anne, accompanied by four dogs – their own and Horatia's – went for a walk; Ida Anna took the jaunting car into Guildford to visit the shops and Horatia, taking a drawing block with her, went to sit on the lawns beyond the courtyard, trying to sketch but really wondering if it might be better to write to Cousin Francis now that he had at long last left. She had heard it said that to announce the breaking off of an engagement by letter was a cowardly way out, but at the moment could see no alternative.

And it was at this point that she heard – very much as she had expected – the silvery notes of a distant flute. Cloverella, either by a sixth sense or by watching the house, probably a combination of the two, obviously knew that Francis Salvin had gone and was making her way up the drive.

But when she rounded the bend Horatia, hurrying forward to greet her, saw that it was not the witch girl playing but a tall handsome lad with a mass of curly dark brown hair and long lean fingers that moved like birds over the reed.

'Jay?' she said, stopping short.

He swept her a deep bow, plucking his cap from his head and brushing the ground with it. And when he straightened up Horatia saw that he was the image of his mother, even down to the strong white teeth. Yet there was something about the set of his eyes that reminded her of someone else.

'You sent for us, my Lady,' he said.

It was not a question but a statement of fact. Whatever ritual Horatia had enacted with the wax dolly had come to fruition. Cloverella and her son had heard her plea for help.

Now Cloverella said, 'How can we serve you?'

Horatia decided to come straight to the point.

'It is about Jackdaw – Major John Wardlaw. I believe that Captain Webbe Weston has spoken to me from beyond the grave. I believe he is trying to tell me that the Major is not dead as everyone believes. What is the truth, Cloverella?'

The gypsy sat down beneath the elm tree, sticking her legs straight out in front of her and producing her pipe from her pocket.

'I'll let Jay tell you that,' she said.

'Jay?'

'Yes, my Lady. He will scry for you.'

'What does that mean?'

'Crystal-gaze, divine. He is better than I am, my Lady. He too comes from the old blood of Dr Zachary and Cloverella the Witch. He will find the answer you seek.'

'Here, my Lady.' Jay's steadfast eyes stared into Horatia's. 'Hold this crystal in your hands.'

His gaze was growing faraway even as he spoke, and his shoulders were hunching. He suddenly looked very

447

wild-blooded and Horatia caught herself wondering who this Dr Zachary could have been to create such a remarkable descendant. But without further indication Jay took the crystal back from her and held it closely, hardly looking at it at all.

'You are very unhappy,' he said. 'But there is no real need for that. Within three years you will achieve your heart's wish.'

'Which is?'

'To be reunited with Major Wardlaw.'

There was a prolonged silence and then Horatia said, 'But I hardly know Major Wardlaw. I doubt that I have met him half a dozen times.'

Jay turned to look at her, and she saw that his face had undergone a transformation. A man looked out at her, a man with strong features yet whose smile was naughty if he chose. She was seeing the boy as he would look twenty years hence and she was amazed at his power.

'Perhaps – but in truth you know Major Wardlaw well, Lady Horatia. It is no good giving conventional answers and thinking conventional thoughts. They are but mouse squeaks in the face of God. You must think on the great scale if you are to achieve wisdom.'

Normally a boy of his background speaking thus to the Lady of the Manor would have had his ears soundly boxed and been put on bread and water for a week. But Horatia made no move. She knew that something else – a force she did not understand – was using Jay as its instrument.

'Then Major Wardlaw is alive?' she said.

'He lives, my Lady. But he is in great danger of his life – not from a particular threat but from the surroundings in which he has been forced to dwell. It is up to you now to keep faith with him.'

'What do you mean?'

448

'If you give your thoughts – and heart – to him, he will know it. It will give him the strength he needs to escape.'

'Then he is a prisoner?'

'Of a kind, yes. But let me tell you this, Lady. It is decreed that you and he should always be together, through many stages of experience, and it is up to you to help destiny fulfil its pattern.'

'Jay, what are you saying?'

His eyes were bright as the evening star as he answered, 'Wait for him. Think of no other. Have faith.'

'And Mr Salvin?'

'That will be made easy for you. He himself will break away.'

'I can't believe it.'

Jay laughed and Horatia saw that he was a youth again; a handsome lean youth who would be so great a person when he came to maturity.

'Watch out for Uncle False-Teeth,' he said.

Horatia looked thoroughly startled. 'But I thought he wanted it – the Lady of the Manor marrying his heir.'

Jay winked. 'Perhaps he drives too hard a bargain, Lady Horatia.'

'What do you mean?'

Jay stood up, still laughing, helping Horatia to her feet at the same time.

'I have told you enough. It is not good to know too much. Just remember that Major Wardlaw needs the power of your thought if what is meant is to be fulfilled.'

Jay's strong teeth flashed into a smile as he looked at Cloverella, fast asleep beneath the elm tree, her pipe still smoking in her hand.

'She is with child,' he said matter-of-factly.

Horatia was shocked. 'Cloverella – after all these years? By whom?'

'Some great man she thought fit to father her daughter.'

449

Horatia shook her head. 'I can't keep pace with you Romanies.'

'It is not intended that you should.'

Horatia looked thoughtful. 'And that reminds me of something else, Jay. Who is *your* father? Is his name known?'

'Oh yes, it's known,' said Jay.

And with that he picked up the flute and played a tune so merry that Horatia lifted up her skirts and – there in the sunshine of Sutton Place – danced as if the world had just begun.

24

That the letter could contain good news did not even go through Horatia's mind. It lay on the silver tray harmlessly enough but there, for a knowing eye to see, was all the evidence that it had been written hurriedly and under a great deal of stress. Algernon's Hicks's usually neat and precise hand was sprawled across the envelope like a child's, and a watery blot lay at the bottom left-hand corner.

Horatia ripped the envelope open with her fingers, not bothering to pick up the silver knife bought in a little shop in Vienna – John Joseph laughing beside her – the place filled with the smell of hot chocolate from the café next door and crowded with dolls and musical boxes.

Her eyes scanned the contents. She read:

Sutton Place,
August 1, 1852.

My very dear Stepdaughters,

I am writing to you in the greatest haste and distress. My beloved wife, your mother, collapsed with severe abdominal pain last night and Dr Thorne was called at once from Guildford. He has diagnosed inflammation of the stomach wall and seems to be treating the matter with some seriousness. Nurse Wood-ware – a blunt woman but highly recommended by the doctor – came to take charge this morning but I would implore you, if you have any love at all for your family, to come immediately. Your mother seems very weak and I do believe the presence of her two daughters might be of great assistance.

I am writing to Annette by the same post but feel that family commitments might preclude her from coming for long.

Yours in great affection,

Algernon Hicks.

Horatia sat down rather suddenly, her blood going cold. For her stepfather to write in those terms must mean that the Dowager Countess's condition was poor; nothing else would induce dear old Algy to sound quite so fraught with anxiety.

Thoughts of her mother went through Horatia's mind. She remembered the beautiful woman, hair swept up into an Apollo knot, on her way to dine with George IV; she remembered the crazy creature who had run round and round the Tribune in grief; she remembered the dear little soul who had married Algernon Hicks in the sweetest wedding ever. Above all she remembered her mother's bravery, her tenacity, her incomparable yearning for life in the face of such hardship. And now – 'inflammation of the stomach wall'. What sinister reality was concealed in those vague words?

The front door opened and closed and Ida Anna, arrayed in sealskin taffeta and sporting fifteen petticoats to hold out the skirt, appeared with Lulie and Porter trotting beside her.

'Oh, my dear,' she said. 'I had such an adventure in the flower market.' She stopped short on seeing Horatia's face. 'What is it?' Her tone changed completely. 'Whatever is the matter?'

'It's Mother,' her sister answered shortly. 'She's seriously ill.'

'Oh Heaven!'

Ida Anna sat down hard on the other chair and there was total silence for a moment or two. Then she said, 'It's not my fault, is it?'

'How could it be your fault?' Horatia answered. 'She has a stomach complaint.'

'Yes, but it could have been brought on by worry. She was so bitterly opposed to my coming to live with you.'

There was silence again while both the sisters thought

of the Countess's letter to Ida Anna written only four months earlier.

'It is hard upon me having two unmarried daughters to lose the society of both in my latter days,' it had read. 'But as it is your wish and pleasure I must submit, and sincerely do I hope that you may be the happier for the change . . .'

'I feel guilty,' said Ida Anna now. 'But I did hate Sutton Place *so* much.'

'So did I.'

'And I wanted to be with you in Leamington, Horry. There's life and fun up here.'

They were both full of remorse.

'Anyway,' Ida Anna went on, 'after Cousin Francis turned you down you needed a companion.'

They both laughed out loud for a moment, thinking of how neatly Horatia had slid out of the commitment. And how Uncle Thomas Monington's plotting had worked so brilliantly to her advantage.

It had been his idea that she should, on marrying Francis Salvin, his heir, give up her allowance of an annual £1,000 on remarriage as stipulated in John Joseph's will. In return, Uncle Thomas Monington would waive his inheritance of Sutton Place, for which he was next in line should she marry again. And at this dear Algy had risen up growling.

'That money was left to you especially by John Joseph,' he had said, standing in the Library and looking furious. 'Horatia, you are not to agree. I shall see Salvin myself and refuse the proposal on your behalf.'

And that had been that! Cousin Francis had told Horatia that he could not proceed with the wedding unless she was prepared to give up her allowance – and she had said, in return, that in no circumstances would she do so. The engagement was over and Uncle Thomas had gone off hissing like a rattlesnake.

'Thank God he did,' said Horatia now. 'I don't think I could have stood all that hawking and hunting.'

'Cousin Francis is very sweet,' answered Ida Anna wisely. 'But not right for you, Horry. Nor for me either,' she added with a sigh.

There was another pause and then Ida Anna said, 'Do you think Jay Blanchard's prophecy is true? That Jackdaw is still alive?'

'I don't know. I pray so. I wish you had been there, Ida Anna. Jay looked so . . . *old*, so knowing. I truly thought I was in the presence of magic.'

'They are a funny couple – Cloverella and her son.'

'There are three of them now. She had a baby girl in February.'

'I know. And called it Bluebell, would anyone believe! Bluebell Blanchard, I declare!'

'I think it pretty,' answered Horatia slowly. 'Bluebell, Jackdaw – both unusual names, and unforgettable.'

Over the snow, over the ice, speeding out of the great mountain pass that reached up to heaven, the tiger came towards the hunting party like a thunderbolt, pausing not at all as it raced forward in full sprint. Every muscle in its body coordinated to produce a glorious effect – fur rippling over sinew, powerful legs leaving the ground with each bound, so that for a moment everyone stood spellbound, finding it hard to realize that in a minute this mighty being would be dead, crunching down on to the ice in a scarlet pool of blood. But, even as it hurtled, guns were raised and the whine of bullets broke the absolute silence of this gateway of the gods – the vast and mysterious border between Siberia and the secret land of Manchuria.

Jackdaw raised his gun with the others but aimed over the beast's proud head. He had no intention of being the one to end that glorious life unless it was absolutely necessary that he should. And then he found that he did, in fact, have to fire again, for the animal charged on unscathed, a flash of steel preparing to defend itself.

The first hunter fell silently beneath its snarling onslaught and the screams of the second were only protracted a moment or two. The third managed to run away and had vanished before the tiger came. So only the fourth was left, standing there in his fur hat and coat, and realizing that it was either he or the magnificent animal that must perish in the snows.

He narrowed his eye and took aim at the tiger's brain. The bullet chamber clicked round and he fired twice more, holding the last two bullets in reserve. Still the creature came on and he fired again at the mighty heart. He saw the tiger leap in pain and then fall, like thunder, at his feet. He could have wept. He, who did not believe in taking life, had been forced to kill one of the most beautiful creations in the world.

And then he realized that the tiger had released him. That by its immense charge against the guns it had rid him of two fellow prisoners and their gaoler. He was free at last – after four years in the Czar's penal colony – to make his way through the mountains and into China. And then back to England.

The thought of Horatia – of her burnished hair and shining beauty – made him look once more at the dead animal at his feet, its fur glimmering like his love. The creature's eyes were open and staring at him mournfully. Just as if it was human he bent to close them – and then a curious thing happened. Quite how it came about he could never afterwards tell but John Joseph gazed at him out of the tiger's eye.

Jackdaw started back in terror, unable to look. But when he regained his composure and stared at the animal once more, he saw that the eyes had now closed peacefully. He knew at once what it meant. In the four years since last he had seen him John Joseph Webbe Weston had died. Horatia was a widow.

As he set his sight towards the perilous mountains through which he must travel to escape, Jackdaw could only think of one thing; that he was going back. Back, to take Horatia away from Sutton Place and the curse that had killed her husband and would surely, in time, find its own way of ending her.

It was extraordinary! Despite the fact of the season's being high summer, Sutton Place had vanished in thick mist. In fact as the carriage bearing the Ladies Horatia and Ida Anna from the railway station came round the sweep of the drive from which the first glimpse of the house was always taken, they saw only a wall of fog. The mansion had disappeared.

'Is it an omen?' said Ida Anna, her eyes fearful. 'I've never seen it – or rather not seen it – as bad as this before.'

Despite being the elder of the two and attempting to be the more sensible, Horatia shivered. She sat opposite her sister, for their huge skirts, supported by layer after layer of petticoat, needed the full width of a seat to allow them to sit at all. But now she leant across and touched Ida Anna's arm.

'I am sure it is not,' she said. 'It is just something to do with the hot days and cool evenings. Look, there are the lights of the house now.'

And sure enough, through the gloom, they could see the gleam of lamps in the courtyard. Yet the feeling of a house cut off from the world persisted, for as the wheels turned over the cobbles there was no familiar clatter and click, but only a strange and disembodied silence. Mr Hicks had ordered straw to be put down so that the Dowager Countess should not be disturbed.

Inside the depressing feeling persisted. There even seemed to be mist in the Great Hall as the ladies, not even stopping to remove their bonnets, traversed the vast space to greet their stepfather, who awaited them in the Library.

They had never seen him so drawn, so quiet, so lacking in merriment. In fact, behind his pince-nez, Horatia saw that his eyes were watery and pink. Dear Algy, who had bounded into their lives and brought them so much in the way of material benefits – and so much, too, in the way of support and encouragement – had been weeping on his own.

She threw her arms around him. 'Oh my darling Father,' she said. She had omitted the 'step' and she did not care. The Earl had been wonderful – handsome, naughty and excellent company – but this dear soul had won all their hearts with his goodness.

He could not speak for a moment or two, clutching Horatia and Ida Anna to him in silent embrace. Then he said, 'The situation is very grave. Dr Thorne believes the disease may have spread to the bowels as well. She is no longer able to eat. You must be prepared for a shock.'

But no words could prepare them for the state of emaciation that had transformed Miss Anne King of Hastings into a ghost. It was terrible – her arms and legs like sticks and her teeth seeming too big in a face drawn to the bones.

Ida Anna let out a great sob but Horatia ran forward to take the frail hand in hers. And after a minute or so the Countess opened her eyes.

'Horry!' she said, her voice a whisper in the shadows. 'You've come. I'm so glad, darling.'

Ida Anna wiped her eyes.

'And I am here too, Mama,' she said, stepping forward.

'My daughters at home,' came the reply. 'I can be happy again.'

The sisters exchanged a glance but said nothing, their only wish to comfort this little mother who was so obviously slipping desperately quickly out of life.

'There is no pain,' Algy murmured behind them. 'The nurse keeps her on doses of laudanum. I have sent for Annette and Archie – and Frances too.'

'Frances?' This from Ida Anna.

'It was your mother's personal wish. Frances has been a good woman of late. A kind wife to old Mr Harcourt – though very frivolous of course. But with never a breath of scandal.'

'Not before time.' Even after all these years Ida Anna had not forgiven the pretty Jewess who had married both of her brothers.

But next day when Frances's carriage came through the morning mist Ida Anna behaved well enough, kissing the cheek of the young Countess warmly and taking her by the hand herself to the Dowager Countess's bedchamber.

Horatia, who had sat beside her mother nearly all night, glanced up to see her sister-in-law, already clad in sombre colours, gazing at her from beneath a dark becoming hat.

'My dear,' she said, rising to kiss her. 'How well you look. How are you? How is Mr Harcourt?'

'Very well,' whispered the Waldegrave widow. 'In fact he is excellent. I can certainly recommend marriage to an older man, Horatia.' She smiled a little. 'They do look after one so. Have you not thought of it, my dear?'

Horry shook her head. 'It is going to be very difficult to find anyone – older or younger – after John Joseph.'

But Frances had turned away, cuddling her ex-mother-in-law into her arms before anyone could stop her, and not listening properly to what Horatia was saying – nor really caring, so shocked was she by Anne's changed appearance.

Throughout most of that day she stayed like that, whispering to the Dowager Countess until their peace was made and old sad thoughts of a flighty young social climber who had married her brother-in-law after only five months of widowhood – flouting convention and breaking the law in so doing – had gone for ever from Anne's mind.

Only then did the erstwhile Lady Waldegrave rise to her feet and kiss her mother-in-law on the brow.

'Goodbye,' she said. 'I promise that Strawberry Hill shall be restored in your memory.'

And with that she was gone, only a whiff of her musky, rather Eastern, perfume lingering to remind them of her extraordinary presence.

The next morning saw Annette – moonstone eyes full of tears – arrive with Colonel Money, very grey of whisker at fifty-three, but still a military man to his fingertips. And within half an hour of those two came Caroline and Francis Hicks to help Algy.

But still that little game fighter hung on to life and it was only in the early hours of the next day, at the time when the soul is most in danger of taking flight, that she finally left the world behind her. Nurse Woodware called the family into the room and so Anne did not die alone. Yet she did not speak to any of them, only opening her eyes just before she went to look at someone who stood in the doorway.

459

But there was no one there to see and Horatia wondered if it was, in fact, the Earl come to fetch his wife. If he stood lounging against the doorpost, one elegant foot crossed upon the other, a smile hovering about his handsome mouth, invisible to all except the Army chaplain's daughter who had borne his bastard son and six more of his children, and whom he had led such a merry dance in this earthly life.

But none of the others noticed and she said nothing, merely putting her hand on Algy's shoulder, where he sobbed in Francis Hicks's arms.

'He must have brandy,' whispered Francis. 'Can you rouse the butler?'

Horatia was glad to leave the room. Glad to walk down the long corridor that led to the top of the West Staircase, passing the bedrooms – nearly all unoccupied now – and thinking not only about her mother but also about the mansion house as it must have been: bustling with life when King Henry and his court had arrived and when the great rich carpet was laid beneath the King's mighty feet.

At the bottom of the stairs she turned into the small hall – wondering if this was where, as legend had it, Charles Edward Stuart had once laughed in the shadows at Melior Mary Weston – and then went left into a corridor. She was in the staff quarters now and a door on her right led into the pantry of Lucas the butler.

It was not necessary to knock but Horatia did so, sure that the poor man was snatching an hour of sleep. Then she went straight in, as her position allowed, and found him in his shirtsleeves dozing before a small and fading fire. He woke up and struggled into his coat.

'The Dowager Countess has died, Lucas,' said Horatia, 'and I know you will be very sorry. But meanwhile Mr Hicks is in a state of shock and I wonder if you could

take the brandy tray into the drawing room and see that
the fire is well stoked up.'

'Of course, my Lady. Please accept condolences on
behalf of myself and the staff. You look worn out, my
Lady. Would you like to sit down for a moment?'

She was suddenly so tired she could faint. In fact the
corners of the room swirled towards her and retreated
again in a spiral of darkness. Horatia sank into Lucas's
armchair and put her head in her hands. How strange to
think of the world without her mother in it. How awful
that she could not ask her advice – regardless of the fact
she rarely took it – ever again.

Horatia suddenly felt very lonely; so few of the people
she had loved were left. John Joseph, J.J., and George
taken away in their sky-blue youth; the Earl on his fiftieth
birthday; and now Anne. Horatia envisaged a desolate
life stretching out before her. She and her sister caring
for their grieving stepfather and living in Sutton Place till
he, in his turn, died. But then Jay had said . . .

She could not think about it any more. It was all too
much for her. Very quietly she began to cry, her arms
falling by her sides as limp as those of a rag doll. And
then her fingers touched something – something which
had lain hidden down the side of the chair, in between
the arm and the seat. She pulled it out, into the palm of
her hand, and there was a marble; a funny, green,
schoolboy's marble. For no reason that she could ever
fathom it gave her a feeling of comfort and she slipped it
into the pocket of her dress, wondering why the feel of it
was so warm to her touch.

At that moment, the moment when Horatia found the
magic sphere where it had slipped from Jackdaw's hand
on the night he had travelled in time, he woke from sleep
and called her name.

461

It was first light over the great mountain range and he stared from the shepherd's hut, in which he had spent the night, into an exquisite and crystal dawn. Despite the blood which seeped through the rags which bound his torn and damaged feet, he felt no pain at all. He was in ecstasy. He had crossed the mountain pass and with it the border; he was in Manchuria and safe, at last, from the jurisdiction of the Czar.

It seemed to matter very little, on reflection, that he had not been guilty of spying for the enemies of the Father of all the Russias – the crime for which he had been sent to Siberia. In fact nothing mattered at all except that his great journey home had begun.

Jackdaw stood up, his jewel eyes bright, his face tanned and healthy from the months spent outdoors. He was ready to start walking. Stopping only to answer nature's call and splash cold water on his face and hands, he set off. If he hobbled he neither knew nor cared. And with the power of his thought he asked only one thing; that Horatia would wait for him until his vast journey was done and he had crossed the mysterious continent of China to the great seaports that would lead him westwards – and to England.

'We shall have to give up the house in Leamington, Ida Anna,' said Horatia. 'We simply can't leave Algy on his own.'

And with those words the trap of Sutton Place was sprung yet again – the Lady of the Manor was to come back to the mansion. Through the goodness of her heart she was about to be immured within, as had been so many before her.

'What a horrible thought! Must we?' Just for a moment the spoilt brat peeped out of Ida Anna's eyes.

'We have no choice.'

'Couldn't he live with Francis and Caroline?'

'No he couldn't. It wouldn't be fair on them. Besides, he has made Sutton Place his home. Until he has recovered from the shock we will have to stand by him.'

'Well, can't the three of us move away?'

'Only if I can let the house to someone else. I need the income from the rent to survive.'

'I shall try and persuade him.'

'I think it might be best if you said nothing for the time being.'

Ida Anna gave a mutinous look but answered, 'Very well – but I intend to try even harder for a husband. As I would advise you to do also.'

She turned on her heel and flounced out of the morning room, her face very cross. She had been unsettled since Anne's funeral and now Algy's grief and dependence on his stepdaughters had put her out enormously. If they could have all three packed their bags instantly and returned to Leamington she would not have minded in the slightest. But there was no hope of that. Mr Hicks – who had always loved the manor house so much – clung to it now for support. For was it not here that the happiest years of his marriage had been spent with that dear little widow who had altered his entire life by agreeing to marry him?

As Horatia crossed the small hall with Lulie and Porter, Polly and Anthus, she heard her stepfather sob somewhere within the house. But she did not dare turn. He was at that dreadful stage where sympathy made him far worse. He was best left to grieve alone and then be forced – as convention decreed he must – to change for dinner and join his stepdaughters at a meal during which he could not force down a mouthful.

As Horatia stepped outside and away from the gloom she noticed that strange difference in the sunshine which told her summer was beginning to end. Though it was only the first week of September there was some subtle change in the atmosphere which heralded the death of the year. Soon it would be autumn and then winter; the time when Sutton Place became impossible to heat though fires blazed in every room. Even the thought of Christmas made Horatia shiver and she took an immediate vow to ask the entire Hicks clan to stay. Or else to hint at an invitation from them. Anything rather than sit pathetically, a tiny lost trio, in that great gaunt house.

As she thought these things she thrust her hands into her pockets, her head tilting forward as she did so. On an impulse she pulled the pins from her hair and saw it fall – glowing as a blacksmith's anvil – about her shoulders. She did not know it but the grief in her life had made her incomparable. She had grown fine with suffering. Her figure filled out once more but her features delicate and sensitive to the nuances of fate.

Rather to her surprise she felt, within the depths of her skirt, the green marble that she had put there on the night Anne died. Once again she retrieved the sphere and gazed at it, wondering to whom it belonged. But the yapping of the dogs distracted her. All four of them had spotted a rabbit and were off, at great speed, to pursue the creature into its burrow.

Looking about her Horatia realized that she had walked a long way, for she stood within the ruins that had once, according to tradition, been the hunting lodge of King Edward – Saint and Confessor. And it was then, standing there amongst that stone old as the Saxon Kings, that Horatia finally raised the silly toy to her eye and gazed into its depths.

Instantly she entered the lair of the dragon who slept at the earth's heart; green convolutes curled about her and stalactites and stalagmites were there to be touched.

But then they blurred as the sound of boys' voices singing filled the air about her. There was the heavy, heady smell of incense and then, as she lowered the marble once more, she saw that she stood where candlelight threw the shadow of the cross, together with that of a crown, upon stone flagging. She was within the Chapel of King Edward as it must once have been and there – gaunt-faced, bearded and crowned with the mediaeval circlet – the King himself knelt before the priest, totally at worship.

And yet there was something frightening about him. He more than prayed – he was obsessed with power. White-faced, white-lipped, he demanded that God should love him for his purity, for his astringent life, for his total forbearance from earthly pleasures. Though she could not have been sure Horatia would have sworn that he wore the penitent's hair shirt next to his skin.

She was too shocked to be afraid; in fact she thought consciously that she was dreaming, that she had fallen asleep in the ruins and that this was where her sleeping mind had taken her. And yet there was a terrible reality about it all. She could smell the spluttering candles, the unwashed bodies, the extraordinary scent that the King put on his hands. But above all she could smell the rain; a combination of wet earth, wet leather, wet horses – and all of it blowing from beneath the Chapel's draughty door.

The whole effect was overpowering. She thought that she must faint where she stood; just behind Edward and able to touch him if she leant forward and put out her arm. But yet she stood stock still, feeling totally swept up with the sounds and the odours and that wild white King taking Christ's blood and body within his lips.

And then at last it was done. The priest blessed the monarch, the gaunt figure rose from its postulant's posture, and the doors of the Chapel were flung open to

465

reveal the rest of the hunting lodge, cold and frightening and filled with the noise of baying dogs.

The King swept past Horatia towards the hunt and she, frightened, ran behind him – terrified to be left alone in that grim Chapel where priest and shadow and altar were all darkly at one. But despite the sound of her feet and her panting breath she realized that none of them – not the King nor the hunting party nor the little boys who had just raised their voices to celebrate the high mass – could hear her. In this dreadful dream she was destined to be the onlooker and never to play a part.

Yet still she ran behind the King to where, outside, the horses were tethered, saddled and ready to hasten them all – monarch and men alike – away into the forest. And then her eye was attracted to something else. Almost opposite the lodge but slightly to the right, standing beneath a clump of trees which grew beside a bubbling spring, was a group of horsemen, amongst which was the cloaked and somehow desperate figure of a woman.

Horatia's heart beat in her breast like a caged bird as she saw the woman, despair in her every movement, break free from the rest and cross the short space that lay between her and the King. He had mounted in that time and Horatia could see that the eyes of the couple were on a level. And what a terrible glance they exchanged – full of hate and love and emotions that delved so deeply into the human soul that they were unspeakable on normal lips.

'Edward,' said the woman, 'you must forgive us. It is still in your power to revoke sentence on the Godwins. Edward, in the name of Christ, for once show your Christian charity. Remember I have committed no sin against you – all I asked was your love.'

Horatia watched aghast as the King did nothing but flicker his eyes over the wretched creature unsmilingly.

The atmosphere was so fraught, so charged with high tension, that she found words rising to her lips.

'Why don't you listen to her? What is the matter with you? What have they done, these people, that you cannot even look her in the face?'

But the Confessor was turning away, bound for the open forest where he could slay creatures to his heart's content. He gave one more contemptuous glance towards the woman and then his back was turned – irrevocably.

As the girl tumbled from her horse – and Horatia realized that she was little more, as the hood fell back to reveal damp strawberry hair and child-like features – nobody moved at all. And then one of her escort hurried forward and knelt by her side.

Horatia knew that the poor creature was having a fit by the saliva flecking her mouth. But what was so terrible – so ghastly to listen to in that dreadful place – was the growling of a human being in despair. It rose from the woman's throat like all the venom of which mankind is capable, horrifying all Christian souls.

'Will! Tom!' said the man. 'The Queen is ill. Look to the Lady.'

But she was beyond help. From the depraved part of her – a part which even the most innocent is forced to bear within them – a curse was rising up; a curse so terrible, calling as it did to old strange gods who had stalked the earth when nature was young and the cost of spring was a blood sacrifice, that Horatia could not bear to listen.

She heard the name Odin mentioned, she heard the Erl – or Elf – King called upon, she saw a mighty ring thrown into the gushing well and steam rise up. Then she saw the Lady grow pale, and appear to die with that dreadful oath.

'Death, madness and despair. Ill upon ill for the Lord of the Manor of Sutton for all time to come.'

Everything was drained of life; all the world had gone still to listen.

'Oh help me,' said Horatia. 'Help me to wake up and escape this terrible nightmare.'

Once more she grasped the sphere and did the only thing possible; she raised it to her eye and stared into its heart. Rushing green, spirals, the end of existence. And then it was over.

Horatia Webbe Weston woke to find herself lying upon the ground, one correct ankle crossed upon the other, a silly schoolboy's marble in her hand. In the distance the dogs were barking as they returned from the rabbit warren.

'Gracious me!' she said. 'What am I doing down here?'

And with that she rose – and walked slowly back to Sutton Place.

25

Once before in the strange tale of the mansion house, the evil web woven by Sutton Place had caught the young Lady of the Manor in its mesh, twining round her until she gave up the hopeless struggle. When Melior Mary – the very last descendant of Sir Richard Weston – the builder – renounced love for the sake of the house and then regretted it bitterly, Sutton Place had never let her go again. There she had lived, growing madder and madder, hating her home and trying to destroy it with neglect, until death had finally released her from her imprisonment.

And now history was repeating itself. Horatia Webbe Weston – not of Weston blood but owner through the legacy of her husband – was trapped as well. For though it would have been easy enough to bid her stepfather farewell and return to Leamington to a happy, contented, aimless life, and leave him in solitary state in the great grim house, the look in his sad spaniel eyes was enough to keep her where she was.

And so the days after the death of Anne, the Dowager Countess Waldegrave, dragged by at stalemate until the weeks eventually turned into months. A miserable Christmas passed, during which the family – though not Catholic – prayed in the Chapel and Horatia thought she heard the sound of sobbing and felt it was the ghost of Giles the Fool.

Since that unnerving dream the previous year she had found herself thinking more and more about the curse and legends of Sutton Place. In fact, if she closed her eyes Horatia could still smell the pungent musk of the billowing incense, the sour unwashed bodies, the guttering tallow grease and, above all, the rain-soaked earth; the odours which had predominated the dream. But worse – far worse – she could, when her lids were closed, still see that tragic young Queen falling to the ground, grovelling in the mud, and uttering words that could have come only from demonic sources.

If Horatia Webbe Weston, twenty-nine years old and brought up as sensibly as possible in the erratic household of the late Earl Waldegrave, had thought such things possible, she might almost have believed she had travelled in time through the agency of a schoolboy's marble and had been present at the actual laying of the curse of Sutton. But as every rational human being knew this kind of thing was absolutely impossible, she dismissed it. Almost . . .

With the horrid solitary Christmas, not relieved by the presence of Francis, Caroline and their horde of children until New Year, finally over, spring showed its face once more in Sutton Park. The jade skies of winter, heavy with indigo clouds, gave way to forget-me-not heavens. There was rose in the dawnings and argent in the afternoons; the sun went down in a flurry of powder pink to show that tomorrow would be fine.

And then the miracle happened again with the year's rebirth. Skeleton branches suddenly held thick determined buds, the river unfroze and a silver fish leapt up, lambs were born into snowdrifts but gamely held on to life.

And with all these signs of the regeneration of the earth's cycle a fever came into Horatia's blood that left her raw with misery. For it was now that she thought of love, of the melting of one body into another and the seed that could have been planted in the heat of such a rapturous midnight. She thought of the child that John Joseph might have given her; the living memorial to him that would have borne her up through all her present difficulties. A child that by its very presence could have banished the loneliness which stalked her day and night.

She had long since given up hope that John Wardlaw would ever come back, knew that Jay – mystic and powerful young man though he might be – had been mistaken. For what clairvoyant does not make an error, misinterpret a signal or sign? And such thoughts made her regret that she had turned down Mr Colquhoun and Cousin Francis – they would have been good enough to sire the longed-for infant if nothing more.

And then she was angry with herself for she knew in her heart that she could never have settled for a life without passion, an existence without love. It was a great puzzle to her: whether to be lonely or to compromise her feelings. But when she spoke of her worries to Mr Hicks he said, '*I* would marry again, Horatia, if I had the chance. Please do not think I could ever love anyone as well as I loved your mother – it is just that I so long for a companion.'

'But, Algy, did I do wrong to refuse Francis Salvin?'

A grin – and some of his old style – returned to her stepfather's face.

'He turned *you* down, my dear. You would not relinquish your jointure if you remember. No, you did quite the right thing. But I wish you were not alone. It is such a pity that you and Ida Anna are really beyond the age for a season in London.'

'Perhaps we should advertise ourselves in *The Times* – "Widower and his two mature stepdaughters available to receive proposals of marriage from respectable people willing to live in doomed manor house in Surrey. Previous experience not essential."'

471

Mr Hicks looked slightly shocked. 'You are not serious, Horatia?'

'No, I am not serious. But, Algy . . .'

'Yes?'

'If one of us three should meet someone with whom marriage could be seriously considered, should we feel able to proceed?'

Mr Hicks looked guilty. 'I feel I am standing in the way of you two girls. I have told you before you are quite free to go. Don't worry about your old stepfather. I will be perfectly happy on my own.'

Horry went over and sat on his lap.

'No you wouldn't. You have your kicked dog expression. But, dearest Algy, won't you think about letting Sutton Place to someone else? In that way we could all go away and have a jollier time.'

'I promise I will soon – when I have recovered from your mother's loss just a little more.'

As she left the room Horatia found her sister outside the door, obviously on the point of coming in but having stopped to listen through the crack.

Ida Anna said, 'Selfish old brute. He *is* holding us back. And I think you are selfish too, Horatia.'

'I? Good God, how?'

'By refusing to leave him. I am twenty-eight this year and firmly on the shelf and you are doing nothing to help me at all.'

'What do you mean?'

'If you would decide to go with me – for how could I set up on my own when that simply is not done? – I might stand a chance. But stuck in this hell hole I've as much hope of meeting eligibles as flying. I think you are thoroughly mean.'

Normally one of Ida Anna's outbursts – which she had from time to time with her eyes snapping like chestnuts –

would have passed straight over Horatia's head. But this day, what with the wildness of spring upon her and thoughts of the baby she never had, Horatia found herself bursting straight into tears and running off across the Great Hall, up the West Stairs and into one of the guest bedrooms. Here she flung herself headlong upon the bed and wept her heart out.

It was one of the smaller rooms of Sutton Place, rather dark, and diminished even further in size by the presence of a huge mahogany wardrobe, the middle door of which consisted entirely of a full-length mirror. Peeping into this now as she wiped her eyes with her sleeve – most inelegant, but then Horatia had never cared too greatly for the niceties of good behaviour – she saw her reflection. The cloud of hair had fallen down and burst about her shoulders, while the storm of tears had wet the full, firm bosom – restored to its former splendour once more. And then she saw John Joseph. He was standing inside the wardrobe and looking out at her – smiling.

She knew the expression 'feet did not touch the ground' – but hers actually did not as she crossed to the wardrobe door and pulled it fully open. Of course he was not really there at all. What she had seen was one of his uniforms – bright blue, frogging across the chest, buttons blazing – hanging where he must have left it when last at Sutton Place.

Impulsively she jumped in beside it, wrapping the sleeves around her. His ambience, his influence – the smell which was his quite individually and could be associated with no other person in the world – was all about her.

'Oh, my darling,' she said, closing her eyes and leaning her head against the jacket chest, 'why did you have to die? Why did you have to leave me?'

Quite suddenly, without her opening her eyes or seeing

473

anything at all, it was no longer an article of clothing hanging in a cupboard and forgotten long since. She felt it grow warm with life, felt the arms tighten about her, felt John Joseph's lips brush her ear as he whispered, 'Goodbye my darling. I have to leave you now.'

Still without daring to look she answered, 'Why, why? Must I be utterly alone?'

'We must both move on,' said that voice from a thousand distances. 'Have faith Horatia. When you hear Giles laugh – that will be the sign.'

He was gone. It was an old empty uniform once more that she held clasped in her arms. John Joseph Webbe Weston had slipped out of her life for ever. And she was alone – standing in a wardrobe like a child – and staring dismally out into the shadows of that little bleak room.

Everywhere the song of April: white birds arcing in an eggshell sky, daffodils flouncing gold as altar cups, trees in their splendid blazing green and hiding in their depths, no doubt, the Green Man himself; Spring incarnate, the creature whom legend was later to call Robin Hood.

The packet steamer that crossed to Dover from Calais came out of a shower-filled mist and into the sunshine, the passengers all gazing up in wonderment as a double rainbow broke the prism and sprang up over the great cliffs.

'It must be an omen,' said a jolly girl, clutching to her side an equally jolly little boy, but sadly minus a husband.

'Yes,' said the man who stood next to her at the ship's rail. 'It is. If we make a wish now I think it has every chance of being granted.'

She glanced at him curiously, her cheerful gaze taking in his dark, slightly greying, hair; his jewel eyes, much lined but still bright for all that; his weather-tanned skin.

He was not in the first flush of youth – probably nearing forty – but still had an attractive air.

So she gave him an extra special smile as she said, 'Have you been away from England long?'

'Too long,' he answered. 'But that's not a mistake I'll repeat again. My wandering days are over, thank God.'

'Oh that's nice.' She gave him an even bigger smile. 'I expect your family have missed you.'

'They believe me to be dead,' he answered, suddenly sad.

The jolly girl could think of no response to that, short of getting involved in long and deep conversation, and as her son needed attention to his nose and the ship's gangplank was rattling down to be clamped on to the quay below, she contented herself with, 'It will be such a lovely surprise for them, in that case, to find you are not,' as she applied a handkerchief and collected her hand baggage all at once.

'Good luck to you,' she said, straightening from her son's nostrils. 'I hope you'll be very happy.' And with that she was gone down the gangplank, with only one backward glance at the attractive stranger whose gaze had gone beyond her to the shore.

'It seems to me, Horatia,' said Ida Anna, 'that you spend all your time mooning round the Chapel these days. I can't think what's come over you. I declare you're growing quite religious. You're not thinking of taking the veil, are you?'

'No,' answered Horatia spiritedly. 'I am not. But if I did I can assure you it would be to get away from you. You have been quite horrid since Mother died.'

The boot-button eyes relented a little. 'I'm sorry. You know why it is. I hate being walled up in this mausoleum.'

''Well we must accept it for the time being.'

'For the time being? Do you have hope of getting away then?'

'Yes,' said her sister in a sudden confiding burst. 'I am sure something is going to happen soon. Ida Anna, you are not to make fun – but I believe John Joseph has spoken to me. He said that when Giles laughed it would be the sign.'

'The sign of what?'

'That I don't know.'

There was a pause and then Ida Anna said, whirling round to look Horatia straight in the face, 'You don't think Jackdaw is on his way back, do you? You don't think that funny Jay Blanchard was right all along?'

'Yes,' answered Horatia, 'no. I don't know.'

'Well, if he comes you are to go with him,' said her sister firmly. 'I will not want to hear any of this "poor Algy" business. I can take care of him. Until you are settled and can send for me, that is!'

'Oh, you minx!' said Horatia, hugging Ida Anna and crying a little.

'But what about the curse of the manor? Can it stop you?'

'Every day I pray that it cannot. That is what I am doing, partly sending up good thoughts – and partly listening for Giles.'

'Oh, how splendid!' Ida Anna clapped her hands together. 'I shall come with you and add my strength to yours.'

And so, with the little pawns in place, it was time for the game to be played finally out. They had both of them – the queen and the knight – borne their hardships well; they had endured suffering, both physical and mental, without allowing themselves to be defeated. They had not been merely passengers on the voyage through the universe.

476

Great laws of action and reaction swung into final place at this; the wheel of fortune began to slow. It was time for the Lady of the Manor to escape the evil which haunted Sutton Place and all those unfortunate enough to be its owners.

And so it was, as Horatia and Ida Anna entered the Chapel on the following morning – the Chapel that had once been Sir Richard Weston's Long Gallery and in which so much in the way of family gladness and despair had been played out in the three hundred years since it had been built – that they heard Giles. Sir Richard's Fool, who had given his faithful heart to all the family, and died in Sutton Forest, had come to tell the Lady, *his* Lady, that she was to be saved from Queen Edith's malediction.

How he laughed! How he jumped and rattled his stick along the wall. They could see nothing, of course, but the sisters knew. They knew that something wonderful and momentous would happen at any minute. So they danced and laughed with him, making a nonsense of time and its separations, as they shared his great and simple joy.

'Quick,' said Ida Anna, 'quick Horry. You must go outside to see. I shall watch from the window.'

And that was how Jackdaw finally beheld his dear love again as his carriage came round the drive's loop – running into the courtyard and on to the lawns, her arms flung wide, and her feet skimming over the dewy grass, her foxfire hair a nimbus about her head.

'Horatia!' he called out, as he jumped on to the gravel. 'Horatia, it's me – Jackdaw. I don't suppose you'll remember me . . .'

But he stopped talking nonsense and rushed forward. For how could she ever forget him? She had known him for centuries and was his soul's own mate.

'Jackdaw,' she cried. 'Jackdaw! You've come. You're alive. Oh Jackdaw.'

They saw so much love in each other's eyes.

'Horatia,' he said as she ran into his arms. 'There is no need to say anything, is there, except will you stay with me for ever?'

'You know the answer to that,' she replied, as she stepped up into the carriage beside him and it turned in the forecourt.

'So at last,' Horatia asked, snuggling against him, 'the story of the doomed Manor of Sutton is ended?'

Knowing that she, at least, was safe, John Wardlaw, aware of old truths, answered, 'Only time will tell that.'

But as the great gates of Sutton Place swung open to let them free, the water in St Edward's Well gleamed like Viking gold.

Bibliography

A History of the British Army, J. W. Fortescue;
Annals of an old Manor House, Frederic Harrison;
The Early Victorians 1832–51, J. F. C. Harrison;
A History of Austro-Hungary, Louis Leger;
A History of London Life, R. J. Mitchell and M. D. R. Leys;
The Late Hungarian Campaign, J. W. Warre Tyndale.